THE SECRET THAT KILLED YOU

Also by Steve Hadden

THE SECRET THAT KILLED YOU

An Ike Rossi Thriller

STEVE HADDEN

MahoganyRow
PRESS

THE SECRET THAT KILLED YOU

Edited by Julie Miller

Cover designed by Damonza

Published by Mahoghany Row Press

Visit the author website:
http://www.stevehadden.com

Names:	Hadden, Steve, author.
Title:	The secret that killed you / Steve Hadden.
Description:	[Daniel Island, South Carolina] : Mahoghany Row Press, [2024] | Series: An Ike Rossi thriller
Identifiers:	ISBN: 978-1-963584-01-1 (paperback)
	978-1-963584-02-8 (hardcover)
	978-1-963584-00-4 (ebook)
Subjects:	LCSH: Private investigators--United States--Fiction. | Drone aircraft pilots--United States-- Fiction. | Cryptographers--Fiction. | Family secrets--Fiction. | Remote submersibles--Fiction. | Safes--Fiction. | LCGFT: Thrillers (Fiction) | BISAC: FICTION / Thrillers / General. | FICTION / Thrillers / Suspense.
Classification:	LCC: PS3608.A27 S43 2024 | DDC: 813/.6--dc23

Dedication

*For Mario, Hildy, Guck, and Dan'l—my lifelong
Pittsburgh friends. Yinz know who you are.*

CHAPTER 1

AMELIA GARCIA PILOTED the remotely operated vehicle and thanked God she didn't have to kill someone again. God knew she'd done enough of that. She sent the underwater craft into a sweeping turn, just above the dark ocean floor five thousand feet below her. While the work was fascinating and fully absorbed her chattering mind, it always reminded her of her time piloting the Reaper drone, minus the killing. She'd told herself she had killed for her country to protect those who couldn't protect themselves. To prevent thousands of her fellow citizens from dying like those who died in the World Trade Center towers. Still, along with that thought, a dark, condemning guilt accumulated in her throat, and she battled it back down with a few deep breaths and patriotic affirmations. While some thanked her for her service, they had no idea what her twelve years as an Air Force remotely piloted aircraft pilot had cost her. She was thirty-five and all her friends were married with children, already having completed the ritual of presenting their firstborns to their parents as precious treasures mined from their shared DNA. While she loved children and was happy for her friends, the endless social media posts and relentless conversations about their children shined a spotlight on a gaping hole in her life, eventually leading to uncomfortable and unanswerable questions. Over time, the gap between her top-secret missions and her friends' lovely family lives became a lonely chasm only breached by annual Christmas greetings. She had sacrificed so much for her patriotic duty, yet the nagging feeling that she was placed on this earth to do something special continued to follow her like a storm cloud. She touched the picture of her older sister resting on the console in front of her and prayed to the dark abyss beyond the ROV's lights that her father's account of her sister's death three years ago had been wrong. She ached for their long conversations and her comforting guidance.

She took each assignment as seriously as any mission, but this one fed both her addictive curiosity and her steadfast desire to serve God and country. This was the first deepwater drilling off the coast of Virginia sanctioned by the US government through NOAA, the agency responsible for managing, observing, researching, and protecting the oceans and coasts of the country. The blocks were held by Falzone Energy, the large oil company headquartered in Pittsburgh that had occupied the headlines for the past year. But based on the parade of government and university scientists regularly arriving for clandestine meetings, she suspected their target wasn't oil. The work and its target were confidential, but their presence wasn't. You couldn't hide the enormous drillship, support vessels, and the Navy cruiser providing security from any prying eyes.

Through the narrow window of the control room tucked into the corner of the deepwater drillship, she saw the first red sparks of dawn reaching the clouds on the horizon. As her anticipation of leaving the ship grew, the hum of the diesel generators that had provided the comforting white noise faded, and the protective shell she'd built around herself with her work melted away. She'd kept her anxiety at bay for a month, but now the last shift of her stay was ending. In three hours, she'd board the helicopter and head onshore for her thirty days off, forced to face the barren realities of her life. She refocused on the controls and the screen in front of her. She scanned the seafloor around the massive blowout preventer one last time.

Once her final inspection was complete, she guided the vehicle past a bed of deepwater coral patrolled by a few ghost fish and headed to a small angular bulge in the smooth seafloor that she'd spotted on descent, one hundred yards from the blowout preventer. The image was clear, but fine silt had covered the object like newly fallen snow. The excursion was not sanctioned by the offshore installation manager or NOAA, but as long as her mission was complete, the higher-ups in her company, including her uncle, ignored her obsession with her miniature deep-sea explorations.

As she approached the anomaly on the sea floor, her pulse quickened. The object was angular, definitely manmade, and had somehow ended up buried in the silt two hundred miles off the coast of the Virginia–North Carolina border. She approached the object until its image occupied the entire screen. The digital readout marked the exact location and depth. Under 4,752 feet of ocean, the frigid water might have preserved the container, but the extreme pressure would have broken most seals and ruined the contents. That is, unless the contents were gems, precious metals, or coins.

She hovered the ROV and snapped a still photo to document the find just in case it was an artifact of interest to the United States regulators in charge of this operation. One 360-degree sweep showed the object was a rectangular box. She guessed it was only a foot and a half long. Her arms tingled with excitement when she realized that the part protruding from the sediment was intact. Guiding the vehicle closer, she gripped the joystick that operated the articulated arm as the thrust from the stabilizers on the ROV stirred the blanket of silt. She reached out with the arm and gently grasped the object. A cloud of sediment enveloped the box as she pulled back on the joystick, extracting the container from the grip of the seafloor. As the cloud of fine particles settled, she carefully stowed the object for the long trip to the surface.

She was one of two pilots on the team that included three technicians and two operators. The trip to the surface filled the balance of her tour, and the daylight crew would be there soon. As the vehicle neared the surface, Gabe Rodgers, the lead operator, entered the control room with his perpetual smile. "Anything I should know about?" he said in his thick Texas drawl.

He was well aware of her hobby of gathering junk from the seafloor for her collection displayed on one side of her two-car garage.

"Good morning, Gabe. And yes. There is one item maybe eighteen inches long."

"Got it. Split the treasure?"

"Half of nothing is still nothing," she said, smiling.

"My usual take, then. I'll put it in your container with your duffel for the trip home."

Gabe laughed, slapped the door, and headed back out on deck.

The recovery went without a hitch, and she was relieved by the new crew who'd just arrived on the chopper. Back in her quarters, she opened the sealed container and examined the heavy metal box. Its weight surprised her, and it appeared thick-walled and watertight. She grabbed a small wire brush she kept in her duffel and scraped away the sediment covering the lid. Her work first revealed an engraving. It looked like the wing of a bird. She scrubbed harder toward the center of the lid, and the image that appeared sent a tremor through her body. It was an eagle clutching a swastika. She immediately recognized it as a Nazi Eagle, and the sudden sensation swept over her that something evil was watching her. She hurriedly stuffed the box back into the plastic container, placed it in her duffel, and headed for the helipad.

At the shore base in Norfolk, Amelia said her goodbyes to the rest of the crew and loaded her Jeep for the seven-hour trip to Kiawah. Once in the Jeep, she called her uncle.

Uncle Billy had been her favorite since she was a child. While he was the founder and controlling shareholder in Winkler ROV Services, he was also her surrogate dad. She trusted him. Uncle Billy and her Aunt Bessie had always been an oasis from her rocky relationship with her father. Uncle Billy had supported her choices and guided her when she'd asked. He'd also given her the job when she'd left the Air Force two years ago.

They lived on Kiawah Island, a private South Carolina island paradise just south of Charleston. Uncle Billy and Amelia's mother had vacationed there every summer as kids and continued the tradition with their families. Amelia loved vacationing with them, her sister, and her cousin. Ten years ago, Uncle Billy had bought a magnificent home on the island. A year later, Amelia's mother and father followed, building a beachfront home less than two miles from Uncle Billy. Both couples commuted to their Highland Park homes in Dallas as needed for business. Uncle Billy had several vacation rentals on the island and kindly rented one to Amelia at a steep discount when she'd started with Winkler ROV.

Uncle Billy answered on the second ring. "Hey sunshine. Headed our way?"

"Hi Uncle Billy. Yes, I am."

"What's wrong?" He'd always been able to read her moods.

"I may have screwed up."

"Ok. I do that all the time," he said. She could hear the grin in his voice. "What's up?"

"You know how I collect the museum pieces?"

"Officially no. But yes."

"I found something at the end of my tour. It was a small strong box. When I brought it to the surface and started to clean it up, I found Nazi markings on the lid."

The silence confirmed her concerns. If it came from a sunken Nazi warship, it was probably protected by the Sunken Military Craft Act. But she'd seen no such wreck. The closest one was eighty miles away.

"Do you have it with you?"

"Yes. Sorry."

"No. Don't worry. Just describe it for me in detail."

Amelia did and when she was done, he said, "Take it home. Don't do anything to it. I'll call a friend I went to school with who's a lawyer at Justice in DC. He'll know what to do."

Having the Department of Justice involved didn't sound good. "Am I in trouble?"

"No. No. And don't worry. I won't use your name. I'll just see what he comes up with. Just come by in the morning once you're settled."

"Okay. Thanks Uncle Billy."

"Don't worry. It will be fine. You driving down here today?"

"I'm going to stop and get some sleep. I had the night tour. I'll drive in late tonight."

"You just drive safe, and your Aunt Bessie and I will see you in the morning."

She ended the call and eyed her duffel in the rearview mirror. Uncle Billy had made her feel a little better, but just a little.

CHAPTER 2

IKE ROSSI WANTED to stop time and stay in this moment forever. He'd never thought he could feel this way again. The glow of pure joy warmed every cell in his body and a swelling pride filled his chest. He leaned back in the Naugahyde booth in Rossi's, the namesake bar and restaurant he'd rebuilt in Bloomfield, Pittsburgh's little Italy, after a bombing that nearly killed his sister Maria. He watched eleven-year-old Jack Cole, who was seated in another booth across from him. Jack studied the chess pieces on the board. He meticulously moved his queen into position and joyfully declared, "Checkmate!" to his fifty-one-year-old opponent. The awkward genius who had always stared at the floor when confronted, Jack had blossomed since Ike had proved him innocent of the murder charge lodged against him for shooting one of his father's killers in self-defense one year ago, setting him free and giving him his life back. After completing the reconstruction of Rossi's, Ike and Maria had hosted Jack, his aunt Lauren, and his cousin Jimmy every Saturday morning for breakfast before Rossi's opened at eleven.

Jack looked over at Ike, flashed an ear-to-ear smile, and pointed at Randy Shane. "I got him again!"

Ike leaned across the aisle and offered a high five. "That you did." Jack slapped it. Ike shifted his gaze to Randy and raised one eyebrow. "What do you have to say to that?"

"The same thing you said to that defensive end that cleaned your clock just before you became a legend of western Pennsylvania football, boss."

Randy had joined Rossi's as a chef six months ago to follow his true passion after completing a twenty-two-year career as a correctional officer. Ike had met Randy in a grief counseling group last year, and they quickly became friends. Randy's wife had been killed after a home invasion by an angry escaped con. Even though Ike had lost his parents to an unsolved murder twenty-three years ago, they'd bonded over their losses. Randy had retired and was adrift in his grief, unable to get meaningful work to fill the void. No one would hire a depressed ex-prison guard. But Ike understood and offered him a job. Randy immediately rediscovered his joy of cooking for others and had accelerated Rossi's comeback with his killer menu and gregarious personality.

Randy turned back to Jack and melted him into the booth with a battle-hardened deadpan stare, but he was a love-and-logic kind of correctional officer, and the stare morphed quickly into a bouncing smile. "Great job, Jacky boy." He high-fived him across the table.

The click of the door latch at the entrance pulled Ike's attention to Rossi's front door as Jenna Price entered, holding her briefcase at her side. Ike's joy was smothered with the murky darkness of uncertainty when Jenna couldn't hold his stare. He was back there again, nineteen and in the athletic dorms at Penn State, lost and alone, after the news of his parents' deaths. Jenna had been Jack's lawyer on his murder case along with her father who owned the two-person law firm. Against impossible odds, and with Ike's help, they'd prevailed. Now, she had more business than she and her father could handle. Still, she'd been carving out time helping Ike uncover the truth about his parents' murders, digging into the evidence of a massive corruption and cover-up scandal within the Pittsburgh Police Department that Ike had exposed while freeing Jack.

Ike felt a hand on his shoulder. He looked up and saw Lauren Bottaro, Jack's aunt and now guardian, with her son Jimmy behind her.

"Hey boys. If it's okay with Lauren, I'll let you test my latest dessert special." Randy stood and was quickly joined by Jack and Jimmy. Upon receiving an approving nod from Lauren, Randy led them to the bar and

stopped across from Maria, who'd been getting ready for the eleven-
o'clock opening.

"You should witness this," Randy said.

Maria glanced at Ike. He nodded, knowing that ever since her brush
with death, she wanted nothing to do with his investigations, especially the
one involving their parents' deaths. She only focused on managing Rossi's.
Randy's arrival had provided a deeper sense of security. He'd demonstrated
that skill on several late-night occasions dealing with overserved patrons
more interested in Maria than leaving. Maria smiled at Randy, and they
disappeared into the back.

Ike turned and looked up at Lauren. They had grown close over the
past year. While they were great friends, Ike sensed they weren't as close
as Lauren wanted. They weren't officially dating, but they'd spent time
together with and without Jimmy and Jack. Ike trusted her completely.
While he still wandered in an emotional desert, he refused to risk touching
the third rail: vulnerability for that deeper connection. He'd tried that once
before and lost. He slid over and patted the open seat. Lauren sat just as
Jenna arrived at the booth.

"Ike. Lauren." A former basketball standout at the University of
Pittsburgh, Jenna folded her thick towering frame into the opposite side
of the booth.

"Hi Jenna. How's your dad doing?" Lauren said.

"Great. Running around like he's on fire. He loves that. He knows he's
fueling the bottom line and securing Michael's future and then some."

"How *is* your brother?" Ike asked.

"Doing great. He moved to a group setting and still works in the
sandwich shop. Dad helped him set up a foundation to help other families
deal with all things related to Down Syndrome. They're both having a blast
helping others."

"Great to hear. So …"—Ike looked at Lauren, then Jenna—"what do
you have?"

Jenna wagged her head. "Not much new. Brooks Latham still won't
cooperate. DA even offered him another sweet deal. Wouldn't budge. He's
afraid of someone."

After waiting more than twenty-three years, Ike still didn't have any answers in his parents' murder case. Vic Cassidy, the discredited detective who took over the investigation into his parents' murders nine years ago, had been a key player in a corruption scheme that involved the cops, the largest law firm in Pittsburgh headed by Latham, and the now-imprisoned Joseph Falzone, CEO of Falzone Energy, a multi-billion-dollar oil company based in town. But Cassidy was killed by Ike's mentor, Mac Machowski, just before Mac admitted Ike's mother was involved in something she shouldn't have been, then Mac took his own life. Latham was their only chance to uncover what happened to his parents.

"Does the DA know who he's afraid of?"

"No. Not a clue."

"Did they find the murder book for my parents' case?"

"No. And the cops are circling the wagons around the department. The DA's investigation has slowed to a crawl." Jenna eyed Ike for a moment, then pulled a manila file from her briefcase and set it on the table. "I did get this from a contact in the department."

Ike opened the file. It contained two pages. When he saw the title of the first page, he was flooded with possibilities.

Confidential Informant Agreement

The tattered form had been heavily redacted with anything identifying either the informant or the controlling agent blacked out. Even the dates on the signature page were concealed. The only information contained in the two pages was that the informant had a spouse and two children.

Ike wasn't sure he'd like the answer to his next question. He asked it anyway. "Where did this come from?"

"It was allegedly buried in Mac's desk drawer. It was hidden under a false bottom."

Ike felt Lauren gently squeeze his shoulder. She nodded when he looked at her, then he refocused on Jenna. "Is it one of my parents?"

"There's no way to tell."

Ike leaned back with the paper in his hand. He scanned the framed photographs that filled the area above the bar. He stopped on the one of him and his mother standing in their kitchen, aprons on, both smiling.

Cooking was their vehicle to connect. They'd talk about everything while he picked up her favorite recipes and the skill to make them. Two themes his mother had promoted came to mind. The first was the value of service to others and how it was the key to a happy life. The second was that Ike should always avoid doing anything at all costs that he wouldn't want to see on the front page of the paper. She'd said that little steps in the wrong direction could lead to big trouble.

He shook his head and looked back at the document in his hand. Neither of his parents could have had a connection in the criminal world. It just couldn't have happened. But the form said two children and a spouse. It fit their profile. Mac had said that Ike's mother didn't know what she was getting into. Ike dropped his head, sagged back into the booth, and looked toward the kitchen and Maria.

"Don't show this to her," he said, "It would crush her." He handed the form back to Jenna.

"We don't know it's one of them," Jenna said, slipping the file back into her briefcase.

"We don't know it's not, either," he said. "But if it is, we have a whole new list of possibilities." That thought burned away his disappointment. It was replaced with a renewed hope that he'd find the people responsible. He sat back up.

"Thanks Jenna. I know getting that wasn't easy."

"We don't do easy, do we?" Jenna said with a smile. She stood with the case. "I've gotta get back and help Dad."

"On a Saturday?" Lauren asked.

"Yes." Jenna said, nodding toward Ike. "Thanks to this guy, our caseload is overflowing." She stopped in the aisle and asked, "How's your work at Minuteman?"

"It's a tight hole. The government has it clamped down," Ike said. "I go out there to check security from Falzone's end for Shannon. The feds do the rest."

After Joseph Falzone had gone to prison, his daughter, Shannon, had taken over the firm and fully cooperated with the government. Thanks to the current administration's stance on offshore leasing, they had the rights to the largest oil find in the last twenty years, the first one off the East Coast, but couldn't produce it. The government wanted to assess the seismic anomaly beneath it that was at the heart of Joseph Falzone's cover-up.

"Well, I'm sure it's in good hands. You two take care. Give my best to Maria and the boys."

"We will," Ike said. "Thanks again."

Jenna gave a wave on the way out the door.

"You okay with that?" Lauren asked, still looking at the door.

Ike shook his head. "No. Not really."

"Let me know if I can do anything."

"I w—" Ike's phone rang. He pulled it from his pocket and saw it was Shannon Falzone.

"Hi, Shannon. We were just talking about you."

She stayed silent a second too long. "We have a problem. The FBI is on their way here."

CHAPTER 3

AT TEN O'CLOCK Saturday morning, Amelia walked into her garage and eyed the eclectic assortment of items covering the rows of black PVC shelving filling one side of her two-car garage. She shook her head as she passed by her makeshift museum and entered her Jeep parked in the far bay. Collecting the artifacts from the deep reaches of the ocean floor was a form of therapy for her. She imagined each owner and the life they must have led. From a colorful coffee cup dropped off a Carnival Cruise ship to a pitted cannonball from God knows when, they all were the source of romantic tales she'd told herself. It had eased the loneliness and isolation she couldn't escape. But now, her latest addition had summoned an evil she'd never understand. For the first time, she'd wished she'd never started the collection.

Despite arriving at the rental home on Kiawah at two that morning, Amelia's circadian clock and her racing, suspicious mind refused to let go of the idea that some evil spirit eyed her. It had robbed her of any sleep. She watched the door roll up in the rearview mirror, inhaled a smooth, deep breath, and let it out as she backed out of the garage. The lush palmettos, the tall, slender pines that reached to the heavens, and the graceful live oaks draped with Spanish moss made Kiawah feel like another world. She relaxed a little and convinced herself that Uncle Billy had solved the problem already, and in five minutes, he'd give her the word that all was well.

While Kiawah was famous for its long ten-mile east-west beach on its south side, her uncle had built his home on the north side of the island, on the banks of the Kiawah River, in a neighborhood known as Rhett's Bluff. She'd spent hours with her uncle on their back deck watching dolphins, herons, and pelicans. As she crossed the berm and spillway that connected the area to the island, the bright fall sunshine warmed her body and thoughts of time with Uncle Billy put a smile on her face. Off to her right, she saw the white herons picking their morning meal from the mucky tidal flats of the river.

She wound around the first curve on the tree-covered lane and spotted a cluster of Charleston County Sheriff's patrol cars surrounding her uncle's home. Instinctively, she spiked the brake pedal. Red and blue flashing lights sliced through the graceful oaks and painted every surface. Her breath quickened when she spotted the county coroner's vehicle. Her hands gripped the sides of the steering wheel and she locked her elbows, trying to push away what her mind was telling her. Panic flushed through her body and tears blurred her vision.

She spotted her father's Range Rover on the side of the road to the right, just short of the skirmish line formed by the emergency vehicles. She wiped her eyes and pulled the Jeep behind her father's SUV. Up ahead, her mother frantically argued with a deputy who was physically restraining her. Tess Garcia had always maintained a put-together and composed public persona. A woman and mother well known in Dallas high-society circles, she occupied a station in life her family had for generations. She never lost control—at least not when she was sober—unless something or someone pushed her too far.

Amelia bolted from the car and sprinted to her mother.

"Let her go!" she yelled.

Her mother stopped fighting and stared at Amelia. The deputy released her mother's arm. Amelia read the news in her mother's eyes, then her mother collapsed into Amelia's embrace.

"He's gone. He's gone!" she sobbed into Amelia shoulder. "They're both gone."

Tears wandered down Amelia's cheeks. "Uncle Billy?" Amelia said, refusing to let her mother's words sink in.

Her mother pulled back, and a haunting composure swept over her. She tilted her head, softened her eyes, and trapped the horrible truth behind her trembling lips.

The October chill seeped deep into Amelia's bones. "Oh no. Not Uncle Billy."

Her mother's expression didn't change.

"Aunt Bessie, too?"

Her mother nodded, then hugged Amelia. A nauseating heat overwhelmed her, and her legs became weak. But she remembered to breathe and caught herself before she went down. She recalled her conversation with her uncle last night. Her body tensed and trembled as her adrenaline spiked, and her mind rejected what her gut told her. Her body couldn't convince her mind there could be a connection. She refocused on her mother.

"How? How did it happen?"

Her mother looked past the crime-scene tape toward the towering white columned home. "Your father is trying to find out."

Amelia spotted her father talking to a taller black man wearing a dark sports coat who was scribbling in his notepad.

"Who's that?"

"I think he's the detective from the sheriff's department." Her mother wiped her eyes, turned, and sneered at the deputy. "And this ass won't let me in or tell me anything."

The young deputy just stared off into the distance, apparently ignoring her mother's insult. She assumed the young man wanted nothing to do with her mother. Amelia's attention shifted toward the house. It was getting windy, and the palms rustled as the gusts assaulted their fronds. Technicians dressed in white suits with hoods covering their heads milled around the front of the house. Three technicians wearing blue gloves and booties were leaving the home. One carried a camera, one an orange tool kit, and the third a cylindrical black object. Through the front windows, Amelia watched as rigid forms methodically moved around the rooms.

Her watch vibrated and a headline from her newsfeed flashed on her screen. "DOJ Deputy Attorney General Dies in Freak Accident." Her arm dropped to her side, and the outward world disappeared. Her mind raced back to the conversation last night. The box, her uncle's assurances, and the call to the attorney in the DOJ. It couldn't be the same one. It had to be a coincidence. She pulled up her iPhone, opened the news app, and found the article. Struggling to read the phone shaking in her hand, she found the name: David Cohen. She opened the browser and looked him up. Her eyes froze on his alma mater—SMU. Southern Methodist University, where Uncle Billy went to school.

She clutched her fists as panic tried to hijack every muscle in her body. She battled the urge to run and anchored her feet in place. Her find had done this. It had gotten her uncle and her aunt killed, along with her uncle's contact at the DOJ. Only one other person knew it existed—her. They'd be coming for her next. She eyed the area again looking for anyone focused on her. She saw her father and the detective headed her way. It forced her to quickly weigh her options. Telling the detective about the box wouldn't ensure her safety. The people involved had power and connections. They'd killed her uncle and aunt on one of the most secure and exclusive private islands in the country and taken out a high-ranking government official at the DOJ. Whoever it was, they wanted the box. And not just the box, but also its contents. Whatever was inside was a threat to the killers. It made sense that whoever controlled the box controlled the outcome. The contents might be deadly to the killers, like kryptonite to Superman.

With her father and the detective stopped and arguing just a few steps away, she decided as long as she had the box, they needed her alive. She had to find out what was inside, and for help with that, only one name burst into her mind. The one man who'd have the best chance. The man she'd met only once on the drillship, introduced to her by another family friend. The man who'd taken on the system and the most powerful family in the country and won. She pulled out her phone and sent a text.

She needed Ike Rossi.

CHAPTER 4

IKE SHIFTED THE deep blue Shelby Mustang into third and felt the horsepower drive him into the seat. Last year the DeSantis brothers had done their magic and returned it to pristine condition after it took two slugs into the engine block while he was working Jack's case. It was nearing noon and the breeze had shifted to the south, making it feel more like summer than mid-October. Traffic was nonexistent, and Ike let his hand ride on the air slipping past his open window. There was always something magical about a Saturday drive, but the image of the redacted confidential informant form gnawed at his mind. It was more like voodoo than magic that attacked his precious memories of his mother. When he spotted his destination in the Pittsburgh skyline, the gleaming Falzone Tower brought him back to the matter at hand. Shannon Falzone had said there was a problem and the FBI was on their way to her office. It wasn't her message but the concern rattling in her voice that compelled him to drop everything and head to downtown Pittsburgh. Since the feds were involved, he assumed it was a problem with Minuteman. Now, he wasn't sure.

He'd given his word to help her with the government's efforts to unlock the mystery of what lay beneath Falzone Energy's blocks. The revelation of the unusual seismic images and the conspiracy to conceal them had set Jack free, but it had created a gargantuan disaster for Shannon. After her brother Patrick had been killed by her half-brother Nick, her father had been forced to kill his son to save his only daughter. Joseph Falzone, founder of one of the largest independent oil companies in the country, had been incarcerated for conspiracy, fraud, bribery, and murder. While his sentence was tempered by his cooperation in convicting two judges, the DA, the assistant police chief, three detectives, and a dozen attorneys involved in the conspiracy uncovered by Ike in Jack's case, there was still a leadership vacuum at the top. Shannon Falzone, at twenty-six years old, was the only family member left to assume the CEO role. She'd asked Ike to help with Minuteman. Because she'd helped Ike dismantle her own family to help Jack, proving she was smart, capable, and honest, Ike knew he had to help.

He exited the Lincoln Highway and squeezed past the towering US Steel building guarding the entrance into the forest of skyscrapers in downtown Pittsburgh. The lush green of Mellon Park gave way to the rumbling cobblestones of Grant Street when he turned left and headed to Falzone Center. A few blocks ahead, he spotted the turreted towers and rough weathered masonry of the Allegheny County Courthouse. At first, a sense of pride filled his chest as he remembered the day he walked out of the courthouse with Jack. But then the failure of the system to find his parents' killer soured his mood, and he turned into the parking garage under Falzone Center.

After clearing security, he took the express elevator to the fifty-second floor. His complete and unfettered access to the building that he now enjoyed was surreal compared to the subterfuge he'd used last year. He extinguished a tinge of guilt for his deception with the fact that Jack was alive and free. Shannon met him as he exited the elevator. Despite the fact she was dressed in faded jeans and a Penn quarter-zip sweatshirt, she still looked confident and in control, but her widened eyes said there was a problem.

Ike threw a nod to the square-jawed security guard stationed at a desk in front of the elevator. "Hey, Warren."

Warren looked up from the monitor in front of him and locked his eyes on Ike. "Hey, Ike."

"Steelers look like they got a shot this year."

"We'll see. Long season." Warren returned his attention to the monitor. Shannon smiled at the guard. "Thanks, Warren."

"You're welcome, Miss Falzone."

They headed down the long mahogany hallway that was the main artery connecting the executive offices. Shannon had done a good job softening the tone to a more welcoming venue for everyone. Portraits and imposing bronze sculptures had been replaced by bright paintings by famous naturalists.

She looked up at Ike as they moved down the long corridor. "Thanks for coming so quickly. I couldn't share what I have over the phone," she said, her face firm with concern. "How is everyone?"

Shannon's concern was genuine, as it always was, so Ike decided to give her the details as they walked. "Maria is focused on ramping up Rossi's reputation as the best Italian restaurant in the city and doing a great job. Randy's doing an outstanding job helping to get that done. He also provides a little backup when I'm gone. Lauren is managing her programming work around Jack and Jimmy, and those two are doing what eleven-year-olds should be doing." Up ahead, Ike noticed that the Falzone Family portrait at the end of the hallway had been removed. He stopped just short of Shannon's office door and turned to face her. "How's your mother?"

"She's better. Last year was hard on her, losing Patrick, then Dad going away. But after the divorce, she's started to get out more and getting a life of her own finally."

"Good for her." Ike liked Erin Falzone. Because she was Jack's grandmother, they'd spent plenty of time together over the past year.

They entered Shannon's office, and Ike took one of the side chairs in front of her desk. Shannon hesitated, then gently dropped into her chair facing him. She'd scaled down the grandeur of her father's old office. She'd donated the old furniture and replaced it with the furniture issued to every other employee in the building. She'd swapped his Remington paintings with framed photographs of groups of Falzone employees from her trips she'd taken to every corner of the operation after she'd taken the job. There were a few photographs of the company's new operations in wind, solar, and hydrogen, probably a reminder of her steadfast commitment to hitting her aggressive greenhouse gas targets. She meant business and put her Wharton MBA and her money fully behind her efforts.

"So, what's going on with Minuteman?" Ike asked.

Shannon gently wagged her head and narrowed her gaze on Ike. Sadness tugged at the corners of her mouth. "I got a call from the FBI."

Ike leaned forward to receive what he wasn't sure he wanted to hear. "What does the FBI want?"

"It's not good news. Apparently, the CEO of Winkler ROV was just found dead in his home on Kiawah Island. His wife too."

"I'm so sorry, Shannon. You all were friends, right?"

"Yes. We've known the Winkler family for a long time. They've been in the business before Dad started ours back in the seventies. Our family offices have worked together for years. I know his sister and their family well."

"Benton and Tess Garcia?"

Shannon appeared surprised. "Yes. How do you know them?"

"I worked on a case for another Texas oil family a couple of years ago. Winkler Oil was their partner in a few big shale finds in the Permian Basin."

"Then you know that Billy Winkler is Tess's younger brother." Shannon shifted her weight back in her chair. "And Minuteman is drilling past fifteen thousand feet. We're in the oil column and headed to the target at eighteen thousand."

"Yes. I've been following the daily drilling reports. They still going to let you stop to log the interval?"

"Yes. But we're getting close to the images. Atlantis, as the crew is calling it. Only three thousand more feet. I think the FBI is nervous that we're getting close to TD and they're investigating—" She struggled to finish as her words choked off her air. Ike noticed a quiver in her chin. "They're investigating Billy's death."

Ike gave Shannon a moment to collect herself.

"Sorry. I can't believe he's gone," she said.

"I understand. Did you get any indication as to the cause of death?"

"Not directly. But the newsfeeds are calling it a murder-suicide." This time Shannon opened a desk drawer and blotted her eyes with a tissue. She sighed and settled her gaze on Ike. "That just can't be. He wouldn't kill Bessie, let alone himself."

Ike nodded, recognizing the pain in Shannon's eyes. "When will the FBI be here?"

Shannon checked her watch. "Any minute."

Ike checked his watch. It was just before noon. "Did they have any children?"

"Yes. A daughter. She still lives in Highland Park. Married. No kids."

Ike could only shake his head. He remembered the numbing shock when they'd called him at the athletic dorm and told him his parents had been killed. Crippling pain had followed and had driven him to his knees. Their daughter would face that now.

"One other thing you need to know," Shannon said. "Billy's niece works on the rig. An ROV pilot. I think you met her."

"I do remember. Very impressive. An Air Force veteran. She and I talked about importance of her blowout preventer inspections." An image came into Ike's mind. A smart, broad-shouldered blonde-haired woman who used to be a drone pilot. Penetrating blue-green eyes.

Shannon's phone rang and she answered. "Yes. Please bring them up," Shannon said. "Yes. To my office." She hung up. "They're here. Security has to bring them up."

Ike realized there was no executive assistant on the floor. It was Saturday. Shannon hadn't called her in.

After a short conversation about their strategy to draw out as much information as they could from the FBI, a firm knock caused Ike to turn and look at the open office door behind him. A large security guard filled the doorway. "Miss Falzone."

Shannon rose and moved around her desk. "Yes, Derek. Send them in."

Ike stood. The guard stepped aside, and a short silver-haired man strutted in as if he'd been unfairly made to wait. His green eyes, shaded by thick eyebrows, narrowed on Ike, but Shannon intercepted him.

"Shannon Falzone." She held her hand out and he shook it.

The agent smiled, almost too much. "Special Agent Curtis Sherman from the Columbia, South Carolina, field office." His southern accent was thick, like molasses.

Ike stepped up and offered his hand, just as the second agent entered. "Ike Rossi. I help Miss Falzone with security."

"I'll be damned. I heard about you, son. Very impressive. You were a hell of a quarterback in your day. That '30 for 30' on ESPN broke my heart."

"That was a long time ago," Ike said, making it clear he didn't want to revisit his past. He glanced over Sherman's shoulder at the approaching agent. He recognized her immediately and the shock made his heart shudder. The woman went straight to Shannon.

"Miss Falzone. Nice to meet you. I'm Supervisory Special Agent Mia Russo out of DC." She shook Shannon's hand. As she turned toward Ike, a flood of joy and regret stunned him. She still looked the same. Short blonde hair, lush red lips, and light blue eyes that both dared and welcomed a person. She locked her eyes on Ike's.

"It's been a long time."

CHAPTER 5

IKE'S FEET WERE planted, as if in cement, yet his skin vibrated with a magnetism that drew him toward Mia. Ten years after he'd let their bond wither, she was back. He reached out across the frigid chasm between them and shook her hand. "Nice to see you again, Mia," Ike said, hoping his smile would leave their past behind them.

Her skin was soft, but her grip was firm and cold. She held the handshake a second longer while Ike remembered the physical contact they had both craved so long ago. She, however, remembered something else. He saw a glint of the pain he'd inflicted still in her eyes, and her forced smile put the blame where it belonged: squarely on him. She released Ike's hand, and they returned to their more stoic veneers.

"So, you two know each other?" Shannon motioned toward the round table near the window, and they headed toward the chairs.

Swallowing his guilt, Ike eyed Mia, then stopped by one of the four chairs around the slate gray table, but he remained silent.

"We met while I was a patrolwoman for the Pittsburgh Police Department," Mia said, not showing any affection for the memory.

"Geez, Russo, when was that?" Sherman said, as if he was owed an answer.

Mia ignored him and tilted her head, stone-faced, pointedly looking at Ike. "Ten years?" In case there was any doubt in Ike's mind, she made it clear she was still upset. She was always what oilfield workers called a short-looper. She never beat around the bush.

Ike decided to play nicely. "Ten years ago. I was working at Abbysis Energy at the time and keeping up with my parents' case with the detective assigned to it. He introduced us."

"They never caught the perpetrators, did they?" Sherman said.

Ike envisioned pounding Sherman while in the ring with him, then took a beat. "No."

Mia eyed Sherman, letting him know he was out of bounds. Then she glanced back at Ike. "Sorry, Ike."

Sherman acted as if he'd sat on a cactus. "No need to treat me like a sinner in church. I didn't know."

With Mia's attempt to call out Sherman, Ike felt the last ember of hope glow a little brighter.

Ignoring the banter, Shannon said, "How can we help you?"

Mia narrowed her eyes on Shannon. "Let me first say, this meeting is confidential. We'd appreciate it if you'd not share it with anyone."

Sherman pulled a pen and notepad from his vest pocket and placed it on the table. "Agent Sherman and I are investigating a very sensitive matter surrounding the death of William and Elizabeth Winkler."

"Billy and Bessie," Shannon said, her face sagging with sadness.

"Right," Mia said flatly. "Because their company was intimately involved with Minuteman, we've been asked to get involved. We'd like to ask you a few questions, and as you know, you're a federal contractor on this project."

Ike assumed Mia thought her warning would increase the pressure on them. It didn't. Ike wanted to respect Shannon's ties to the Winklers but pressed through his reluctance to upset her. He knew she was stronger than that. "Agent Russo. Can you tell me why the FBI is investigating when the local authorities suspect it to be a murder-suicide?"

Mia didn't lift her gaze from Shannon. "No, Ike. And we'll be asking the questions."

Sherman stopped writing and said, "Let us get to the questions and then we'll see what other comments y'all might have."

Mia glanced at Sherman, silently scolding him, then turned back to Shannon. "How long have you known the Winklers?"

"Most of my life. My father had several partnerships with the Winkler family in the seventies and our families remained friends. Our family offices also worked together over the years."

"What do the family offices do?" Mia asked.

Shannon's watch lit up, and she glanced at the message, cleared it, then said, "They manage the families' wealth, charitable work, and family income."

"When was the last time you spoke with either one of the Winklers?"

Shannon checked her watch again for a moment, then said, "It was last Thursday afternoon. I called Billy."

"And what did you talk about?"

"We talked about the schedule for Minuteman relative to his ROV services, how his operations were going, and how his niece was doing on the drillship."

Mia leaned forward. "His niece?"

"Yes. His niece works as an ROV pilot on the ship."

Mia raised one eyebrow. "And what's their relationship like?"

Ike saw Shannon's jaw go taut. "I'm not sure what you're implying, agent," Shannon said.

Louder, Mia said, "I want to know if you know anything about the relationship between Billy Winkler and his niece."

Ike had enough. He put both palms on the table. "Agent Russo. Is there something you're not telling us?"

Mia's eyes flashed a warning at Ike. "You can be assured there are things we aren't telling you."

Ike ignored her warning. "Is the niece a person of interest?"

Mia leaned across the table toward Ike. "We're asking the questions here."

Ike pushed himself up from the table. "Were the Winklers murdered?" Ike realized they were both standing with Shannon and Agent Sherman seated, watching. Shannon's composure was stretched, and Ike realized what he'd implied about her friends' deaths. "Unless you're willing to share, Agent Russo, we're done here without our attorney present."

Mia stared at Ike. It felt as if she were saying *I can't believe you did this to me.* The lump in Ike's throat said that deep down, he felt the same.

Shannon stood. "Thank you for your time, agent." She offered Mia her hand.

The room went silent. Ike and Shannon held their positions.

Mia shook Shannon's hand and looked at Sherman. "Let's go."

Sherman stood, and Mia dropped her card on the table. "If you think of something that can help us, call me." She dipped her head toward Shannon. "Miss Falzone." Then she glanced at Ike and held her gaze a second longer. "Ike." She led Sherman out of the room.

Shannon deflated like a balloon. "Do you think they were murdered?"

Ike reached out, cupped her shoulder, and spoke softly. "I don't know. Sorry, but they wouldn't be involved if that wasn't a possibility."

Shannon walked to her desk and picked up her iPhone. "That message I received was from Amelia. The niece."

"What did she want?"

Shannon read the message on her phone. "She wanted to know if I could connect her with you."

A primal warning ran through Ike's veins. His life had just settled. He had a steady stream of low-risk clients in his business, mainly kidnap-and-ransom seminars instructing overconfident executives about how their arrogance could get them killed, and he'd promised Maria he'd not take any more risks that would jeopardize what remained of their family.

Shannon typed, then waited. "She won't tell me why. We have to meet her in person."

It was a request, not a statement. Ike could see that in Shannon's eyes.

"I can't, Shannon."

"She's a great person. A patriot who gave twelve years of her life to the Air Force, most of it as a drone pilot. You wouldn't believe what she had to do to keep us all safe. It took a big toll on her. I've helped her get back into civilian life. Since her sister died three years ago, she's all alone. She was closer to Billy than her own father, and now he's gone. After this last visit, it sounds like she could use your help. I could take you down there and just talk to her."

Ike didn't respond and turned to look at the Pittsburgh skyline. He knew this had all the markings of something big. Two killings and the FBI investigating. And Amelia had just lost the person she was closest to. Ike knew what that felt like. He also knew that the system rarely delivered closure, and the FBI, part of that system, just pegged his uncertainty meter on high. He was sure their next stop would be Amelia, and her life would get very complicated quickly. Shannon had called her a patriot. Ike wondered what kind of patriot. The politicians had usurped that word to mean selfishly radical for your own cause. Ike hoped Shannon meant Amelia had made a great sacrifice to help her country, the entire country, even those with whom she disagreed. With that assumption, the urge to help her was strong, but he remembered Maria when she was in the hospital bed. He'd made a commitment to her. They'd just got Rossi's back on its feet and that helped Maria in her recovery. He couldn't put his family at risk again. However, there was a security problem on Minuteman. While the FBI was responsible for security relative to the United States' interests, he was responsible for security for Falzone Energy and its people relative to Minuteman.

"At least just talk to her. Meet with her. That's all I'm asking. We can take the plane and be there in a couple of hours and back early this evening."

Ike turned and said, "I'll talk to her and ensure Falzone's interests are protected. But that's it."

Satisfaction radiated from Shannon's face, and she immediately started texting. Ike let out a long breath, but it didn't ease the suspicion swimming in his gut as he wondered what kind of patriot Amelia Garcia would be.

CHAPTER 6

AMELIA BATTLED HER nerves as the detective and her father approached. Her uncle had been killed because of her, and she was trapped between the icy fear blowing through her and the pacing anger that fueled a grinding desire to avenge his death. She wanted to know who'd killed him, but to get that answer, she needed to know what was in the box. She'd buried that thought where she kept her deepest secrets, and as the detective strode up, she readied her lies. Telling the truth might help the detective find her uncle's killer, but she doubted it. She knew lying to the police was never a good idea. Eventually, the truth had a way of seeping into daylight and coming back to punish the liar. But she needed the box, and she needed time. She casually wiped the beads of sweat forming on her forehead.

The detective's tweed jacket clung to his body. Not tailored but filled out to its fullest. She recognized the clean jawline and tight smooth skin of a man who knew his way around a gym. He stopped, facing her, pulled one side of his sports coat back to expose the badge on his belt, and locked his glassy, dark brown eyes on hers. Just then, her watch vibrated. She glanced at the text. Shannon was bringing Rossi.

"Amelia Garcia?" he asked as he pulled a small notepad from his breast pocket.

"Yes," she said.

"Detective Clarence Jefferson Wilson."

She watched her father walk up to her on the right. He reached out and hugged her, but she kept her arms limp at her side. As usual, he was putting on a good show for his audience. He awkwardly stepped back to her right.

"Amelia. This is Detective Wilson of the sheriff's department. He wants to ask you a few questions, but remember, you don't have to answer. I've got our lawyer on his way."

Wilson scowled at her father, then turned his attention back to Amelia. "Miss Garcia. It would be very helpful if you'd answer a few questions. It would help us with the investigation into your aunt's and uncle's deaths."

The words made Amelia's eyes fill with tears again and her lower lip started to quiver, so she bit it. Then she inhaled as much air as she could and hissed it out. "What happened to them?"

"That's what I'm trying to find out. I have two victims, both with fatal gunshot wounds to the head."

A gruesome image burst into Amelia's mind and stunned her. She imagined that was Detective Wilson's intent.

"Now. Your father tells me you were close with your uncle?" Wilson stared, expecting an answer.

"Yes. We were close."

"When was the last time you spoke with him?"

Amelia's mouth began to dry out. "I spoke to him yesterday."

Amelia heard her mother walk up behind her. Wilson tilted his head slightly but kept writing on his pad. "What time was that?"

"I'd just arrived onshore from my job, so around two p.m."

"What job is that?"

"I work as an ROV pilot for my uncle's company."

"ROV?"

"Remotely operated vehicle. Mainly in deep water."

Wilson kept writing, not looking up. "And what did you talk about?"

Amelia ignored the adrenalin spike rippling through her body. "We just chatted about my tour and when I'd be arriving back on Kiawah." She steadied her nerves and hoped nothing signaled her lie.

Wilson stopped writing and eyed Amelia. "That was it?"

"Yes."

"Did he mention anything unusual?"

"No."

"And what time did you get to Kiawah?"

"It was late. Right around two this morning."

"And you live on Kiawah?"

"Yes. On Gadwall. One of my uncle's rentals."

"And can anyone vouch for that?"

Amelia's father couldn't hold his mud any longer. "Detective, I think that's enough questions."

Wilson leaned toward her father and said, "Just a few more." He turned back to Amelia. "If that's all right with you?"

It was best not to have anything to hide. Or at least appear that way.

Amelia waved off her father. "I'm okay, Father." She returned her attention to Wilson. "The main gate would have that data. I used the right lane with the reader."

"But no one saw you?"

"No." Amelia was getting uneasy. She was conscious of everything: her blinking, her breathing, her swallowing.

"Can you tell me how your aunt and uncle got along?"

Amelia suddenly wanted to attack, and she felt flush as the hair tingled on the back of her neck. It was the same feeling she used to get piloting the Reaper and awaiting the approval to strike a high-value individual. "What do you mean?"

"Did they have a good relationship?"

"What are you implying?" her mother said, stepping into the conversation.

"Mrs. Garcia, right? I'll talk to you in a minute. I'm not implying anything. It's just a question I have to ask."

"Are you implying that one of them did this to the other?" Amelia heard the words her mother said but didn't believe them.

"I'm not implying anything." Wilson stepped a little closer to Amelia. "Now. What was their relationship like?"

"They loved each other. Always. They were happy. I can only hope I'm that happy someday."

Wilson finished writing. "Will you stay on Kiawah?"

"I'm not sure that's any of your business."

"She'll stay with us," her mother said. "And I don't have anything else to add. I love my brother and I haven't talked to him in three days. And we talked about the weather, golf, and dinner plans for this weekend."

"Did yo—"

"We're done, detective," her father said.

This time Wilson just folded his notepad and slipped it into his jacket. "Thank you, folks. I'm certain we'll talk again."

As he walked away, her mother said, "Can I get in there?"

Wilson turned with a look of concern on his face. "I'm sorry ma'am. It's an active crime scene. I wish I could let you in, but I can't. I'll be sure y'all are notified as soon as we're done. I gave my number to your husband. Call if you have any other questions." With that, he turned and headed back into the house. That left Amelia and her parents in an awkward silence.

The tension attacking Amelia's body abated, but the crushing, thick guilt remained stuck in her throat. She wanted to disappear, but now both parents trapped her. She wasn't sure what to say that wouldn't betray her secret.

Her mother rubbed Amelia's back and looked lovingly into her eyes. "What is it, Amelia honey?"

"What?"

"Is there something you're not telling me?"

Amelia glanced at her father standing in the grass just a few feet in front of her. He was scrolling through his phone. He rarely paid attention to her. At least never gave her the attention she deserved. He looked up from his phone and gave her that expression: a look that said she was a disappointment. They never talked about it. She didn't have to. She hated the feeling it fed of never being enough.

"Honey?" her mother said again.

Amelia noticed the tear streaks on her mother's face. "I'm sorry, Mom. I'm just numb. Shocked. I can't imagine how you feel, too."

Her mother studied the spectacle unfolding at the house. Technicians and uniformed officers were covering the scene. Then her mother turned to her father. "You need to find out what's going on here." Her voice was sharp and she'd stopped crying.

Amelia's father was a short man with plain features and a little boy's haircut, simply parted on the left side with short bangs sweeping across his small forehead. He'd appeared cute in her parents' wedding pictures, but keeping the same look as a tween boy and aging it fifty years had turned cute into just short of creepy. Amelia thought someone with north of ten billion dollars could afford better.

He looked up from his phone, aggravation twisting his face. "I'm working on it."

Her mother wasn't having any of that. She turned for a full-frontal attack. "I can't understand why anyone would want to hurt Billy and Bessie."

Amelia had seen this a million times.

Her mother stepped even closer to her father, who ignored her, his nose in his phone. "Your little club wouldn't have anything to do with this?" she said.

Her father dropped his phone to his side and glared at her mother. "No," he said. His thick sarcasm coated every word. "The club, as you call it, would have nothing to do with this. I can't believe you'd even ask that."

Amelia knew her mother was talking about the Texas oilmen who were silent power brokers and controlled politics and regulation in the state. They'd gotten another one of their chosen few in the White House three years ago and were plotting his reelection.

She stepped in between her parents to break up the contest. "I'll talk to the detective when they're done." It was an easy offer knowing that Ike Rossi would be helping her, but she couldn't tell them that.

Her mother's shoulders sagged. "Still, I'm not leaving. He's my brother."

"I'll stay with you."

Her mother hugged her again. "Then you can come home with me."

Amelia needed to get back to her house. She'd hidden the box, but someone could find it if they searched hard enough. And these killers were clearly highly skilled and connected. Shannon and Rossi were on their way too, and she couldn't involve her parents in that mess. They wouldn't understand. But she couldn't bear the thought of abandoning her mother when she needed her the most.

"I'll need to go back to the house. I've been gone for a month. I've got some things to do."

"It can wait. I don't want you being alone." Her mother pointed to her brother's house. "Not after this."

"Your mother is right," her father said, still not looking up from his phone.

There was no way around it. She'd have to tell them. Shannon would want to talk to her parents anyway. And when she'd convinced Rossi to help, he'd need to talk to them too.

"Ok. I'll do a few things, then come right over. But I've got something to tell you."

It must have been something in her voice, but her father put his phone away, and her mother turned and stared at her. Her mouth went dry, and she had to clear her throat.

"I told Shannon Falzone about it. Shannon is coming down. She'll be here in less than two hours."

"Okay," her mother said. "She's like family."

Her father shrugged then reached into his pocket for his phone again. "Shannon's a good friend. She's dealt with her share of tragedy, too."

Amelia and her mother both looked at her father, then at each other, wagging their heads at his insensitivity.

"But there's one more thing," Amelia said.

Her father kept his phone in his pocket. He'd apparently read the guilty expression on Amelia's face. "What?" he said, flatly.

"She's bringing Ike Rossi."

CHAPTER 7

AMELIA PULLED INTO the driveway of the rental house and her heart sank further. She stopped the Jeep and eyed the sprawling live oak that guarded the forty-year-old house. The ranch style home's light-beige exterior was in flawless condition and the manicured landscaping welcomed its occupants. Everywhere she looked she saw her aunt's and uncle's care for the happy families visiting this unique vacation spot. When she'd left thirty-one days ago, she didn't think her life could get any lonelier. Now, they were gone, and the universe had proved her wrong. She rolled down the window and let the gentle breeze cool her tears, then pulled to the garage.

She pressed the opener, but the door didn't budge. She pressed it again. Nothing. It had worked an hour ago. She leaned back into the seat and rubbed the back of her neck. Glancing to the right, into the kitchen window, she froze when she realized the kitchen light was off. She'd left it on. The key to her survival, the box, was inside. They'd found her. She closed her eyes for a split second and reminded herself of her resilient warrior mentality from her time in the Air Force. Dialing 911 wasn't an option here. It was up to her. Inside, the answer to her questions roamed.

She grabbed the keys, eased the driver's door open, and slipped out. Scanning the front of the house, she detected no movement and no forced entry. She crept quietly to the front door. If they were armed and waiting, it was over. So be it. All she needed was ten seconds to get to her Beretta after she opened the door. She sneaked up the stairs and slipped the housekey into the deadbolt. She eased the key counterclockwise, slowly enough to avoid the noise from turning the cylinder or the bolt leaving the jamb. The front door opened onto the small entry facing the living and dining rooms. She could see into the kitchen to her right. Clouds had moved in, and with no inside lighting, a gray hue blended with the shadows. Satisfied that the rooms in the front of the house were empty and with her back against the wall, she slid six steps to the left, stopping just short of the entry to the utility room. She paused, held her breath, and listened. Hearing nothing, she kept her eyes scanning the path forward and crept to the cabinet over the dryer. She stopped and listened again. She could hear a rustling outside, probably the wind. She pulled out the gun safe, unlocked it, and removed the Berretta and a magazine.

With the gun in her hand, she had at least evened the odds. She furrowed her brow, set her jaw, and tightened every muscle as she shifted her focus from being hunted to being the skilled hunter that she'd been as an RPA pilot. Capturing the intruder would be her ticket to her uncle's killer. She raised the Beretta and moved to the doorway, pressing her back along the jamb. In one fluid motion, she cleared both directions in the hallway. The back of the house had less natural light, and she moved much slower, her eyes straining to clear every hiding place. She heard every breath, every heartbeat, and the subtle sound of her Allbirds flexing against the hardwood floor. Running her hand along the wall, she found the light switch. She flipped it on. Nothing happened. After tiptoeing further down the dark hallway with her Berretta leading the way, she cleared the back bedrooms. That left the garage. Her museum.

Retracing her steps into the utility room, she went to the thick white door leading to the garage and stopped. She pressed her ear to the door and listened, but only heard the beating of her racing heart. Then she heard it. It was barely audible, but she was sure it was the rattle of the garage door.

Stepping back and spreading her stance, she stretched out with her free hand and swung the door open, ready to fire. The garage was darker than she expected. The window at the opposite side of the garage had been covered by a shrub. The rattling had stopped. From her vantage point on the single step into the garage, she could see the garage door. There was no indication of an intruder. In front of her, the first row of storage was four shelves high. Large gray Tupperware storage tubs occupied each shelf and blocked her view to the next row. Some of the items inside the tubs might stop a bullet, but not all of them. She eyed both ends of the shelving and decided to go around to the left. Quietly she moved down the step and onto the concrete floor, keeping her gun in firing position in front of her as she approached the end of the first set of shelves.

In an instant, with no warning, someone yanked something over her head and tightened a cord around her neck. Terrified, she felt a hard body pressed against her back for leverage with a force strong enough to lift her off her feet. She wanted to aim the Beretta over her shoulder, but her survival instinct caused her to drop the gun and reach for her neck with both hands to grab whatever was choking her. She found the extension cord around her neck. Her fingers couldn't get under the cord, and unable to breathe, panic set in. She could feel herself losing consciousness. Then, her attacker dropped her back to her feet, keeping pressure on the cord. She sucked in enough air to quell her panic and avoid fainting, but still couldn't get her fingers under the cord.

"Where is it?" The voice was sharp and gravelly. He lifted her back off her feet. "Where?" he growled and dropped her back down. Amelia knew if she told him, she was dead. She thought about Uncle Billy.

"Screw you!"

"Bitch."

The cord went slack and she felt a sharp pain at the base of her skull, then nothing.

She awoke with her cheek against the cold concrete, disoriented. Her nose tingled with pins and needles as her sense of smell rebooted, filling her nostrils with a damp, dusty odor. She couldn't remember how she got here at first, but then the memory of the attack came rushing back. She pressed herself into a seated position and surveyed the garage. It was dark and she could hear rain hitting the roof as she struggled to focus on anything. Then, it hit her. *The box.*

She scrambled to her feet and hoped the attacker was gone. A wave of dizzying nausea buckled her knees, and she dropped to all fours. She felt the painful bump at the base of her skull, then scoured the cold garage floor with both hands. Finally, she found the Barretta and her eyes focused. She saw that the magazine was gone and the chamber empty. Dashing into the house, she found the breaker box and flipped the power on. She swept through the house, turning on lights as she went. It looked as if a tornado had hit: overturned furniture with gashes in the upholstery, cabinets and drawers hanging open with their contents strewn on the floor. But no intruder. She waded through the pots and pans and broken dishes in the kitchen. Pushing the debris to the side, she dropped to the floor beside the dishwasher. Under the cabinet, she tapped the kick plate. It dislodged and she removed it. She reached in and pulled out the box. She held it up in the light. It was still frozen shut. Whatever was inside had saved her life *this* time—but she knew she couldn't last on her own.

She eyed the flashing clock on the oven and remembered Shannon was bringing Ike Rossi down to Kiawah. She pulled her phone from her pocket and texted her to meet her at her parents. Her father had security at the house, and this was one of the few times in her life that she needed her father.

CHAPTER 8

IKE DROVE THE rented SUV and admired the sprawling marshland, split by the meandering Kiawah River. Shannon looked up from her phone and her face relaxed, smiling at the sight of a pelican effortlessly gliding overhead. The sun hung between two rainclouds in the sky and illuminated white and blue herons peppered through the marsh grass. But as they traversed the small two-lane bridge onto Kiawah Island, the battle in Ike's gut became more intense. While he was eager to meet a patriot and help her in any way he could, the invisible headwind of betrayal howling its warning was intensifying with every mile. Ike had made a promise to his sister not to take another assignment like the one that had nearly killed her, and now he had Lauren and her two boys to consider, too.

After showing a digital pass to one of the guards at an impressive, manned security gate, they entered what looked like a Hawaiian island retreat. They passed a lush green golf course with brilliant white sand bunkers that quickly gave way to graceful palms and majestic live oaks decorated with Spanish moss hanging from their thick twisting branches like pale green tinsel. The oaks formed a canopy over the well-kept two-lane parkway that wound through this fantasyland. As a longtime Pittsburgh resident, he'd only associated palms with vacation. He'd never seen so many varieties in one place. Tension began to naturally drain from his body, and he understood why Shannon had said the ten-mile island was one of the greatest vacation spots in the country.

They cleared a second security gate two and half miles later.

"I see why you called this a private island," Ike said.

"Yes. It's a great place to live if you want your privacy. That's why the Garcias and Winklers spent most of their time here. You can't get on the island unless you have business or vacation plans here."

"Who can grant access?"

"The homeowners or the resort. That's it."

Ike had studied the area on the plane. The island was bordered by a long flat beach that reached into the Atlantic on the south side and the Kiawah River on the north side. While access was controlled on the roads, anyone could gain access from the water.

"Security patrols?"

"They have a few, run by the HOA," Shannon said as she looked at her phone. "Amelia just texted. She wants to talk to you without her parents. There's something that she doesn't want them to know."

"Any idea what that is?"

"No. But I'm sure it has to do with Billy and Bessie."

Following the GPS, Ike turned off the main throughfare and wound down a street lined with luxury homes. They entered a section where the homes weren't visible from the road, then turned into a long winding driveway. Ike readied himself for the encounter with Amelia and her parents. He'd met her father a few years back. Ike's read on him was that he was either a brilliant introvert or an asshole. Ike was ready for either. But Amelia's mysterious secret had his interest piqued, and he looked forward to hearing her story.

They stopped at an iron gate with a small guardhouse. Shannon leaned forward as Ike rolled down his window.

"Shannon Falzone."

The guard wore a dark-blue golf shirt and tan shorts. Ike noticed the Glock on his hip. He leaned in toward the open window. "Ahh. Miss Falzone. Nice to see you again." He waved them in.

They pulled down the drive and around a large fountain in the middle of a cobblestone court in front of the sprawling home. Ike stepped from the SUV and felt the cool sea breeze on his cheeks. He could hear the breakers on the other side of the beachfront home. The house rested on a large substructure that kept the first floor for living about fifteen feet off the ground. The house stood two stories above that. It had a gray cedar shake exterior trimmed in copper with brass fixtures. Four giant white columns supported the front porch that stretched the entire length of the house. It looked like a Cape Cod beach house on steroids.

Ike joined Shannon on the other side of the vehicle.

"Hey, Shannon!"

Ike looked up the wide stairway and spotted a woman dressed in faded jeans, a loose-fitting sweatshirt, and a pair of black Allbirds. She was tall, thick, and broad-shouldered with a square jaw and a decent tan. She had thick blonde hair pulled back with a hairband. Oddly, she had a silk scarf around her neck. Ike pegged her at five eleven. As she trotted down the stairs, Ike noted the square, shoulders-back posture of an Air Force Academy graduate. He remembered her from the drillship.

Once at the bottom of the stairs, she embraced Shannon. "It's so good to see you. I'm grateful you could come down."

"Don't mention it. You'd do the same for me." Shannon presented Ike. "Amelia, this is Ike Rossi."

"Mr. Rossi." She extended her hand.

Ike shook it, noting her puffy green eyes, firm grip, and rippling forearms. "Call me Ike."

"Thank you for coming, too, Ike."

"Sorry it's under these circumstances. My condolences."

Amelia's face saddened, and Ike felt like a heel for reminding her of her devastating loss. She flashed her eyes wide and forced a smile, then rolled her eyes at Shannon. "Mom and Dad are waiting inside. Dad is dying to see you both."

"I'll bet he is," Shannon said.

They started up the stairs together.

Ike got the message. Benton Garcia was a third-generation Texan handpicked to run the Winkler oil empire by his wife's father. Both men were Texas A&M graduates, and Ike assumed that connection had given

Benton the edge over Billy, who had chosen to study law at SMU. Despite Billy being his only son, the old man had chosen Benton. Ike had met him a few years ago while working an oil-theft ring for a company that had shared working interest in several large fields outside of Midland. Benton came across as capable, but also as a man who closely guarded his power.

When they entered the home, Benton and Tess Winkler stood in the center of the marble compass rose in the middle of the foyer. Benton was shorter than Tess and his sports coat was slightly larger than necessary for his small frame. His dingy brown hair parted on the left along with the loose-fitting blazer made him look like a sixty-year-old student in *Dead Poets Society*. Tess stood proud, her chin up, her silver hair in a pixie cut, wearing pressed blue jeans, boots, and checked pearl-buttoned blouse. She looked like the heir to one of the largest personal fortunes in Texas.

"Mom. Dad. You know Shannon."

"Hi, Mr. and Mrs. Garcia. Nice to see you again."

Tess hugged Shannon and gave her an air kiss. "Always so good to see you, honey."

Benton awkwardly hugged Shannon. "How do you like running the whole enterprise?"

Shannon stepped back and politely smiled. "It's a challenge, but I'm up to it."

"Your green initiatives are making some of us look bad," he said with a half-serious expression.

"It's a new world out there. And it's the only one we have. We're only doing what I think is right for us."

Benton tossed his head back and grunted. Then he stepped up and seemed to force his hand in Ike's direction. He was missing the tip of his middle finger, the result of an oilfield accident before college. Ike shook his hand. He was weaker than Ike had remembered. "Mr. Rossi. I'd say nice to see you again, but there is nothing nice about these circumstances."

"I agree, Mr. Garcia." Ike looked over to Tess. "My sincere condolences to both of you."

Amelia cradled her mother's shoulder and introduced her. "Mom, this is Ike Rossi. Mr. Rossi, this is my mother, Tess."

Her hawklike blue eyes searched Ike's face, probably judging his sincerity. Ike didn't mind. He'd been there too. "My pleasure, Mrs. Garcia."

Her stoic face broke into a gentle smile. "Please call me Tess."

Now something deep in Ike's gut doubted *her* sincerity. "Of course, ma'am. Please call me Ike."

"Y'all come into the family room. We can talk there." Tess turned and walked down the corridor.

Benton extended an open palm and silently waited for the group to go ahead of him. Shannon and Ike followed Amelia and her mother, with Benton behind them. Being wedged between Tess and Benton gave Ike an uneasy feeling. They'd both given Ike their best façade, but Ike suspected Amelia wasn't the only one to have a secret in the Garcia family.

CHAPTER 9

IKE SAT IN THE tan leather chair, gazed over the sand dunes, and watched the flashes of lightning drop from the dark clouds over the Atlantic. The stormfront had passed the South Carolina coast, and the late afternoon sun illuminated the cavernous living room. The leather furniture with heavy iron frames, twenty-foot ceilings with towering windows, and collection of paintings and personalized memorabilia from the most recognized athletes associated with the state of Texas, were certainly intended to impress or intimidate guests. The place screamed money. Ike watched Tess collect a tray that held six iced teas from one of her attendants, then presented them one by one around the room. When she reached Ike after serving everyone else, she had three left. Ike swore he smelled bourbon.

"Thank you, Tess. These look great." Ike took a sip. It was iced tea. "Can I ask who else is joining us?"

Tess smiled, her lips sealed, and turned away with the tray toward Benton.

"I've asked my head of security to join us," Benton said. "Here he is now."

Ike recognized Trent McCallum as he entered the room from the back of the house. He immediately felt as if he needed a shower. McCallum, a decorated Army Ranger veteran, had been associated with Benton Garcia since the beginning. Ike had encountered him on several assignments for

Texas clients. At around six one with salt-and-pepper hair and a build like a free safety, he moved like a man who could handle any situation that presented itself. While his methods were harsh, his results were outstanding. He was also the tip of the spear for the political arm of the well-funded band of Texas families that controlled most of the politics in Texas. He had more mud than the Mississippi River on every politician in the state and had utilized it to destroy candidates not aligned with the club's best interests, both at the state and national level.

He stopped and stood next to Benton who sat in the opposite chair. "Rossi. Surprised to see you here."

Ike doubted McCallum was surprised by anything. "McCallum."

McCallum pulled out a small, folded note and handed it to Benton, then moved to the fireplace just behind him and rested his elbow on the mantle.

Benton read the note and put it in his breast pocket. "Mr. Rossi. While I appreciate you coming all the way down here, I'm afraid you've wasted your time. This is a private family matter, and as you know, I have Mr. McCallum and his team to deal with anything that may come up."

Ike ignored the urge to smack the smugness from Benton's face. He looked at McCallum, who grinned, then he focused on Benton, pausing long enough to clear the fake smile from Benton's face.

"Father!" Amelia said. "I asked Mr. Rossi down here."

Ike smiled. Knowing she had to deal with her father every day of her life, he decided to provide cover for Amelia's secret, whatever it was. "Mr. Garcia. While I'm quite familiar with Mr. McCallum's talents, I think I need to remind you of several things." Ike stood and walked to the massive window, scanning the angry surf. "First, your brother-in-law was under contract to Falzone Energy. In turn, Falzone was under contract to NOAA on one of the most sensitive and public undertakings in decades. Your daughter worked for him." Ike turned from the window and eyed Benton. "Now, I'm head of security for Falzone Energy on Minuteman, and I'm conducting an investigation in that capacity."

"Investigating what?" Benton said.

"The killing of the head of a major contractor working for Falzone on Minuteman."

Benton wanted to say something, but he sat back and folded his arms.

"Mr. Garcia," Shannon said. "I've asked Ike to look into this matter and see what our exposure is and what measures, if any, we need to take to ensure the security of our operations and our people." Shannon looked directly at Ike. "I've asked Ike to move as quickly and as discreetly as possible."

Benton uncrossed his arms and dismissed Shannon with a wave. "Whatever. You're both wasting your time."

Ike had had enough. Before he could intervene, Tess said, "I think what Benton means is that y'all are welcome to look into my brother's killing." Tess paused, took a large sip from her glass, and gathered herself. "Please be quick and discreet about it."

Ike suspected she had the bourbon in her glass. He didn't blame her. He remembered the feeling when his parents were killed.

Benton glared at Tess, but Tess ignored him, looking a little more relaxed. "What questions do you have for us?" she said.

Ike glanced at Shannon and she nodded. He sat back down in his chair but turned toward Tess and Amelia who were seated together on the sofa, locked his fingers, and rested his elbows on the armrests. He softened his expression and leaned closer to Tess. Despite Tess's impeccable exterior, Ike could feel her grief. It was all too familiar.

"Thank you, Tess. I do have a couple of questions, but only if you're up to it."

Amelia wrapped her arm around her mother's, taking her hand in hers. Tess's lower lip quivered, then she stiffened and pulled her shoulders back. "Go right ahead, Ike. Ask away."

"When did you last speak to your brother?"

The corners of her mouth turned down and she sighed. "Three nights ago."

Ike noticed the guilt written on Amelia's face. He refocused on Tess. "What did you talk about?"

Benton interrupted. "That's none of your business, Mr. Rossi."

Ike ignored him and kept his attention on Tess.

She eyed Benton. "I'll handle this." Then she took another drink and looked back at Ike. "We talked about some Winkler Foundation business, then just small talk about our family."

"What was his demeanor?"

Tess's eyes flashed. Ike had hit a nerve.

"My brother was happy. He was always happy. He wouldn't do anything to hurt Bessie or himself."

The sadness in her eyes was gone, replaced by a seething anger.

"I'm sorry if I've offended you," Ike said. Tess stole a look at Benton. Ike thought he saw him subtly wag his head. Tess snapped her gaze back at Ike. "Anything else?"

Ike knew he wouldn't get any more meaningful information. "Just one more thing. Do you know of any threats against your brother or his wife?"

"No." Tess stared at Benton. "They were loved by everyone."

Ike didn't believe her. "Okay. Thank you."

He turned quickly back to Benton. "Mr. Garcia, when did you last speak to your brother-in-law?"

Benton seemed surprised and froze. He looked at Tess and Amelia.

Ike could see in their faces that he'd hit a family minefield.

Benton's face reddened as the ladies didn't bail him out. "We spoke at the last board meeting at the family office."

"When was that?"

"Nearly three months ago."

Ike knew Benton had taken the job that Billy had probably assumed was his. Maybe that bad blood ran deeper than he thought. The tension in the room was now palpable.

Amelia stood. "I need to speak to Ike alone."

"You won't speak to anyone about this without me or our lawyers," Benton said.

Ike saw Amelia ready to rebuke her father. Benton's face hardened. Ike didn't want to commit to helping her. He couldn't. He'd made a commitment to Maria, but he could see the trepidation in Amelia's eyes. Her father was a bully. Ike stood up. "Mr. Garcia, Amelia is a contractor whose firm was under contract with Falzone Energy. I'll need to speak with her alone."

Ike could tell Benton didn't like that idea.

Before he could say another word, Amelia grabbed Ike's arm. "Let's go down on the beach, Ike."

McCallum stepped forward. Ike locked his eyes on him and stepped up to meet him.

Amelia wedged herself between them, facing McCallum. "I'd like your men to give us some privacy."

Ike fixed his eyes on McCallum's until McCallum turned to Amelia.

"We'll keep a safe perimeter."

"Fine."

The fact that Amelia required security reminded Ike of the scarf around Amelia's neck. He suspected she needed protection, but from whom? Ike followed Amelia out of the room.

CHAPTER 10

IKE FOLLOWED AMELIA down the long wooden boardwalk straddling the sand dunes that protected the island from Atlantic hurricanes. She walked with the confidence and purpose of the tough-minded warrior Ike had expected. The RPA pilots he'd known were disciplined, highly skilled, and honorable. They were hunters and protectors who were asked to kill to save troops in harm's way or to take a high-value terrorist off the face of the earth, sometimes at great personal costs that they rarely spoke about.

When they'd cleared the dunes, a stiff onshore breeze pushed against him as they made their way to the beach. It wasn't nearly as strong as the memory of Maria's words warning him not to get involved. It was low tide, and the long flat beach led to the churning, foamy sea, aggravated by the storms just offshore. Amelia reached the end of the boardwalk and reached down to remove her Allbirds. Her scarf slipped up her neck, exposing a bruised ligature mark.

She smiled at Ike. "It's best to leave your shoes and socks here. The sand is very fine in spots and will seep into your shoes, especially with this breeze. There's a foot wash at the house to clean up before you go back."

Ike removed his shoes and socks and followed her onto the beach. The sand was cool and still damp from the storms that had moved out to sea. Seeing four men in a diamond formation spread out along the beach, he stopped in his tracks. They were at least thirty yards away, and with the crashing waves and gusty wind, they'd never hear their conversation.

Amelia turned back to Ike. "Let's head down by the water."

"Before we do anything you'll have to tell me how you got those marks on your neck, and why you have such a tight security net."

Amelia's confidence waned but she pulled her shoulders back and gathered herself with a deep sigh. "I was attacked this morning."

"Are you okay?"

She reached up, her hand shaking, and rubbed her neck. "I think so."

"Where did it happen?"

"At my house here on the island. He was waiting for me when I got back from Uncle Billy's."

Ike knew he was getting pulled into something he wanted no part of, but he still had to ask the next questions. "Who did it?"

"I don't know. That's why I need your help."

"How did you get away?"

"When I wouldn't tell him where it was, he knocked me out. When I came to, he'd trashed the place, but he was gone."

"Where what was?"

Amelia scanned the beach, then scoured the sky. She settled her eyes back on Ike and leaned closer. "A box I pulled from the seafloor two hundred yards from Minuteman's blowout preventer."

Ike ran through the facts instantly: the FBI, two killings, an attack, the box. A box from five thousand feet under the ocean. The spike in adrenalin supercharged his focus. Amelia must have seen the shock on Ike's face. Her eyes had widened and for the first time Ike saw fear.

Ike forced himself to calm down. "Tell me about the box."

"About eighteen inches long, six inches wide, and a few inches deep. Has the Nazi Eagle on it."

"What's inside?"

"I don't know. I couldn't get it open."

"Where is it?"

Amelia looked around again. "It's here."

"On the island?"

"No. Here at the house. I've hidden it."

"Will you show it to me?"

Ike saw her eyes fill with tears. "Ike. I think they killed Uncle Billy after I told him about it. He was like a father to me. I can't believe he's gone. And it's my fault."

Ike reached out and put his hand on her shoulder, but she pulled away. He hated seeing this woman who'd given so much for her country in the same spot he'd been in twenty-three years ago. "I'm so sorry. I know what that's like. It will be okay."

She dropped her head and studied the sand for a minute.

"Can I ask a few more questions?"

She raised her head and nodded.

"Any idea why they would kill your uncle?"

"No. All I know is that he called one of his friends from SMU that worked at the Department of Justice to see what I should do with it." She wiped a tear away. "He's dead too. Killed last night in a car wreck."

Ike pulled back, as this latest piece of information brought the dark cauldron of facts in this case to a boil. The body count was already up to three. He'd wished she would have led with that information. What was a difficult murder investigation had just become a deadly conspiracy, maybe at the highest levels of government. "Did you tell anyone else about this?"

"No. I didn't even tell the detective at Uncle Billy's. The only thing keeping me alive is that box. Everyone who finds out gets killed." Realizing what she'd just done, she covered her mouth. "Sorry!"

Ike had just become the next target. But somehow it didn't bother him. Amelia was up against some unknown force. Alone, she wouldn't make it. Her father would be of little help.

"Will you help me?" she asked.

Ike looked out to sea. The storms stretched to the horizon and looked as if they went to the edge of the earth. He thought about Maria in her hospital bed and the fire that had destroyed Rossi's.

Apparently sensing Ike's hesitation, Amelia said, "I know this isn't your problem. It's mine. I have to know who killed the most important people in my life. The two people responsible for who I am today." She paused and swallowed hard. Ike noticed moisture in the corners of her eyes. "When my sister died three years ago in Europe, I was helpless. I'm not now. But I think there's something bigger here. They killed my uncle, aunt, and the second in command at the Justice Department for whatever is inside that box. And it must be someone powerful in Washington. I can't let them get away with it. Yes, I want answers and maybe revenge, but I also took an oath to protect and defend the Constitution and protect people like my aunt and uncle who couldn't defend themselves, against *all* enemies. That didn't change when I left active duty. I'll do whatever it takes. Risk everything. You don't know me, but I can assure you I can handle whatever you need me to do. I just need your help." She reached out and touched Ike's arm. "So please, help me."

The determination in Amelia's eyes reminded Ike of his own determination to close the painful wound of his parents' unsolved killings. Ike now understood what Shannon meant by *a patriot*. Amelia knew what she was up against, yet she was still committed. He'd learned a long time ago that you had to move toward what frightened you to defeat it. Amelia was doing just that. He remembered what he'd promised himself when he'd hit a dead end in his parents' killings. It was why he'd gotten into this business. *If not for me, then for them.* If he couldn't get closure, he'd get it for others. And maybe someday, the karma would come full circle and give it to him.

"Can you show me the box?"

Amelia gave him a hopeful smile. "So, you'll help me?"

"Let's start with the box."

Amelia paused, then said, "Fair enough. But we'll have to keep it from my parents. They can't know about it."

"I understand. Let's go."

They headed back toward the dunes. On the boardwalk, they picked up their shoes and headed over the dunes.

Once inside, Amelia whispered, "Follow me." Ike followed her down a set of stairs into the substructure of the house. She moved quickly down a white clapboard hallway and opened a second door. She flipped on a light illuminating a cavernous room with cinder-block walls and pillars supporting the massive house. He followed her through the darkness to a small door. She opened it, and Ike could see the underside of the massive back deck. Light filtered through the spaces between the planks. She turned right and went to the far corner of the deck. She removed a board resting between the deck and the cinderblock and pulled out a plastic container. Turning to Ike, she opened the container and presented the contents to him. It was just as she had described. The sight of the Nazi Eagle triggered a chilling evil that shivered through him.

"May I?" Ike asked as he reached for the box. He tried to open it, but it wouldn't budge. It was crusted with scale and the thick hasp had it securely locked.

Above them, he heard a sliding door open, then close. Through the spaces between the decking, he saw two people step onto the deck. Then he heard Tess's voice.

"Why is the FBI here?"

"I don't know. Probably that Minuteman project," Benton answered, his words coated with contempt.

"Is there something else going on?" Tess shot back.

"Don't ask me that!" Benton stomped back toward the door.

Ike put his finger over his lips as he handed the box back to Amelia. He couldn't let Mia and the FBI get the box. Not until they knew who and what they were dealing with. Amelia slipped it into the slot and covered it. He heard the sliding door open and close again and quietly followed Amelia inside.

CHAPTER 11

IKE FOLLOWED AMELIA down the ornate hallway that led back to the living room on the first floor. His emotional radar was on high alert. Clearly, despite their deceptive façade, a deep-rooted wound festered just below the surface between the Garcias. Ike sensed that any marital trust that had existed was gone, replaced by a mutual contempt. Neither seemed to be backing down, both trapped in an indignant power struggle, like a cage match until death do they part. He didn't know what secrets they held, but he knew he needed answers. Ahead, he could hear strident voices thundering through the house. One was unmistakable. He tried to quell the intoxicating anticipation about seeing Mia again. While he was certain she was a tough investigator, he'd known her in a different life. A life for which he secretly longed. As usual, he reminded himself that the emotions of the past were always an illusion that led to a maze to nowhere.

Filling his lungs with the over-air-conditioned air, he refocused on the moment at hand. He noticed a family portrait hanging on the wall. He stopped for a second and examined the picture. Tess and Benton were in the center, with Amelia next to Tess and another more stunning young woman next to Benton. They were all dressed in formal attire and Benton was beaming with pride, as was his other daughter. Amelia and Tess were posing more than enjoying the moment. Benton's favor for his older daughter was obvious. A wave of empathy for Amelia washed through Ike.

Another sign of a family in turmoil. He turned away, trotted, and caught up with Amelia, who hadn't noticed he'd stopped. He reached ahead and gently touched Amelia's shoulder to silently get her attention before reaching the living room. She pulled it away as if it were a snake bite. Ike wondered what was going on. When she turned back, her expression warned him not to do it again.

"Be careful with answering questions when we get in there. You don't have to say a word," he said.

She silently acknowledged Ike's advice and headed toward the foyer that led to the living room.

When he walked into the room, it went silent. Everyone was standing and all eyes were on Amelia. Lurking in front of the oversized sofa, Benton was silhouetted against the massive windows framing the churning seascape behind him, McCallum rigid at his side like a well-trained Doberman. Tess stood far to his right, next to Shannon, beside one of the leather side chairs with her arms crossed. Shannon caught Ike's attention, wagged her head, then cut her eyes toward Benton. She looked as if she'd rather be anywhere but here. Mia and Agent Sherman had their backs to Ike but strained to look over their shoulders at him. Mia's eyes widened with an intensity he remembered from the few arguments they'd had. Benton waved at Amelia to join him, which she did. Ike moved past the FBI agents and into the no-man's-land between the two groups.

"We're glad you could join us," Mia said. She walked to Amelia, giving Ike the cold shoulder on the way past. She leaned over the coffee table and offered her a card.

"I'm Agent Russo from our Washington, DC, field office. This is Agent Sherman."

Amelia took the card and read it but stayed silent.

Mia stepped back to Sherman. "We'd like to ask you a few questions."

"Agent Russo, I told you, she won't be answering any questions," Benton said. Ike never thought he'd be happy Benton was an ass. Still, Ike didn't trust him. No telling what he was hiding.

Mia ignored him. "Ms. Garcia?"

Amelia glanced at Ike and stayed quiet.

Mia snarled at Ike, then glared at Amelia and waited for a reply. When it didn't come, she turned to Ike and said, "Can we talk outside?"

Her tone was suddenly cooperative, and Ike decided he might get more information by hearing what she had to say. He'd also get Mia farther away from that box. "Sure." He looked at Shannon then Amelia. "Excuse me for just a minute."

"Mr. Rossi. If you're working for my daughter, I don't want you talking to these agents without McCallum," Benton said. It sounded like an order.

McCallum stepped forward.

Ike put his palm up and locked his eyes on McCallum. "No way. I talk to who I want, when I want. I'll do this alone."

"It's fine, father," Amelia said.

Benton wagged his head at McCallum. McCallum smirked sarcastically at Ike and stepped back.

"Let's go out front," Ike said. He headed out the door and Mia followed. When he reached the cobblestone at the bottom of the steps, he stopped and turned to Mia.

"This okay?"

Mia gave Ike a genuine smile. "It's fine. How are you, Ike?"

Surprised by her sudden change in disposition, Ike hesitated.

Apparently still able to see right through him, Mia said, "Look. There's no reason we can't put what you did to the side."

"What I did?"

"Ike, you dropped me out of the blue. Things were going great, for both of us I'd assumed. Then, with no warning, you told me we should end it. That somehow it wouldn't be fair to me."

"I'm sorry."

"Sorry doesn't cut it. I spent the next year trying to find what was wrong with me. Why you did it. It was torture."

Ike still didn't want to tell her why. "I didn't mean to hurt you."

Mia put her hand up and deflected Ike's apology. "Don't worry. I'm over it. But like I said, we can be adult about it." Mia looked up the stairs to the house, sighed, shook her head at Ike, then said, "I didn't want to get into that." This time she forced a smile. "All right. Now, how are you doing?"

Ike felt like shit, but let it go. "I'm doing fine. Pretty busy."

"I know. I saw your case last year. Quite a mess. How's your sister?"

"Better."

"Still single?"

"Maria?"

"No." She laughed. "You."

"Yeah. You?"

"Yeah."

The pleasantries led to an awkward silence. One that despite Mia's scolding, Ike's mind filled with old possibilities. Finally, Mia said, "Look Ike, I didn't want to say this in there. We've been asked by someone in the White House to look into this."

"The White House? Who?"

"Don't know. You know I couldn't tell you if I did. The deputy attorney general was killed last night. A one-car accident. Some on-board computer glitch. We ran his calls from yesterday, and there was one from Billy Winkler."

Ike decided she knew him too well for him to act surprised. "What do you make of that?"

"I don't know. But the last person to talk to Billy Winkler was Amelia Garcia. I need to talk to her about that call."

"Doesn't look like she'll talk to you right now."

Mia's face lit up, perhaps realizing Ike was firmly on Amelia's side. "You're representing her?"

Ike didn't say anything, but he didn't have to. She could always read him like a book.

Mia's face deadened and she locked her eyes on his. "Ike, don't do this. Don't get involved."

Ike's face flushed as it usually did when people told him what not to do. "I'll do whatever I please, Agent Russo."

"No, Ike. I mean it. There's something going on here. I don't know what yet, but I don't think you want any part of it."

A righteous anger anchored Ike where he stood. He trusted Mia was sincere, but he had no idea who was involved. He certainly didn't trust the justice system to deliver security or closure for Amelia. It hadn't for him. He figured that Mia was probably in as much danger as Amelia. The only difference was that Mia had a badge. And he agreed with Amelia. Right now, that box was keeping her—and Ike—alive. "Thanks for the concern. But I'll do what's right."

Mia stepped back, pressed her lips together, and stared at Ike.

Ike could see she was genuinely concerned. "If you think she's a suspect, I'll drop her," he said.

Mia wagged her head. "She's not. She has a rock-solid alibi."

"Then the best I can do is get your number and call you if I find something. She won't talk to you today."

"The best you could do is to get her to cooperate." Mia shook her head again as she wrote something on the back of one of her cards and handed it to Ike. "I guess I'll be seeing more of you."

While Ike knew the excitement that sparked inside him when he visualized her words was based on what they used to have, he wondered if they'd ever have a chance to be together again. He leaned in, took the card from her fingers, and read the personal cell phone number on the back. He kissed her on the cheek, surprising her. She still smelled like lavender.

"I'll look forward to that." He headed up the steep stairs.

"You can get me on that number any time, day or night. Send Agent Sherman back out, please. I don't need that exercise." Ike turned and thought he saw Mia blushing. "Will do, Agent Russo. Will do."

CHAPTER 12

AS IKE HEADED UP the front steps, he knew they didn't have much time. He needed to get Amelia off the island. With open access from the river and sea, she was a sitting duck. She'd already been attacked and now a federal investigation was ramping up. The investigation itself wasn't bothersome, but the reason behind it had to be something that the highest levels of government wanted to control. Judging by the response, whatever was in that box was never supposed to see the light of day. It would only get worse from here. The FBI was conducting the above-board investigation, but something or someone else was working below the surface on a clandestine effort to get the box and keep its existence secret, and they were willing to kill to do it.

Ike returned to the living room where everyone was seated except for McCallum and Agent Sherman. Sherman was casually looking at every item in the room without touching it while McCallum tracked close behind him. Benton was seated in one of the side chairs thumbing his phone, and Amelia sat between her mother and Shannon on the sofa. Shannon looked up from her phone and mouthed the words *We need to go.*

Ike acknowledged her with a nod. "Agent Sherman? Agent Russo said to tell you she's waiting outside."

Sherman turned away from the pictures on the small shelf and moved toward the front door. "Y'all have a beautiful place here. You have our number if you change your mind."

Ike waited for the front door to close. "Amelia, you should gather your things. We need to get going."

Amelia stood.

"Hold on. She's not going anywhere," Benton said.

"That's not up to you," Amelia said as she moved toward the hallway. McCallum blocked her exit. Amelia leaned into McCallum's face. "Unless you're planning on becoming a soprano, I'd step aside."

"We have security here. You think you'll be safe with him?" Benton asked. "I can make one call and get to the bottom of this."

"Is that the same contact you used to keep Harper safe?" Tess said.

Ike could see her eyes boring into her husband's.

"You don't know what you're talking about. Harper went to Belgium of her own accord."

"But you set it up. You got her the job with the Janssens family's conglomerate."

Benton cut his eyes to Ike then back to Tess. She, too, quickly eyed Ike then settled back into the sofa. Ike suspected there was more to Tess's anger, but it was a family secret, the toughest to uncover.

"Move!" Amelia said. Benton wagged his head at McCallum as Amelia pushed past him and disappeared down the hallway. McCallum didn't follow her. Ike tried to hide his relief and hoped that would give her time to get the box. The DeSantis brothers could easily open it and not say a word.

"Where are you taking her?" Benton asked.

Shannon stood. "We're headed back to Pittsburgh. I'll help keep an eye on Amelia. We have our own resources there."

Benton pointed at Shannon. "You're out of your depth, young lady."

"That's one opinion. I don't happen to share it. I trust Ike's judgment here."

"I do too," Tess said as she stood. "I let you lose one daughter. I'll not lose another."

Tess reached out and hugged Shannon. "You and Mr. Rossi bring her back to me."

"We will," Shannon said. She released Tess and walked to join Ike at the entrance to the room. She showed Ike a report she had on her phone. Minuteman was approaching the target. "We can monitor this from the Real-Time Remote Operations Center at the office, so we've got to get back."

Ike had forgotten about Minuteman for a few hours. In a matter of days, the specialized diamond drill bit would be attached to a core barrel and whatever was down there, placed there 160 million years ago, would be brought to the surface.

Amelia returned. "I'm ready to go."

"Where's your bags?" Ike asked, thinking more about the box than her luggage.

"All loaded in the car. One of the security people helped me."

"You're making a mistake. I can protect you here," Benton said.

Amelia didn't reply. She walked to her mother and hugged her. "I'll let you know when I get there." Then she walked over to her father and hugged his neck. He stood, rigid, not returning the hug. "Bye, father."

Benton's expression sagged in resignation. "Goodbye."

Amelia rejoined Ike and Shannon. Tess walked with them to the door.

"Take care of her," Tess said.

"I will," Ike said and followed the women down the stairs to the SUV.

CHAPTER 13

IKE WATCHED AMELIA in the rearview mirror as they cleared the main gate leaving Kiawah. Looking over her shoulder, she stared out through the back window of the SUV long enough to signal her concern over what or whom she was leaving behind. Ike wasn't sure if it was her aunt and uncle, or if her parents were tugging at her heart, but when she turned forward again, her face seemed empty under the weight of her loss, her eyes glazed with sadness. Somewhere down deep, the gaping emptiness in Ike's soul that opened twenty-three years ago stirred.

Ike decided Amelia needed a distraction. In his case, distraction was like lidocaine for his grief. He glanced at Shannon in the passenger's seat who was reading something on her phone. She looked back at him. He cut his eyes toward Amelia. Shannon put her phone away, then faced Amelia.

"How are you holding up?" Shannon said.

"I'm doing okay. It's hard being around my parents without Harper."

"I can't imagine how much you miss her."

"I talk to her all the time. She was the one person in my family who always had my back."

Ike glanced at Amelia in the mirror. "Can I ask what your sister was doing in Europe?"

"She was a lawyer for a Belgian family. They ran a big industrial conglomerate. Dad got her a job with them in their family business."

"Where did she go to school?" Ike asked.

"University of Texas. Dad got her summer jobs in DC with his connections there. When she graduated, she worked for a law firm in DC. She got a job in the State Department that she wouldn't talk about. Then suddenly, she wanted to go to Europe. She worked for the Janssens for seven years. Then, one night three years ago, a boat she was on exploded just off the Sicilian coast. I was on active duty by then, stationed in New Mexico. The person I looked up to most in the world was gone, and I couldn't do anything. The local authorities, INTERPOL, and the State Department were all brought in. My father saw to that. Mom thinks she never should have gone and blames Dad for getting her the job. Anyway, someone contacted my father and told him she'd died. They interviewed over sixty witnesses that were on the beach at a resort. They confirmed there were no survivors. They never recovered her body."

Amelia's face saddened again. Ike decided to change the subject. He'd noticed the large four-foot by four-foot road case she'd loaded in the back of the SUV along with a large duffel.

"So, what's in the road case?" he asked, returning his attention to the road.

"It's a drone. I thought it might come in handy at some point."

"Tools of the trade?"

"Yes." Looking at Ike in the mirror, Amelia grinned. Ike felt better for her and returned his focus to the gentle curve ahead in the two-lane road. "Interesting term," she said. "I never considered it a trade, but it was a skill that transferred to my current job. But the skill was only part of it."

Ike glanced back in the rearview. "How's that?"

Amelia gazed out the side window. "For me, learning how to control your emotions was the most important skill."

Shannon put her phone back in her lap. "I imagine that was hard on you."

"It's hard on all RPA pilots. We just don't talk about it." Amelia forced a sarcastic chuckle. "And not talking about it makes it harder. For me, after I got out, I felt like I just didn't fit in anywhere else."

"Fit in?" Ike asked.

"Yeah. When I was on active duty, I'd work twelve-hour shifts; sometimes a TIC situation would come up. Troops in contact with hostile forces. More often than not, an ambush. We'd have to get into position and take out the enemy. Other times I'd follow a high-value target for days or even weeks: to soccer games with his kid, to dinner with his wife, or just at home. Then, when the right situation presented itself, I'd notify the operations center and get a call from someone authorizing the strike. I'd take the target out. I did my duty and would do it again, but when the shift was over, it all stayed confidential. I still had to carry it around. I couldn't talk to anyone about what I'd done. Even if I could have, they had no idea what it was like to kill people, even remotely. It was no video game. It was very real when you'd see the non-combatants come out and pick up the pieces of his body. I felt different. Like I didn't fit in. Didn't belong anywhere. That's one reason I'm still alone. That and about a dozen bad decisions I dated. I think the dating apps are convinced that my phone is a graveyard where first dates go to die."

"I get that," Shannon said, giving Amelia a knowing grin.

Ike felt his connection to Amelia growing. He could relate to her feeling of not fitting in. He'd fit in on the football field, with his teammates and friends, but that was ripped away by his parents' murders. He instantly had become a novelty. The best that never was. The blue-chip quarterback that had quit to raise his nine-year-old sister. A nineteen-year-old orphan. The sympathetic looks simply felt like pity. He ignored it all and focused all his time on his parents' case, pivoting away from his chemical engineering studies at Penn State to an internship with the Pittsburgh Police Department, and earning a master's degree in criminal justice at Point Park University.

"I know you've heard it before, but I have to say it," Ike said. "I respect and appreciate your service and all that you've done for us."

"Thanks, Ike. But I feel like I should apologize for my parents back there," Amelia said.

"No apologies needed," Shannon said.

"Thanks, but I get embarrassed with Mom's drinking."

"She didn't seem any worse than anyone else who'd just lost their brother," Ike said.

"You didn't stay long enough," Amelia said. "She can get pretty wound up late."

"I'm sorry, Amelia. I never knew," Shannon said.

"That's okay. No one does outside our family. Father won't talk about it at all. He's never talked to me about it. But I've heard Mom late at night. She blames Father for Harper's …" Amelia paused. "For her death."

Ike suspected there was much more behind it, but for now, it was none of his business. In the rearview mirror, he noticed a black SUV closing on them quickly.

He sat up in the seat and put both hands on the wheel. "Make sure you guys are belted in." The digital display on the dash said they were doing fifty. On either side of the road, the bulging trunks of the thick live oaks seemed to move closer to the road. They were adjacent to the white line marking the edge of the lane. For some of the larger ones, the line pinched the lane smaller to go around.

"How far to the executive airport?" Ike asked.

Shannon and Amelia looked back at the SUV.

Shannon opened her iPhone and said, "Three miles."

The SUV was four car lengths back and closing. Ike accelerated but still braced for the impact. "Hang on!"

The impact jolted their SUV and Ike corrected the slight skid and moved to the middle of the road. They'd die instantly if they hit one of the oaks racing past on the shoulder.

He heard Amelia unbuckle and saw her reach over the back seat and open the road case. She pulled out a Berretta, cocked it, and opened her window on her left. She eyed their pursuer. "Can you get him beside us?"

Amelia seemed calm and calculating. Ike guessed the warrior ethos had taken over. He immediately trusted her in this situation. He moved into the oncoming lane and waited for the SUV to close again. It did. Eyeing the row of oaks on his right, he hoped the tires on the rental would hold. He swerved to his right. The passenger's side mirror exploded against one of the massive trunks, and Shannon screamed. He slowed down and the attacker's SUV catapulted beside them.

Amelia fired once, disintegrating the right front tire. Ike accelerated as the other vehicle flipped and was crushed like a beer can against one of the oaks. Ike slowed and heard Amelia roll up the window and buckle back in, her eyes fierce and face stoic. Looking ahead, he pulled back into his lane and saw Shannon shaking in her seat. "You okay?"

With wide eyes, she turned to Ike. "Who was that?"

"That's a great question." Ike thought about the box and what was inside.

"It's them," Amelia said. "The same people who killed my aunt and uncle."

Shannon held up her phone. "Do we need to call the police?"

In unison, both Ike and Amelia said, "No."

Ike saw the sign for the Charleston Executive Airport. He slowed and made the right turn to the airfield. "Let's just get to Pittsburgh. I have someone there who can help us."

CHAPTER 14

IKE PULLED HIS Shelby Mustang into his usual spot behind Rossi's and rehearsed his introduction one more time. He'd texted Maria before leaving Charleston and explained that he'd had no choice. He had to bring Amelia to Pittsburgh. He'd asked Maria to simply meet Amelia. Then, if she was still against him getting involved, they'd work out an alternative. After arriving at Falzone Enterprises' hangar on the northwest side of the Pittsburgh Airport, Ike had dropped Shannon at her Squirrel Hill townhome, then headed to Rossi's with Amelia. He hoped that given time, Maria would come around and support him taking on Amelia's case.

It was just before ten and the streets of Bloomfield were winding down. While Liberty Avenue still had a few bars and lively taverns fueling the Saturday night's young, trendy revelers, the rest of what was called Little Italy was settling in for the night. Settled mostly by Italian American families at the beginning of the last century, Bloomfield had been home to the Rossi family for as long as Ike could remember. Most of the shops and restaurants still had that heritage on display today, and neighbors and shop owners still looked after each other. It was nice to be home.

Ike checked the alleyway. From the corner of his eye, he saw Amelia scanning her surroundings, wide-eyed and sparking with anticipation.

"Don't worry. My sister will love you."

Amelia sighed, then stared ahead at the brick wall in front of them. "I hope so. I'm out of alternatives."

Ike's heart ached. He felt Amelia's desolation. He knew what it felt like to feel so alone, hanging on to your last hope by a thread. After a few seconds of awkward silence, he said, "I hear you. I've been there, believe me. But you'll get through this."

She pressed her lips together firmly, then gave him a confident nod.

"You ready?" he said.

"I'm good."

Ike opened the car door and got out. The brisk October air was refreshing and probably thirty degrees colder than the Lowcountry evening on Kiawah. He stepped to the trunk, opened it, and pulled out the road box and the duffel.

"We'll take these inside just in case."

Amelia closed the passenger's door and looped around behind the car. "Let me take that."

Ike handed her the case and walked to the rear entrance to Rossi's. After unlocking the new steel door they had installed, he led Amelia inside and down the hallway. He heard Maria's precise fingerpicking on her Takamine guitar as she sang the last words to the song, "One Last Time," that she'd written for their parents. She ended every evening the same way. He entered a code into the keypad adjacent to the door to the upstairs office and living quarters they'd upgraded during the rebuild, then opened the door and dropped the duffel at the base of the stairway.

"You can put it in here. Safe and secure."

After putting the road case inside, Amelia followed Ike into the restaurant. Maria had finished and half of the crowd was filtering through the restaurant as they headed for the front door. Ike spotted Randy behind the bar cleaning up, while the regular bartender tabbed out the last few customers.

Ike walked up to the bar. "What's up?" Ike asked.

"Hey, Ike. Another good night," Randy said, tossing the bar towel over his shoulder. "And who is this?"

"Randy, this is Amelia,"

Randy wiped his hands on the towel and extended his hand. Amelia squared her shoulders and shook it.

"Amelia Garcia."

"Nice grip," he said.

"You too," she said, smiling but not giving any ground.

"Ike tells me you're an Air Force veteran."

"That's right."

"Named Amelia. After Amelia Earhart?

Amelia hesitated, then the corners of her mouth barely turned up in a smile. "My mother says she named me after the strongest woman she could think of at the time. Said she thought I might need the inspiration. Looks like she was right. But the Air Force was all my idea."

"Well, thanks for your service."

"You're welcome. Have you tended bar here for long?"

Ike choked off a laugh.

Randy grinned and said, "A little while."

"And how long were you a corrections officer?"

Randy's face went slack. "How did you know that?"

Straight-faced, Amelia said. "It shows. Vice grip, back to the wall, eyes always moving, keys on the belt, high and tight haircut."

Randy appeared puzzled. Then Amelia's composure gave way to a smirk.

Ike laughed and Amelia joined in. Randy too, once he realized she was joking.

"Ike told me about you on the way in."

"You'll fit in perfectly with these guys," Randy said, looking at Maria approaching behind Amelia.

Maria walked up. "What's so funny?"

"Amelia here appears to be a pretty good poker player. And a great comedian," Randy said.

Maria offered Amelia her hand. "Maria Rossi. Welcome to our little slice of heaven."

Ike noted his sister's tone was more marking her territory than greeting a guest. He decided to play arbitrator. Firmly, he said, "Maria, this is Amelia Garcia, the person I told you about."

Maria got the message and softened her look. "I'm so sorry about your loss."

Ike saw the anguish tug on Amelia's smile as she battled to keep her composure. She lifted her chin and pulled her shoulders back. "Thank you. My aunt and uncle meant everything to me."

Maria looked past Amelia to Ike, who stood on the other side. He'd seen that look before when Maria was about to push back against a limit Ike had set when he was trying to parent his then nine-year-old sister. Randy eyed the two of them, then raised his eyebrows, "I need to help Ben." Then he retreated to the other end of the bar.

Maria squared up to Amelia. "That's what Ike had said. He also said there was some trouble you were asking him to investigate."

Amelia seemed to sense Maria's reluctance for her brother to get involved. "Look, Maria. While I don't know you and can't imagine what it feels like to go through what you have, I have an idea of what you're probably feeling about your brother risking what you two have to help me. I know you and your brother went through hell last year. Ike told me about the bombing, your hospital stay, and how you two have rebuilt this wonderful place. The last thing I'd want is to do anything to hurt that."

Maria took a beat, then said, "Thanks, Amelia. I am worried. I'm worried about losing my brother."

"I get it. Ike is all you have left. I also know you know something about devastating loss, and I want you to know a few things about me. My aunt and uncle were like parents to me." Amelia stopped and Ike saw tears glaze her eyes. "Growing up, they were my oasis. Between my mother's alcoholic unpredictability and the constant look of disapproval in my father's eyes, they provided structure and guidance in my life. They and Harper. I adored my older sister. She was beautiful, smart, and tough. I looked up to her. She taught me so much. We would go everywhere together. She even took me to her High Power Rifle Championship that she won when she was a senior in High School. Taught me how to shoot. But when she disappeared and was presumed dead when her boat exploded off the coast of Italy three years ago, I felt alone. Uncle Billy and Aunt Bessie helped me get through." Amelia wiped the tears from her cheek and stood tall. "Someone took them away from me, and I want to find out who and why. I need your brother to help me. I realize these people may be dangerous, but I promise you, I'm a very capable person, and I'll do everything to see that Ike comes back to you. Making the killers pay will not fill this black hole of loneliness in my soul, but I owe it to Uncle Billy and Aunt Bessie to stop them from doing it again. I became an RPA pilot in the Air Force to help people who couldn't defend themselves. This is no different." Amelia reached out and gently touched Maria's shoulder. "But I, of all people, understand. If this is too much for you, just say the word, and I'll be on my way."

Maria's eyes misted and she turned away and scanned the empty bar. She settled her gaze back on Ike, then said to Amelia, "Go do what you need to do, just bring him back to me."

CHAPTER 15

IKE DROPPED THE duffel into the trunk of the Shelby as Amelia got into the car. Hesitating before he closed the lid, he reminded himself to stay focused on the box and the secrets it contained. He was well aware of the threat it represented to him, his sister, and everyone around him. He knew the only way out of danger was to push through this mystery quickly, and the DeSantis brothers were the key to discovering what was inside.

Maria and Randy had supported Ike's suggestion that Amelia stay in one of the three apartments above Rossi's. During the rebuild, Ike had the contractor install bullet-resistant glass, steel-reinforced doors, and state-of-the-art security and fire suppression. He'd been splitting his time between his Mount Washington townhome and one of the apartments and planned to stay in that unit as long as Amelia was in the other. Despite her protests, he'd convinced Maria to stay in the third apartment, instead of their parents' house where she stayed regularly anyway. Randy had agreed to share Ike's apartment above Rossi's for the duration of the investigation to ensure both Maria's and Amelia's safety. The large gun safe in Ike's office provided all the necessary firepower, if needed. Because Ike had uncovered corruption in the police bureau in Jack Cole's case last year that had resulted in the bombing of Rossi's, patrols around Rossi's had increased dramatically and had stayed that way for the past year.

Ike entered the driver's side and buckled in. "It's just two blocks away," he said to Amelia already in the passenger's seat. Ike started the car and backed into the alley.

"Who are these guys again?" Amelia asked.

"The DeSantis brothers. I grew up with them. Their dad ran the auto repair shop back then. After he died, Vinny and Danny took it over. They have a huge shop and the equipment necessary to access the box without destroying the contents."

"But can they be trusted?"

"Absolutely. With my life. They've gotten me out of many a nine-line bind."

Amelia scrunched her nose. "What did you say?"

"A nine-line bind. It's oilfield slang. Means a total mess."

"Funny. In my old line of work nine-line meant attack orders."

"That's interesting. But seriously, these guys can be trusted," Ike said.

Amelia focused on the alley way ahead.

Ike wasn't convinced she believed him. He thought he'd better prepare her for the DeSantis experience. For those that didn't live in that world, their first impressions could be unsettling. It was near midnight and there was no traffic in the alley.

Ike slowed the Shelby, then stopped. "There's something you need to know about these guys."

Amelia eyed Ike. "What is it?"

"They are the best mechanics I've ever seen. They specialize in vintage muscle cars, but I've seen them work on everything from snowmobiles to vacuum cleaners. They're throwbacks, wrapped in the early eighties. Their dad got them hooked on eighties rock when they worked in the shop with him. I've known their family for years, and they knew mine. Vinny is a year older and Danny a year younger than me. They did everything for my sister and me when our parents were killed. Vinny even picked up Maria from grade school that day because I was still in State College. They aren't polished by a long shot, but I trust them."

Amelia seemed to relax a bit. "Okay. I trust you. You trust them. I'm good."

"Great." Ike turned left and drove to the entrance to DeSantis Auto two blocks down. He pulled up to the chain-link gate, rolled down his window, and pressed the button on the rusty speaker box. He checked his watch and noted it was after midnight. He surveyed the security camera mounted on the pole ahead and hoped the boys were partied out—and alone. Texting or calling ahead wasn't an option. He didn't want to leave any electronic trail to the DeSantis brothers.

The box crackled, then Ike heard "You Really Got Me" by Van Halen in the background.

"Hey, Ikey boy!"

Ike glanced at Amelia and smiled. She was already grinning.

"Hey, Vinny. Sorry about the late hour, but I need some help."

Ike waited for a reply. Then Vinny said, "Prego!"

Ike pressed the button and said, "Grazie."

The gate rattled, then jerked and rolled open. Ike pulled ahead as the middle of three white shop doors rolled up. Vinny stood to the right side in boxers and a Metallica t-shirt, holding a sixteen-ounce Pabst Blue Ribbon beer. His thick black hair was pulled behind his ears in a ponytail. When he spotted Amelia, he pulled the bottom of his t-shirt down to cover his fly and brushed some crumbs from his chest onto the shiny gray garage floor.

"Sorry, dude. Didn't know you had a date."

"Not my date, a client." It was the first time Ike called her his client. It felt right.

Vinny stepped aside and Ike pulled behind a metallic-blue Chevelle. Vinny clicked the remote in one hand, chugging what was left in the can with the other as he walked to Ike's window. Leaning in on both forearms, he eyed Amelia, then Ike.

"Hey, man. How's things?" He offered Ike a fist and Ike bumped it. Vinny smelled of beer, as he did most nights, and his eyes were glazed but active.

"I'm good. Maria too. How are you and Danny doing?"

"The same," he said, then he grinned. "Awesome!"

"Vinny, this is Amelia Garcia," Ike said.

Still leaning on the window, Vinny raised one hand.

"Hey, there. You as tough as you look, young lady."

"Tougher," Ike said. He reached for the door handle. "Let me out of here."

Vinny stepped back and tossed his beer can toward a steel drum against the wall near the door. It clinked on the lip and dropped in. Most people measured therapy in hours. The DeSantis brothers measured theirs in ounces.

"That's a pretty good shot," Amelia said, climbing out of the car.

Vinny covered a belch. "Lots of practice."

"Where's Danny?" Ike asked.

"Takin' a leak. He'll be here in a minute."

Ike stood at the trunk. "Before I show this to you, you need to know that everyone who has seen this has been killed or become a target."

Vinny thought for a moment. "Have you seen it?"

"Yes."

"Then I'm not worried. Let 'em try something."

Ike walked to the trunk and opened it. He unzipped the duffel, then looked at Amelia. "You do the honors."

Amelia stepped up, pulled the sealed container from the bag, and set it on the edge of the trunk.

Vinny examined it. "What is it?"

"I think it's a German strong box from some ship. Got it in five thousand feet of water," Amelia said, as she opened the container and showed Vinny the box.

"May I?" Vinny said reaching for it.

She placed it on his outstretched hands. He surveyed the box from all angles and stopped when he saw the eagle and swastika. "Wow. I know some skinhead assholes who'd cream their jeans over this."

"Over what?"

Ike looked over the car and spotted Danny coming toward them. His thick lips were stretched into a wide smile, and his teeth were darkened, stripped of their enamel. A year younger than Ike, Danny had been the fiercest middle linebacker Ike had ever seen at Peabody High. His career ended one winter when he broke his leg hanging Christmas lights while traveling hand over hand from the second-story gutter. But he'd quickly become the best muscle-car mechanic in the tristate area.

"Hey Danny," Ike said as they shared a bro hug. "This is Amelia. She's a client."

"Hey there." He offered her his hand, and they shook. Danny gave her the once over. "You play?"

"I did. All the way up until high school. They wouldn't let me play after that." Danny shook his head. "Jagoffs."

Amelia appeared a little confused, then smiled.

"Check this out," Vinny said.

"We need to open it. Carefully. Without affecting what's inside."

"What's inside?" Danny said.

"That's what we're here to find out," Ike said. "But this is just between us."

Vinny and Danny shared a look. Danny nodded.

"You got it, dude," Vinny said.

"Let's get it into the machine shop," Danny said.

The brothers headed for the room in the far corner of the large garage and Ike and Amelia followed. Ike estimated they'd passed half a million in custom vintage muscle cars in the four bays along the wall to the left. When they entered the machine shop, he was confident Vinny and Danny would get the box open. He wasn't so confident about what they'd find inside. Whatever it was, he was about to bet their lives he could figure out what it was and why it was so deadly.

Ike looked at Amelia, who slowly shook her head and said, "This should be interesting."

CHAPTER 16

BENTON GARCIA DID his best to hide the fear clawing at his confidence from inside. Billy had refused his offer of security when they'd set up on Kiawah, and now, he'd paid for that bad decision with his life. But despite the team of trained security personnel guarding the Garcia compound, Benton knew there was always a way in if the killers were committed. He and Tess could be next.

He looked up from the matrix of phone messages on his desk and watched the storms drifting away out to sea. He wished the storm he was dealing with was headed out to sea with them, but based on the twenty or so messages his secretary had delivered just after ten p.m., this storm was just getting started. The lightning flashes were barely visible in the distance, but they illuminated the choppy seas churning just beyond the dune that sat a few feet from the window in front of him. He'd built this wing for his home office to the edge of the dunes, as close as the island's strict regulations would allow. For him, the ocean represented power, and he wanted to see and feel that boundless force to remind him of the power that he had—and how it could be washed away like a retreating wave.

Glancing back down at the messages, he knew any one of them could be the beginning of the end. The messages were collected this afternoon at the business center in Kiawah's Freshfield's Village where he'd rented offices for his secretary and himself when he was on the island. Despite his gut telling him to get to Dallas, Billy's killing dictated that he remained on Kiawah with Tess to show her family his commitment. After all, one of the last remaining heirs to the Winkler fortune had been killed, and the other family members would be watching Benton closely. He knew he had half the family in his corner; the other half thought Billy should have been chairman and CEO. But after old man Winkler had died, Tess was always the deciding vote, and the leverage he had on her ensured he remained in power. Despite the sale of forty percent of the company to a New York–based private equity firm to raise cash for the family, he still held his job. The family vote was his firewall.

The phone messages on his desk were from a mix of family members, board members, and principles of other Texas oil families. He knew the family members had two issues: what happened to Billy and his wife, and whether they themselves were safe. The board members, some of whom were family members, wanted to know the same thing, plus, they wanted details on what was going on and what would be the spillover into Winkler Oil since a family member had been killed. Everyone wanted to know how and why it happened. Was it a murder-suicide as some news outlets had hinted? Had both Billy and Bessie been ruthlessly killed in their own home? Or was it something more? Several had heard the FBI had gotten involved. Was it because of Billy's company's work in Minuteman or was there another reason? The heads of the other Texas oil families had said they were offering their sincere condolences, but for a subset of them, Benton knew there would be a much more pointed discussion about what was going on, why the FBI was involved, and what it would mean for the political landscape in Texas and Washington, DC. And whatever it was, did Benton have it under control?

Control. That was what The Club had always done. It had always been that way, ever since the first gusher at Spindletop in 1901. Since then, the group, or some subset of it, had used their money and power to control Texas politics. Later, that influence had spread to the White House, placing several of Texas's favorite sons into the most powerful office in the land. The latest success, President Richard Reed, had been Benton's proudest moment. But that moment had come with responsibility. He'd taken the lead to quietly get Reed elected, and that success made Benton the de facto leader of The Club. With that power came the responsibility to be the point of the spear for The Club's interests.

Trent McCallum walked into the office wagging his head. "No one in DC is talking much. The second in command at Justice was killed last night. An alleged one-car accident. Justice wants to be sure, hence the FBI. That's all I could get, other than the fact that there is an invisible hand guiding the investigation."

"A hand from where?"

"It's not Congress. So I think it might be the White House." McCallum ended that sentence with a raised eyebrow and a *What are you gonna do?* look.

Benton knew this was how the game was played. The powerful rarely went toe to toe unless their representatives had done their groundwork first. The next move was his to make.

"I'll call my contact in the White House," Benton said.

"Okay," McCallum said, then turned his attention quickly to the hallway leading into the office from the house. Benton listened for a moment, then heard ice cubes rattling against a highball glass coming from the hallway. Every muscle in his body went taut and his stomach fluttered. His mind prepared to repel the attack he was sure was coming. McCallum looked back at him, and Benton signaled for McCallum to leave.

From the darkness of the hallway, Benton heard, "Benton." The voice was Tess's, but it was drifting in and out of its lane due to the bourbon that had been assaulting her brain for the last five hours.

"Benton!" Her words were slurred and wobbly.

"In here," Benton said as McCallum left the room.

Tess passed McCallum in the hallway. "Where are you going?"

McCallum didn't answer and left.

Tess staggered to Benton's desk, steadying herself on the back of one of the side chairs. "You need to find out what's going on."

"I'm working on it."

"Well, work faster. You want to hang onto that job, don't you?"

"I'm doing all I can." Benton pointed to the messages on his desk. "You see what I'm dealing with here."

With her face twisted with anger, she appeared to read a few of the names and numbers on the message forms. One of them turned her face slack and sad. Her eyes welled, then she looked up and zeroed in on Benton. "Don't screw this up like you screwed up with Harper."

Regardless of being three sheets to the wind, she knew how to hit below the belt. Even though he was ready for it, her words easily penetrated him and infected him with a sickening guilt that froze him in his chair. He thought about Harper, and the last time they talked. She was worried about what the agency had asked her to do. Benton brushed her concern aside and said it was part of the job. He'd vouched for her to get her the job and was more worried about what they would think about him instead of his daughter's welfare. Those were the last words they would speak.

"Well?" Tess said, her eyes filled with resentment.

"You need to go to bed," he said firmly.

"You need to help Amelia." She drained the last of the bourbon in her glass. "You never treated her as well as you treated Harper."

"I wonder why that was?" he said. It was his turn to hit below the belt.

Tess absorbed the words like a punch to a boxer about to go down. A tear ran down her face. She turned and headed to the hallway. "Asshole."

Benton sighed and pulled out the phone he reserved only for these calls and dialed. He heard the person on the other end pick up the call but say nothing. "We need to talk."

CHAPTER 17

IKE TRIED TO suppress the anticipation vibrating through his nervous system. The excitement of discovering what was inside the box was tempered by his concerns. Whatever was in there had already proved to be deadly. Once his lifelong friends had seen the contents, they would be targets too, along with Amelia and anyone he cared about, until he could uncover the truth. Harnessing his surging energy, he narrowed his focus on what he needed to do next. On the top of his list, he needed to alert Randy and take measures to protect Maria, Lauren, and Lauren's kids. Once protective measures were taken, he hoped whatever they found in the box would allow him to move quickly to expose the killers. The longer it took, the longer they were all in danger.

Under the bright fluorescent lights dangling from the ceiling, he watched Danny place the heavy box between the steel jaws of the vice on the air float table of the large valve seat and guide machine that looked like a massive drill press on the far wall of the shop. Flanked by a bright red spray wash cabinet that looked like an industrial dishwasher on his right, and a faded blue blast cabinet on his left, Ike knew the DeSantis brothers would make short work of the box. Danny swung a large magnifying glass on its articulated arm over the box, while Vinny shrugged on a pair of coveralls to cover his boxers. He rolled the top down and tied the sleeves around his waist. The vice floated on the table, and Danny rotated the box in the vice as he examined the outside. Vinny opened one of the drawers of the huge toolbox on the far wall and removed a small hammer and small steel punch and moved next to Danny. After Danny showed him the box through the magnifier, Vinny carefully tapped the steel punch against the box. The sound was low-pitched, as if the walls of the box were thick. The brothers shared a look but remained silent. Then Vinny nodded at Danny, who looked over his shoulder at Amelia.

"How deep was the water where you found this?"

"A little over forty-seven hundred feet."

Danny looked up, then closed his eyes. "That's seawater, so a pressure gradient of just under half a pound per foot of depth." He turned to Vinny wide-eyed. "That's over two thousand pounds per square inch."

Vinny turned to Amelia. "How cold?"

Standing next to Ike behind them, Amelia gave Ike a bewildered look. Ike knew the brothers were sneaky smart and surprised most people with their intelligence. Ike nodded toward them.

Amelia turned back to the brothers and said, "Thirty-seven degrees."

Vinny read the digital readout on the wall to the right of the machine. "It's seventy-six in here." Then he locked eyes with Danny. "Double it." They froze for a moment, then moved slowly away from the table.

Ike stepped back, pulling Amelia with him.

She leaned into Ike. "What is it?"

"They're worried about the box being pressurized. Four thousand pounds of pressure could turn that thing into a grenade."

"You're damn right, dude," Vinny said as he and Danny used their arms to herd Ike and Amelia out of the shop.

Once outside, Danny said, "If I try to open that and it's under pressure, it's all over."

"So what can we do?" Amelia asked. "We need to know what's inside."

"If it is under pressure, we can't carry that thing around anymore, either," Ike said.

"If it's under pressure," Danny said, "it will probably explode when I drill into it. But the pressure would have had to equalize in the box, then the box would have had to reseal itself."

"Right," Vinny said. "It's thick-walled, and based on the lack of corrosion, it's some type of stainless alloy. Could have held its seal the entire time."

"If that's the case, it wouldn't be a problem. It wouldn't be pressurized." Danny said.

"Did I see an X-ray machine in there?" Amelia said.

"Bingo!" Danny said. "We can X-ray it first. Then see what we got."

Danny ran across the garage and disappeared through the door he'd originally entered. Ike knew it led to the business office, then to the stairs to the living quarters on the second floor.

"Where's he going?" Amelia asked.

"He'll be back," Vinny said, smiling. "He does that sometimes. Hopefully it's not the scoots."

Amelia looked at Ike and shook her head. But Ike wasn't worried. He knew the look that had spread across Danny's face. He had had an idea.

The three of them waited in silence, until Danny burst back through the door. He looked like an armored armadillo. A black helmet rocked back and forth on his head as he ran and shrugged on a bulletproof vest with POLICE emblazoned on the front. He stopped in one of the bays, disappearing behind the bright yellow Barracuda parked over the lift. He trotted out from behind the car looking like a bulldog, carrying a welder's mask in one hand and his helmet in the other.

He stopped, proudly standing in front of Ike and Amelia.

"My PPE." He leaned closer to Amelia. "Personal protective equipment!" he said with a grin. "I'll go in and X-ray it. Stay out here."

"Awesome outfit, bro," Vinny said, laughing as he gave Danny a fist bump. Danny pulled the welder's mask down over his face and put on the helmet. He went back into the machine shop. Amelia and Vinny walked to the window in the door, and Ike stood behind them, looking over their heads. Being six four still had its advantages.

Danny carefully removed the box from the vice and slowly carried it to the red refrigerator-sized box in the corner of the machine shop. Opening the square gray door, he positioned the box inside and closed it. He stepped to the computer monitor attached to the machine. He typed something on the keyboard, then turned to them, dancing to whatever rock song was playing in his mind, the SWAT helmet bouncing on his head and the welder's mask, still covering his face, rocking to the beat of his earworm. An image came on the screen, and he stopped, turned back, and focused on the image. After examining it, he raised the mask, pulled off his helmet, and waved them inside.

Vinny opened the door and Ike followed him inside with Amelia close behind him.

Danny pointed to the image on the screen. "See that. No fluid inside. For the pressure to have equalized, there had to be seawater in there."

"The damn seal held. All those years," Vinny said. "I'd like to meet the German engineer that made it."

Ike studied the image on the screen. It was varying shades of gray. The box was mostly empty. Its thick walls were obvious on the screen. But there was one object, very light gray, that looked like a miniature roll of paper. "What do you guys make of this?"

Danny and Vinny leaned closer to the screen.

"Can't tell till we get that sucker open," Vinny said.

"It could be something like a teletype paper," Amelia said, leaning in over Danny's shoulder.

"Smart *and* she looks like she could still hit like a defensive end," Danny said, looking back at Ike. "Let's get it out of there."

The group stepped back, and Danny pulled the box out. "This will take a few minutes. Yinz might want to get a beer."

Ike started for the door, but Amelia stood still, scrunched her nose, and stared at Danny as he took the box to the spray wash cabinet. Ike realized she hadn't been exposed to the Pittsburgh slang.

"Come on," Ike said to Amelia as he headed for the door. "I'll explain outside."

CHAPTER 18

IKE LED AMELIA to a cable spool turned on its side, serving as a table along the back wall of the shop. The makeshift break area had four tattered lawn chairs scattered around the wooden spool and was centered on one of the few windows in the brick structure built sometime in the early 1950s. The dim lighting in the garage did little to illuminate the darkness and gave the cars, most of which were built in the seventies, a haunting, retro presence. It was just after two, and the grief that had taken up residence in Ike's heart when he learned of his parents' murders seeped out as it always did when he was up at this hour. Over the years he'd grown used to it, but he could see in Amelia's eyes that her grief was still new, raw, and toxic.

The only noise came from the machine shop and sounded like a high-pressure car wash. He slid one of the chairs from the table and offered it to Amelia. She sat, and he pulled another chair out and sat beside her.

"How are you doing?" Ike asked.

Amelia glanced at the door of the machine shop, then turned back. "Yinz?"

Ike laughed. "Yeah. Some of the folks here use that in place of y'all."

Amelia's gaze drifted around the shop as if she was avoiding Ike's question. He knew from experience that was a flawed strategy.

"How are you doing?" he asked, again.

Amelia settled her eyes on Ike and hissed out a deep breath. "All I can do is think about Billy and Bessie. How terrified they must have been. I can't believe it. I keep yearning for the great times we had together, but then I realize those will never happen again."

Ike knew she needed a vessel. Someone to stand witness to her pain. He'd been there. Even though it had been twenty-three years, the pain, when he let it surface, was as fresh as the day he'd first felt it. He remembered the words the therapist had taught him to use with Maria when she was ten years old and struggling with their parents' deaths and Ike was struggling to play the role of a parent. "I hear you. Tell me more."

She wagged her head. "Not much else to say. I got them killed and lost the only people who were helping me build a happiness I had never had."

Ike had to respond to Amelia's pain. He wasn't built to ignore it. "I won't bullshit you and tell you I know exactly what you're feeling, but I know a little about what you're going through."

"How did you get through it?"

"I didn't," he said, staring off into the distance. "It will never go away. It will stay with you forever. But it will find its place in your life. It won't get better, but it will become a part of you. You will revisit it often, sometimes by choice and sometimes not. And for me, it drives me."

Amelia thought for a moment. Then her eyes flashed, her breathing sped up, and she tightened her focus on Ike. "I'll use it, too. To get those bastards that did it. I'll make them pay."

The warrior had returned. Ike was sure it had never left. He noticed the noise had stopped. Amelia did too. The door to the machine shop opened, and Ike looked over Amelia's shoulder.

Vinny stepped out. "You'll want to be here for this."

The words were like a siren's call, triggering a flood of curiosity that pulled Ike to his feet. Amelia glanced at Vinny then back at Ike. Her eyes narrowed, and she jumped to her feet, heading for Vinny. As Ike followed Amelia to the door, his enthusiasm was throttled back by his concern over what they'd find. A dark foreboding over what they were about to unleash swept over him.

Entering the shop, Ike spotted the box in the grip of the rotating vise floating on the air table. Danny stood proudly beside it with his safety goggles sitting atop his slicked blond hair, still wearing the bulletproof vest, his arms crossed and biceps bulging. The box was clean, shimmering like a large stainless steel jewelry box. They had removed the scale and grit that had marred the outside and partially covered the insignia on its top. The Nazi Eagle now arrogantly glowed, projecting its evil spell throughout the room.

Amelia walked up to the box. "This is what I found?"

"It is," Danny said, rotating the box in the vise. He stopped it with the thick locking mechanism facing up. "I think if we drill this here, it will open."

"Let's get to it," Ike said, stepping closer.

Danny pulled his goggles over his eyes. He pointed to the floor. "Okay. Step back behind the yellow line," he said. After lining up the latch on the box with the bit above it, he locked the vise in place, adjusted a couple of handles, and typed something into the keypad on the machine. The bit began to spin.

Amelia stepped back and stood between Ike and Vinny as they watched Danny grab the handle on the side of the machine and carefully pull the drill bit down to the lock. Ike leaned closer waiting for the lock to give way. Amelia glanced at him for a moment, and he saw the fear and excitement in her eyes. With a high-pitched screech, the bit dug into the lock. Curly strips of the alloy peeled out of the hole and dropped to the table. The smell of hot metal filled Ike's nostrils. The screech became a grinding, then the bit jolted when it broke through the lock. Danny returned the bit to its starting position and shut down the machine. He pulled the box from the vise and set it flat on the table. He stepped back and focused on Amelia.

"You want to do the honors?" Danny said, offering her his gloves.

She glanced at Ike.

"It's all yours," he said.

She stepped across the yellow line, took the gloves, and stopped in front of the box. Pulling them on, she reached down and grabbed the box with both hands. Ike saw her forearms ripple as she strained to open the box. Just then, Vinny stepped forward and handed her a metal wedge and hammer. Turning the box on its hinges, she placed the wedge on the seam and with one powerful swing, popped it open. She caught it halfway open and set it down on its bottom. Setting the tools aside, she grabbed the top and opened it. Her eyes widened. "Oh my God."

Ike looked at Vinny on his right. He shrugged. He then eyed Danny on his left who just shook his head. Ike stepped up next to Amelia and peered into the box. There was a small roll of paper that appeared as if it had been baked in an oven. It was browned with age. Looking more closely at the paper, he saw perforations peppered on it in seemingly random patterns. The rest of the box was empty. He raised up and saw Amelia staring at him, shocked with a tear running down her face.

"I got them killed for nothing." She began to cry. "They were killed for nothing."

Danny and Vinny stepped up and looked inside while Ike grabbed Amelia by her shoulders. She dropped her gaze to the floor.

"No. We don't know that," Ike said. Amelia didn't look up. "Look at me," Ike said. Slowly, she raised her head and Ike looked into her eyes. "It looks like a tickertape. It could be some sort of code."

"I think Ikey boy may be on to something," Vinny said.

"Me too," Danny said. "Don't worry, Amelia. Remember those jagoffs that wouldn't let you play?" He didn't wait for her to answer. "Doesn't look to me like you let them make you quit? This could be World War II spy stuff." She gazed at Danny.

"Danny's right," Vinny said. He looked at Ike, nodding. He stopped and tilted his head. "You know what I'm thinking?"

Ike read Vinny's mind. He'd been thinking the same thing. "Mister McNally."

Danny folded his arms and grinned at Amelia. "Mister McNally."

CHAPTER 19

IKE DROVE THE Shelby through the gates of DeSantis Auto and onto the naked streets of Bloomfield. Ike was tired, but his neurons were firing, reacting to challenging questions and possibilities that forced his mind to deal with the tiny roll of paper in the box. The seductive combination of curiosity and anxiety had his blood pressure up, and he felt every heartbeat in his chest. Despite his fatigue, his eyes were active. It was three in the morning, and traffic was scarce on the backstreets of Bloomfield. The black streetlights stood witness to the still silence of the neighborhood. Cars sat motionless in their spots. Homes were dark, awaiting the lights of the early risers, workers readying for early morning shifts and retirees whose bodies awakened them from their slumber due to either ailments or habit. Peacefulness always made Ike uneasy because it was where his haunting memories lived. Amelia sat next to him at attention, holding the container that made them both targets. He could see the frustration building as her jaw silently flexed, and she gritted her teeth. She knew the longer it took to unravel the mystery inside the box, the longer they risked the lives of anyone they contacted.

She caught him eyeing her. "Can you tell me more about Mr. McNally and when we'll see him?"

"Mr. McNally lives alone. He's ninety-seven. We don't wake him. He's up every day at six. Showered and ready by six-thirty, done with breakfast by seven. We'll head there then."

"You know a lot about him."

"We all do."

"Everyone?"

"Those of us whose families have been here for generations. We look after each other, but we especially look after our seniors. I used to mow his lawn when I was a kid. After his wife died, the people from the neighborhood started looking after him. We do whatever he's comfortable with. Fix up his house, take him to appointments, visit on the porch with him."

"That's quite nice of you."

"We just do it. We don't do it to influence what other people think about us. It's part of the fabric of the old neighborhood. It's the way it was always done."

"That's pretty rare these days."

"It is. We do have some folks who have moved into the area who aren't from around here. Most don't participate, and that's okay. They weren't aware of that tradition. But those that do seem to love it."

Ike pulled down the alley behind Rossi's and parked. Randy stood at the steel security door, waiting. Ike turned to Amelia. "I texted him that we were coming back." He turned off the car and got out.

"Hey, Randy."

"Hey, Ike. Amelia."

"Hi, Randy," Amelia said, as she headed to the door.

Randy's eyes scoured the roadway in either direction with his arms crossed, positioning one hand above the Glock in his belt.

At the door, Ike stopped and let Amelia carry the container inside. He went inside, and Randy closed the door, joining them at the stairs off the back hallway.

"Get some rest," Ike said to Amelia. He nodded to the container. "I'd let Randy put that in the safe." Ike checked his watch. "We'll leave here at six forty-five. I'm going up to the office to check on a few things."

Amelia handed the container to Randy. "I'll give it a shot. No guarantees I can sleep." She headed up the steps.

Randy followed Amelia and glanced at Ike over his shoulder. "Jenna was here last night and dropped something off for you. I put it on your desk. She said you'd want to have a look at it."

"Okay. Thanks." Ike walked back and checked the steel door, then headed up to the office. He'd built it at the end of the hallway, away from the residences. He quietly closed the door and noticed that Randy had left on the copper lamp sitting at the corner of his desk. The rest of the office was dark, other than the diffuse, haunting glow from the streetlights on Liberty Avenue framed in the window behind the desk. Centered on the black desk blotter, he noticed the letter-sized brown envelope. A chill swept through him.

Jenna had been working on getting more information regarding the confidential informant form that pointed to his mother somehow being involved with the FBI. He moved to the desk, picked up the envelope, then dropped into his high-back chair. Opening the envelope, he pulled out the two pages inside. A handwritten yellow sticky note was at the top. The cursive penmanship reminded Ike of when he was a young boy attending Saint John's Elementary and the sessions with his mother helping him with his penmanship. The note read:

Ike,

This was all I could find. Sorry I couldn't find more.

Jenna

He pulled the note from the paper. It was an ancient photocopy of what appeared to be the same FBI confidential informant form Jenna had given him yesterday. Just as before, the form was heavily redacted with blackout lines in most of the boxes. As his pulse raced, Ike found the box containing the informant's name. It had been blacked out. Jenna had highlighted two boxes with a yellow marker. The first was a section with what appeared to be an FBI confidential informant number. It was an alpha-numeric:

PIT-237-OC. The other highlighted box had its title blacked out but had *Tier 1 OIA* entered onto the form. He leaned back and exhaled, calming himself. He still couldn't imagine his mother as an informant. She couldn't be. Not his mother. But now he had two more clues. Clues that might lead him to the truth, and maybe to his parents' killers.

He opened the laptop on his desk and launched Google. Ike knew that unless his mother testified in a trial as a confidential informant against a defendant, he'd never identify her. Instead, he searched the meaning of the letters *OC* contained in the number. The result on the screen sickened him.

Organized Crime

Ike knew exactly what that had meant in Bloomfield. The Giordano family.

"No, Mom. No," he whispered to the photograph on his desk.

Ike's movements became deliberate, and an invisible resistance worked against him. Part of him wanted to stop. To go no further. He didn't want to infect his memory of his mother. Reality said otherwise. To get to her killer, he had to get to the truth. He entered another search, this time on the Tier 1 OIA designation.

Otherwise Illegal Activity

Ike shoved the laptop away. This was not his mother. No way. That designation meant that someone in the FBI sought to get approval for the informant to conduct illegal activity under their supervision with immunity from prosecution. She was the kindest, most gentle person he'd ever been around. She was loved by her family and friends. She'd guided him away from drugs and gambling and into sports. Every accolade he'd earned he'd credited to his mother's love and support. Picking up the form, he stared at it, magically hoping it would somehow change. He thought about Maria. This would crush her. When she'd lost her parents, she was only nine, and her mother and father were like gods. He didn't want to destroy that memory. Maria had suffered enough.

After a minute or so, acceptance robbed him of his fantasy. He had to follow the facts, no matter where they led. He hated himself for continuing, but he knew it was the only way. He also needed help. He needed a contact in the FBI who could be trusted. Someone who'd be willing to help him find the truth. But to find the truth, he'd have to risk all that he and Amelia had been working on. He'd have to call Mia. He had trusted her right up until he let their relationship die to preserve his bond with his sister. He was trapped, and the only way out was through. He pulled out his phone and searched for the cell phone number Mia had given him.

CHAPTER 20

IKE REMEMBERED THE look on Mia's face when she warned him not to get involved in Amelia's case. If he was going to reach out to Mia, he had to trust her. He had years before, and they'd had a bond that couldn't be broken. Until *he* broke it. Staring at the screen of his iPhone, he decided calling Mia just after four in the morning was not the way to win her cooperation. She was probably sound asleep in DC. Instead, he texted her, asking if she would text him back when she was awake. He slid the phone back into his pocket. Before he let it go, the phone vibrated with a reply. He pulled it back out and read her response.

You can call anytime.

Suddenly the past wasn't so distant, and the bond between them seemed stronger than he had initially thought. He made the call.

"You're up early," she said, her tone bright and welcoming.

"Look who's talking," Ike said.

She giggled in a way that made Ike feel she was flirting. "What's up? Do you have something for me?"

Ike immediately felt the pressure ramping up. While he'd thought she was flirting, she may have been simply disarming a source. He never betrayed clients and sharing anything about what Amelia had found felt like a betrayal. He wanted Mia's help more than anything, but it could cost him his ethics.

"Yes. But it's not what you think. It's personal."

The silence that followed was unnerving. "Oh," she finally said.

"You know I've been working on my parents' murders, forever."

"I do. I'm so sorry no one has come up with any answers after all this time. I know how much pain that brings you."

Ike was drawn back to the nights they'd spent together sharing each other's dreams and the mountain of pain they'd each faced in finding the courage to move forward. Her empathy felt good, and the strong desire for a deeper connection to Mia barreled out of the cage of denial he'd built when their time together ended. He felt worse about what he'd done and what he was doing now. It was like running into a blind alley with no escape. Not only was he betraying Amelia, but now his feelings for Mia were a betrayal of Maria. And he'd be using his past connection to Mia to get information about his mother.

"I appreciate that," he said. "You were always there for me back then."

She hesitated, then said, "We did have some wonderful times."

Ike relaxed a little more. "We did. Boston, New York City, skiing in Crested Butte."

"Too bad it had to end," she said tersely. "What's up?"

She'd set him up to make her point. Her reply reminded Ike that back when it was first recognized as a human condition, nostalgia used to be treated as a disease and that it came from the Greek words *nostos* and *alga* for homecoming and pain. He needed a cure for his nostalgia. He needed to focus on the present.

"This needs to be off the record. I have something I'd like you to look at, but I need to give it to you in person. I can get to DC in a couple of days."

"That sounds a little cloak and dagger," she said, letting her words hang in the air for a few seconds before continuing, as if weighing her options. "I'm at the Renaissance hotel here in Pittsburgh. Can you come over?"

"You're here in Pittsburgh?" The shock of that revelation rifled through Ike. If she was in Pittsburgh, was she following Amelia and him? Did she know about the visit to the DeSantis brothers?

"Yes. On official business. But I have some time right now."

Now Ike was weighing *his* options. He no longer felt guilty; he felt betrayed. He was nothing more than a person of interest to her. While his guard went back up, he decided to go ahead. Showing her the form and asking her to find out what his mother was doing, if indeed it was his mother, would cost him nothing.

"I can be there in fifteen minutes," he said.

Ike headed to the Shelby, form in hand. He arrived at the Renaissance in ten minutes due to the empty streets and a string of green lights all the way into downtown. He slipped the sleep-deprived valet a twenty-dollar bill to hold the car out front, then entered the lobby. He spotted Mia in the far corner sitting in one of two high-back chairs with a table holding two steaming cups of coffee between them.

As he approached, he noticed she'd done her lips and hair but had no other makeup on. She was always beautiful to him, makeup or not. A few strands of her short blonde hair dipped across her left eye. As he got closer, she smiled, and despite his best efforts to remain stoic, a warm heat spread over him. He took the chair beside her, and she handed him the cup of coffee.

"Sorry about that comment on the phone," she said.

"No worries. I deserved it."

"Yes, you did," she said. "But I can't fathom what you've been through these past twenty-three years. What can I do to help?"

Ike settled himself and handed the form to Mia. "I've found this form."

Mia scanned the first page, then lifted it, and scanned the second.

"What I've found so far indicated that my mother could be the informant."

Mia's red lips parted, her eyes wide with surprise. "No."

"That's what I said at first. But the details that aren't redacted match our family profile back then, and it was found under a false bottom in Mac Machowski's desk."

Ike searched her eyes trying to find the trust they once had, hoping it was still there. "I need you to see if you can find out if this was her and what she was doing."

Mia remained silent and looked back down at the form.

"I know what I'm asking could get you fired, maybe put in jail. I understand if you can't do it."

Ike waited for Mia's ask. He fully expected a quid pro quo from her involving information relating to what he'd found so far in the Garcia case. He was getting close to the answers he'd sought since he was nineteen years old. He'd told himself he'd do anything to solve his parents' murders. For once, he didn't know what he'd do if she insisted on information in return. He didn't know what the contents of the box found in the deep black sea meant, but it meant something. Something worth killing for. Mia represented the US government, and based on what he'd found so far, they couldn't be trusted.

Mia looked up from the form in her hand. "I'll see what I can do."

There it was. No ask. She'd do it and perhaps end the years of torment and anguish for Ike. Driven by excitement and joy, he lost himself in the moment. He shot up, and she stood with him. He hugged her, and she pressed her body against his. For a moment, they went back ten years, bonded by trust and desire.

She pulled her head back and fixed her deep dark eyes on his. "Do you want to come up?"

CHAPTER 21

IKE FELT TRAPPED by Mia's invitation. After ten years of what ifs, Mia had spoken the words that just might be the beginning of a second chance. The chance he'd thought was gone. One he'd thought of in those rare quiet moments when he'd emptied his mind and listened to his heart. Accept it, and he could start down the road to repair the relationship he'd let die. The threat of her ex's accusations of an affair between them were echoes from the distant past. Ike and Mia had started dating two years after her marriage had ended. Before Mia's divorce, they were friendly co-workers, accepting the moat of respect that surrounded married women, at least in Ike's mind. Still, after their divorce, her then-husband accused Ike of having an affair with Mia while they were still married, instead of accepting responsibility for his own terrible behavior being the driving force for their problems. He threatened to go public if Ike didn't end their relationship. Her ex's lies had been baseless, but as a then-thirty-two-year-old surrogate parent, Ike had mistakenly thought he had to remain flawless in his little sister's eyes. He decided not to tell Mia because no matter what happened, he still couldn't risk the accusation going public. He'd just cause more problems for Mia. While he'd known Mia could have been The One, back then he was certain he could have never revealed their relationship to his little sister. Because of the false accusation, there was a risk Maria would believe it. Ike thought she just wasn't ready for that, even at twenty-two. Now, Maria was in her thirties, and his relationship with her had never been stronger. She'd understand. But accepting Mia's invitation this morning would come at a cost. Amelia was waiting, lives were in danger, and time was running out: for her, for Ike, and for everyone involved. Ike couldn't break his word. In this moment, he hated that part of himself that he usually cherished. Mia couldn't know why, but he'd have to decline.

As Ike searched a quagmire of shit for the right words, Mia's eyes changed from soft to uncertain. She could still read his mind. He felt strangely vulnerable and stripped of his armor. She could see right through him, and his deepest secrets were hers. Mia had earned that right through long nights helping Ike navigate the dark potholes on the road to getting answers to his parents' murders. She'd also shared her secrets back then. The biggest had led to her role in the FBI and being ostracized from her family, all relatives of the head of the Giordano family. While most were law-abiding citizens, none of them had wanted her to poke the bear.

Ike's hesitation said it all. Mia knew his answer before he could say the words. As the disappointment spread across her face, he felt the tide, filled with ten years of regret, rising again.

"Ike?"

Ike couldn't believe what he was about to say. "I'm sorry. I can't."

"Did I misread what was going on between us?"

"No. My timing is crap. There's nothing I'd like more than to be with you this morning, but there's something I have to do."

Mia studied the form in her hands, then raised her head and locked her eyes on Ike. This time they had the familiar fire he'd seen before.

"The Garcia case?"

"Yes."

"I warned you about taking that. It's dangerous."

"Danger is nothing new to me."

"You don't know what you're getting into."

There was something in Mia's tone that had shifted. She was brutally honest most of the time. Now it was as if she'd memorized each word she spoke. Ike watched a man in a suit walk through the empty lobby.

The woman behind the desk eyed him, then dropped her gaze back to the monitor in front of her. Suddenly he felt watched.

"You know anything about a one-car accident on the road to the airport just before you left Charleston?"

Ike remained silent.

Mia pressed him. "Tell me what's going on."

Ike was getting backed into a corner. He couldn't tell Mia what he'd already found. She worked for the US government, and he'd already concluded that they couldn't be trusted. The conversation had quickly turned into a scripted interrogation. He'd have to conduct the investigation on his own. Once he uncovered the people behind Amelia's uncle's killers, he'd reach out to Mia.

"If I get something I can share with you, I will."

Mia leaned deep into the back of the chair and raised the paper in her hand. "I'll do what I can here," she said, resting the form back in her lap. She leaned forward. "But I have to do my job, and you continuing with the Garcia case might put us on opposite sides of the law. If that happens, I won't be able to help you."

"What aren't you telling me?"

Mia rose and started to walk away. Ike stood up, his anger overcoming his desire. "Mia!"

Mia stopped with her back to Ike and scanned the lobby. Over her shoulder she softly said, "The Garcias are not what they appear to be." She turned and walked away, shaking the confidential informant papers over her head. "I'll let you know."

As she walked away, he believed he was watching his chance at love—a deep belonging he'd ignored since they'd last been together—fade into the early morning light. He was heading back into the emotional desert. A familiar anger rose and burned away the regret. On the way out the lobby doors, he pulled out his phone and made the call to The Farm.

"It's me. Set it up for tonight."

CHAPTER 22

IKE IGNORED THE cold, biting mist assaulting his cheeks as he walked from the hotel, nodded to the young valet holding the car door open, and gave him another ten dollars as he entered the Shelby. The hardworking kid finishing the graveyard shift deserved it. A cold front had blown into the city in the short time he'd been inside. It wasn't nearly as cold, or as intentional, as Mia's frosty departure. Heading back to Bloomfield, his windshield was quickly coated with the fine mist, and he flicked on the wipers to clear his view. The coating gave the streetlamps a haunting aura that reinforced the growing sense of resentment building in his gut. The Garcia case was becoming a black hole, whose gravity was pulling in people he cared about. Maria, the DeSantis brothers, and now the ninety-seven-year-old war hero who'd been a mentor to him since his high school days. Mia's warning loomed large. She rarely gave them. And while he knew all families had secrets, whatever the Garcias were hiding sounded deadly.

By the time he reached Rossi's, the first glints of dawn were leaking through the few gaps in the overcast. He parked the Shelby in back and pushed his door open against the wind from the mounting storm. Sprinting to the back entrance, he entered the code, opened the door and was inside before getting soaked. Walking down the hallway, he smelled the dark Italian roast coffee from the machine behind the bar. When he entered the bar, he saw Amelia on a stool, facing him, looking eager but fatigued. Her red-rimmed eyes said she hadn't slept, but Ike could sense the need for revenge fueling her. She was nearing the end of her rope. Randy was busy setting up and awaiting the first pot of the day. Ike noticed the box sitting on the bar. Amelia stood.

"Where did you go?"

Ike read her as angry, but her tone was panicked. He took a beat before he reacted, trying to give her the benefit of the doubt. Over the years with his clients, he'd learned that people under pressure were just doing the best they could. He'd been there himself. Still, in the back of his mind, Mia's warning about the Garcias echoed. He wondered what she was hiding. He glanced over her shoulder and Randy made eye contact and wagged his head.

"Let's back it up, Amelia. What's wrong?"

"What's wrong is that I hired you to help me. You said we go see that Frank McNally," she pointed to the box on the bar, "to help find out what this is and find my aunt's and uncle's killer. But you disappeared for an hour and a half."

"You hired me, but you didn't buy me. I had another prospective case I had to follow up on. That's all."

Ike heard Maria behind him. "What case was that?"

Ike turned to see Maria, sleepy-eyed in her jeans and his old Penn State sweatshirt. It yanked him back to when she was nine and their parents were gone. His heartbeat raced, and he tried not to reveal his dilemma. He'd never lied to Maria. He'd made that promise to himself the day he came back to take care of her. He'd lived up to that promise all their lives, until now. He couldn't bring himself to tell her about Mia.

"Just a prospective client who wants to remain anonymous," Ike said.

"Can we take this to Frank, then?" Amelia asked.

Ike turned back to Amelia and saw her with the box in her hand.

"First of all, it's a little too early. I'm not going to wake up a ninety-seven-year-old man early on a Sunday morning." Ike pointed to the box in Amelia's hand. "Second, we're not taking that."

Amelia made herself appear bigger and stepped a little too close to Ike, standing on her toes to get eye to eye. "Why not?"

Ike held his ground, along with his temper. He'd had enough of this and eyed her without saying a word. A few seconds passed and she caught herself. She dropped her gaze, stepped back, and raised one hand, apologetically. "I'm sorry. I just don't want to fail here. People are counting on us to figure this out and if I don't do it, my father will step in, and believe me, neither of us want that."

Ike took a second to relax. "Look. One lesson I've learned is that you need to use your own yardstick. Don't measure yourself by what anyone else thinks. Even your father. It will drive you crazy. And I get what you're going through. No one deserves to have anyone taken from them, especially people as precious to you as your aunt and uncle. I give you my word, we'll get to the bottom of this quickly. But I can't risk other peoples' lives without them knowing what they are getting into, Frank included."

"I don't think you should get Mr. McNally involved," Maria said as she walked to the bar. "As a matter of fact, I'm starting to think *we* shouldn't be involved at all."

"What?" Ike protested.

"You promised you wouldn't put us in this position again, and yet, here we are. I feel for you, Amelia, I really do, but my brother is all I have left." She looked back at Ike. "It's getting more dangerous. I can see it in your eyes."

"What do you suggest we do?" Ike asked.

"Turn it over to someone else."

Ike didn't have the heart to tell Maria that if they stopped now, they'd all be dead soon. "I'm not doing that. I gave her my word."

Maria leaned toward Ike. "You gave it to me, too."

Randy set four mugs on the bar. "Coffee anyone?"

"Not now," Ike said.

"Hey. I worked hard on this contraption you Italians love just to make these for you inmates. Show a little appreciation," Randy said, grinning as he picked up the thick white mug, the handle between his thumb and two fingers with his pinky extended.

Ike had to chuckle even though he knew what Randy was doing. Randy picked up another mug and offered it to Maria. She sheepishly took it. Ike walked over next to her and took the other two, handing one to Amelia.

"Now," Randy said. "You all have something in common. Someone has taken something very precious to you and you all are pissed as hell about it. Rightly so. But I'd suggest you use that energy on whomever did this to you instead of yourselves. And as far as your safety goes, Maria, I will guarantee that."

"I'm sorry, Ike," Maria said.

Ike hugged his sister. "I'll be careful."

He turned back to Amelia. "We'll go see Frank but let me take the lead." Ike pointed to the box again. "And we're not taking that."

CHAPTER 23

IKE TURNED THE corner and let the Shelby idle down the street he'd traveled most days in his youth. Craggy trees, their decades of growth represented by the uneven, broken sidewalks, were shedding their leaves, laying a brown and crimson lining along the edges of the rain-wet street. Brick homes, with comfortable, columned front porches, stood with pride in the dingy gray light of the dull morning skies. The occasional construction dumpster in the front yard signified the new generation of Bloomfield residents moving in and moving up to be within walking distance of the Montessori school, their money enough to displace the patriarchs and matriarchs of the proud Italian families that had built them. He remembered the safety and comfort of the old neighborhood, and it settled his nerves.

Frank McNally had always been there. To call him the pillar of the community was an understatement. A World War II veteran, he'd served in the Army Signal Intelligence Service and secretly in the Office of Strategic Services and had returned to Bloomfield a hero. He'd gone to school on the GI bill and received his master's in mathematics from the University of Pittsburgh. The rumor was he was at the top of his class and took a job working for the fledgling National Security Agency. When his only son died in a car crash in 1966, he and his wife, Bella, moved back to Bloomfield, and he took a teaching job at the high school. His spare time was spent helping children, including fundraising and volunteering at the Boys and Girls Club and helping senior citizens in the neighborhood any way he could. By the time Ike came through his senior year of high school, Mr. McNally was seventy-three years old and had touched most every life in Bloomfield. He retired that year and the entire town lined Liberty Avenue for his celebration one week after graduation.

Ike had first met him through his parents when he was a young boy. Ike was fascinated by the detailed models of different mechanical contraptions Mr. McNally had scattered throughout his home. Those led to detailed conversations about how everything worked. As Ike grew older, the questions changed to dating, reputation, and service to others. Mr. McNally was there for *The Play,* the last play of the state championship game where Ike relied on the self-confidence and discipline that Mr. McNally had taught him. Ike credited Mr. McNally with his choice to study chemical engineering when he received the scholarship from Penn State. Since Ike's parents' deaths, he'd become a mentor and a friend.

Ike spotted the red brick two-story on his left and slowed the Shelby.

Amelia fidgeted in the passenger's seat. "Does he know we're coming?"

Ike shook his head.

Amelia's voice got louder. "Shouldn't we text him before we just show up early on a Sunday morning?"

Ike had to laugh. "He's old school. He doesn't text." Ike scanned the front of the house. "He's ready."

Amelia leaned forward, squinting through the windshield at the house. "How can you tell?"

Ike nodded toward the porch. "The flag. Puts it up every morning then has his coffee on the porch."

The American flag was proudly displayed in its holder on one of the four large columns on the front porch. Ike pulled into the narrow driveway leading to a one-car garage.

Turning off the car, Ike faced Amelia. "I'll introduce you. Believe me, he'll love you. But let me ask about his help with the box first. Just follow my lead. Frank is special to me. I don't want to pull him in unless he can help."

Amelia gave Ike a smile that said she understood. "I'll go easy."

Ike opened the door and headed to the stone stairway that had welcomed him so many times before. It was much colder now, but at least the rain had stopped. Amelia stayed close behind him.

"I thought that was you," Frank said from his wood rocker on the porch. He was dressed in what he called his uniform. A gray t-shirt, a pressed blue-and-white checkered shirt, a pair of khakis, and brightly colored Nike running shoes. He'd added a bomber jacket for the cold morning air.

"It *is* me," Ike said, smiling but fighting off the guilt in the back of his mind about getting Frank involved in this potentially deadly case. But he had no other option. "Sorry to bother you. Do you have a few minutes?"

"Do you even have to ask?" Frank said smiling. He spotted Amelia and stood.

Ike was still impressed with Frank's physique. At ninety-seven, he still stood at attention, shoulders back, chest out, and just a couple of inches shorter than Ike. His close-cropped gray hair was neatly combed. He didn't wobble or hesitate to offer his hand to Amelia. Ike noticed Amelia, shoulders back and chest out, looking at his hand, probably noting how smooth his skin was for a man his age.

"Frank, this is Amelia Garcia."

Amelia shook Frank's hand. "Nice to meet you, sir."

"The pleasure is mine, young lady." His voice was deep and booming, not weak and shredded by his years. Frank gripped her hand for a few seconds longer. "Air Force?" Frank appeared as if he were a magician about to make the big reveal.

"Yeah, Air Force. Thank you for all you've done for your country."

Frank's grayish-blue eyes glowed, and he kept them locked on Amelia's. "I'm sure it wasn't easy, Airman."

Amelia kept her hand in his. "How did you know?"

"I just know. You've seen combat?"

"I have."

Frank let her hand go, plucked his coffee mug from the small wooden table beside his chair, and headed to the front door.

"Let's go inside. It's a little chilly this morning." Frank opened the storm door then the thick front door, stepping back to allow Amelia and Ike to enter. Amelia slowed when she passed Ike and gave him a *what gives?* look. Ike shrugged and followed her inside.

Frank closed the door and directed them into the living room on the left. Amelia's gaze drifted around the room. Ike could see the same wonderment in Amelia's eyes that he'd had the first time he'd seen it. The room was finished in dark maple with detailed millwork adorning every window, entry, and the large fireplace on the far wall. Ike knew homes back then were built by craftsmen and not corporations. Placed neatly around the room were fine wooden models with levers, shining silver balls, wheels, troughs, and bases that were works of art, complementing the Victorian-like furniture. Each one looked as if it required an engineer to design and operate it. One table against the wall held a forest of family photos. The room was spotless and had a light scent of cedar.

"You built all of these?" she asked.

"I did, Amelia."

"He has quite a woodshop out back," Ike said.

Amelia stopped and admired one of the faded family portraits. Frank, a beautiful glowing woman, and a young boy were in the photo. Ike knew it was from the 1950s.

"Is this your family?" she asked.

"It is. That's my Bella and our son, Finn."

"Does your son live close by?"

Ike made eye contact with Amelia then subtly shook his head.

Frank put his hand on Ike's shoulder and his eyes went soft. "It's okay, Ike." He looked at Amelia. "My son died in a car accident in 1966."

"I'm so sorry. I didn't know."

"Please don't be. Bella and I had him for seventeen wonderful years. And I had the privilege of having my Bella as my wife for sixty-eight years. Not many people find the love of their lives, let alone have them for nearly a lifetime."

Amelia started to smile until her lower lip quivered. "How wonderful. Where did you meet?"

"We met here. I was seventeen and palling around with my friends one day in the hallway at school. I saw her walk by, and I knew that she was it. She was the one. A real looker, too. I stopped her and asked her to a movie, and she said no. Over the next two months she said no six times. On the seventh, she said yes. We dated for a month before I enlisted early in the Army. My parents signed for me. She waited *four years* until I made it back to her. We were married three weeks later." He took another sip, then said, "I'm the luckiest man on earth."

"Well, I hope I can find a man like you," Amelia said.

Frank grinned. "I'm single!"

Amelia set the framed picture back among the others. She picked up another and showed it to Frank. "What's this one?"

Frank's easygoing demeanor disappeared, and he squared his shoulders and raised his head. "That's my last salute."

Amelia showed the picture to Ike. Frank was dressed in a warm black coat and black gloves. Amelia looked at Ike for an explanation. Ike decided it was Frank's story to tell.

"That was November of 1947. Homestead Cemetery. That's the day the greatest patriot I knew finally came home. And I mean a true patriot."

"A true patriot?" Amelia asked.

"Yes. I think of someone being patriotic as someone who supports our country and the values it was built on. And mind you, I take nothing away from all of those people. But a true patriot bravely gives of themselves, making great sacrifices, so others can live with truth, justice, freedom, liberty, and the pursuit of happiness, all intended in the Constitution. Our country hasn't gotten it perfect yet, probably never will. But the greatness lies in the fact that we can constantly change to become a more perfect union."

Amelia held up the picture. "Can I ask who this was?"

Frank bobbed his head and started his story. "His name was Joe Bernardi. He was older than I was, but I had known of him in high school. Joe enlisted in the Army at the beginning of the war. Later he volunteered for the OSS. He was part of an operational group that was charged with helping the French Resistance fighters behind enemy lines.

I was in France trying to bring several resistance fighters to a safe house. They'd intercepted several high-value messages between Hitler and his field marshals. We got trapped in a small town, and he and his team parachuted in from a low-altitude flight behind enemy lines with only moonlight to guide them. Only he made it to us. He guided us toward the Swiss border, but we got caught in a firefight with a German patrol. We fought our way out, but he jumped on a live grenade, covering it with his helmet, saving me and the resistance fighters. He had a letter to his wife in his pocket in case he was killed. Before he died, he asked me to personally deliver it." Frank's eyes turned glossy. "He said he fought for his family, for his friends, but most of all for his country. A country that had a goal to provide freedom and justice for all so people could be whatever they wanted to be. He said freedom wasn't a zero-sum game. No one had to lose it for someone else to win it."

Frank pointed to the picture in Amelia's hand. "That cemetery is just down the street."

"You said it was 1947?" Amelia asked.

"It took that long to get his body back home. Bella, my wife, snapped that picture. That day I saluted a true patriot who left behind a wife and five children. I promised myself I'd never salute again in order to honor his sacrifice."

Amelia was speechless, her eyes wide. "Thanks for sharing that, sir." Amelia gently returned the framed picture to its place.

"You're welcome, Airman."

Ike loved the connection Amelia had made with Frank, but it didn't make what he was about to ask any easier.

Frank shifted his attention to Ike. "Can I get you coffee?" he asked, hovering by a high-back chair.

"No thank you, Frank." Ike said.

"No thank you, sir." Amelia added.

Frank pointed to the sofa. "Have a seat."

Amelia took the side farthest from Frank.

Frank took a slow sip of his coffee, eyeing Amelia then Ike. "So, how's Maria doing? It's been a while since I've been in to see you all."

"She's great. She's written seven new songs. Played them this week during one of her sets. The crowd loved them. She has Rossi's doing great, too."

"And how's that new chef working out?"

"Great. He's a great add."

"Nice. And Amelia, tell me little about yourself."

"I'm from Dallas but now live on Kiawah Island."

"Kiawah's a great place. I had a friend who lived there back in the eighties."

"It is. I left the Air Force two years ago after twelve years of service, mostly as an RPA pilot."

Frank set his mug down. "You have seen some tough duty, then."

Amelia seemed to relax and appreciate Frank's recognition. "I have. But I left to become an ROV pilot for my uncle's company, Winkler ROV Services."

Frank's expression turned sullen. "Please accept my condolences. I read the articles in the paper and saw the news reports. I'm so sorry for your loss."

Amelia appeared surprised at first, then Frank's words settled in. Her eyes glazed with tears.

He gave Amelia a gentle smile. "Well, nice to have you here. Any friend of Ike's is a friend of mine."

Frank turned to Ike. "I assume that's why you're here?"

As usual, Frank was always a step ahead. "Yes. Amelia is my client. There are some circumstances around her aunt's and uncle's deaths that we don't quite understand. There is one aspect you might be able to help us with."

Ike felt as if he were on the edge of a cliff looking into the abyss. "Before I show you something, I want to tell you that I think anyone who looks at this may become a target of Amelia's uncle's killers."

Frank rubbed his chin and stared off into the distance. Then he said to Ike, "I'm ninety-seven. I'm not worried. If I can possibly help, I want to."

Ike and Amelia told the story of how she'd found the box, its location, and the subsequent killings. Frank listened, his blue-gray eyes widening with every detail. When they finished, Ike pulled out his phone and pulled up the pictures he'd taken of the box and its contents and handed it to Frank.

Frank stopped on the first photo. His expression turned serious, as if he'd seen the devil himself. He flipped through the other pictures that showed the contents of the box, then handed the phone back to Ike. He leaned back in his chair, gazing at both of them, carefully weighing what he was about to say. "This is most likely from the German High Command, back in World War II." He leaned forward. "Can you show me where you found this if I pull up a map?"

"Of course," Amelia said.

"Come with me," Frank stood, and Ike followed Frank and Amelia to a small office in the back of the house. It was well organized, the walls lined with books, and a large desk sat against the window looking out into the backyard. A large monitor hooked to a docking station and laptop sat in the center. Frank sat at the desk, pulled out the keyboard and in seconds had a map of the Atlantic coast of the US. Ike and Amelia watched over either shoulder. It showed various shades of blue representing the depth of the seafloor. There were yellow dots scattered offshore.

Frank turned to Amelia and slid the mouse to her. "Show me where you found it."

Amelia slid the mouse to the position off the Virginia/North Carolina border. A yellow dot was just inland of the location.

"Thanks." Frank took the mouse and clicked on the dot. Data on a sunken German U-boat appeared. Frank pulled his head back, as if surprised.

"What is it, Frank?"

"See this date?"

"Yes," Ike said. "April 30, 1945."

"That's the date the boat was sunk. Probably by an ash can—sorry—a depth charge. I'm thinking your box came from that boat."

Ike wasn't getting Frank's point. "I'm not sure I understand."

"That's the day Adolf Hitler killed himself."

A cold wave surged through Ike's body. He still didn't know exactly what that meant, but his gut was telling him it wasn't good.

"So what was inside the box?" Amelia asked.

Frank closed the browser then cleared his history and disconnected the Wi-Fi. He shut down the laptop and pulled it from its docking station. He stood and said, "I think I know how to find out, but you don't want to do this, Ike. You're getting into something you may regret."

"We need this," Amelia said. "What is it?"

Ike didn't like her accusatory tone. Ike tried to burn a hole in her with his stare. "Hold on." She backed off.

"What are you not saying, Frank?" Ike asked.

Frank gazed at Ike and took a beat. "You know I was in the Signal Intelligence Service in the war, right?"

"Yes."

"I've seen this before. It's not good. You don't want to pursue this. That's why people are getting killed."

"What's it say?"

"I don't know. I think it's a code."

"On the paper tape?"

"Yes."

"Can you decode it?"

"Not here."

"Frank. I have to do this. If you're worried about your safety, just point me in the right direction. I understand."

"I'm not worried about my safety. I'm worried about yours."

"Can you break the code?" Amelia asked.

Frank exhaled a surrendering breath. "Come back tomorrow."

Ike looked at Amelia, then focused on Frank. "Time is critical here." Ike said.

"Come back tomorrow!"

"It can't wait," Amelia said.

Frank stepped close to Amelia. "Believe me, Airman. You'll want to wait before opening the gates of hell."

CHAPTER 24

IKE INHALED THE scent of garlic and wings as he entered Rossi's from the back hallway after spending the last few hours at the Real-Time Remote Operations Center at Falzone Energy getting updates from Minuteman. It was just after three and the patrons were glued to the big-screen TVs, their chatter building with each play the Steelers ran. It was late in the fourth quarter, and they trailed by four. With every first down, the patrons' energy pressurized the room, anticipating a jubilant eruption. Maria bantered with the customers at the bar, while Randy helped the servers deliver his Sunday specials, pollinating each table with his smile and hilarious wit. Seeing Maria happy reminded Ike of his commitment to insulate her from the dangers of his job, and according to Frank, they were about to open the gates of hell.

Amelia sat at the end of the bar looking like a haggard warrior who'd just returned from a losing battle, unknowingly broadcasting her grief and loneliness into the room. It wasn't right that someone who had sacrificed so much for others should carry the same burden Ike had carried since his parents' murders. His credo he'd adopted echoed in his head: *If not for me, then for them*. He walked past a few tables and joined Amelia at the bar. When she spotted him, she pulled her shoulders back and emerged from her trance, the burning desire to find her uncle's killer flaring back into her eyes.

"Did you get any rest?" he asked Amelia.

"Enough. How were things on the ship?"

"Still drilling below sixteen thousand feet and headed to the core point."

"What are they looking for?"

Ike eased back and sized up Amelia. Every fiber of his body said she'd keep the secret. After all, she'd kept hundreds of missions confidential throughout her military career, some that would threaten the political life of those on the other end of the kill order, perhaps even the president. If it were up to Ike, he'd tell her. But the confidentiality agreement meant something to him. He'd given his word not to tell anyone outside the key few people who knew or needed to know, and his father always said that breaking your word, even on a small issue, was like drilling a hole in the bottom of a pool—eventually all the trust leaks out.

"I can't say," he answered.

"Copy that." She checked the distance to the closest customer at the bar, then leaned closer to Ike. "Do you know what Frank meant this morning?"

"Not exactly, but he rarely issues warnings like that. Being in the SIS, he's intimately familiar with codes, secrets, and the extent people will go to protect those secrets."

Maria spotted Ike, finished her conversation with a customer, and strolled to his end of the bar. "Hey, brother."

"Hi, Sis." Ike scanned the restaurant. "Looks like another great game day."

"Yeah, it does. Now if only the Steelers can pull this one out, I'll stay in a good mood." She touched the bar in front of Amelia. "Can I get you anything?"

"No thanks, Maria."

Maria studied Amelia for a moment. "You know what? I've got just the thing for you."

Maria stepped down the bar and made a tall drink that looked like iced tea.

"Try this." Maria said, grinning. "A John Daly. It's a Sunday tradition like no other."

"I'm sorry. I usually don't drink."

Maria looked aghast. "Oh. I didn't know." She moved the drink in front of Ike.

Amelia glanced at Ike, then back at Maria, as if gauging their trustworthiness. Finally, she said, "It's because of my mother's problem."

Ike remembered Amelia telling them about her mother's alcoholism. At the time, he'd sensed that this was a family secret. While this was one in many families, he felt there was something bigger besides this one, based on his read of Tess and Benton Garcia.

"You know, I don't know anything about your family," Maria said.

Ike could see that Maria had decided to go on a fishing expedition. Amelia appeared as if she didn't suspect anything and gave Maria a gentle smile. "That's fair. My father is Benton Garcia. He went to Texas A&M and graduated as a petroleum engineer. My mother is Tess Winkler Garcia."

"I read the article. She's your uncle Billy's sister."

Amelia tersely corrected Maria. *"Was.* My mother's family, the Winklers, are big shots in the oil business in Texas. My grandfather handpicked my father to run his company years ago, before I was born." Amelia paused.

"How about you?" Maria asked.

"I was born in McKinney, Texas, just north of Dallas. Moved to Highland Park a few years later. I had a sister, Harper. She was a lawyer who went to work in Europe. She died three years ago while I was on active duty."

"Sorry to hear that," Maria said. "I know what that's like."

Amelia glanced at Ike again. "I know you do." She settled her gaze on her hands resting on the bar. "Anyway, if you read the news, you know the rest of the story."

"Your father is a kingmaker in Texas politics, right?" Maria's tone had changed. She sounded more like a prosecuting attorney. She'd been holding back on what she knew.

Amelia puffed up and knitted her brow. "Yes, he is."

Maria's eyes darted to Ike and back. Holding a bar rag, she rested her fist on her hip. "Doesn't he have people that can help you?"

Ike's anger spun up, and his face felt afire. "That's enough!"

"No. I want to know why her own family can't solve her problem instead of involving ours."

Ike shot up and his bar stool hit the floor. "That's my business and none of yours."

Randy appeared at Ike's side. Picking up the bar stool he said, "You kids might want to take this upstairs."

Ike looked at Randy, who nodded toward the tables. Ike saw half the restaurant looking at them. He stared at Maria.

She stared back for a moment, then turned away in disgust. "I'm done," she said, then tossed the bar rag in the sink and walked away.

Ike sighed as Randy patted him on the back. "I'll talk to her." Randy headed back to the kitchen.

Ike refocused on Amelia, who looked ready for battle. "I apologize for my sister."

Amelia turned away and slowly shook her head. "No need to apologize. She's right. My father should help me. But he won't. He'll just cover his own ass."

"Still, she shouldn't have done that."

Amelia kept her focus straight ahead. "I would have done the same thing if I thought it would have kept my older sister safe."

Ike could tell there was much more to Amelia's family. He'd heard one secret but could tell there were more. Ike wanted to ask Amelia about Mia's warning about the Garcia family, but this was not the time. Amelia's family had secrets. Whose didn't? But he wanted to be sure that hers wouldn't kill what was left of *his* family. He'd also brought Frank into this, and deep in his gut, Frank's and Mia's warnings boiled over. He balled his fists and stood up.

"I'll be gone for a while. But I'll be back later this evening."

"Where you headed?" Amelia asked.

He wasn't in the mood to provide an explanation. "Out. Stay here. If you need something, ask Randy."

"I'd like to go with you."

No client ever went with Ike. "No. You can't."

Ike turned away, knowing that what lay ahead up north was the best thing for him. He went upstairs, grabbed a duffel, and was in the Shelby heading north to The Farm in minutes.

CHAPTER 25

IKE DROVE NORTH, out of the city, and jammed the Shelby into sixth gear as he merged onto I-79 north and headed toward The Farm. The opposing forces of Mia's warning—Frank's pending revelation that he'd promised would lead to the gates of hell, and Maria's frontal attack on his client— were closing in on him, building up pressure and suffocating his thinking.

He stuck his hand out of the window, deflecting the cold October air onto his face. The familiar rumble of the powerful engine gave him some sense of control over something. The red glow of sunset was muted by the cloud layer, and the chilly fall weather, the harbinger of the first frost, reminded him of the simplicity of his playing days. Back then, conditioning, preparation, and relentless practice had prepared him for anything a defense could throw at him and his teammates. At six foot four, he could easily read the defense's scheme and change the play at the line of scrimmage if necessary. But this was different. Trapped between his responsibility to protect Maria and his commitment to help Amelia, the frustration boiled his blood. Both Mia and Frank added fuel to his fire with their warnings. Now, he was doing the only thing that could release the pressure, clear his head, and give him a path forward. It was quicker than therapy, and Ike looked forward to the release.

When he exited the interstate, he began his prefight ritual that he and his father had carefully crafted more than twenty-nine years ago, envisioning every move and every counter. His father had used the same ritual to become the tristate kickboxing champion decades earlier. Ike knew that once in the ring, any inattention on his part would be met with brutal pain. He'd learned that painful lesson at his father's hands as his teenaged sparring partner.

After winding through the rolling farmland just outside of Harmony, he pulled the Shelby between the split in the whitewashed fence and stopped at the call box just short of the black iron gates.

Ike pressed the button.

"Yes?"

"It's me."

As the gates parted, Ike felt his adrenaline spike. Easing the car into first gear, he let the Shelby idle along the paved drive flanked by thick evergreens. Daylight was fading, and the Shelby's headlights reached out into the dusk. The tree-lined road opened to a small white gravel parking lot next to a large, white, corrugated-steel building. One of the four large doors was open, and Ike could see the crowd milling around the ring inside. To his right, the lot was filled with expensive exotic sports cars. The owners were sports figures, bankers, company founders, and a few ancient former Mafia bosses.

The Moretti family had made their fortune in the glass business while also running numbers for the Mob. They'd gone legitimate a generation ago, and Phil Moretti had taken his share, bet it on the fledgling natural gas business in western Pennsylvania, and made another fortune. Ike pulled next to Moretti's Lamborghini and got out. Moretti appeared in the open door, dressed like an Ivy League alumnus attending a football game, chewing on a cigar. He was a trust-fund baby and braggart who'd made it big, amplifying his blowhard personality. But his family had run these unsanctioned fights since Ike's father's days. The matches were fair, not rigged, and the payoff was in cash that Ike planted firmly in the hands of the Boys and Girls Club after every fight.

Moretti waved Ike over. "Man, you're still the best draw I have." Putting his hand on Ike's back, he guided Ike to two older men who looked as if they could kill you with one look.

"Just as promised gentlemen. I'd like to introduce you to Ike Rossi."

Neither man extended a hand nor offered their names. Ike noticed a scar running between the wrinkles on one man's face.

Ike nodded. "Gentlemen." He'd seen these types before in Bloomfield. Definitely Mob.

"You fight as well as you played football?" Scarface asked.

Ike didn't answer.

Scarface turned to the other man. "This guy was the best quarterback I've ever seen. I made thousands betting on him." He turned back and locked his eyes on Ike's. "That is until he had to quit." Scarface held his stare and smiled.

The image of the confidential informant form he'd uncovered in his mother's case barged into his mind. Ike felt the rage rising from his chest and filling every muscle. Ike stepped within inches of the man's face. He felt Moretti tug at his arm. Ike held his stare for a few more seconds, then let Moretti pull him away.

As they walked away, Moretti said, "You don't want to tangle with him."

Ike yanked his arm away, ignoring Moretti, and headed to the makeshift locker room. Alfredo, a barrel-chested, sixty-year-old Mexican immigrant who'd helped his father decades ago, sat on a bench waiting. Ike hugged him. Ike could feel Alfredo hugging back. The tension drained from his body, and he swore he felt his father's presence. He dropped his duffel on the bench and changed. Alfredo pulled tape from his bag and wrapped Ike's hands. As he pulled the lightweight gloves over the tape, Alfredo said, "I'd ask if you wanted to do this again, but I know the answer."

Ike grinned and glanced down at Alfredo's work. "After all these years, you know I have to."

Alfredo nodded as he finished lacing the gloves. He offered both fists to Ike, and Ike bumped them with his gloves. Alfredo made the sign of the cross. "May God be with you."

Ike slammed his gloves together and turned to leave. "I don't think God wants anything to do with this."

Ike stopped in the doorway and ignited his fury. He thought about his mother and the look on the mobster's face. He let the searing conflict between his commitment to protect Maria at any cost and his promise to Amelia—a patriot who'd sacrificed most of her young life to protect others—to find her uncle's killers, rise from the dark depths of his soul. All this in the face of dire warnings from the people he once trusted the most in his life.

To ready himself, he imagined his body was solid steel, tensing every muscle in his body, then relaxing them. Ignoring the raucous crowd, he slammed his gloves together again and parted the throng of spectators.

Approaching the ring, he spotted his opponent. He looked like one of Ike's former Samoan teammates, with a broad body that filled the entire corner. His bronze skin glistened in the bright lights. His bald head could have been mistaken for a boulder, and his fists were the size of basketballs. He snorted like a bull, his dark eyes focused on Ike. Moretti was trying to give Ike his first loss, again.

As Ike slipped between the ropes, his impression of the man shrank as he reminded himself that size didn't matter. While Ike was well known, Moretti had made it a point to never reveal names of his opponents, so Ike nicknamed this mountain of a man *Rainier*.

"Okay gents," Moretti yelled from the side of the ring, "betting is closed." Moretti picked up a brass bell and struck it with a small hammer.

Like an angry sumo wrestler, Rainier trudged to the center of the ring. The canvas shook with each step. Ike moved to the center of the ring but then drifted to his left. Rainier's eyes tracked him like prey as he turned his thick body in Ike's direction. Ike jabbed him with a left, his punch flattening against Rainier's skull with no effect. Suddenly, Rainier began to dance to his right. Nimbler than Ike had estimated, he was on Ike like lightning. He threw a right, and Ike raised his glove to block it. Ike's own glove slammed against his head. Rainier was strong *and* quick. Ike took two steps back to his right, staying out of the corner, and waited. Rainier threw a left jab again, and Ike stepped into it, planting his left foot hard, deflecting it with his left and countering with a right, putting his full body weight behind it. It caught Rainier by surprise, and his eyes lost focus for a second. Quickly regaining his footing, Rainer charged and hit Ike with a right to his side. Ike heard a muffled crack and every ounce of air left his body. The impact lifted him from his feet. Instinctively, he dropped his left to cover the pain. Rainer reloaded and hit Ike in the cheek. Ike's face stung, and he could smell the blood running from his nose. He stumbled but caught himself and kept from falling. He wiped his nose with his glove and spotted the blood. With his legs back under him, he gathered himself.

Smelling victory, Rainier snorted twice as hard. Ike narrowed his eyes on him and imagined his parents' killer. Amelia's painful look burst into his mind. Ike knew the anguish and rage she must be feeling. He felt it too. He thought about losing Mia by putting his client first. Amelia had earned that. His anguish transformed into determination and flowed from his chest and charged his fists. What was happening to Amelia was wrong, and a strange feeling that it was bigger than any one person swept over Ike. It involved evil, and someone killing to hide a secret. He knew what had to be done.

Ike stopped dancing, lowered his head, and dropped his shoulders. He focused on Rainier's chin and waited. The move seemed to baffle Rainier, but he swung anyway. Ike slipped the punch, landed a right uppercut, and left his feet with the follow-through. It crushed Rainier's jaw. The crowd roared. Rainier was stunned, and his arms went limp at his side, dropping his guard. Ike hit him with a combination, and Rainier stumbled backward. Ike followed him into the corner and finished him with another right uppercut. The Samoan went down. Ike knew he wasn't getting up. The doctor entered the ring, and once Ike saw Rainier was okay, he turned toward his corner.

Ignoring the raucous crowd, Ike ran to his corner. "Can you get these off here?" he asked Alfredo. Alfredo nodded and unlaced and removed the gloves. Moretti jumped into the ring and grabbed Ike's arm to raise it. Ike held it down and reached out with his other hand. Moretti shrugged, reached into his green blazer, and laid a thick envelope in Ike's hand. Ike pulled out a wad of hundreds and handed it to Alfredo, then leaned in and hugged him.

"Next time, my friend. I've gotta go."

In minutes he was changed and on his way back into the city. No one should have to feel the way he had for the last twenty-three years. Especially not a patriot like Amelia. He'd help her and solve the mystery of the box, even if it led to the gates of hell. After all, he'd been there before.

CHAPTER 26

BENTON KNEW SOMETHING was wrong. He could feel his power vaporizing. As he walked to the long window of his Kiawah office, examining his reflection, he pulled his shoulders back, tucked a fold in his golf shirt into his pressed slacks, and eased out a sigh to eliminate any external sign of distress. Stopping inches from the window, he scanned the moonlit sea. Above it, the blanket of stars chased the moon across the sky. Yesterday's storms had cleared the atmosphere and left a dome of still cold air covering the island. None of it cooled his fraying nerves. He hated the waiting.

The call he'd placed last night received a terse response, and, for the first time since the Texas congressional primary thirty-five years ago, he was told by the people he'd put in the White House they'd have to call back. Through the glass, he glanced to the right and spotted Tess, buried under two blankets and half a bottle of bourbon, asleep on a chaise lounge on the Brazilian hardwood deck. She'd been right about Harper, but he couldn't admit it, to himself or to her. And despite Tess's constant accusations, he did care about Amelia. He assumed many on the outside simply concluded he had a better connection with one child than the other. That was fine by him. She was part of the family, but with Amelia now the subject of an FBI investigation, he had to minimize his exposure.

Turning away from the window, he focused on McCallum, who was sitting in one of the leather side chairs with his nose buried in his phone. "Found anything yet?"

McCallum looked up. "A little. Lots of quiet activity happening up there, but it's not centered around the Oval Office. The advisors are taking turns in Kara Williams' office. No one is talking."

The mention of the president's sister made Benton's skin crawl.

"What's going on?"

"I can't tell you. They won't talk to me. My sources say everyone is tight-lipped."

"Look. I pay you to be in the know. My family is under investigation by the FBI, for Christ's sake. They are after my daughter for some reason. Suddenly, people who couldn't find their way out of Lubbock think they did all of this on their own." The image of Harper stuck in his mind, his guilt building into a quiet rage that made him quake. He let the anger overtake him—rage felt good—and he charged the desk and shoved the pile of papers on the floor next to McCallum.

"Find out, damn it!"

McCallum squared himself in the chair and scowled. He bent down and started snatching the papers off the floor. "Your best bet is Knight's call."

Benton checked his watch. It was 7:14 p.m. "He's late."

"He's always late."

"Not for a call to me!"

While Michael Knight had been a valued lawyer in the Winkler Family Office for twelve years, Benton was now losing his patience for him. Benton had given him his start. He'd also used him extensively to handle any family problems that weren't for public consumption. But he'd always shown deference to Benton, feeding him information on his boss and those around him, especially after Benton had gotten him a position in Reed's Texas gubernatorial campaign. Knight's success with the governor led to a position as senior campaign advisor in Governor Reed's run to the White House. Now he was a fixer for President Reed. While Knight was a fixer extraordinaire, he always knew who put him and Reed in the presidency and always kept Benton in the loop.

President Thomas Reed was older than Benton and had helped Benton early in his career. When Benton was driven from his childhood home in Odessa by his stepfather and started a one-truck water-hauling business, Reed had given Benton's company enough work to earn credibility with the heavy hitters in the Permian Basin oilfields. That had led to a sale of the business, Benton entering Texas A&M, and ultimately to the invitation from old man Winkler to run his company.

Now, the seventy-six-year-old president understood that much of his power came from Benton and The Club. He broadened that base by masterfully tapping into the fears and anger of the middle class. But there was one other person that had always been by Reed's side. His younger sister, Kara, had always protected him. She was involved in every campaign, and since she had her brother's ear, she wielded significant power. She was a threat Benton had successfully managed by always playing to her outsized ego. He'd gotten the feeling she was doing the same with him. Secretly, he'd held her responsible for the pressure to send Harper to DC. Now, according to McCallum, she was controlling the flow of information, probably without the knowledge of her brother.

The phone rang and Benton headed to his desk, giving McCallum a dead-eyed stare. Benton sat in his chair, keeping his eyes fixed on McCallum, and let it ring again. When it rang a third time, he calmly smiled and reached slowly for the burner phone.

"It's about time."

"Sorry Benton. I couldn't get free until now," Knight said. "You know how this works. You don't want them to know I'm doing this."

Benton relaxed his death grip on the phone. While he wanted to chew up Knight and spit him out, he knew Knight was right, and crossing him would be stupid. Benton was well aware of the things Knight had done to people who'd crossed him.

"All right. Why is the FBI harassing us?"

Knight's silence on the other end of the call fueled an undeniable suspicion in Benton's gut. Something was wrong. Instantly, he felt as if he was locked out in the cold. "Look, Benton, your brother-in-law was mysteriously killed. Then the last person he spoke with, the second in command in Justice, was killed. Your brother was involved in Minuteman, the most sensitive, public, high-profile activity we have going on. They have to be sure there is nothing else happening here."

"My brother-in-law committed suicide."

"That's the leading theory."

Benton paused and moved the phone away from his ear. He knew those things could be staged. He suspected Knight had arranged such things as Reed's fixer. He moved the phone to his other hand and put it to his other ear.

"I don't need theories. I need the truth."

"I don't know what to tell you, Benton."

While he didn't trust Knight, he had to ask. "Is Kara Williams behind this?" He looked over at McCallum who was leaning on the edge of the desk. Knight said nothing for a moment. The silence told Benton everything he needed to know. Benton felt his power and position circling the drain.

Finally, Knight said, "Anything else I can help you with? I've gotta get back."

Knight was useless. Still, he didn't want to show his hand. "No. Thank you." He hung up.

He tossed the phone onto his desk and leaned back in his chair, staring at the burner. Rubbing his chin, he looked up at McCallum. "We have a problem."

CHAPTER 27

AMELIA UNLOADED THE warm glasses, arranging them neatly on the shelf behind the bar. In the mirror, she watched Maria help the last server close out so she could get home early and see her kids before bedtime. After the Steelers' victory late in the fourth quarter, many of the customers had ordered dinner and a few drinks to celebrate the win. They'd all left within fifteen minutes of the nine o'clock closing time.

Amelia knew the danger she'd brought to Rossi's wasn't Maria's fault and didn't involve her family. While that guilt distracted her from some of the frustration over Ike's absence for the last few hours, it did nothing to quell the disgust she directed at herself. She couldn't believe she'd put herself in this position. She refocused on the dishwasher trays full of glasses that Randy had delivered from the back and kept stacking the highball and beer glasses on the shelf. Staying busy was always the key to settling her chattering mind.

"Oh, Amelia. You didn't have to do that," Maria said after magically appearing at the bar.

Amelia looked down at the last glass in the last tray and realized she'd lost track of time. Placing the glass on the shelf, she turned to Maria. "I couldn't just sit here after watching you help that girl get home to her kids."

Maria looped around behind the bar and joined Amelia. She grabbed a spray bottle and rag and began to sanitize the counter. Without looking up, she said, "Well, thank you. You look like you've done that before."

Amelia stacked the tray on top of the others on the corner of the bar. "I worked at a restaurant in Dallas during summer break when I was in high school."

Maria kept cleaning. "You go right from high school into the Air Force?"

"Yes. I got an appointment to the Air Force Academy when I was a senior."

Maria paused, looked up at Amelia, and smiled. "Of course you did."

"What do you mean by that?"

"Your father."

Amelia forced herself to ignore the dig. "It wasn't that way. He didn't want me to go."

Maria placed her fist on her hip and leaned into the bar. "Really? How's that?"

"He wanted me to go to Harvard. I'd already been accepted. He thought it would be more appropriate for a young woman." Amelia left out the part about his concern regarding the investigation into her assault charges, which she'd faced after her senior prom, getting into the public eye.

Maria wasn't buying it. Amelia could see that the sixth sense most women possessed had broken her code.

"Appropriate for a young lady? Sounds like he had other expectations for you."

"He did. He wanted me to be more ladylike, as he'd say."

Maria folded her arms across her chest. "Now you have me curious. What were you like in high school?"

Amelia sensed Maria's concern. She didn't know why, but she decided to open up a bit.

"I was like I am now. Tough. Strong. Didn't take any shit. I'd competed against boys all my life. Tackle football until high school. I think that pissed off my father the most. He rode me all through high school. Even forced me to go to the debutante ball with some guy from another Highland Park family. He never supported what I wanted. I was never enough. All that year, he kept riding me and insisted I go to the prom. He was relentless, more afraid of how it reflected on him. I finally gave up and agreed to go to the prom with the high school quarterback to get dear old Dad to shut up. When Mr. Football of Texas tried to rape me that night, I broke his throwing arm. My father was livid and paid off the cops and his family to cover it up. He was ashamed of me. That made *him* give up. The next week he kicked me out of the house, and I went to the Academy."

Maria's mouth had dropped open. "What did your mother do?"

Amelia's eyes involuntarily drifted to the bottles behind the bar and settled on the row of bourbon bottles. As the words came to her, her heart sank into a place where she was never good enough, as it always did when she thought of her mother. "She tried but she had her own problems."

Maria appeared speechless.

Amelia continued. "It's okay. Back then, my older sister was still alive, off at law school. She talked me through it all. I served for twelve years in the Air Force, and I'd do it again."

"I'm so sorry, Amelia. I didn't know."

"It's okay. I'm sorry too. I know this mess isn't your fault at all and it has nothing to do with your family. I wish I'd never started to collect things from the seafloor."

"Can I ask why you do that?"

Amelia figured she'd gone this far. "I guess it gives me comfort. I can imagine how the items got there and think about the romantic stories that could be behind them."

Now Maria looked sad.

It made Amelia uneasy, standing on emotional quicksand, the loneliness, sadness, and shame of not being enough for her mother to stop killing herself, pulling her in. She took a second to re-center herself, then shifted the focus of the conversation away from her and back on the mission. "But I'm committed to find out who killed my aunt and uncle. I sure wish your brother didn't leave this afternoon. We could have made more progress."

Maria pushed herself away from the bar and started cleaning again. "Believe me, you wanted him to go. His fights clear his mind. He's usually much better afterward. I don't like it, but I like the result."

"Fights? How's that work?"

"It brings him peace."

"Fighting brings him peace?"

Maria kept her focus on cleaning, not looking at Amelia, but kept talking. "I know it sounds weird, but my dad used to kickbox. Ike learned from him. They would train together and go to tournaments. Dad won a bunch of individual titles. Then, when Ike came home to take care of me, he was sad and scared. I could tell. He tried not to show it, but he was a kid too. He was going to be drafted by the NFL near the top. All of a sudden, it was gone. Replaced by a nine-year-old who cried every day. One day, Alfredo, my dad's trainer, came by the house. They went into another room, and when they came out, my brother was different. More confident. Alfredo took him to his first fight after he left Penn State. Then he started to figure it out. One day at a time. He took great care of me. When he'd get stressed, he and Alfredo would go off to a place they called The Farm to fight. He'd come back relaxed and focused, and we'd go on. I never ask him about it or even if it's legal. I don't care. It helps him and that's good enough for me."

"So you think it will help me, not hurt me?"

Maria stopped scrubbing the sink and looked up at Amelia. "That's what I've been trying to say. He'll think much more clearly and have laserlike focus. Believe me."

Amelia's phone vibrated in her pocket. She pulled it out and read the text from her father.

You need to get back to Kiawah now. You're in danger.

"Tell me something I don't know," Amelia said to herself and shoved the phone back into her pocket.

Maria looked up again. "What did you say?"

Amelia didn't want to upset Maria at this point. Maria already knew they were in danger. Amelia could see it in her eyes.

"Nothing. My father just texted me something stupid."

But as the words soaked in, Amelia realized it wasn't stupid. It was the first time her father had shown any concern for her in years. He knew something. Just what, she'd have to find out.

CHAPTER 28

AFTER TURNING RIGHT onto a deserted Liberty Avenue, Ike watched a ghostly cloud emerge from the rooftop heating unit of West Penn Hospital. It drifted down to the shining wet street in front of him, its translucent gray thickening as it absorbed the fog already in the cold night air. Glowing in the golden aura of the streetlights, the cloud waited for him on the empty street as if it wanted to swallow him up. Ike shook off the chilly night air funneling through his open window. As usual, the fight had cleared his mind of any uncertainty, and he knew exactly what he needed to do. But the cloud reminded him that any chance he had with Mia, no matter how nebulous and diffuse it was, stood between him and the truth. The loneliness he'd concealed behind a life committed to helping others selfishly clawed at his resolve to help Amelia. But by the time he reached the darkened storefront of Rossi's, he'd already told his self-pity to go screw itself. Downshifting in front of Rossi's, he turned right, then right again into the alley. Parking behind the restaurant, he exited the car and went inside.

As he made his way down the back hallway, he stopped at the picture of his parents on the wall. Touching his bruised cheek, he examined his face in the reflection in the glass. He entered Rossi's, and a hint of bleach filled his nostrils as he spotted Maria with a spray bottle in her hand rubbing the far end of the bar with her rag. Amelia leaned against the back wall about halfway down the bar, her arms folded. He acknowledged Amelia with a nod as he passed her and stopped next to Maria.

"Hey, Sis. How are you?"

Not looking up, Maria made tighter circles on the bar with her rag.

"I said, hey, how are you?"

She looked up at him. "Oh. I didn't see you come in." She was pissed.

"Look, I'm sorry but I made my decision. I have to help Amelia."

"That's not what I'm upset about." Maria sarcastically chuckled then went back to wiping down the bar.

Amelia kept her arms crossed and seemed bemused at his predicament. His face warmed as his commitment to always be there for Maria ground against his determination to help Amelia. He wanted to rip that sinking feeling of going against Maria's wishes from his chest.

He turned back to Maria. "What then?"

Maria finished and slipped past Amelia, stuffing the bottle and rag under the bar. She turned and faced Ike. "If you're going to help her, help her. Stop wasting time."

Maria might as well had been speaking another language. Her words didn't make sense. She'd been against helping Amelia from the start.

"Like I said," Maria moved next to Amelia and leaned against the back of the bar with her. "Stop wasting time."

"What about you?"

"What about me?"

"You're okay with Randy's promise to keep you safe?"

"Yes, I am." Maria smiled at Amelia, touched her arm, and headed for the kitchen. Randy met her on the other side of the bar with his phone in his hand. "Speak of the dev—" Maria stopped in her tracks. Ike noticed the pointed expression on Randy's face.

"We have a visitor," Randy said as he held up his phone and showed the image in the security camera app on his screen.

Amelia squeezed past Randy and Ike and disappeared from the back hallway, her footsteps fading up the stairs. Ike stared at Maria, who raised both hands giving him a perfect *I don't know* emoji. Turning back to Randy,

Ike slipped behind him and looked at the screen over his shoulder. Maria joined them and looked over Randy's other shoulder.

Randy pointed at the screen. "That car pulled up a couple of minutes ago. Someone is just sitting there looking at the front door."

It was a dark, late-model sedan with a masked man at the wheel.

"Not a government car. They wouldn't wear a mask anyway and wouldn't be alone," Ike said.

Ike heard Amelia's footsteps racing down the stairs. He pulled out his Glock.

"No. I've got this one," Randy said as he handed the phone to Ike and headed out the back hallway door.

Ike realized Amelia didn't come back into the bar. From the back, he heard Randy say, "Good idea." The back door slammed shut, and Ike heard footsteps echoing back up the hallway. Amelia barged in carrying a large square controller with an antenna.

"I'm in the air," she said as she moved between Ike and Maria. On the digital screen in the controller, Ike saw two images. One was an aerial view that moved over Rossi's then the street. The image was as clear as the 4K TVs they'd installed earlier in the year. A second window showed the drone's view straight ahead. Soon, Randy's shadowy image appeared at the corner of Rossi's. He dashed across the street. Moving behind a few parked cars, he worked his way up behind the masked driver's sedan. As Randy stood to approach him, the car leapt from the parking space and raced down Liberty Avenue.

"I've got him," Amelia said calmly. With an easy flick of her wrists, the drone dropped down and positioned itself right on the masked man's tail. Amelia hit a button and a screen shot disappeared into the corner of the frame. "That will get the plate if he has one," she said. Then the drone instantly closed the distance to the car and raced up to the driver's side. Amelia adjusted the camera angle, and the screen displayed a perfect image of the driver. But the car suddenly screeched to a stop. "Red light," Amelia said. The drone swooped up, above the car again, as the vehicle turned left and raced down the tree-lined side street.

"What's your range?" Ike asked.

"About eight miles. I can follow him for a while."

Ike focused on the screen. "Wait. That's Frank's Street!"

The car stopped under a tree near the street corner adjacent to Frank's house.

"No! Let's go!" Ike raced through the hall to the alley.

Amelia was right behind him, the controller raised above her head. "I'm coming with you."

He scrambled into the Shelby. Amelia was barely in the passenger's seat when he lit up the tires and spun into the alleyway.

"Can you see him?" Ike asked without taking his eyes from the road.

"Yes. He made his way across the street to Frank's."

Ike downshifted and floored it through the turn onto Frank's street. Ike steered the car down the road, pinning the accelerator to the floor and praying he wouldn't be too late. If the thug was watching Rossi's, that was because someone was already entering Frank's house.

"You armed?' he asked.

She showed him her gun. "Yes."

"When we get there, go around back. There's a lockbox on the gas line going into the house. The code is 4579. Use the key inside. Don't let anyone get out. Do you remember the layout?"

"Yes."

"Okay. Then work your way to the living room after you clear the office. I'll meet you there. Be careful."

Amelia set the controller on the floor and racked the slide on her Beretta.

Ike slowed the Shelby, stopped two houses short of Frank's, and slipped out of the car. Amelia followed him. They worked their way along the parked cars on the street, one by one until they could sneak into Frank's driveway, taking cover against the retaining wall. The cold mist numbed Ike's cheeks as he looked to the right, across the street, at the masked man's car. He signaled to Amelia to go around back. She disappeared over the fence on the left side of the house. Ike started up the steps from the driveway to the front porch.

Once on the front porch, Ike pressed his back against the brick wall next to the door and listened. He spotted the infrared camera mounted on the corner of the porch aimed at the front door. All he heard was his pounding heart. He'd brought these killers to Frank's doorstep. He didn't want to find his ninety-seven-year-old hero dead. Carefully working the latch, he realized the door was locked. He reached up, slid his fingers along the backside of the mailbox mounted next to the door until he felt the hide-a-key, pulled it out, and removed the key. He slid it into the lock and raised his Glock. He gently turned the key until he heard the tumblers fall into place. Listening again, he heard nothing. Gently, he opened the door.

CHAPTER 29

AS IKE READIED to enter Frank's house, an anxious energy ricocheted throughout his body and put his senses on high alert. He assumed one man was already at Frank's when the other rushed in to warn him. That gave the advantage to the intruders. It was nearing ten on a Sunday night. The street was deserted and there were no lights in the adjacent houses. Before entering, Ike envisioned what he'd face on the other side of the door. With no lights on inside, the mercs could pick their location, lie in wait, and, with Ike silhouetted in the dim light from outside, pick him off any time they wanted. They'd have Frank, probably bound, and most likely beaten, if not already dead. Pushing the door open, Ike could smell cedar. That triggered thoughts about everything Frank had done for him throughout his life. An angry burst of energy supercharged his senses. He'd have to stay low and be ready to react.

Reaching into his pocket, he pulled out his phone and turned on the flashlight. While it might mark his location, it would also give him enough light to spot them in time to shoot and not hit Frank. His phone vibrated and a text appeared. Amelia was entering through the kitchen door. Leading with his Glock, he squatted and entered the home.

The light from his phone quickly faded in the distance. Shadows drifted along the hallway as the light washed over furniture and Frank's hand-carved picture frames that hung on the walls. The effect looked like a cheap grade-school funhouse, but this funhouse could kill him. Ahead, he could see the entrance to the living room on the left and dining room on the right. In the distance, he could barely see the stairs that headed to the second floor. Behind them, Amelia would be making her way from the kitchen into the office. Ike paused and heard nothing but the sound of his own breathing. After reaching the entrance to the dining room, he edged around the corner and quickly swept the room with the light. Nothing. He turned his attention to the living room and crept across the hallway. The various models and structures played with the light, projecting fleeting images around the room and causing him to target the movement with his gun. He approached the large sofa near the far wall. A noise in the hallway tripled his heart rate. He spun, taking aim at the entrance.

"It's me," Amelia said before entering. She appeared calm and her eyes were still, locked on Ike. "Nothing in the back of the house other than the freezer door was left open."

Amelia looked puzzled. Ike had no idea what that implied. He didn't have time to ask questions. "They're either in the basement or upstairs," he said.

"Or that douche bag just ran through the house and left."

"They're here. I feel it."

Amelia nodded toward the hallway. "Basement?"

"Basement. Let's go."

Ike led Amelia down the hallway and carefully curled around the stairs to the thick wooden basement door. The alarms going off in his gut said they were somewhere behind the door. Ike grabbed the doorknob and stopped to look at Amelia, who raised her gun.

"I've got your six," she said, with more confidence than Ike had expected.

Ike nodded, relieved that she knew what she was doing. Leading with his Glock, he opened the door, but it creaked about halfway open. Ike winced and his heart felt like it jumped into his throat. Peering down the stairs into the darkness, he heard movement and readied to fire.

"Ike? That you?" Frank said from somewhere in the darkness. Ike assumed they had Frank at gunpoint. Making him lure Ike downstairs.

"You all right, Frank?" Over his shoulder, Ike shared a look of concern with Amelia.

"I'm fine. Hit the light and come on down."

Ike decided to call their bluff. He took aim at the bottom of the stairs. "You come to the bottom of the steps." He flipped the light switch on. A shadow moved toward the stairs. Amelia moved beside Ike, taking aim down the stairs too.

"Don't shoot," Frank said as he walked into view with his hands up.

"Where are they?" Ike asked, holding his aim on Frank.

Frank smiled and dropped his hands. "They're sleeping."

CHAPTER 30

STUNNED, IKE LOWERED his Glock, stuffed it in his waistband, and headed down the basement stairs. As Amelia followed him down, he wondered where the hell the two intruders were and how this ninety-seven-year-old had defeated them. When Ike hit the last step, he carefully scanned the room and felt as if he were entering a time machine. In all the years they'd known each other, Frank had never let him come downstairs. The room was finished in lacquered knotty pine and had the feel of the summer home Ike's parents had rented along the Allegheny River when he was a teenager. A small bar filled one corner. Atop the bar, a lava lamp and a bar light with a hula girl shade from the sixties glowed in the low light. Looking over his shoulder, Ike eyed Amelia as she walked by the lamp, shaking her head. Frank led them to a powder room door adjacent to the bar. Opening the door, he stepped inside, and pressed a three-masted schooner on the nautical wallpaper.

The wall opened, and Ike felt his jaw drop. Frank threw a fiendish grin at Ike and stepped through the secret doorway. Wide-eyed, Ike looked at Amelia, whose expression seemed to indicate she shared Ike's wonder. The room was battleship gray: on the walls, on the floor, and on the ceiling. The walls appeared spongy, with the texture of a waffle iron. Ike recognized the soundproofing foam used in some recording studios. Light rock drifted from the two flush-mount speakers in the ceiling. Frank turned around, folded his arms, and leaned against the long cabinet system that ran along the entire length of the back wall. It held dual computer monitors, a keyboard, and several devices that looked like miniature cameras. He nodded to his right, the grin still on his face. Two men, dressed in black, lay side by side, unconscious. Ike could see their chests rise and fall.

"How did you do this?" Ike asked.

Frank reached behind him and produced a gun.

"Dart gun with frozen neurotoxin projectiles. A little insurance policy my old friends allowed me to keep."

Amelia chuckled and her eyes found Ike, then Frank. "Allowed you to keep it in the freezer?"

Ike knew Frank had been involved with some clandestine work for the government. But he was only aware of Frank's ties to the SIS and later the NSA. As far as he knew, Frank was a codebreaker, not a deadly operative.

"How did you get them down here?" Amelia asked.

Frank pulled an iPhone from his pocket, opened an app, and the soft rock volume blasted.

"I lured them down here," Frank yelled and held up the dart gun. "This did the rest."

Ike knew the thugs hadn't had a chance. They would have never suspected that from an old man.

Frank lowered the volume again and returned the phone to his pocket of his tan khakis. "They're professionals. Mercs. The boys at the Company used to use agents like these overseas. But not here at home."

Amelia stepped deeper into the room, her eyes burning a hole in the men lying on the ground. "Who hired them?"

"Airman," Frank said in a tone that drew Amelia's attention away from the intruders. "The first question is whether you really want to know. That thing you found is lethal. To anyone that possesses it."

Ike could see that Frank knew much more than he'd shared. "What did you find out about what's in the box, Frank?"

Concern washed away Frank's confident grin, and he rubbed his chin then stared at the floor for his next words. Amelia squared up in front of

Frank, shoulders back and expecting an answer. "You don't need to worry about me, sir. I'd risk anything to get to the bottom of this."

Frank raised his head and locked eyes with Amelia. The two stood frozen in each other's gaze, as if communicating with some sort of telepathy. One warrior to another. Both were clear-eyed and their commitment to their causes was obvious. The silence didn't matter. They were communicating far beyond the realm of words. Observing the silent exchange, Ike didn't feel left out. A strange reverence washed through him, and his respect for each of these people grew.

Frank broke first, with a smile and a nod. Amelia relaxed and nodded too.

"The box you lifted from the ocean floor should have stayed there. It is property of Adolf Hitler. We'd seen a few of these during the war. He used them to communicate directly with his top generals. He'd send five messengers out with five identical messages, sometimes each in a different encrypted form. If one or more were intercepted, the others would get through."

Ike had suspected as much. "If that's the case, it came from that U-boat that was sunk the day Hitler killed himself. And if someone, even today, nearly eighty years later, would kill to keep the contents secret, it must have been intended for someone in the states. Right?"

Frank glowed with pride like Ike's father used to. "That's right." He motioned toward the thugs on the floor. "And whoever it is will do anything to stop you."

"Let them try. I welcome the attempt," Amelia said. "You said there was a coded message on the paper tape. Can you break it?"

Frank's eyes moved from Amelia to the two men still unconscious on the floor. "Not here," Frank said as he herded them out of the room and closed the soundproof door. He walked to the bar and stopped. "The paper was from an old teleprinter. The messages are coded using a German ciphering device called a Lorenz machine."

Ike had heard of the Enigma machine. He'd even seen *The Imitation Game*. But he'd never heard of this device. "Lorenz?"

"It's a twelve-wheel cipher machine that was used to encipher messages sent by a teleprinter that used five-bit punched paper tape."

Amelia looked confused.

"Coded radio messages," Frank said. "Hitler started using it extensively in 1944 to send the highest-level top-secret messages from German headquarters to his generals and field marshals."

"What would that have to do with anything here?" Ike asked.

"The right question is why did a U-boat have the message? The Germans communicated to their U-boat commanders using the Enigma, not the Lorenz. And what was in the box was the coded teleprinter tape that had been received, so they had the Lorenz on board."

Ike let his mind grind through the new information. If the U-boat was carrying a top-secret message from Hitler, and it wasn't from an Enigma machine, who was the intended audience? Then it hit him. He focused on Amelia. "The U-boat was delivering a message from Hitler to someone in the US government."

They both looked at Frank.

"I'd heard rumors of such an attempt back then, but no evidence was ever uncovered," he said.

"What was the rumor?" Ike asked.

"That Hitler was wanting to make a deal."

"With us?" Amelia said.

"Apparently we didn't like the message and killed the messenger, that U-boat." Frank said.

"Can you break the code?" Ike asked.

"Lorenz was far more sophisticated than the Enigma. But the British broke the code."

"So you can break it?" Amelia said.

As he considered his reply, Frank's gaze drifted around the room and then landed on Amelia. "I'll need an old teleprinter. And the easiest way to break it is with a Lorenz machine. But I'll need to figure out the wheel settings."

Amelia looked like she was ready to burst. "Okay. Let's do it."

"Hang on," Ike said. "Where is this Lorenz machine?"

"DC," Frank said.

"Then if someone in Washington is killing people to hide this secret, they'll know the Lorenz would be the key, too."

Frank tried to smile but couldn't. "There's a problem." He crossed his arms. "The only Lorenz machine is in the NSA museum in DC. It's adjacent to the NSA building at Fort Meade. There's no way to get in and out undetected, and if the Lorenz machine is removed or borrowed, it will raise red flags."

Ike knew a dead end when he heard one. Trying to get into the NSA was a death sentence. Amelia looked as if she'd been gut-shot.

Frank continued, "That's why I warned you both. You're entering a dark world of death and deception. We're about to enter the gates of hell. It's the world I left behind, and for good reason. No one is guaranteed a way back. Not even me. I'm willing to help you get to the bottom of this, but there will be a cost. For me, it won't matter. I've lived my life. You two are in a different situation."

Amelia stepped forward, shoulders back. "I'm in."

Ike felt the focus in the room shift to him. The chill in his spine told him he was at the abyss again, looking in. He looked back at the secret room holding the men on the floor. The prospect of facing professional killers, perhaps hired by a radical and powerful foe in the US government, wasn't his first choice. The US had emboldened extremists at both ends of the political spectrum, thanks to the rhetoric of the current president. Anything was possible. He'd be risking the life he'd carefully rebuilt this past year, with Maria, and with Lauren, Jack, and Jimmy. Any closure for Maria regarding his parents' deaths could die with him. And then there was Mia. Any chance of reconnection with the woman he'd thought was The One would evaporate if someone in the US government was involved.

Rising from someplace he could never identify, a single thought filled him up, pushing any doubt or fear aside. He looked at Amelia staring back at him. *If not for me, then for her*, echoed in his head again. The words were automatic. "I'm in."

Ike thought for a moment. They had the tape—the answer to this problem—they just needed to break the code. "There has to be another way."

Frank's gaze drifted around the room. He was trying to pull something out of his failing memory. Then he snapped his attention back on Ike. "There is. I think I can do it manually, but it will take days or maybe a week."

"Too long," Ike said. "We'll be dead by then."

"Then I need a teleprinter and a computer that can simulate the Lorenz."

"Where can we get that?' Amelia said, the high pitch of desperation in her voice.

The answer hit Ike like a lightning bolt. "I think I know where."

Frank locked his eyes on Ike and Amelia. "Then we have to get there now. Our risk of certain death is increasing by the second."

CHAPTER 31

IKE JAMMED THE Shelby into third gear as he raced away from Frank's. According to Frank's last warning, time was their enemy. A desperate sense of urgency turbocharged his body and accelerated every thought and action. It was almost eleven. They needed to quickly retrieve the box from Rossi's, get an old teleprinter, and find a Lorenz simulator before someone figured out what was happening. To avoid detection, they'd agreed to meet at DeSantis Auto. There they'd have a little better security, and the DeSantis brothers knew almost everyone in the area. Ike had remembered one customer, a Carnegie Mellon grad turned tech entrepreneur, who might be able to help. As he raced down Aiken Avenue, his darting eyes were drawn to every pocket of darkness, searching for another threat. When he reached Liberty Avenue, he glanced across at Amelia, who was silently checking her drone.

Bloomfield felt like a ghost town. Liberty Avenue was still devoid of any traffic. To his right, West Penn Hospital remained quiet. He turned right and headed toward Rossi's. He slammed on the brakes when he noticed Mia's government ride parked in front of his restaurant.

Ike yanked on the steering wheel with both hands. "Shit!"

Amelia looked up and spotted the car. "FBI?"

Ike's face suddenly turned hot as his focus narrowed, and he felt his pulse pounding in his ears. Mia was alone with Maria. Any miniscule hope of starting over with Mia was dashed against the jagged rocks by a tidal wave of anger. Furious, he jammed the car into first, raced around the corner, and turned right into the alley. Sliding into his parking space, he was out of the car and storming to the door before Amelia unlatched her seatbelt.

"Hey! Wait!" she said.

Racing down the hallway to the restaurant, he caught himself and stopped. Closing his eyes, he reminded himself he had no idea what Mia might have said. He needed to be careful not to overreact and give his sister more information than she needed to worry about. Gathering himself, he stepped into the bar area. He spotted Randy leaning against the back of the bar, arms crossed, staring at Maria and Mia who were seated facing each other at the bar. Upon seeing Ike, Maria jumped up and marched toward him. Ike could see the tears twisting down her cheeks. A familiar guilt rose from his gut and stuck in his throat. He couldn't stand to be responsible for his sister's sadness. Mia remained seated with her back to them.

Maria stopped inches from him, stood on her tiptoes, and glared at Ike. "You lied to me."

"I don't know what you're talking about. I didn't lie."

Maria pointed behind her, toward Mia. "She said the government is handling whatever you're working on and that you'd be arrested, hurt, or killed if you got involved."

Ike pushed past Maria and looped around Mia to face her. "What did you tell her?"

Still seated, Mia calmly looked up. "The truth, Ike. I warned you not to get involved in a federal investigation. You need to stop. Now."

Ike felt the red-hot passion of their old fights return. "That's not going—"

"Hold on there," Amelia said, storming past Maria. "You have no idea what you're talking about."

Mia stood and faced Amelia's charge. She pulled her jacket back, exposing her badge and her gun. "Why don't you enlighten me?"

Now standing behind Mia, Ike eyed Amelia over Mia's shoulder and silently shook his head. Amelia needed to calm down. The less Mia knew, the better. Amelia got the message and shut it down. But Maria saw Ike's signal.

"I don't know what you two have going on, but you need to give it all to Agent Russo," Maria said.

Amelia spun, targeting her ire toward Maria. "Maria! We talked about this."

"You didn't tell me that the FBI could handle it. You didn't tell me that my brother would get arrested or killed."

"My aunt and uncle were killed," Amelia said.

Maria moved closer to Amelia. "And I don't want you to add my brother to that list."

"Maria," Ike warned.

Amelia leaned closer until she was nose to nose with Maria. "You don't get to tell me what to do."

Maria put her index finger into Amelia's chest. "Get my brother out of this."

Amelia swatted Maria's hand away. Randy leaped over the bar and was between them before Maria could retaliate. "All right. Let's take it down a notch or three."

Ike needed to get control of the situation. He felt like he was on a griddle. Nothing he could say would make all three women happy. The frustration fed a growing anger. In the back of his mind, he was thinking about his mother. Mia could provide the answers he'd been seeking for twenty-three years. But the chances of that happening were evaporating by the second.

"Mia. Why don't you and I go talk about this, privately," Ike said, his instinct to fight dwarfing any inkling of flight.

Mia faced him, and Ike noticed deception in her eyes. She was hiding something. Not anything about the case she was working on. That was a given. Just part of the job. But this was personal. Something she wanted to tell him but couldn't. He couldn't explain it, but he could feel the deception between them.

Mia nodded. "Okay. Where to?"

"I want to know what you tell her," Maria shouted.

Still standing between Maria and Amelia, Randy calmly said, "Come on Maria. I'm sure you can trust your brother. Let them talk." Randy glanced at Amelia, then back at Maria. "Let's go ladies. I've got some coffee and carrot cake in the back."

Ike thanked God he'd hired Randy. He had a demeanor that was gentle but firm and people trusted him, instantly. After both women glanced at Ike, they followed Randy into the kitchen. That left Ike and Mia, still standing and facing each other. Mia pulled out a barstool and sat, arms folded, waiting for Ike to speak. Ike knew she was holding something back, and while her body language radiated power and strength, her eyes were still begging for help. She'd crossed the line by talking to Maria, and she knew it. As far as Ike was concerned, it was the first time she'd ever tried to manipulate him. Ike stared at her, then released his anger with a sigh. He pulled out a barstool and sat facing her, their knees nearly touching. Despite his displeasure with her, he still felt her gravity pulling him in.

"Look. I told you I'd let you know if we found something I thought would be of interest to your investigation. But I have an obligation to my client, and I plan to honor that."

Mia's expression softened, and she leaned forward, placing her hand on his knee. Her touch was electric. "Ike. You need to stop what you're doing. It won't end well for you. I'd like to think that you and I still have a connection. One that has possibilities. I can feel it, and I think you feel it too. But you have to stop. You're hurting more people than you know."

He couldn't believe his ears. It was the first time she'd openly acknowledged the rekindling of her feelings for Ike. Ike felt his heartrate pick up and for a moment he let his body enjoy the brief flood of endorphins. But those buoyant thoughts were quickly dragged back to earth by the weight of his obligations and suspicions. Betraying Amelia now, especially to a government agent, would result in her death, and probably his and Frank's too. He had a path to the truth, albeit a dangerous long shot. Decoding the message in that box and discovering who was behind the killings was the only way out. Mia couldn't be a part of that. He knew his next words would send him back to the emotional desert he knew all too well. He leaned in and placed his hand on hers.

"There's something you're not telling me. I wish I knew what it was. Maybe I could help. But I can't do what you are asking Mia. I just can't."

For a moment, Ike could see her disappointment and sadness fill her eyes. She looked down at their hands, pulled hers away, and stood. Locking her eyes on Ike's, she gently shook her head. She walked around him and headed to the front door. She unlocked it, paused, and looked back over her shoulder, her eyes hawkish and cold.

"I'll do what I have to do."

Then, she was gone.

CHAPTER 32

IKE TURNED INTO DeSantis Auto and pulled to the chain-link gate again. He remembered all the times he and the brothers had bailed each other out since grade school, and that memory fed his faith that the DeSantis brothers would have the answers they needed. That quelled the trace of doubt that vibrated through him. Between them, they knew most everyone in the area, especially in the burgeoning tech community around Carnegie Mellon University. He rolled down the window and reached for the talk button on the rusted box. His breath formed a pale cloud that drifted over the box. He checked the temperature on the dash. It was twenty-eight degrees, yet he hadn't felt the biting cold. The digital clock subtracted another minute from what little time they had left.

On the way over, he'd thought about what lay ahead. Amelia and Frank were his responsibility. Amelia had been uncharacteristically quiet on the drive, but Ike remembered what it felt like when his parents' killings sank in. Despite her coldness toward him, he felt their connection. It was like a force field between them that formed an unspoken bond. It was why he'd taken the case.

Ike knew the killings would continue until they exposed those behind them, and the deeper they dug, the deadlier the coded message became. Maria had made it clear she'd be waiting for his safe return, and he planned on doing everything in his power to make that happen. He didn't like

149

leaving her behind, but he didn't have a choice. While Randy could protect her for now, whoever was behind this would come looking for her if Ike didn't find them first. Mia had walked out, along with his hopes of getting the details about his mother's work as a confidential informant for the FBI. Those thoughts hardened his focus: on breaking the code, exposing those behind it, and coming home in one piece. A plan was coming together in his mind, and the first step started here.

Before he could push the button, the gate jolted, clattered, and rolled open. Vinny had gotten Ike's WhatsApp text. Across the lot, he saw the center garage door roll up. He looked at Amelia.

"Here we go."

She glanced at Ike, then stared ahead. "Copy that."

Ike spotted Frank's car and pulled in between it and a black Suburban with dark tinted windows. With Van Halen's "Panama" playing in the background, he threw a nod at Danny, who was pressing the button mounted on the back wall to close the door. Ike got out and Amelia joined him in front of the Shelby.

"Hey, Ikey boy. Two times in a weekend. Feels like old times," Danny said as he walked over to them in rhythm with the music, his barrel chest and hulking shoulders stretching his faded ZZ Top t-shirt. He gave Ike a fist bump and offered one to Amelia. She looked down at it.

"Hey, Amelia. Don't leave me hanging. You'll break my heart," Danny said with a grin.

Amelia cracked the first smile Ike had seen from her in a while, and she fist-bumped him.

"That's what I'm talking about." Danny spun and headed for the door at the back of the garage. "Wait here," he said over his shoulder. Amelia followed him with her eyes, still smiling, then she apparently realized Ike was watching and stopped. Danny opened the door. "Let's rock and roll, guys!" he shouted. He held the door open, bouncing and singing the chorus, until Vinny and Frank emerged from the shop.

Vinny went straight to Ike, shook his hand, and hugged him. "You hanging in there, brother?"

"I'm good. How 'bout you guys?"

"The usual. Fabulous!"

Frank slowly shook his head. "I can vouch for that."

Ike immediately thought about the two thugs in Frank's basement. "Did you have any problems getting out?"

"No. I've got a cleaning crew taking care of things. They'll put those two fish on ice for three or four days."

Frank was still full of surprises.

Frank checked his watch. "We need to get going."

"Right," Vinny said. He looked at Ike. "Lay it on me."

"We need to find a techie that can help us," Ike said. "Frank can give you the details."

The group formed a circle. Frank eyed Amelia, apparently seeking her permission to talk about the box. She nodded.

Frank began his explanation. "We have an old teleprinter tape that needs to be read, and we need a computer simulation of a thing called a Lorenz machine. It's German. From World War II."

Vinny and Danny both raised their eyebrows and shared a bewildered look.

"What's a teleprinter?" Danny said.

"It's an old device that was used to send and receive coded messages during the war. It converts radio pulses into holes on a paper tape and vice versa," Frank said.

Danny eyed Vinny. "This is gettin' good. You thinking what I'm thinking?"

Vinny nodded.

"Do you have a name for me?" Ike asked.

This time, they nodded together. Vinny said, "Dominic."

Ike ran through the deep recesses of his mind but couldn't come up with a Dominic.

"You remember," Danny said. "DM."

An image took shape of a scrawny pale kid from the neighborhood who was rarely caught outside all the way from grade school through high school. He'd lived two blocks over. Ike had lost track of him when he'd left for Penn State. "Dominic Massaro?"

"I remember him," Frank said. "One of the brightest young men I've seen, that is, when you could get him to talk."

"Yeah. That's him," Vinny said. "Went to CMU and dropped out his sophomore year. He founded three start-ups he sold for millions. Now he runs an incubator for ideas that he'll invest in."

"I should have studied harder," Danny said, straight-faced.

"Don't worry, bro. He can't hold a candle to you in the restoration business. That's why he comes here."

"He a client?" Ike asked.

"Yeah. We've filled his twelve-car garage with our work. He loves muscle cars."

"He's the one who took that Super Bird," Danny said.

"He still has strong ties to CMU. Given them millions. Even had a building named after him. If anyone can get this teleprinter thing, he can. CMU has a bunch of old stuff that led to the computer. He'd probably be able to hook you up with this Lawrence thing too."

"Lorenz. L-O-R-E-N-Z," Frank said.

Ike was leery of getting another person added to someone's hit list. "It's the same deal, guys. Anyone who sees this thing or helps us will be in danger."

"No worries, Ikey. This guy lives in a freaking compound in Mars. Top-notch security. Better than we have. He's not afraid of anyone," Danny said.

"Little Dominic?" Ike said.

Grinning, both brothers shrugged, raised their eyebrows, and silently nodded.

Amelia leaned into the circle, checked her watch, and said, "It's zero one hundred. Can we go wake him?"

"The dude never sleeps," Vinny said, pulling out his phone. "Let me send him a message."

Vinny stared at his screen for a few seconds, then held his phone up to the group. "See. He said come over."

Ike glanced back at the Shelby. It was getting late, and the risk of another attack was increasing by the second.

"Take this," Vinny said, apparently reading Ike's mind.

He walked between Ike and Frank to the Suburban. He knocked on the passenger's side window. "Multi-layer ballistic glass." He patted the roof. "Anti-mine protection on the roof and floor." He opened the back door. "And hardened ballistic steel protecting the passenger compartment." He closed the door and kicked the back tire. "High performance run-flats."

Danny wiggled between Ike and Amelia to join his brother. "Yeah. We call it The Stallion."

"Stallion?" Amelia said, rolling her eyes.

"Yeah," Danny said, slightly offended. "You know. Like the Italian Stallion." Danny stopped, waiting for Amelia to get it. She didn't.

"Rocky!" he said and started shadow boxing. "Takes a beating but still wins!"

"Where did you get it?" she asked.

Vinny and Danny shared a look.

"A prominent local family," Vinny said.

"Very prominent," Danny said. "They were done with it, so we traded for it."

Ike knew exactly who they were talking about. So did Frank.

"Who is that?" Amelia asked.

"Never mind," Ike said. "Let's get our things."

"Oh. I forgot." Vinny opened the rear tailgate. He lifted a hatch. "Concealed storage for your goodies."

Danny just smiled.

"Got it," Ike headed for the Shelby and opened the trunk. He grabbed a black duffel. Amelia stepped beside him and grabbed the road case and a smaller duffel. Ike eyed the case. They'd placed the box inside. He was certain the contents would reveal the killers. They'd have to guard it with their lives until then. Frank headed to his SUV and retrieved a leather duffel. They met back at the tailgate of the Suburban and loaded their things inside.

Vinny walked up, cocked the gun in his hand, and shoved it in his waistband. "I'll get you in. Danny will follow in the Chevelle and bring me back here."

Frank stood firm, showing the confidence of a man half his age. Still, he was Frank. A legend in Bloomfield and respected by anyone who mattered. He was ninety-seven, and Ike was putting him in harm's way.

"I have to ask," Ike said. "Are you sure you want to do this?"

Frank dropped his head and chuckled at the ground, then looked up at Ike. "Don't worry about me. We're entering my old world. It's a world where thinking like that will get you killed. Everyone will have a job to do. Focus on that. You need me to get through this and break that code." Frank walked toward the back passenger's door of the car, looking at his watch again. "Let's get going." He got in.

Amelia shrugged her shoulders at Ike, smiling at the admonishment he'd received, then walked to the front passenger's door and got in. Vinny hopped in the other back passenger's door. Ike headed to the driver's door and grabbed the handle. Before he got in, he wondered what the gates of hell would look like. He studied the Stallion. He thought about the innocent people who were dead and channeled his anger into a solid commitment building in his body. Maybe he'd already seen them.

CHAPTER 33

IKE STEERED THE Stallion down the dark winding road, being careful not to overdrive the headlights. At two in the morning, the trip north out of the city had taken forty minutes, but they were minutes he couldn't spare. They were somewhere on the outskirts of the town of Mars, and Ike thought it ironic that in the dense darkness they could have been on the dark side of the red planet itself and not known it. Seeing only what the headlights allowed, he felt the heavily armored vehicle slog back and forth through the curves. Still, as he pressed on, the weight of his own determination pushed him deeper into the darkness propelled by the faith that somewhere out there was the answer that would give closure to Amelia and get them all out of danger.

"It's up here around the next curve," Vinny said quietly as he looked over at Frank who was napping next to him.

As they crested a small rise in the middle of a curve in the road, the dark tree line abruptly ended. To the right, Ike spotted the dim landscaping lights of a massive house resting in the miniature valley. The lighting traced a winding drive that connected to the road up ahead.

He heard Amelia unbuckle. "I'll get the box," she said.

In the rearview mirror, he watched her lean over the backseat and heard her open the road case. When she turned back to her seat, she had the box and her Beretta in her hands. "From now on, where I go, it goes."

155

Frank opened his eyes and lifted his head from the headrest.

"We're here," Amelia said.

Ike turned right and followed the drive until they approached a massive iron gate. The wall that surrounded the house was three times taller than the front of the Stallion. Ike estimated it was over twelve feet. It appeared to be made of solid concrete painted a brilliant white. Topped with a conglomeration of sharp concrete spikes, Ike thought it was nearly impossible to climb over. To Ike's right, a small lighted gatehouse stood sentry. A thick man, the size of a defensive end, stepped out of the gatehouse. Vinny rolled down his window.

"Vinny here to see Dominic."

The man leaned in and eyed Frank, then Amelia, and looked at Ike. "He's expecting you," he said, stepping back as the thick iron gates magically parted. He waved them through.

"Impressive," Frank said.

"Jesus, who is this guy?" Amelia added.

The LED landscape lights on each side brightened as they approached each one, as if leading them to the large circle in front of the house. The house was a towering Tudor made of thick granite blocks. A large turret adorned the right side and two symmetrical roof peaks reached to the sky on the left. In the center, an arched double wooden door trimmed in black bolted metal stood protected by a large, well-lit porte cochère. Farther to the left of the house was a long garage that looked like a horse stable, if it weren't for the dozen double wooden garage doors.

Ike pulled to the entrance and stopped. He slipped the Glock from his belt and checked the magazine. Vinny and Amelia did the same. He scanned the surroundings one more time, then said, "Let's go."

They exited the Suburban and made their way to the front doors. An infrared bullet camera stared down at them. Vinny pressed the digital doorbell and in seconds the door opened.

The man inside was tall, maybe six two. His limbs were thin and seemed uncoordinated with the rest of his body. His close-cut black hair looked as if his barber were a sheep shearer. Flecks of gray peppered his temples. His eyelids looked like they weighed a ton. But Ike could see brilliant green eyes scanning the group through the slits. The man had a Red Bull in his hand.

"Hi, Vinny," he said, opening the door wider. His voice was high-pitched but clear. "Come in."

Vinny led them inside and they followed Dominic down a long hallway. Ike noticed the elaborate alarm system and the digital frames along the wall. Most contained beautiful nature scenes, but a couple, evenly spaced down the hallway, had the eight squares showing the view from what must have been security cameras stationed around the property. Ike watched Danny pull to the gate in his Chevelle on one.

Dominic walked like an alien. His thin form flexed with each step, and his arms floated out of rhythm with his strides. Ike didn't remember him being that tall in high school. He'd been a quiet mouselike skinny kid and the target of pranksters and bullies. He turned left through an archway and opened another pair of thick wooden doors. They entered a library that looked like it belonged in an Ivy League college. Stained oak bookcases lined the walls, separated by spans of smooth panels. Brass rails decorated the space and green shaded lamps were on each polished table in the room. He led them to a large hearth and to opposing sofas flanked by two high-back chairs meant for a king or queen. He stopped at one of them.

He motioned to the sofas with his Red Bull. "Please, have a seat." He took a drink.

Vinny and Ike sat on one sofa, and Frank and Amelia sat on the other.

"What can I do for these people, Vinny?" he asked.

"Dominic, this is Ike Rossi," Vinny said.

Dominic acknowledged Ike with a nod followed by another sip of his drink.

"He's helping Amelia here find out who killed her aunt and uncle, and they need help breaking a coded message." Vinny hesitated, then said, "From World War II."

Dominic's eyebrows shot up. He eyed the box in Amelia's lap.

Vinny continued. "You know Mr. McNally. He's helping us break it."

Dominic smiled at Frank. "Hi, Mr. McNally. Do you remember me?"

"Yes, I do. You were one of my brightest students. And it's Frank."

Dominic shook his head. "Even after all these years, I don't think I can call you that, Mr. McNally."

Vinny stood. "Now that I've made introductions. I'll leave you all to it." He leaned down and shook Dominic's hand. "Thanks for doing this. I'm meeting Danny outside." He looked at the rest of the group. "Don't want too much information."

Dominic raised his hand to get Vinny's attention. "Tell Danny that sixty-nine Barracuda is a beast!"

"Will do." Vinny saluted with two fingers and left the room.

Holding the box, Amelia leaned toward Dominic. "We need your help breaking this code so we can find the people behind my aunt's and uncle's murders. They were great people, and they meant the world to me."

He extended his hand, and she handed him the box. He examined it. He ran his fingers over the Nazi emblem. Ike could tell by his expression that Dominic wasn't sold. Dominic returned Amelia's glare and said, "That's not a good enough reason to risk my life and all I have." He handed the box back to Amelia.

"What?" Her eyes flared, and Ike thought he saw her reaching for her Beretta.

Before she got to it, Ike said, "Hey, Dominic."

Dominic turned his attention to Ike. The stern look on his face immediately melted away.

"The people behind this are trying to hide something. They're killing innocent people who can't defend themselves to do it. Breaking this code will stop them." Ike could see he'd hit a nerve.

Dominic folded his hands in front of him. A pleasant expression swept over him. Looking off into the distance, he seemed to be remembering something. "I remember you, Ike. You were one of the few people who were kind to me."

Ike wasn't sure where Dominic was going with this.

Dominic settled his gaze on Ike. "Do you remember that time in the cafeteria?"

Ike was drawing a blank.

"It was just before Christmas our senior year and three other football players were trying to get me to eat a fly they caught. First, they offered me money. Then they threatened me. Everyone was watching. As soon as you came in and saw what was going on, you came over. You were the big-time quarterback. The big man on campus. And I ..." Dominic's face turned sad. "Well, you know what I was. Nobody." He shook off his sadness and continued. "Anyway, you told them to knock it off. You even grabbed one of them and told them you'd see that they'd be kicked off the team. You told them to leave me alone. Everybody heard you. Then you got your lunch and sat with me. You asked if I was okay, and you actually talked with me."

As he told the story, Ike remembered it. He'd been livid and couldn't stand his teammates.

"You changed my life that day. It was the first time someone really saw me. I realized that I was someone, and I committed to believe in myself just like you believed in me. No one bothered me after that. As a matter of fact, I even made a couple of friends before I graduated." He gestured around the room. "I have all of this, partly because of you."

Ike was uncomfortable with the compliment. "I appreciate you saying that, but I'm sure you did this on your own. But will you help me?"

Dominic looked down at the floor in thought. After a few seconds he raised his head. "You stuck up for me back then. So, yes, I'll return the favor."

"Thanks, Dominic. I'll owe you," Ike said.

Dominic leaned on his armrest toward Ike. "You owe me nothing." He sat back up in his chair, his green eyes now fueled by the Red Bull. He turned his attention to Amelia and Frank. "Tell me what you need." His matter-of-fact tone, completely devoid of any emotion, impressed Ike.

Amelia gave Ike a *what the hell?* look as if insulted by Dominic's sudden change of heart. She handed the box to Frank. "Frank can fill you in," she said.

Frank took the box, examined it, then held it up. "We believe this is a message from Adolf Hitler intended for someone in the US." He pointed to the lid. "These markings are identical to those used by Hitler." Carefully prying open the box, he tilted it and pointed to the rolled-up teleprinter tape. "It's a coded message using a Lorenz machine. It's on this tape using a five-bit Baudot code. I could use an old teleprinter to read this quickly, then start trying to break the code."

Dominic had been nodding while Frank spoke. "Got it. The teleprinter may take a little time since the one I know about is in the CMU archives. Lorenz is another story."

Ike's stomach dropped, and Amelia's face turned sour.

Dominic apparently had seen their reactions. "Not a bad story. A good one," he said as a smile grew across his face. "I know of several online Lorenz simulators that with a little tweak could work well. We can get access from here. I'll just need the wheel settings. There's twelve of those, you know."

Amelia stood, unable to contain her nerves. "We don't have time to go to CMU and back again. We gotta get going now." She glanced at Dominic, then Frank. "How can we do this without the teleprinter?"

"She's right," Ike said.

"Then I'll transpose the teleprinter tape by hand," Frank said. "Then use a section of the code to try to break it and get the wheel settings."

"You'd have to know what that section said to do that," Dominic said with challenge in his tone.

"I know the last line of all of the messages sent by Hitler."

"What was it?" Ike asked.

"ADOLF9HITLER9FUEHER9. He signed all of his messages that way. The nine represents a space. They used the twenty-six-letter alphabet plus six other characters. During the war, the boys at Bletchley Park in London showed us how to do it."

Dominic looked impressed.

Ike stood. "Let's get to it, then. I'll assist Dominic, and Amelia will help Frank, if that works for everyone?"

There were nods all around.

"All I need is a pair of gloves to handle the tape, a pencil, and a tablet," Frank said.

"A pencil?" Dominic asked, puzzled.

"Old school," Frank said, standing. "Old school."

CHAPTER 34

BENTON GARCIA CRUSHED another empty coffee cup and tossed it into the wastebasket in the West Wing lobby. He stared at the painting of Washington's crossing of the Delaware River. Despite the chaos going on around him as Washington's troops battled the icy currents of the river, Washington held his powerful pose. But Benton could feel *his* power leaking away. It was just a trickle, but a trickle could quickly become a raging river that would sweep him away into obscurity. It was already ten a.m., and Benton had waited for two hours when he'd normally be whisked straight into the Oval Office or that of the president's most trusted adviser. His anger built inside with each tick of the antique clock on the wall.

Kara Reed Williams was making him wait. The president's younger sister and senior advisor had guided the president from his first run in congress, to his victory in the Texas gubernatorial race, through the primaries, and into the White House. Now, she was ramping up his campaign for his second term. She'd taught him how to use the media to his advantage and how to discredit their reporting when needed. She'd helped him demonize his opponents and define the other side early in the races with his sharp tongue and quick wit. Benton had bankrolled their campaigns from the start, lining up donors, political action committees, and SuperPACs to propel them to victory.

"Ms. Williams will see you now," the middle-aged secretary said.

Benton huffed and followed her down the hallway to Kara's office.

"Mr. Garcia, ma'am," the secretary said, then disappeared back down the hallway.

As Benton entered the office, Kara lifted her eyes from the document she'd been reading and removed her reading glasses. She glowed with the fitness of a woman half of her seventy-one years. Her features were sharp, and her penetrating blue eyes felt as if they could stop a train. The row of wrinkles between her eyes, her taut jawline, and complete lack of a smile intimidated even the most seasoned staffer. The tight navy pantsuit didn't have a thread out of place. Benton was used to her, but he needed to be careful. He was walking a tightrope between projecting power and retaining his access.

She stood and offered her hand. "Hello, Benton. This is a surprise."

Benton shook it, and she offered him a seat at her side table. They both settled in and folded their hands in front of them.

"I flew up this morning, Kara. I need some help. I don't understand why the FBI is questioning me and my family."

She eyed him and cocked her head. "How was your trip?"

Benton slowly hissed it out: "Early. Now what can you tell me."

"You know we don't get involved in FBI investigations."

"And the Easter Bunny is real. Come on, Kara. You and the president know exactly what's going on. I need some answers."

Kara looked to the side in thought, then turned back to Benton.

"You have a daughter, right?"

"I *had* two." Benton felt his pulse pounding at the thought of losing Harper. He knew Kara had a hand in that, but he let it go for now. She waited for his real answer. "Her name is Amelia."

"Right. Amelia. Air Force, right?"

"Yes. For twelve years. Now an ROV pilot for my brother-in-law's company."

"Former."

"What?"

"Former brother-in-law. Wasn't he killed a few days ago?"

Benton just nodded.

"I understand that daughter of yours was the last one to speak with him before he died."

Benton felt as if a trap door was about to open and swallow him up. He tried to hide the uneasiness flipping in his stomach. "What's that have to do with anything?"

"Well, the second in command at Justice was killed right after that following a call between him and your brother-in-law."

"So what? She's his niece."

"She started the dominoes falling, it seems. And every time another one falls, someone dies. The FBI is trying to figure that out."

"There's nothing to figure out."

"Then you have nothing to be concerned about."

Kara's eyes shifted their focus, and she couldn't hold her gaze on Benton. He knew she was either lying or holding something back. Something that could hurt him.

Benton pulled back from the table. "There's something you're not telling me."

"Where is she?" She raised an eyebrow this time with her focus firmly on Benton.

"No!" Benton said.

"What?"

"You leave my family alone. You already cost me one daughter."

She shook her head, leaned back, and checked her nails. "All I did was get her the job you wanted. She wanted to work for the agency."

"I'm sure she didn't want to die."

"No officers ever do. There are one hundred thirty-nine stars on that wall. She's only one."

Benton desperately needed leverage. "I've funded every one of your brother's races."

"And we appreciate that. But with a popular incumbent president, we've built a large war chest. So you need to think about *your* future." She looked up from her nails. "You realize this can go one of two ways. You're viewed as cooperative, and you get the sympathy of those around you, or you're viewed as part of the problem—a liability—and you lose everything you've worked for. One call or tweet from the president and your so-called friends will drop you in a second. So where is she?"

Benton thought about Amelia. She'd battled him at every turn. She'd rejected all of his advice and his efforts to shape her thinking. She'd been a thorn in his side since the beginning. Harper was the opposite. When she died, Amelia blamed him. He didn't have the connection to her like Harper did. He knew one thing. He needed to keep his reputation intact and that meant keeping his access.

He swallowed hard. "Pittsburgh."

"Pittsburgh?"

"She's with a guy named Ike Rossi."

Kara just nodded again as if she already knew.

CHAPTER 35

IKE STRODE CONFIDENTLY down the long hallway carrying his Glock and checking the security cameras as he passed each of the framed screens. At nearly ten-thirty in the morning already, he knew time was not on his side, so precautions had to be taken. The gun was weighty, loaded with its seventeen rounds. It wasn't the force multiplier he'd need in any attack, but it would have to do. Ike's focus was now on one thing: get the teleprinter tape deciphered. The plan was solid and gave him a certainty that centered him. That invisible force surged inside him, driving him forward with righteous determination in every move he made. But the process was taking time he didn't have.

As he walked past the library, he glanced in and noticed Frank carefully handling the paper tape in his gloved hands and transposing the perforations into one of the thirty-two characters he'd said each line represented. Earlier, they'd agreed that a couple of hours of sleep would clear Frank's mind and allow him to do the painstaking work. He appeared fresh and alert as he looked up at Ike.

"You doing okay? Need anything?" Ike said.

"I'm good. How's it looking out there?"

"All quiet. Dominic is across the foyer in his office making progress with the simulator."

"Good. Come on in," Frank said as he stripped off the gloves and rubbed his eyes. "I could use the break. I'm nearly done with this first process. It will give me the encrypted character strings, then the hard work starts."

Walking to the table, Ike scanned the library. "Where's Amelia?"

"I guess the pace was too slow for her. We agreed she needed some air."

Ike looked down at the paper tablet in front of Frank. It was all in pencil and looked like a cat had been walking on a keyboard. Each line had five dots or Xs followed by a character or number. Reading down the page, he noticed that the column of characters at the end of the lines were letters and numbers haphazardly interspersed. He noticed the number nine separated some groups of letters.

Frank must have read the expression on his face. "Don't worry. This is the messy part. The raw Baudot code and corresponding characters. Looks like there are fifteen hundred and eight characters, and I'm almost done."

Ike had no idea what Frank was talking about. He didn't need to as long as he had Frank. "What's next?" he asked.

"Once I finish manually reading the tape, I'll start my breaking work. If this is from who I think it is, I know how he signed off every message. Once I get that break, I'll try to push it at least fifty characters back. That might give me enough to get the wheel settings for Dominic's work."

Ike knew time was critical. "Can we help with any of this?"

Frank shook his head. "Not unless you know German and have all of the nine hundred and ninety-two possible combinations of each character of the Baudot code added to all other characters of the code memorized."

"You still remember all that after all these years?"

"Surprisingly. It's all coming back to me."

Ike was shocked by Frank's degree of recall. Ike only hoped if he made it to ninety that he could at least remember his name. Frank's attention snapped to the doorway.

"Are we close?" Amelia asked, hope emanating from her face. She walked into the room with her Beretta hanging from her hand, barrel down.

Ike turned back to Frank. "What's your best guess as to when?"

Frank rubbed his face this time and let out a loud sigh. "I'd guess another three or four hours, at least."

Amelia rolled her eyes. "Ugggggh!"

"Amelia," Ike warned.

"What? I'm frustrated." She narrowed her eyes on Frank. "Can we help?"

"I already offered. We don't know the language or the code," Ike said.

Frank pulled his gloves back on, picked up his pencil, and resumed looking at the tape. "The sooner you impatient iPhone-carrying young people leave me alone, the sooner I'll be done."

Ike eyed Amelia, then nodded toward the door. She followed him to the threshold.

"You stay here with him. Let me know as soon as he has something. Dominic is making progress with the simulation. I'll stay with him. Stay alert. We've been here too long."

"No shit."

Ike ignored her frustration. He had enough of his own. "I'll be in the office with Dominic. If something happens, get to his safe room. It's behind the office. Across the front foyer."

"Copy that," she said, lifting her Beretta and heading back into the library.

Ike made his way back down the hallway and entered the office. Dominic hunched over the wireless keyboard and concentrated on the large monitor on his desk. Three empty cans of Red Bull cluttered one side. A fresh one was sweating droplets onto his desk blotter. Ike grabbed the iPad from the corner of the desk and pulled the perimeter cameras back up.

Dominic stopped his manic typing. Leaning back in his chair, he took a long pull on his Red Bull. Ike recognized the chair as the same RECARO x Porsche gaming chair he'd given Danny for his help on the Jack Cole case.

"What's up, Ike?"

"Frank is making progress. He said he'd have the wheel settings in a few hours."

Dominic burped. "Sorry." He wiped his mouth with the back of his hand. "That'll work. I've worked out a few bugs in the code and can use that time to test it for accuracy." He threw a nod towards Ike. "What's up with the cameras?"

"Just checking."

Dominic shrugged. "Okay. Remember I got the safe room if we need it. Secure, bulletproof, fireproof, and wired."

Ike didn't want to tell him there was no such thing in his world. He acknowledged the comment with a quick nod, then looked out the window behind Dominic. A few rays of sunshine had broken through the overcast. Ike grabbed the iPad and checked the cameras. What he saw launched him from the side chair. Holding the iPad closer, he examined the images again. Each of the eight cameras showed the dim light of the overcast on the security cameras. He knew the bullet cameras had infrared capability, but that feature only made darkness appear brighter. He selected the front gate camera and expanded the screen. It was still overcast in that image and the infrared hadn't kicked in. He examined the tiny digital clock in the upper-right corner. It had frozen at 10:38. He checked his watch. It was 10:41. He threw the iPad to the floor and cocked his handgun.

"What's wrong?" Dominic said.

Ike trotted to the office door and stopped. He pointed the Glock down the hallway that led to the foyer and front door. Looking over his shoulder he said, "Get your stuff to the saferoom. Don't close the door until I get back with Frank and Amelia."

Dominic jumped up, snapped his laptop shut, stuck it under his arm, and grabbed his Red Bull.

"Why?" Dominic said.

"We have company."

CHAPTER 36

IKE SPRINTED DOWN the hallway, harnessing the adrenaline coursing through his body. He had to get Frank and Amelia to the safe room before the attackers breached. He reached the massive marble foyer, stopped, and looked to his right to check the thick oak front door. It was still intact and locked. As he started across the foyer, a deafening concussion came from his right and knocked him to the cold floor. Fragments of wood dug into his skin. Stunned, with gunfire ripping into the wall just above him, he pulled himself up on all fours and scrambled back to the hallway, hoping the walls would stop a bullet. He looked down in his hand and realized he'd held onto his Glock. Sitting on the floor with his back against the wall, his mind quickly caught up, and without looking, he squeezed off six shots in the direction of the door. A hail of bullets ate away at the drywall above his head, and he could see bits of the concrete core.

"Come on, Ike!" Dominic called from the safe room.

"Do not shut that door!" Ike ordered.

Confident the wall would hold, he stood and fired six more shots at the jagged doorway as he tried to move across the foyer. Rapid fire coming from the open doorway forced him back to cover. He couldn't get to Frank and Amelia. Now a steady stream of gunfire clipped the battered corner of the wall, spraying concrete chips in his face. He squeezed off the last five shots in his magazine, then stopped to reload. The gunfire got heavier, and he turned away to protect his eyes. Then he heard Amelia's Beretta from across the foyer. The barrage of bullets stopped. Ike thought she'd hit one of the gunmen. He turned back, looked across the foyer, and spotted Amelia on one knee firing at the door. Ike targeted the doorway too, firing quickly and heading to her position. But the gunfire returned and strafed the marble in front of him, chasing him back toward the office hallway. He slammed his back against the wall and slid down to a squat.

Then he heard it. The grenade rattled along the floor, hit the elevator doors, and ignited. Smoke started to fill the foyer.

"Ike!" Amelia yelled.

Ike spotted her. She was still firing at the door but looking at Ike. He saw Frank just behind her slide something next to her. It was a small box. He moved up and shoved it as hard as he could. The box spun slowly but kept racing towards Ike. It was going to stop short. Amelia increased her firing rate, and Ike lunged for the box and yanked it back behind the hallway wall.

The smoke thickened, and now he could barely see Amelia. She stopped firing. She was out of ammunition. "We're not going to make it. Finish it!" she yelled.

As Amelia disappeared in the smoke, Ike looked down and checked the cardboard box. It held Frank's tablet and the Nazi strongbox. He knew if the attackers got that, it was over for Frank and Amelia for sure. He gave one more look at the thick smoke concealing every inch of the foyer. Still squatting, he checked the box again. He couldn't do it. He couldn't leave them. Four more shots ricocheted off the wall above him. Turning back down the hallway toward the saferoom, Ike gave the box a shove along the smooth floor.

"Dominic. Come get this and get in the safe room. Now!"

He ejected his last magazine and checked it. Eleven rounds left. Reloading it, he cocked the gun. He waited for a break in the gunfire, then opened fire on the doorway. Just as he started across the foyer, he heard something rolling along the floor again. A searing flash burned his eyes, then a split second later an explosion knocked him to the floor. Blind, with his ears ringing and his mind blank, he felt someone dragging him by the collar of his vest. He tried to move, but his limbs wouldn't respond.

"I got you, man." he heard from a voice above him. His mind began to reboot.

"Dominic?"

"Yeah."

The thud of the thick door and the hiss of the seal locking punctuated a terrifying thought. *They had Amelia and Frank.*

CHAPTER 37

CHOKING ON THE smoke, Amelia picked herself up off the marble floor. She staggered to Frank who lay face down and motionless. Despite her ringing ears and the confusion trying to overtake her, she forced her mind to focus. With no return fire, she knew they'd be coming in for them in seconds. She put her hand against the wall and leaned on it for a moment, coughing heavily. Her lungs felt as if they'd been tossed into a fire, and her head throbbed with a vice-like ache. Staring at Frank, still face down on the floor, she shook her head, pushed her hair away from her face, and dropped to one knee. She squeezed his shoulder.

"Frank."

At first there was no movement. At ninety-seven, it would be a reasonable assumption that he didn't survive the concussion grenade. Stroke, heart attack, or just giving up after a very long life. Then his head moved, followed by his legs. She helped him turn onto his back.

"We gotta go, Frank."

His eyes widened as he apparently regained his faculties. "Help me up."

Throwing his arm over her shoulder, she helped him to his feet. His body felt light and brittle, but she knew they didn't have any time left. She dragged him down the hallway, his legs regaining their balance and strength with each step. They entered the library and with her free hand, she closed the oak pocket doors behind them. She heard their assailants enter the hallway from the foyer as she fumbled with the latch until it locked. She scanned the room for any potential exit.

"I'm okay now," Frank said, pulling his arm from her shoulder.

She let go and spotted the large window behind the heavy wooden desk.

"Over here," she said as she ran to the window.

She pulled her Beretta from her waistband, striking the window hard. It didn't break. The pocket doors shook, their killers pounding them with something heavy, probably their gun butts. She struck the window again. Still no breakage.

Gunfire erupted just outside the doors, and they splintered around the latch.

"Get in here," she said, guiding Frank under the heavy desk.

She checked the desktop for something that could be used as a weapon and found nothing. Then she bolted toward the stacks of bookshelves, grabbing Frank's pencil from the table on the way past. The pocket doors shattered, and two masked men entered. She pulled back behind the last bookshelf.

Both men had MP5s equipped with lights, lasers, and suppressors. Illegal for the public, the only time she'd seen those weapons was a video of a SEAL team drill. They split up at the door, one heading right toward Frank, the other toward her. The first attacker swept the path ahead of him with his rifle up, creeping slowly toward her. Through the books on the shelf, she could see the other attacker closing on Frank.

Amelia positioned the pencil in her fist, pressing it in with her thumb. She pulled out her personal phone with her other hand and turned it on. As the attacker approached, she pushed a book through the shelf. The book on the other side hit the floor. The man lurched in that direction, and she grabbed him from behind, jamming the pencil into his eye socket. He fell limp to the floor. She picked up the MP5 and turned to fire.

"Don't do it," the other man said. He was holding Frank as a human shield with the MP5 pressed into his cheek.

"Shoot," Frank said.

She couldn't. Not only was he an elderly veteran, Frank was the only one who could break the code. Killing him would be the end of it for them all. She remembered her Survival, Evasion, Resistance, and Escape training. She'd *act* like a model prisoner. She let the MP5 go limp in her hand and dropped it to the ground. Frank looked angry, but *he* didn't know her plan.

CHAPTER 38

IKE SAT WITH his back against the silver door of the safe room gathering his senses. His body felt stiff and unresponsive. Despite every effort on his part, he couldn't clear his head. In the thick morass circulating in his mind, images of Amelia and Frank, bound and in trouble, floated past. He knew he needed to act—now. Slowly, his mind was getting traction, but the pace was too slow. The room appeared to be moving and everything was coated with a thin white haze. All the product of the concussion. His vision began to clear, and he took in the room. It looked like an oversized elevator car. A large digital screen covered the back wall. Eight squares, each containing a rotating wheel, filled the display. To the right, he spotted Dominic at a small digital display mounted on the wall.

Dominic looked back at Ike, panic in his eyes. "I rebooted the cameras. That should clear them, but it will take a minute or two."

Dominic lifted his hand and readied to push a button on the control panel. "I'm going to release the knockout gas. That'll stop them."

It took a second, but Ike's mind flashed a warning. "No. Stop."

Dominic pulled his finger an inch away from the display. "Don't worry. It's a new generation of knockout gas."

"Don't do it," Ike said, ignoring the pain and struggling to his feet. "It might kill Frank. I'm sure they didn't test it on ninety-seven-year-olds."

Dominic pulled his hand away from the panel.

Ike listened through the door as he regained his balance. The gunfire had stopped. He guessed they were in the house. He wondered about Amelia and Frank.

"I gotta get back out there." He reached for his Glock, but it was gone, and that realization hollowed him out.

"You looking for this?" Dominic held up Ike's gun and a new magazine.

Ike wobbled over and took it. He reloaded the weapon and cocked it. Then he heard a click against the door. "Get back," he yelled, shielding Dominic. A loud thud shook the room, but the door didn't budge.

"Told you," Dominic said. "They can't blow it open."

A crescendo of rapid-fire thuds came from the door. Ike knew someone was showing their frustration by emptying their magazine into the thick steel. Ike remembered the box Frank had slid to him and glanced at it sitting in the corner. They couldn't get to it. And that was good. But they wouldn't necessarily leave empty-handed. Unless they died in the attack, they had Amelia and Frank. And Ike was certain they'd use them as currency to trade for the only thing they wanted. But even the thought of the possibility of their deaths saddened him. He pushed that image from his mind and convinced himself they would be kept alive—for now.

Just then, the back screen came to life. One by one, the eight cameras went to their live feed. It was just in time to see a black Lincoln Navigator, much like the Stallion, pull away and through the broken gate, turning left at the end of the drive.

"Open it," Ike said.

"Are you sure? There could be more of them," Dominic said, his body quivering.

Ike stepped to the door and pointed his gun at it. "Open it."

The hum of the motor was followed by the short hiss of the seal breaking. The door slowly rolled open. The scent of motor oil filled the air.

"What's that smell?" Dominic said, still far back in the safe room. Ike quickly cleared the area through his gunsight. "C4. Close the door until I get back."

As the door rolled shut, Ike worked his way through the debris from the failed attempt to breach the door. He cleared the short hallway to the foyer, then stopped before entering. He felt a light breeze from the opening that was once the front door. Listening, he heard nothing but the wind and a few chirping birds. He could see the Stallion parked just outside, its front run-flat tire shredded. There'd be no chasing them. He moved quickly over the rubbly marble floor crunching under his feet. In seconds, he'd cleared the hallway. He stood at the shattered library doors, gun raised, his stomach twisting as he imagined the overwhelming firepower that had done the damage. Amelia hadn't stood a chance. He braced himself to find their bodies inside.

There was no damage inside the library. He assumed Amelia had recognized the futility of a battle and surrendered, probably for Frank's sake. But Ike believed she wouldn't surrender unless she had a plan. He wished he knew what that was.

He moved quickly past the desk and saw the cracks in the unbroken window. Reading the etching in the lower-right corner, he knew why Amelia had failed to escape. Dominic had used the same bullet-resistant glass Ike had installed at Rossi's during last year's rebuild. It stopped most gunfire and break-ins, but it trapped the occupants inside. He targeted the stacks next, row by row, until he reached the last one. He lowered his gun. There, on the floor, he saw the blood. A lot of blood. This was a wound that was probably fatal. For a split second, his gut twisted again. But there was no body. He noticed the broken stub of the eraser end of a pencil and a book in the center of the pool. He examined the floor, then the adjacent bookshelf. One was in backward, pages facing him instead of the spine. Carefully examining the shelf, he spotted the open shelf space on the other side where someone had pushed a book through. Relief swept over him when he visualized Amelia creating a distraction and killing an attacker with the pencil. If it was Amelia's blood, she most likely would have been shot and her body left behind.

Moving to the other side of the shelf, he found the vacant space between two thick trade paperback books. The one on the right had an image of a pencil on the spine. *Thinking, Fast and Slow* was the title. Looking closer, Ike noticed hurried writing, in light pencil, along the spine.

3 atkrs

1 dwn

√ UR Phn

Ike pulled the book from the shelf and sprinted back to the safe room. The door was open, and Dominic and the front gate guard were inside. The guard was rubbing the back of his head and apologizing to Dominic.

"They disabled the cameras and the security system. No call went out. I'm sorry, boss."

"That's not necessary, Derek," Dominic said as he moved behind Derek and checked his scalp. "How's your head?"

"I'll be fine."

They both turned to see Ike standing with the book in his hand. He held it up.

"Amelia left a message. There were three of them. She took one out. They took the body with them. She and Frank are alive."

"How do you know that?"

"No bodies. They'd have no reason to take them. Just one of their own."

Ike tossed the book into the corner. "How long would it take to get that teleprinter?"

Apparently, surprised by the information, Dominic raised his eyebrows and raised both hands out to his sides. "Uh, I'd say as long as it takes us to get to CMU. But we'd have to get approvals and get someone to unlock the lab. It usually takes a day or two."

Ike went to the box and pulled out the Nazi strongbox and Frank's tablet. "Too long. We'll break in. If your security is all right, let's get going." Ike headed out the door.

"I'll be fine. Go," Derek said.

Dominic caught up. "What are you going to do with the teleprinter?"

"Save Amelia and Frank. We'll have to take one of your cars. And we have to get there fast," Ike said as they sprinted out of what was once the front door. Dominic froze when he spotted the disabled Stallion. Ike kept running toward the twelve-car garage, then stopped.

Out of breath with one hand on his knee, Dominic caught up, pulled out his phone, and tapped the screen. The second door rolled open.

In between his heaving breaths, he said, "This will get us there fast."

Ike couldn't believe his eyes. It was a '69 burnt orange Plymouth Barracuda Hemi in mint condition. He remembered Danny saying fewer than four hundred were made.

"I'll drive." Ike headed for the driver's side door.

"The keys are in it," Dominic said as he reached for the passenger's side door.

They got in and Ike fired it up. The car rumbled and vibrated, then smoothed out. Ike shoved it into first, floored it, and with tires screeching on the painted floor, headed out of the garage. "We have to make one stop first."

"Where's that?" Dominic asked, bracing himself with his hand on the dash.

"Rossi's."

CHAPTER 39

AMELIA WORKED HER wrists against the thick zip-tie handcuffs pinning her arms behind her. The seatbelt bound her to the second-row captain's chair of the Lincoln Navigator and limited her movement. Sticky duct tape sealed her mouth, forcing her to breathe through her nose. Despite her quick surrender to the two goons in the front seats, she was determined to end them. These were most likely the killers who murdered her aunt and uncle just three days earlier. Anger bled from her pores, as her carefully controlled breaths, drawn through her nose, channeled that energy deep inside where she could use it when the opportunity presented itself.

The thick tinted windows made it look like nightfall outside, but she knew it was just past noon. Their captors had removed their balaclava masks, probably so they wouldn't draw the attention of passing motorists. The driver had a shaved head, his brown skin glistening in the sunlight coming in through the windshield. His passenger had thick red hair and a stubbled beard. They were moving fast along a wooded two-lane road. Not fast enough to draw the attention of the passing traffic, but fast enough to make her wonder if Ike could get to his phone in time. She'd stuffed her phone inside the dead man's vest when he fell. They'd executed a thorough search of her body before she entered the SUV but left his alone. She could smell the stale butcher store scent of death coming from the back. She knew at some point they'd arrive at their destination or stop to dispose of the body. Either way, the phone would most likely be separated from her location or be discovered and disabled and she'd lose the one advantage she had.

Frank sat next to her, his head resting against the seat. His face was haggard and drawn, probably the result of his lack of sleep, smoke inhalation, and the physical demands of the battle he'd just fought. She saw his chest heaving as he struggled to breathe through his nose. His eyes were open, and he rolled his head to face her. He still had the fire of a warrior in his eyes. She'd seen it in others throughout her time in the Air Force, and those who had it had never let her down. She gave him a confident nod. He appeared unimpressed and returned to staring at the ceiling.

If it weren't for Frank, she would try to take out her aunt's and uncle's killers right here. But Frank held the key to breaking the coded message that could reveal the people pulling the strings. People, perhaps, in the US government. These were just their pawns, and killing them, risking Frank's life, would not allow her to live up to the enlistment oath she'd taken to uphold the Constitution against all enemies, foreign and domestic, and to obey the orders of the president of the United States. But at some point, she'd want to eliminate these mercenaries. It would come down to them or her. She knew their MO. They'd use Frank and her as bait to attain what they really wanted. Then, if they could, they'd kill them all. But dying had never scared her. She wondered about how her sister felt at the end of her life. To drown in the Mediterranean one hundred yards offshore with dozens of witnesses standing on the beach of the Italian resort had to have been terrifying. Amelia was certain her end, if it came to that, would be more violent but much quicker if she had anything to do with it.

The SUV slowed, and they took a right past a mailbox shaped like a farmhouse with white siding and a black roof. Black numbers hung below the mailbox: 403. The thick woods hugged the one-lane drive. She'd wished they'd blindfolded them, but their captors seemed to not care. That meant they'd planned to kill them no matter what. As they cleared the woods, she spotted a large farmhouse that looked like the mailbox. Clusters of trees and shrubs hugged the farmhouse and made it seem like the owners took great pride in their home. A small, circled drive split off the main driveway that continued to the large white barn about fifty yards away. The structures were surrounded by tree-lined fields and green pastures that covered the gently rolling hills and portrayed a dreamlike fantasy of life on a farm. The acreage ended in thicker forest displaying the bright colors of mid-fall.

As they approached the barn and slowed down, she knew that this Norman Rockwell setting was intended to be her grave. She wouldn't let that happen. When the situation presented itself, she'd do what she could to make these men pay. The SUV stopped and the merc on the passenger's side got out and opened the barn door. The other man pulled the Lincoln inside, then the other closed the door. The inside of the barn was pristine. Concrete floor, lacquered wood framed stalls, and no sign of any livestock, equipment, or feed. She'd guessed this was either an established safe house or a city slicker vacation rental. The trip had only taken around fifteen minutes, not nearly enough time for Ike to get to his personal phone. His burner didn't have the features of his iPhone. She wished it had. She needed more time.

As the driver got out, Frank raised his head from the headrest and looked at Amelia. He nodded slowly indicating he was on board with whatever she had planned. Redbeard appeared at her door and opened it. He pressed the barrel of his MP5 to her chest and leaned in to release her seatbelt.

"Don't move, sweetheart," he said.

It was just the right thing to say to her. Her blood boiled. The last man to call her *sweetheart* got a broken arm. Skinhead opened Frank's door and Redbeard glanced at him. In that moment, Amelia drove her knee up, knocking the barrel away from her chest and catching Redbeard under the chin. She braced herself for what would come next. It was going to hurt but it would buy precious time. Redbeard recoiled, shook his head, then drove the butt end of his rifle into her jaw. For a split second, the right side of her face exploded with pain. Then she blacked out.

***

Amelia awakened with someone gently tapping her foot. Disoriented with an aching jaw, she felt the cold concrete on her face. As her blurred vision came into focus, she saw Frank sitting against a beautifully finished stable door. He was tapping her foot with his while watching someone to his left. She pressed herself up and, still seated on the cold floor, rested her back against the stable door. With his mouth still taped, Frank peered at her as if to say, *Are you okay?*

Amelia nodded. Her ploy had worked, but she had no idea how long she'd been out. She'd guessed she'd needed at least fifteen more minutes for Ike to reach Rossi's. She leaned forward, looked around Frank, and saw both men checking their equipment. Redbeard immediately saw her and stopped.

"Sleeping Beauty is up," he said as he stood and moved toward them. Skinhead followed him. When he reached her, he bent down and yanked her up by her arm. "Let's go." He clearly was not happy. Skinhead silently pulled Frank to his feet and led them past the SUV toward the door beside the large barn doors. As they passed the SUV, Amelia looked into it through the open tailgate. She stopped midstride and choked off a gasp. The body was already gone. The adrenaline, the bad kind, sent her insides into a spiral. She'd bought less time than she thought. Redbeard must have noticed. He shoved her forward and placed the rifle at the back of her head. "Get going."

Frank was ahead of her and looked back. She was sure he saw the disappointment in her eyes. He turned back toward the house and kept walking. If Ike hadn't made it in time, she knew they were on their own. They'd lost the element of surprise. The people behind this, whoever they were, now had full control. They'd set up the exchange on their terms and Amelia and Frank, along with Ike, would be dead immediately after. This would now come down to her and Frank against these two trained killers. It saddened her to think of Frank dying. She'd do anything to not let that happen, including giving her life for his. If she died, she'd only have one regret: that she died alone, just like Harper. She'd never get to live the lives of the characters in her fantasy world she'd built around the treasures she'd found under the deep black sea. At least she'd die for a patriot. That was all she could ask for now.

CHAPTER 40

IKE SWUNG THE Barracuda into the parking space behind Rossi's and checked his watch. Thanks to the 'Cuda's 426-cubic-inch Hemi and Dominic's state-of-the-art radar detector, they made the forty-minute drive in twenty-four minutes. He wasn't sure that was fast enough, but he'd decided not to risk calling Randy and asking him to check his iPhone. It would have saved the drive in, but he was certain the FBI was nearby and maybe monitoring calls. No telling who else was too. He needed the element of surprise for his plan to work, and the call might have tipped someone off. Propelled by his determination to get Frank and Amelia back, he threw open the door, launched himself from the seat, and headed to Rossi's back door. Dominic followed behind him, carrying the strongbox. Ike barreled down the hallway, squeezing past Maria.

"Sorry, Sis."

Startled, she yelled, "What's wrong?"

"I'll tell you in a second," Ike replied as he burst through the doors and up the stairs, two at a time. He reached his office, ran to his desk, and grabbed his iPhone that was charging on the blotter. He opened the Find My app and selected Amelia's name. Quickly, the map appeared showing her location: 403 Harriet Creek Lane. It wasn't far from Dominic's, and when he switched to satellite view, it looked like a secluded farmhouse. He knew Amelia or Frank didn't have the phone on them when they left the house. They would have been searched. That meant Amelia planted it on one of the attackers, probably the dead one. He tossed the phone back on the desk and raced back down the stairs. Maria was waiting with Dominic.

"Who's this?" she asked.

"Dominic, this is my sister, Maria. Maria, this is Dominic. He's helping me with something."

Ignoring Dominic, she moved in front of Ike. "What's going on?"

Ike could see the worry in her eyes. "They have Amelia and Frank."

"Who does?"

"I don't know. But I know where they are."

"Call the police," she insisted.

"Can't. Where's Randy?"

"I don't like this."

"Me neither, Sis. This is on me. I gotta get them."

Ike could see tears filling his sister's eyes.

"I knew this was a bad idea," she said.

He took a couple of steps into the hallway to the door into Rossi's and pushed it open. "You can hang out here for now, Dominic."

"I'm going with you," Dominic said.

"No. You stay here and see if you can get that teleprinter. Or just a printed tape. It has to be that five-bit Baudot code, though."

"What should it say?"

"Doesn't matter. Just make it as long as the other message. We may need it as a backup. And secure that thing in the safe. Randy can help you."

"Okay. Got it."

"And don't let anyone follow you."

Randy was at the bar talking with Jenny, one of the servers. Ike calmed himself so as to not raise suspicion. "Randy. You got a second?"

Randy threw a nod in Ike's direction and excused himself from his conversation.

"Ike!" Maria was now crying.

Ike turned to her, reaching out to comfort her. "What is it?"

"I can't go on if you get killed. You and I are all we have now."

"I know. But I'm right here. I'll be fine."

"But what if you're not? You said you wouldn't do this again."

"I didn't have a choice."

Randy came through the door. "What's up, boss?"

Ike turned away from Maria. "I need to get a message to Vinny or Danny. Can't have anyone else access it."

Ike turned to see Maria walking up the stairs. "Maria," he called.

She ignored him.

He turned back to Randy, who said, "The best way to do that is with a written note hand delivered. No calls, no text, no trail."

"Can you do that for me? It's gotta get there fast."

"No problem. I can get it there right now. What is it?"

Ike went into Rossi's and pulled a pad and pen from next to the phone. He wrote the message and handed it to Randy. Ike pointed his thumb at Dominic. "I need you to help Dominic here, too."

"Got it." He held up the note. "It will be there in five minutes." Randy folded the message and headed toward the kitchen. "I'll be back in a second, Dominic," Randy said over his shoulder.

Just then, the phone behind the bar rang. Jenny answered it. She held up the receiver. "It's for you, Ike."

Ike stepped to the bar and took the phone from Jenny. "Thanks, Jenny." Jenny went to the other end of the bar.

"Rossi," he said.

"If you want to see them again, bring what you have to the entrance of the old Carrie Blast Furnaces at midnight." The caller hung up.

Ike pulled the phone away from his ear and hung it up.

"Who was that?" Dominic asked.

He put his hand on Dominic's shoulder. "Just get that teleprinter tape. I gotta go."

Ike walked into the kitchen. Denny, a giant nineteen-year-old who lived just six blocks away, was standing at the steaming industrial dishwasher. He had a faded yellow Pirates ballcap on backward and Ike spotted his denim shirt hanging on the hook on the back wall.

"Hey, Denny. I need to borrow your hat, your shirt, and your bike."

Denny eyed Ike, then his shirt on the hook. He shrugged. "Sure Ike." He gave Ike the combination for the bike lock.

"Thanks, man. Grab one of the hats from the merch closet. I'll get all this back to you."

Denny pulled off his cap and pulled his shoulders back. "You need me to help?"

Ike took the hat, hiding a smile at the offer. "No. This is more than enough. Thanks again."

Fifteen minutes later, Ike was headed out Rossi's back door with the cap pulled down to the aviator sunglasses covering his eyes. His jeans matched the faded blue denim Denny had on, his black, long-sleeve t-shirt covered by Denny's thick denim shirt. The heavy scent of cheap cologne assaulted his nose and made his eyes water. He tried to remember what it was like to be nineteen, but all he could remember from his nineteenth year was his parents' murders. As he thumbed the wheels on the bike lock, he swept the alley with his eyes. While he didn't see anyone, his skin tingled as if an audience stared at him. He wasn't sure if the uneasiness swirling in the pit of his stomach was caused by that or by the urgent need to peel Frank and Amelia from the grip of those mercenaries. He shook off the sensation, hopped on the bike, and rode the six blocks to Denny's house. After chaining the bike to the railing on the steps from the driveway, he walked around behind the house and cut through the yards to the next block.

Reaching the sidewalk, he looked left, then right, hoping his note reached the brothers in time. There was no time to waste. He spotted the old Nova immediately. Rusted light blue with gray primer doors and no hubcaps, it stood out among the cars parked on the street that were easily forty years newer. As he walked down the sidewalk to the Nova, he scanned both sides of the street. It was after one in the afternoon on a Monday. The neighbors' day jobs along with the overcast and threat of rain had the street deserted. Reaching the car, he grabbed the keys from atop the right rear wheel. Unlocking the door, he opened it, cringing at the metal-on-metal groan. He slipped into the car, noticed the black windbreaker and black ball cap on the passenger's seat, and started it. He made his way north, painfully hugging the speed limit. He'd passed through Cranberry forty-two minutes later. The paved parking lots and brick buildings quickly gave way to thick trees, lining the road and flaunting their bright fall colors. A light drizzle had started, and the Nova's wipers streaked the windshield.

In four minutes, he was on Harriet Creek Lane. The road was tree-lined and had a narrow shoulder. Ike passed very few mailboxes, the huge distance between them indicating the size of the small number of farms that remained in the area. When he reached 402, he began to search for a turnout. Ahead on the right, he spotted a small indentation in the tree line, adjacent to a creosote power pole. He pulled in and shut off the engine. He could see the white-and-black mailbox at 403 up ahead. There was no indication anyone was at the entrance.

After waiting for a car to pass by, he took off Denny's hat and shirt and slipped into the windbreaker and dark cap. He opened the door slowly, and it groaned again like an old man with arthritis. He went to the front of the car, opened the hood, pulled a wire loose from the distributor, and closed the hood. Everyone would expect this wreck to have broken down. With one last check of the road, both ways, he ducked into the woods. The trees dripped as the drizzle accumulated on their leaves then dropped to the forest floor. Ike zipped the windbreaker up to cover his neck. With each step through the damp woods, the fire, fed by his determination and anger, grew inside him. He'd get his friend and his client, no matter what it took.

When he reached the edge of the tree line on the other side, he crouched down with a clear view of the farmhouse. The were no lights on inside, and the house and the barn beyond it stood quietly. His phone didn't have enough detail to know whether they were being held in the barn or the house, but his plan had taken that into account. He wasn't worried about his plan. He was worried about Frank and Amelia. He had to assume they were still alive based on the call arranging the exchange. But as tough as Frank was, he was nearing one hundred years old, and Ike wasn't sure how much his failing body could take.

He knew he had to wait for the cover of darkness. Everything depended on that. Still, waiting for that tactical advantage battled against the eruptive force mounting inside him. He had to get Frank and Amelia before those behind this could kill them all. Dragging a fallen log into position, he sat with a concealed view of the house and barn, checked his Glock, and waited for dusk. It would be a long wait.

CHAPTER 41

AMELIA KNEW THEY needed to be ready, whether Ike had discovered their location or not, because if they weren't, she and Frank would die today. Amelia sat on the creaky maple kitchen chair. The smell of damp dirt and clay clogged her nostrils. In the dim light provided by a single light bulb dangling from its wire at the base of the ancient wooden stairs, she could see Frank across the room. Anchored to another chair, he was facing her but searching the room with his piercing eyes. She'd examined every wall and corner and concluded that there were no clear options for escape. The heavy door at the top of the stairs had been dead-bolted by their captors after dragging them into this windowless cellar. The crude, lime rocks cemented together to build the walls showed signs of leaching but no signs of failure. They were bound and trapped below ground in this tomb with no way out.

She'd played the role of the perfect prisoner, other than agitating Redbeard to knock her out to buy time. She'd seen their type before when she had rotated through a forward base in the Helmand Province in Afghanistan as a Launch and Recovery Element Reaper pilot. They were contractors. Hired killers and some of them she'd encountered were first-class misogynists. These two were cut from that same cloth. She'd decided early that warped perspective would be their weakness: underestimating her abilities. That element of surprise might just save them. She only needed an opening.

Above her, she heard footsteps. Two pairs moving slowly towards the door. The clunk of the tumblers in the dead bolt made her heart accelerate, but despite the tape still covering her mouth, she breathed deep to slow it down. Redbeard came first, followed by Baldy. They both had sidearms, holstered under their arms. When they reached the cellar floor, Baldy checked his phone, read something, and stuffed it back in his pocket. Redbeard made his way to Frank, while looking back at Amelia with a sickening grin. When he turned back to Frank, every muscle in her body burned with adrenaline. She was the reason Frank was here. She'd dragged him into this. He'd been an elderly icon of the community living out his last days in peace, until she came along. Yelling through the tape, she strained against the ties holding her arms behind her back. "Leave him alone!"

Redbeard slapped Frank with an open hand. Frank's head snapped to the right with the slap. Frank brought his head back slowly, his face already reddened. Redbeard hit him again. This time he knocked Frank over and into the dirt. Amelia yelled again, then stood with the chair caught in her wrists behind her. Suddenly someone grabbed her shoulders and shoved her back to the floor. She looked over her shoulder and saw Baldy directly behind her. She felt the barrel of his gun press against her neck.

"We'll get to you, honey."

Redbeard picked up Frank, still bound to the chair, and set him upright. Frank's nose was bleeding, and Amelia had no idea how much his body could take.

"Don't break any bones," Baldy said. "At least not yet."

Without turning back, Redbeard said, "I was just getting this old man's attention." He grabbed a corner of the tape covering Frank's mouth. "Let's see what he has to say." Redbeard ripped the tape from Frank's mouth.

Redbeard dropped down until he was face to face with Frank. "Okay, old man. You get one shot at this. What was in that strongbox?"

Frank stared at the man, defiant in his silence.

Redbeard slapped him again.

Again, Frank slowly moved his head upright. He spit blood on Redbeard's foot.

Amelia yelled and tried to stand again. While he was most likely a well-trained killer, she wanted to rip Redbeard's guts out. At least take a shot at it. She hated seeing Frank being dishonored. Baldy stepped in front of her, cocked the pistol, and pressed it against her forehead. "Enough!"

"It's okay, Amelia," Frank said, a calm confidence in his voice. "I'm just about done with him."

Enraged, Redbeard punched Frank in the jaw. Frank went limp and his head hung down, his chin on his chest.

"Great job," Baldy said, sarcastically.

Redbeard stuck his fingers on Frank's neck to check his pulse. Amelia held her breath. "He's still here." Redbeard turned back to Amelia and Baldy. "You're up."

Baldy pressed Amelia's head back with the gun. She hoped he wouldn't fire. She knew she was trade bait and was no good to them dead. At least for now. She wanted to tell Baldy to stick that gun up his ass. But Amelia had a role to play. She'd save that for later. Baldy ripped the tape from her mouth.

Her cheeks were on fire. "Please don't hurt me. I'll—I'll tell you."

"Then tell me," Baldy said, easing the gun's pressure on her forehead.

"It's some kind of a paper tape. That's all we know."

She forced herself to start crying, knowing these dipshits couldn't handle that.

"That's it?" Baldy asked.

Amelia just kept crying. Baldy turned back to Redbeard.

Redbeard kicked Frank's foot. "He's still out."

"I'll tell you where it is if you leave him alone."

The men shared a laugh.

"We know where it is. Rossi's. We just can't get in there. FBI has it under surveillance."

Baldy examined Amelia's face again. "I think that's what we need for now." He holstered the gun and started for the stairs.

"What about the tape?" Redbeard asked.

"We don't need it anymore. No one will hear them down here," Baldy said.

Redbeard shrugged and followed Baldy up the stairs. After they latched the door, Amelia scooted her chair to Frank.

"Frank. Frank!"

Frank opened one eye. "They gone?"

Amelia felt a wave of relief sweep over her. They'd underestimated Frank, too.

"Are you okay?" Amelia asked.

He ran his tongue along his lower teeth. "Other than losing that loose cap, I'm fine."

Blood had run down Frank's nose to his shirt.

"You don't look fine."

Frank grinned, showing the missing cap on his lower-right tooth. "Good." He sat up straight in the chair. "Now, can you get yourself out of that chair? Maybe get your arms in front of you?"

Amelia studied the thick legs of the chair. "I think so. It might make a little noise, though."

Frank looked up the stairs. "They won't hear it."

Amelia stood then waddled to the wall. She twisted, and with all of her might, she slammed the chair into the wall. She heard a crack but nothing gave way. She repeated the maneuver, this time letting her full weigh slam into the wall with the chair. The legs shattered and the seat separated from the back, and both fell into the dirt. She dropped to the ground and slipped her wrists underneath her, then under her legs and over her feet. She thanked God for her thirty-five-inch sleeve length and her Pilates instructor as she stood up.

"Okay. Come over here. Get one of my laces untied," Frank said.

Amelia walked over to Frank and studied his black boots. "Laces?"

"Kevlar." Frank gave Amelia a devilish grin. "It will cut through those nylon cuffs."

Amelia knelt, wrists bound together, and using her fingers unlaced one shoe.

Frank looked down and watched her finish. "Loop it around my other ankle and then tie it off."

Amelia left the lace looped through the top eye of the boot and tied it off around the opposite ankle.

Frank pulled the laces taut between his ankles. "Now saw the locking bar on the cuffs."

Amelia placed the thick white bar on the lace and moved it back and forth, keeping the pressure constant on each stroke. The lace began to cut through the nylon, the white residue accumulating on the lace then falling like snow into the dirt. Each stroke sounded like a nylon zipper being pulled up then down. She could smell the nylon heating up. Above them, she heard footsteps again. Looking up, she stopped and listened. It was only one set of footfalls, headed toward the door. Each step fed the fire growing in her gut.

She looked up at Frank, and he pulled the lace tight. She frantically sawed back and forth on the thick locking bar. With the chair shattered, she had no choice. She had to get the cuffs off before they came down and spotted her. She was about halfway through the locking bar when the footsteps reached the door. They stopped, but then kept going. She sawed the cuffs and pulled them apart at the same time. Finally, they snapped in half, and her hands were freed.

She untied the lace and yanked it from Frank's shoe. She went behind him and in less than a minute had cut through his locking bar.

Frank stood, wobbled a bit, then rubbed his wrists. "What now?"

"They're going to wait for the cover of darkness. That's what I'd do. If Ike got the message, he'd have to do the same thing. There's not enough cover between the woods and the farmhouse."

"They'll want to make a trade," he said.

"Then they'll kill us all." Amelia walked to the bottom of the wooden stairs. "The good news is they won't do it here. That means they'd have to take us to the site of the swap. I'm guessing we've been here for three hours. That puts us around five. Sun goes down around six-thirty." She scanned the room. Walking over to what was left of her chair, she picked up one leg, then broke off the support. "I think I can surprise them." She went to Frank and handed it to him. "You'll have to finish them."

Frank pounded the leg against his other hand. "My pleasure."

CHAPTER 42

IKE ANXIOUSLY EYED the farmhouse as darkness finally swallowed it up. For the past hour, an avalanche of guilt about what might be happening to Frank and Amelia had swept over him, burying him in pointless rumination that sent his blood pressure soaring. Deciding it served no purpose, he cleared his mind of the toxic debris and harnessed the energy to forge it into action. The bright fall colors were now dark shadows reaching out toward the house and barn, and he carefully plotted his pathway to each of them. Faint light suddenly appeared in the front windows of the farmhouse because someone turned it on or a timer had reached its programmed interval. His watch vibrated, and he turned the alarm off. He pulled back through the damp brush and headed for the car.

As he reached the old Nova, he spotted the flareside Ford pickup approaching. It pulled to the shoulder behind the Nova, gravel crunching under its wide tires, and the headlights went out. The truck had a gray-primer hood and a faded red paint job, probably from twenty years ago. Ike walked to the driver's door.

"Hey, Ikey boy. Got your message." Vinny said, his elbow resting on the open window frame. The truck smelled like a brewery. Ike looked over at Danny, who was chugging a sixteen-ounce Pabst Blue Ribbon. When he finished, he smiled at Ike and belched, tossing the empty can into the bed of the pickup through his open window without looking.

"I especially liked this part of the plan," Danny said then grinned, pulling another can from the twelve-pack at his feet and popping open the tab.

"Just don't overdo it. These guys are tough," Ike said.

Danny chugged the beer. When he finished, he said, "I get stronger with every ounce."

"He does, man," Vinny added.

Ike pulled out a folded piece of paper and opened it. "Here's the layout. The road in is here." He traced it with his finger. "The house here and the barn here."

Vinny eyed the paper. "Got it."

Ike folded the paper and stuffed it back in his pocket. "There was a light that turned on inside the house. I think they're in there. But I'll get to the barn first and check it. I'll signal you once I clear it. Do you have the Maglite?"

Danny opened the glove box and passed the flashlight to Vinny, who handed it to Ike.

Ike turned it on and off. "Good." He put it in his jacket pocket. "Once you get the signal, you're on. As soon as you're done, I'll go in."

Danny popped the top off one more beer. "Got it. It won't take long."

"You guys ready if they start shooting?"

Vinny grinned and lifted his sweatshirt, revealing his gun.

"All right. Here we go." Ike started toward the front of the truck to head back to the woods and stopped. He walked back to Vinny's window. "Thanks, guys. I owe you."

"You owe us nothing," Vinny said as he started the truck.

Ike headed into the woods, crossed the driveway, and stopped at the tree line behind the barn. After zipping up his jacket, he pulled out his Glock and crept toward the back of the barn. He hadn't noticed any cameras or windows in the back, just a large barn door. In seconds, he was leaning against the wall, sliding toward the door. Once there, he quietly listened. No noise came from inside. He carefully pulled on one of the large black door handles, easing the sliding door open, and looked in. He spotted the SUV that had been at Dominic's. It was dark inside, and the rest of the barn was empty.

Moving to the other side of the barn facing the drive, he pulled out the Maglite and gave one brief flash toward the road. Immediately, he heard the truck's radio blast "Hollywood Nights" by Bob Seger. The pickup's engine roared, gravel hit the fenders as the headlights appeared, and the truck rocketed down the driveway. Vinny was singing along, loudly, and Danny began to yell.

"Linda! Hey, Linda!"

The pickup swerved onto the cement circle in front of the house, its tires screeching to a stop.

"Linda!" Danny yelled, leaning out the window and holding a beer can like the Statue of Liberty. "Hey come on, Linda. Come out with us."

The door flew open and a man with a shaved head stepped out. He held a rifle at his side, a Doberman-like expression on his face.

Danny kept going. "Hey! Send Linda out, man."

The man stepped off the small porch and stopped halfway down the sidewalk. "There is no Linda here. Now get going."

"Awe, man. Don't be a jagoff. I know she lives here. Has for a long time." Danny held the beer can out the window again. "Hey. You want one?"

The man wagged his head. "There is no Linda here. Get going!"

Danny opened his door and fell to the ground, still holding the unopened beer. He stood up and sloppily brushed himself off. He held the beer in front of him and staggered toward the man. "Here, man."

Seeing the man's attention fully occupied, Ike dashed to the side of the house, staying low to avoid the windows. He moved around the far side and stopped at the front corner, about twenty feet from the front door. He ducked behind the bushes bordering the foundation.

When Danny was about ten feet from the man, the man lifted his rifle. "Stop right there." Ike's heart pounded in his throat.

Danny stopped, still holding the beer out. "What's wrong, man? You don't want a beer?"

"No. I want you to turn around, get in the truck, and get out of here."

"But Linda lives here, man." He stuck the beer out again and began to stumble forward. As he started to fall, the man lowered his rifle to catch him. Danny moved like a panther. Pouncing on the man, he took his legs out in one move and swung around behind him, quickly locking his thick arm around the man's neck, trapping him in a sleeper hold. The man dropped his gun and tried to yank Danny's arm from his throat. Flailing and gasping, he couldn't reach Danny.

Ike sprinted to the door. It was locked. Then he heard a burst of gunfire coming from inside the house. All he could think about was Frank and Amelia. Gritting his teeth, he pulled back and kicked in the door. Ike charged inside, his gun drawn and ready. He felt someone behind him. Glancing over his shoulder, he saw Vinny.

"Let's go."

The gunfire had stopped after a short burst. That meant either the shooter had been stopped or he'd hit his targets. As Ike moved forward through the living room toward a short hallway that led to the kitchen, Vinny moved to a different hallway that headed to the bedrooms at the back of the house. Halfway down the short hallway, Ike noticed a heavy wooden door. He guessed it was the cellar. He slipped past it and cleared the kitchen. Returning to the door, he pressed his ear against it. Nothing but his own pulse throbbing in his ears.

Reaching down, he made sure the dead bolt was open then grabbed the doorknob. Leading with his Glock, he eased the door open and looked inside. A single light dangled from a wire at the base of the stairs and swung back and forth, causing the shadows on the cellar floor to dance.

He pressed the door fully open, and someone behind the door grabbed his gun hand at the wrist and yanked him toward the stairs. Instinctively, he grabbed the door jamb with his free hand to anchor himself. At the same time, he dropped the Glock and twisted his gun hand around, grabbing his attacker's wrist, thrusting his shoulder forward, and turning to get leverage. Using the door jamb as an anchor, he dragged the person toward him and pinned him to the landing with his knee, face down. He recognized Amelia immediately. She continued to fight against his weight.

"Amelia. It's me. Ike." He eased his knee up and she relaxed. He helped her to her feet. She turned and hugged him. She seemed to catch herself and pulled back, surprise in her eyes.

"Where's the other one?" Ike asked.

She pointed down the stairs. Frank came into view holding the bloodied chair leg.

"He's done." Frank dropped the leg and plodded up the stairs.

"You okay?" Ike asked.

"A little bruised, but I'm okay," Frank said, brushing the clay from his clothes. "What about the other one?"

"I put him to bed." Danny said as he and Vinny appeared in the doorway.

Danny squeezed past Ike and hugged Amelia. "Nice to see you again, gorgeous."

"You smell like a kid after a kegger."

Danny smiled. "Part of the plan."

Amelia chuckled and wagged her head. "It's good to see you too, Danny."

"We gotta go. We're running out of time." Ike said as he picked up his Glock. "Grab what you can from here then we'll head back."

"Ike. They said the FBI is watching Rossi's," Amelia said as she brushed herself off. "And they know what we have. They know it's there."

Ike felt the seconds ticking away. If everyone knew what they had was at Rossi's, it wouldn't be long before they tried to take it. And Maria, Randy, and Dominic would be no match for whoever was behind this.

"We got this, Ike," Danny said. "You guys get to Rossi's."

Ike fist-bumped Danny. "Thanks again." He turned to Frank and Amelia. "Let's go. We've gotta break that code. Now."

CHAPTER 43

KARA REED WILLIAMS knew it was bad news before the words left Michael Knight's mouth. The one man with no official title in the White House who could fix anything had entered her office just after seven p.m. Standing before her, her desk lamp providing the only light in the office, his face took on a haunting glow. Unconstrained by the limits of the law, he'd taken care of the things that could have destroyed all that she had worked for. The president's habitual affairs, business transactions in their family oil firm that had drifted outside of the ethical lines drawn by the woke public, and potential witnesses bribed by the Department of Justice with sweeping pardons. All were neutralized, buried in a morass of misinformation, clever honey traps, and accidental deaths. But this could not be fixed.

"The Pittsburgh teams failed again," Knight said with no emotion, as if reading a headline from the sports page.

Unable to get details of the failure and demand accountability from the dolts that had failed, Kara focused the rage tearing through her body on Knight with her scorching stare. She knew she needed to be careful. Projecting the immense power she held by proxy and demonstrating total control of her emotions kept people like Knight in line. More important, maintaining deniability would be a key to her defense if it ever came to that.

"Can you achieve the objective? That's all I want to know."

"I can. But there's a problem," Knight said.

Kara dropped her head in disappointment. She forced herself to breathe normally despite the internal pressure suddenly growing in her chest. "Is it one I really need to know about?"

"Yes."

"Go on."

"The FBI is in the way."

"How so?"

"The item in question is at Rossi's restaurant. That target had been hardened last year. We'd have to go in loudly, but the FBI has the place under surveillance."

Kara leaned back and hissed out her disgust with Knight. She reminded herself of a core principle she'd drilled into her brother. *Believe your lies and they become the truth.*

"You're aware that this item is very important?" She didn't give Knight the opportunity to answer. "These people are a threat to national security. They are getting close and need to be dealt with, and this morning I had a meddlesome donor barge into my office asking questions that you don't want me to answer. You have to fix this. Now!"

"Benton Garcia won't be a threat. He's trapped by his need for power and money."

Kara leaned forward. "He asked about his daughter's death."

Knight remained stoic. "That's no problem. She's a star on the wall at Langley. End of story."

Kara eyed Knight for a few seconds. Knight didn't blink.

"She's gone along with anything she knew," he added.

"You'd better hope so." Kara stood, walked around her desk, and sat on the corner. "Don't worry about the FBI. I've taken care of that."

"So I can go in hard?" Knight asked, looking like an eager six-year-old.

"No. We have to find another way."

"What way is that?"

"Family ties."

"Family ties?"

"Just be ready to head to Charleston. I have to take care of a few things. Keep working the problem but don't share anything. Especially not with that nosy chief of staff Clark or the president. Only you and I need to know about this."

"Will do."

Knight turned and left the office. Kara remained seated on the corner of the desk. While she was still unsure about the severity of the threat, she knew even a ten percent chance of taking a bullet to the heart could kill a person if the odds went against them. Her mother had warned her to be aware and alert. The trip wires she'd planted throughout her brother's administration were made up of people indebted to them, and that line of defense had worked. The call from the Justice Department official was the first warning flare. It had cost him his life. Now, she wasn't simply protecting her family, she was defending democracy, the democracy they'd defined for the common citizen. Like a wolf in sheep's clothing, she knew ways to get into the hearts and minds of the unassuming American public—the people that had given them power. The secret she and her mother had shared wasn't just theirs, but it fell to them to guard against it ever seeing the light of day. She picked up the picture of their then-ninety-eight-year-old mother standing between her and her brother at the inauguration. She'd made her a promise fifty-three years ago, and she intended to keep it—no matter what it cost them.

CHAPTER 44

BENTON KNEW THIS would be a difficult conversation. Tess was a ticking time bomb, unpredictable and volatile, especially when Amelia was involved. His influence in the White House was fading, and he needed her support to maintain his standing in The Club to apply the pressure necessary to regain his leverage over Kara and the president. Tess held the controlling interest in Winkler Oil, and the board always followed her lead. Without Tess's support, he'd not only lose his job, but The Club would shun him into obscurity.

He exited the back seat of the Escalade and shut the door. The thick humid air condensed on his skin, a reminder that Kiawah could still feel tropical this time of year. The driver pulled around the circular drive and parked in his usual slot. Standing at the bottom of the stairs, Benton buttoned his suit coat and admired his beachfront home, glowing in the soft decorative lighting. He hoped to avoid Tess, but he spotted her eyeing him from the sidelight window to the left of the door. While the flight back from DC was rough, with thunderstorms turning the flight into a rollercoaster, he knew what was about to happen would be ten times rougher. He waved, pulled his shoulders back, then headed up the lighted stairway to Tess.

Opening the door, he did his best to smile, knowing it probably wouldn't matter. She had moved to the center of the foyer, carefully positioned directly below the twenty-thousand-dollar chandelier and on the rose compass embedded in the polished marble floor. The queen was demanding an audience. Her eyes were clear and locked on Benton. He could tell she hadn't been drinking. At least not yet. Her hands were in front of her, locked together by her interlaced fingers. Her posture had a lean to it, as if readying for a fight.

Benton walked over to her and kissed her cheek. "Good evening, dear."

"How was it?"

"The trip was a bit rough on the way back."

"I don't want the weather report. What did Kara say?"

There was no way to avoid it. He'd have to deal with her now. He sighed and centered himself. "I asked her why the FBI was asking questions of our family. She said it was because of Amelia."

Tess's eyes flashed wide open. "Amelia. What did she say about Amelia?"

Benton knew this was dangerous territory. Amelia was always a conundrum. One that held the potential for the mutual assured destruction of them both. They each held the key to the other's undoing, but for thirty-five years they'd lived up to their agreement. It hovered over them anytime Amelia came up in conversation. To Tess, she was a loving daughter who could do no wrong. To Benton, she was a problem. A thorn in his side, despite his efforts to help her. Ignoring his advice, she'd turned out to be the exact opposite of what he'd want in a daughter.

"Apparently she was the last one to speak with your brother before he died."

"Why is that a problem? She wasn't even here when they died."

"Immediately after they talked, Billy called the number-two guy in the Department of Justice. He was found dead later that night."

"They're connected?"

"That's what the FBI is trying to find out."

Tess's eyes roamed back and forth, searching Benton's face. Then, like a missile system finding its target, they locked on his.

"What did you do?"

"Nothing."

"What did you tell her?"

Benton found himself looking at the floor.

"Benton?"

Benton didn't want to speak. Mutually assured destruction. For him, that meant Tess pulling her support and the board would send him packing. Everything would be stripped away, and he'd be left with nothing.

"Tell me."

"Fine." Benton started pacing. "She asked me where Amelia was."

Tess cut him off and stepped in front of him. "And you told her?"

"I didn't have a choice."

Tess went limp and looked like she'd seen a ghost. "You know what they do to people."

"I didn't tell her anything she didn't already know."

"But you know what she's capable of. And Knight. Good God. You know firsthand what he can do. He destroys people." Tess turned her back to Benton and started to walk away. Then she stopped and faced him again. "Why Amelia?"

"What?"

"Why does she want Amelia?"

"She just said she was the last person to talk to Billy. She said she started the dominoes falling."

Tess's unfocused gaze roamed back and forth, searching the floor for a clue. "She must know something or have something. And why would Kara Williams be interested in that? It must be something that's a threat to her or their agenda." She suddenly looked up at Benton. "No!"

"What is it?"

"You're an asshole."

Tess pivoted and headed down the hallway toward the back of the house. Benton trotted behind her.

"What are you going to do?" he yelled.

Tess shouted over her shoulder but kept walking, "What I should have done a long time ago."

CHAPTER 45

IKE DROVE THE old Nova down Liberty Avenue. The stiff steering and the deep rumble vibrating the floorboards made him feel like he was in a time machine. The night had turned clear and cold, and the heater blasted dry, antifreeze-scented air into the passenger's compartment. He wondered how he'd survived his high school days. His eyes scoured the road ahead, powered by his determination to precisely execute the plan in his head and break the code.

As he approached Rossi's, he spotted the government car. Parked directly across the street from his restaurant, the FBI had given up on concealing their surveillance. There were two occupants in the black sedan. A warning tingled up his spine. The FBI never did anything without a purpose. This was either intimidation or protection, both of which were not good news.

"Our friends are being pretty obvious," Frank said from the passenger's seat as they drove past the car, turned off Liberty Avenue, and swung into the alley behind Rossi's. Ike studied Frank. Dried blood spotted his face and covered his shirt. Ike's heart fractured a little at the sight of the grey-haired neighborhood treasure bruised and beaten because of him. Somehow, he'd make them pay.

"FBI?" Amelia asked from the back seat.

"Yes, on both counts. We need to move quickly. Now that they've shown their hand, we won't have long," Ike answered.

"Why are they being so obvious?" Amelia asked.

"Either they're applying pressure on us or sending a signal to someone else. Someone who's a threat."

"They know about the mercenaries?"

"Maybe." Ike killed the engine, and they all headed into Rossi's.

It was just after nine, and the Monday night crowd was winding down. Ike was pleased to see the customers still inside. Their presence assured no one would try anything during business hours. Except, of course, the FBI. As he walked down the back hallway, Maria emerged from the restaurant and ran directly to him.

"I'm sorry about before," she said, hugging him. "I was being selfish." She pulled back, still looking at him. "You do what you have to."

A warm wave of gratitude washed over Ike. "Thanks, Sis. It's you and I together. Always will be as far as I'm concerned." They hugged again.

"Oh my God," Maria said when she spotted Frank and Amelia over Ike's shoulder. She released Ike. "Let me help you." She went to Frank and helped him down the hallway. "I'm taking them upstairs," Maria said, looking back at Ike. "Dominic is in the bar talking with Randy."

"I'll see you in a bit," Ike said. He headed through the doors and into the bar. Dominic was on the first stool at the end of the bar, leaning on his forearms and talking with Randy, who stood on the other side. Several tables were finishing as they watched the final inning of the National League Division Series game seven. Ike made sure they were out of earshot and took the stool next to Dominic.

"Dude. Did you get them? "Dominic said.

"We did. They're upstairs with Maria. Frank took a bit of a beating," Ike said.

"Frank? Is he okay?"

"I think so."

"That's one tough old man."

"More than you know."

Randy leaned closer, his elbows on the bar. "Did you see our friends?"

Ike nodded. "How long have they been there?"

"A few hours."

Ike turned back to Dominic. "You get what we needed?"

"Yes. I was able to get the teleprinter tape. I aged it with a little lemon and a light bulb. Looks just like the other one."

"Good."

"I also have the laptop loaded with the Lorenz simulator. We won't need to get online now whenever Frank gives me the coded message and the wheel settings."

"Great."

"Will he be able to finish?"

"Yeah. We have to." Ike threw a nod to the front window. "We're out of time." He stood and offered his fist to Randy. "Thanks for holding things together here, Randy."

Randy bumped it. "No problem, boss."

"Let's go upstairs," Ike said to Dominic. Dominic finished his beer. "Thanks, Randy." He followed Ike out of the bar and up the stairs to Ike's office.

Ike spotted his phone where he'd left it on his desk. He had one text message. It was from Jack. Ike thought back to the time he'd spent with Jack on Saturday morning and how much his life had changed in only three days. The message said: *Can you come over this Friday and throw a football with me?* Jack had touched his heart in so many ways. He never wanted to disappoint the twelve-year-old. Ike wanted to get back to that life.

He set the phone down when Frank walked into the room. He had on a clean black shirt, had replaced the lace on his boot, and moved without any sign of a limp. Other than the shiny red welt below his right eye, he looked much better. He had the pad of paper he'd been using to decode the message in one hand and the strongbox in the other.

Dominic walked to him and gently embraced him, then pulled back. "You okay, my friend?"

"I'm ready to go." Frank sat at one of the side chairs facing Ike, setting the pad and the box on the desk. "Okay if I work here?"

Ike offered his high-back desk chair. "You want to sit here?"

"No. I'm good." Frank flipped to a page half full of characters and opened the box. He pulled the teleprinter tape out, pulled on his gloves, and began his work.

Dominic took the seat next to him. "I've got the simulator ready."

Ike sat down in his chair. "I hate to ask after all you've been through, but how long before you're done?"

Frank looked up from his work. "Let's see. I've got to finish transposing the characters from the remainder of this tape, then I need time to get some clear text, text where I've broken the code, then extend that break far enough to get the wheel settings. I'd say somewhere between six and eight hours at the earliest."

Ike shifted his focus to Dominic. "How long for your part?"

"We'll have to feed the transposed characters from the message into the simulator manually, but after that, it should be a matter of minutes, if not seconds. An hour total—tops."

Ike knew that would have to do. But they didn't have that much time. He'd have to find a way to stall the FBI. "Any idea who might be behind this? That's what we really need."

Frank held up the teleprinter tape. "Without knowing what this says, it will be impossible to know or to make an educated guess." He carefully set it back on the corner of the desk. "We do have a few clues though. Like the fact that Hitler usually sent out five messages using five different couriers and routes. This was World War II, and many didn't make it to their destination. He had to be sure one got through. I suspect this one was thought to be lost forever when that sub was sunk. Someone may have directed the Navy to sink that specific U-boat to do just that, not knowing that the U-boat commander had tossed it into five thousand feet of water."

"But who was it?" Ike asked.

"You know that Hitler had to be sending a message to the president or someone in his cabinet," Frank said.

"So that would have been Truman?" Ike said.

"Yes. Roosevelt died April twelfth and he assumed office. Hitler died later that month on April thirtieth. The same day that U-boat was sunk."

"All those men are dead. Why would it matter what the message was now?" Dominic asked.

All three men looked at each other hoping one of them had an answer. They didn't.

"That's why we need to break this coded message. Whatever it says will answer that question," Ike said.

"I'll get after it," Frank said, as he picked up the teleprinter tape and his straight edge.

"I'll leave you to it," Dominic said as he stood. "I'm gonna put that decoy message together just in case."

"What decoy?" Frank asked.

"It's just a backup. In case we need it. A teleprinter tape that looks like that one." Ike said as he walked to the door.

As Ike and Dominic were leaving the office, Ike heard heavy footsteps running up the stairs.

In the hallway, they ran into Randy sucking in air to catch his breath. He had the bar phone in his hand. "It's—it's for you. Mia—with the FBI."

CHAPTER 46

AS IKE ENTERED Randy's empty office, holding the phone while closing the door with his foot, he noticed it suddenly felt warm. He unzipped his sweater and wrestled it over his head, tossing it on the desk. This would be a tough conversation. Regardless of what Mia wanted, he knew this was another step toward the end. The end of a dream he'd secretly held onto for years. One that had kept his loneliness at bay with the hopeful thoughts of mending their hearts and renewing the only love he'd ever felt. But this conversation required deception. He needed to buy time to break the code before the FBI surrounded Rossi's and took whatever they wanted by force. Dropping into the chair, he sucked in most of the air in the room, then let it out.

"Hi, Mia."

"Hey Ike. Just a heads up, this call is business, it's not personal."

"It's all personal to me." Ike surprised himself with his honesty.

"I know what you mean." There was a long pause. "Look, Ike, we need to meet."

"Why?"

"Because there are some things I need to tell you. I can't do it on the phone."

Ike was curious. "What kind of things?"

"Not on the phone. What I can tell you is if you don't cooperate, we will be forced to detain you and forcibly take whatever you have."

There it was. The end of their relationship. Prisoners of their obligations, neither could do or say what was in their hearts. At that moment, Ike decided he wouldn't let her see his sadness. While he felt raw and exposed, as if she could always see right through him, he knew that vulnerability would be the source of the courage he needed to face her head on. Mia had been The One. The only woman he'd truly loved. Now, for the second time, he'd intentionally deceive her. He was certain that would be their death knell. Lonely or not, he'd go on with an empty heart. He'd already done it for years. As long as he stayed busy, he could do it for a lifetime.

"Is that what you want?"

"It's my job, Ike," Mia said, protesting. She took a beat to gather herself. "This is worse than you can imagine."

"Believe me, I don't have to imagine."

"I know there are people after you."

"Who?"

"We don't know. But I can't protect you anymore."

"Protect me? From whom? You've done anything but that. You've been working against me and the truth that I've been seeking from the start."

"Ike, please. Just meet me. I'll tell you what I can. But you have to tell me what you're working on. That's the only way this goes. Otherwise, I'll have to arrest you."

Ike felt the last thread connecting them stretch tight, their tug of war about to snap it. "For what?"

"Obstruction, among other things."

Ike resented Mia's aggression. "So that's what we're reduced to?"

Mia hesitated before replying. Each second, two things happened. Ike's heart fell deeper into the abyss, and a speck of hope tried to pull it back out.

"I don't have a choice ..." Mia said, trailing off at the end.

Now Ike felt as if he were in an elevator in a freefall from the fiftieth floor. Loneliness, disconnection, sadness, and resentment: Ike pushed it all down into that corner of his heart that he rarely visited and locked his heartbreak away. They were distracting emotions he couldn't afford. Like the third rail in a subway, they could kill him if he touched them.

"What about the information on my mother?"

"I'm willing to exchange it for whatever you have."

Whatever was left between them had been transformed into a simple negotiation.

"All right, Agent Russo. Ten a.m. in Mellon Park. Take one of the benches facing the fountain. Come alone. If I see anyone else, it's off." Ike hung up, and disgusted with the mess this case had created, tossed the phone onto Randy's desk.

Turning around, he stared out onto the dark street and the FBI sedan sitting squarely in front of Rossi's. One thing Mia had always been with him was honest. But there was something in her voice. He knew there were things she couldn't tell him. That was part of her job. What nagged him was something different. Her words were saying one thing, but the way she'd said them almost begged him for help. Not with the case. With something else. The more he thought about the call, the more the sense grew that she needed help.

The phone rang again, snapping him out of his trance, and he immediately thought of Mia. Spinning back to face the desk, he snatched the phone and answered, hoping it was her.

"Rossi's"

"Mr. Rossi?" The voice wasn't Mia's. The woman's voice was older and even more pointed than Mia's. Then, it finally registered. "Mrs. Garcia," he said.

"I need to speak with Amelia. It's urgent." Tess Garcia's insistent tone was intensifying with every word.

"Mrs. Garcia, can I help with something?"

"It's Tess, and you know, Mr. Rossi, I know you mean well, and I actually like you, but this is between Amelia and me. Very urgent, very sensitive, and very private. So I need you to please get her on the phone."

Ike stood and headed for the door. "It's Ike, and the way this case is going, if it affects Amelia, it can affect us all."

"I'll leave that up to Amelia. If she feels she needs to share it with you, I'd appreciate your respect and discretion with the information."

Ike stopped, pulled the phone from his ear, and eyed it as if he were holding a venomous snake. He headed down the hall to find Amelia.

CHAPTER 47

AMELIA BRUSHED HER wet, blonde hair, examining her face in the mirror. The scent of Maria's lavender shampoo had replaced the thick heavy smell of clay and wet soil that had penetrated her nose in the farmhouse cellar. Maria had gently covered the bruises on Amelia's face with a few brushes from a makeup kit that looked like a tackle box. Inspecting her look in the mirror, she finished brushing her hair and laid the brush on the white quartz vanity. Dressed in her trademark black shirt and jeans, there wasn't much to inspect. If it was good enough for Steve Jobs, it was good enough for her. She smiled as she remembered Frank's prediction that in eight hours or less, they'd have the answers they needed to end this mess.

Maria had gone downstairs to help with closing. Amelia walked to the window and parted the blinds. The FBI was still parked across the street. That made her nervous. They were too close to have the feds screw up everything now. A knock on the apartment door drew her attention away from the window.

"Come in," she said.

Ike walked in with a phone in his hand. His eyes narrowed on her, his face expressionless, and his usually taut jaw slack. He almost appeared shocked.

"What's the matter?" she said as he approached with the phone.

"It's for you." He handed her the phone. "It's your mother." Ike stood there for a second, as if wanting to warn her, then left the apartment.

Amelia raised the phone to her ear, not knowing what to expect. It was after nine-thirty and by this time her mother was usually drunk.

"Mom?"

"Hi, sweetheart. Are you alone?" Her mother's words were crisp and clear. She wasn't drunk.

"Hi, Mom. What's wrong?"

Her mother took a while to answer. Amelia's mind filled every second with worst-case scenarios.

"I need you to come to Kiawah."

Amelia didn't anticipate that request.

"I can't right now. We're close to getting some answers. Plus, it would be too dangerous for you and Dad. Is everything okay? Is someone hurt? Is it something about Harper?"

Amelia heard a long sigh on the other end of the call. "You're in danger. More than you can imagine. I don't know what you're involved in, but you need to come here before you do anything else."

Amelia felt like she was back in high school, having her life dictated to her by her parents. But her mother was dead sober. This wasn't one of her fragmented conversations that always ended with her hanging up or walking out of the room in tears. "I just told you I can't." She switched the phone to her other ear. "Why do I need to come there? I can't just drop everything. Why can't you just tell me now?"

"Because this is the kind of thing that one would never tell her daughter over the phone. All you need to know is that your life and your future depend on it."

Her mother wasn't letting up. She was lucid, clear, and Amelia could hear the concern in her voice. Maybe her father or his asshole goon, McCallum, were causing problems. "Is Dad part of this?"

"Just promise me you'll come talk to me before you do anything. There are people after you that you want nothing to do with. I've made arrangements for a jet to be waiting for you at Falzone Energy's hangar at

Pittsburgh International tomorrow morning. After you hear me out, you can do what you wish. But believe me when I say you'll want to hear this."

Amelia knew she had to move fast. Whoever was trying to kill them had already demonstrated they wouldn't stop. She glanced at the window. The FBI was closing in and could stop them in their tracks any second. The only way to keep everyone she cared for alive was to solve the code and expose the perpetrators. Flying to Kiawah would delay them. She wasn't sure if her father could keep them safe—keep her safe. He never showed up for her in a big way. Why would he start now? As crazy as it sounded, with his connections in Washington, DC, he or McCallum could be part of this. But her mother had never sounded so concerned. Amelia believed her but would have to convince Ike that the time would be worth it.

"Amelia?"

"I'll do what I can."

"There's nothing more important …" Her mother's voice cracked and trailed off into a sob. "I love you."

"I love you too, Mom." Amelia ended the call.

CHAPTER 48

AMELIA EASED THROUGH the back door leading into the restaurant. Frank and Dominic were hard at work upstairs in Ike's office, but everyone else was in Rossi's. Randy was behind the bar, carefully lifting bottles and meticulously positioning their colorful labels facing out, noting the inventory of liquor on a small digital tablet in his hand. Ike and Maria floated from table to table around the restaurant like a brother and sister who'd known each other for a lifetime in what looked like a carefully choreographed dance, kidding and laughing as they cleaned the tables. The light scent of lemon and bleach filled the air, and the bright lights gave a sparkle to the richly stained wood and shining brass accents around the restaurant. Amelia imagined what it would be like to feel the close sense of belonging she saw between Ike and Maria. She hated the part of herself that was about to ruin their fun. Ike spotted her, said something to Maria, dropped his rag on a table, and walked over. He was still grinning when he reached her. He suddenly looked taller than six four. She girded herself by thinking about the warrior's ethos she'd learned in the Air Force.

"How'd it go?"

Amelia didn't know how to start, so she did what she usually did in that situation: just say it. "Not good."

"What is it?"

"We need to go to Kiawah."

The smile left Ike's face. "Kiawah? We can't."

"My mother said she had to tell me something before we did anything else."

Ike checked his watch, then locked his eyes on Amelia's. "Was she ..."

"Sober? Yes. Very clear-minded and insistent that I get there to hear what she had to say."

Ike wagged his head. "We can't do that." He pointed toward the front window. "They won't let us. If we try to go without dealing with them, they'll arrest us. Game over. They'll take what we have, and we'll be done. All of us."

Amelia raised her arms out to her side and shrugged. "Don't know what to tell you. She said my life depended on it. And I believed her."

Ike looked away and seemed to hesitate. She wondered what he was thinking. Maybe he was just so pissed he'd started counting to ten. When they'd first met, she thought he was just a washed-up jock who had to feed his ego. But the last three days had proved otherwise. He'd put everything on the line for this case. He'd earned her respect. She didn't want to alienate him, but she had to make her point.

"Look, Ike. She's sending a plane. It will be waiting at Falzone's hangar first thing in the morning."

Ike's eyes bored into her. "You know we have to break that code then figure out who is behind this and expose them. It's the only way this ends well for any of us. Any delay could be deadly."

"We can all go. Frank can keep working on the plane."

"That won't work. I have to meet with the FBI tomorrow or it's over."

"Meet with them?"

"Yes. I have to give them something to get them off our backs."

"What will you give them?"

"I can't say."

"Why not?"

"It's better if you don't know."

Amelia's heartrate shot up and her cheeks felt flush. She felt mansplained. "I'd like to be the judge of that." She looked up and saw Maria standing off to the side, hands on her hips, listening. Over her shoulder,

Amelia spotted Randy standing behind the bar, arms crossed, seeing how this battle would end. She was at a crossroads. Trust her mother and go to Kiawah—alienating Ike, risking her life and those of everyone here—or ignore her mother's warning. But there was something in her mother's voice that tugged at her. She believed her.

"Ike, please. I've never heard my mother like that. She knows something. Something we need."

Ike glanced at Maria, then at Randy. "I have to think about everyone here. We can't go."

Amelia decided to drop the hammer. "I'm the client. I say we go."

Ike pressed his lips together tightly. Amelia could see his jaw muscles flexing. He stepped within inches of her. "That's not how this works."

"What if you went after?" Maria's voice cut through the air like a song. Ike stared at her.

"Don't give me that look," Maria said smiling. "You remember what it was like when those cops stonewalled you about Mom and Dad's case? You were willing to do anything to get that information." Maria let that comment soak in.

"She's got a point," Randy said.

Amelia felt buoyed by their support.

Ike eyed Randy, then Maria. He dropped his head and hissed. He looked back up at Amelia, his face softened with understanding. "Okay. I do know what it's like to lose someone and not know why. You know your family better than anyone. You've sacrificed a lot for others, and you earned the right to have your request honored. We can go right after I take care of the FBI. But we can't stay at your parents or anyplace associated with your family. I'll see if Shannon Falzone can use one of their subsidiaries to get a place under an alias."

"Thank you, Ike."

"No need to thank me. You deserve an answer. What do you think your mother has?"

"I don't know. I can't imagine what it is. You know about my father's connection in Washington. Maybe it's something she overheard."

"What did she say to you?"

"She said she had something to tell me. She said she knew there were people after me. That I was in danger—more than I could imagine."

"That's a—"

Suddenly it sounded like a stampede coming down the back stairs. The door burst open, and Dominic and Frank shot into the restaurant. Frank held his yellow tablet and pencil in the air like a trophy. Dominic had his laptop under his arm. Both were out of breath.

"He did it," Dominic said, still huffing and puffing.

"Did what?" Ike asked.

"He got the first break in the code. You gotta see this."

Suddenly Amelia felt as if she was on a highwire in a tornado. It was the same feeling she'd had before the first time she had to kill a high-value target. With the code nearly broken, the pressure would be on to find out who was behind this, and what she'd heard in her mother's voice may have been just that.

Frank went to one of the cleaned tables and placed his tablet and a few papers in front of him. "Come look at this."

Amelia and Ike stood on either side of Frank, while Dominic watched the screen from behind. Frank pointed to a series of twenty-one characters of the code. It looked like gibberish. But beneath those characters was a simple but stunning line.

ADOLF9HITLER9FUEHRER9

Looking over Frank's head, Ike shot Amelia a look she'd never forget.

"The message was signed by Hitler. He signed most of the messages that way. That allowed me to break in here …"—Frank pointed to the last line of another piece of paper with a much longer series of characters on it—"… on the last line of the code."

"What's the rest of it say?" Amelia asked. She realized she was clenching her fists. She was getting closer to her uncle's killer.

"I have to take these twenty-one characters of clear text and extend the break-in backward about fifty characters or so. Once I get that, we'll have the settings and patterns for all twelve wheels."

Dominic held out his laptop. "Then all we need to do is run it through this Lorenz simulator and we'll have the message."

Both Amelia and Ike spoke at the same time. "How long?"

"I need to take a break. I'm spent. I can't break any more tonight. It's tedious work. I haven't slept much and that beating at the farmhouse really took it out of me. I'll only need a few hours of rest, then I can get back to this. All in, probably five or six hours after I'm refreshed."

"Can't you do it now?" As soon as the words left Amelia's mouth, she wanted to take them back.

Frank looked up at her, wearily.

"I'm sorry, Frank," she said.

"No need to be sorry. You've lost a lot here."

"Let's let Frank get some rest," Ike said. "I'll meet with the FBI and get them off our backs in the morning. Then we head to Kiawah while Frank breaks that code."

Frank gathered up his papers and headed upstairs. Dominic followed him.

"Hitler sent the message," Ike said, eyeing Amelia. "But what was it doing two hundred miles offshore at the bottom of the ocean? Frank said the U-boat that sank was eighty miles closer to shore."

Amelia felt exonerated and guilty at the same time. Her discovery had resulted in three murders. "Don't know," she said. "But if it was a message that the Germans didn't want anyone to see, maybe they dumped it in the ocean thinking it would be lost forever."

"If it came from Hitler, who was it going to? Had to be someone high up in the US government," Ike said. He looked around the room. "But that was seventy-eight years ago. What on earth could it be that would cause someone to risk killing the second in command in the Justice Department?"

Amelia went through what they'd discovered so far. "It was around the time of Hitler's death. Do you think it had something to do with that?"

"I don't know. The Russians were bearing down on him. He didn't want to be captured so he killed himself." She could see Ike's mind grinding through the facts. Then he paused.

"What? What is it?"

"It had to be a transaction: something Hitler wanted for something we wanted. That's the only thing that makes sense."

"Something that no one knows about? Even today?" Amelia said, thinking out loud. Every cell in her body was suddenly electrified. This was beginning to feel like the reason she was put on this earth. She didn't know what secrets the code held, but she was sure whatever it was could never be put back into that box again. A lump stuck in her throat when she told herself they'd find out tomorrow—along with another secret. One her mother had implied could kill her.

CHAPTER 49

KARA REED WILLIAMS knew this meeting would be a knife fight. Her network was sending up warning flares that this threat was very real. While she was unsure about the severity of the threat, she'd learned from her mother that if it ever came to light, it would be deadly to her family. Even a small chance of destroying everything they'd built was well worth avoiding. The fears they had manufactured, preying on the disenfranchised and disillusioned, had put her brother in the White House. The real truth could throw them out.

As she walked down the hallway past the vice president's office, she was happy to see he wasn't there. Probably working on one of the "high-profile" initiatives she'd carefully laid out to the president. While it had been difficult to fill that position, finding someone in the party who polled well with voters but whose political ambition dwarfed their intelligence had worked out well. He'd stayed out of their way.

Turning the corner, she stopped at the chief of staff's aide's desk in the small reception area just outside his office. As she looked into his office, the young aide raised her head and whispered that he'd already left for the meeting. Kara shook her head and smiled. The ambitious twenty-six-year-old former political science major and congressional intern now held the title of special assistant to the president, thanks to Kara. Once again,

Kara's network had paid off. She thanked the aide and headed toward the Oval Office.

Jackson Clark wasn't her idea for chief of staff, but her brother had insisted he was necessary to be the face of diversity in his administration. Clark was a Boy Scout who'd risen to partner in one of the largest hedge funds on Wall Street and had become one of her brother's favorite supporters. However, Clark viewed his role as preventing the president from making impulsive mistakes, which he was prone to do, by controlling what was placed in front of him for signature or decision. He'd set the meeting for eight-thirty and gone in early. She hadn't been invited, but she always knew her brother's schedule. The president had requested an update from FBI Director Welch this morning on the killing of Deputy Attorney General Cohen over the weekend. Both Welch and Jackson avoided her at every turn, but with her network of spies carefully placed throughout all branches of government, she was always in the know.

She slowed her pace as she walked down the beige carpeted hallway and admired the antique furniture topped by brass lamps with crisp dark-blue shades. Her brother would stall until she arrived, and her late arrival would signal to Welch and Jackson where the power in this place really resided.

When Kara entered the Oval Office, the president was still seated at his desk reading a single sheet of paper. Two tan sofas faced each other with the canyon between them filled by a small coffee table. With Welch occupying the middle of one sofa and Clark centered on the other, they looked as if they were about to engage in a high-stakes chess match. Both men scowled at her as she rounded the sitting area and stopped in front of the president.

Kara looked her brother in his eyes. "Sorry, Mr. President. I was detained by another pressing matter."

Taking the cue, the president stood. "Glad you could make this briefing." He guided her to the sitting area, and he took the armchair at one end of the sofas. Kara circled him. She stopped on his left but remained standing, her hand resting on the chairback.

"Bill. What do you have for me on that guy's death?"

Welch looked at the president then at Kara. He dropped his balding head and pulled some papers from the file sitting in his lap. His stocky build and wrinkled face made him look like a bulldog: one Kara needed to control.

"David Cohen," Welch replied, still looking at the paper.

"What?" the president asked.

"The man's name was David Cohen."

"Yes. Cohen. Go on."

"We have twenty agents working on this. So far, they've uncovered an anomaly in the car's on-board computer."

"Anomaly?"

"Yes. It appears someone hacked into the speed-control code for the cruise control. It caused the car to jump into cruise control at a high rate of speed, resulting in the loss of control and a fatal accident."

"How fast was he going?"

"One hundred and ten."

"Jesus. So someone killed him?"

"Yes. We're now internally calling it an assassination."

The words hit Kara hard. This was a problem.

Clark leaned over the coffee table. "Whoa, Director. Let's not call it that."

"Yes. Let's not call it that," The president said. "Suspects?"

"Mr. President, we think it was a professional. Someone obviously very well trained. We have a long list of domestic terrorist groups we're working through. Cyber is trying to trace the hack."

The president turned and looked up at Kara. "Can we use this?"

Kara knew she had to walk a fine line. She needed to give the president some information, but not enough to penetrate the veil of plausible deniability.

"We can put out a statement that says you've directed any and all resources to be put on solving this terrible crime."

"That's good." He turned back to Clark. "Do it." Clark made a note and then glanced at Kara, huffing in silent protest.

Welch pulled out another sheet of paper. "We do have another person of interest."

The president leaned forward with his hands folded in front of him. "Who's that?"

"A woman named Amelia Garcia."

That name sent a jolt through Kara that she tried to hide.

Her brother seemed stunned. "Garcia? Any relation to Benton?"

"Yes. It's his daughter."

"Oh Christ."

Something in the president's eyes triggered another tremor in Kara's body. There was something going on that she didn't know about.

The president stood. "How the hell is she involved?"

"We're not sure. She was the last one to speak to her uncle before he and his wife were killed, and her uncle was the last one to speak to Cohen before he died."

The president dropped back in his chair. "Oh shit. She's a suspect?"

"No, Mr. President. She was nowhere near the killings. She alibied out. But we think someone may be trying to get to her. Perhaps for what she knows."

"We need to get out in front of this. Let's discredit her in the media. Anything else that comes up, we'll call nothing but a political hit job. I'll send out a series of tweets about it and get Benton Garcia out of the picture. We have an election to think about."

Kara could see that Welch and Clark had noticed exactly what she had in her brother's overreactive demeaner.

"Mr. President," she said, placing her hand on her brother's shoulder. "I don't think Director Welch said she was a suspect." Despite what she'd said to Benton yesterday, they still needed his full support.

"Can you arrest her?" the president asked.

"Not at all," Welch said, his eyes widening at the question. "She is of interest in the investigation but not a suspect in the killings. She's committed no crimes as far as we know. I have one of our toughest agents taking the lead on that side of the investigation. We have eyes on them around the clock for now."

Welch was a pigheaded dolt as far as Kara was concerned, but he was doing her work for her by giving a convincing argument that Amelia Garcia was not a threat. At some point, she might need to advise her brother otherwise, but not now. It was better to leave her brother in the dark. If she didn't, he'd be like a dog with a bone. He wouldn't let the issue go until he destroyed her. He'd also lose plausible deniability. Instead, she needed him to focus on reelection. The political machine she'd built over their lifetimes was too valuable to risk now. The shame of being a one-term president would be too much for both of them. She pulled out her phone and sent a quick text.

Kara knew it was time to end this meeting. "Mr. President, I'd suggest you have Director Welch provide daily updates, more frequent if something comes up, and have Mr. Clark work with the press secretary on the press release."

"Good idea. Thank you, gentlemen." The president stood. As did Clark and Welch. In seconds, they were gone.

The president returned to his desk, but before he sat, he furrowed his brow and said, "I don't want that Garcia woman anywhere near here." His tone was terse and firm. "Now, I've got work to do."

He sat, ignoring Kara, who still stood in front of his desk. She hated being reminded that *he* was the president. She was the one who should be sitting behind that desk. He was too arrogant to realize she was the only reason he was there. She turned and left the office.

Michael Knight was waiting for her in her office. "Got your text."

She closed the door. "You have to stop them. Now."

"What exactly is it that they have? It would help to know what we're dealing with."

"You don't need to know." Kara walked past Knight to her desk and dropped into her chair. "You don't want to know. All you need to know is that they are a threat to national security." She looked out her window. "The director has the FBI protecting her. I know he does. He's loving this." She spun her chair back to face Knight. "It's time to play our trump card."

Knight put both hands on her desk, leaned closer, and whispered. "She's already in play."

CHAPTER 50

IKE WALKED UP Sixth Avenue wondering if this was the last time he'd see her. He checked his watch for the third time and noted it was five minutes to ten. He sensed this would be one of those moments in life he'd look back on and wonder about what could have been. While his goal was simple—deceive the FBI and buy some time—its execution required Ike to lie to Mia. Not only was it a crime, but it would also ensure he'd never see her again. Without that deception, they were done. The FBI would come in and take the coded teleprinter tape. Amelia, Ike, and those he cared about would be left to deal with whomever was trying to kill them on their own. As he trudged uphill toward Mellon Green, fighting a reluctance that felt like an invisible gale-force wind, he repeatedly convinced himself he had no choice.

He'd chosen to park on Fifth Avenue, walk to Sixth, and use the bustling traffic, both vehicular and pedestrian, as cover. In typical Pittsburgh fashion, the late-fall weather had turned warmer overnight. Dressed in jeans, a black t-shirt, and his favorite tweed sports coat, he broke into a sweat and wished he could take off the coat. But it covered the Glock on his belt. In his hand, he carried a small black duffel. Bright morning sunshine reflected off the windshields of the cars on Sixth Avenue and assaulted his eyes. He ignored the glare and kept his eyes moving, looking for any threat among the cars and pedestrians on the street. Buses chugged up Sixth, and the cacophony of city traffic competed with the occasional chatter from the few birds and pigeons perched on the rooftops and in the trees whose trunks were imprisoned in the concrete sidewalk. He felt as if he were walking through time when he passed the Duquesne Club. Its members included some of the wealthiest industrialists of the last century. The rugged stone structure opened in 1889, according to the historic landmark plaque, and he wondered how many titans of industry had made this same trek to clandestine meetings designed to crush their competition.

Looking ahead, he spotted the entrance to the Mellon Green. The modern park was an oasis in the concrete and cobblestone of downtown. This was where they'd met, years before, sharing countless lunches and the secrets of their lives until they'd fallen in love. Now, it was where they'd end whatever they had left for good. Half a block away, Ike heard Amelia say "All clear" in his earpiece. She'd volunteered to fly overwatch with her drone. Ike glanced up but couldn't see the small aircraft. Still, he felt better under her protection. Looking down a small alley, he spotted a pair of boots next to a red dumpster. No one was around to claim them, at least that he could see. He wondered what happened to their owner.

He reached Grant Street. While he waited at the crosswalk, he scoured the area for any sign of the FBI. Cars rumbled along the cobblestone street, but he saw no trace of the Feds.

"Still all clear," Amelia said in his ear.

Ike crossed the street and entered the small park. His pulse immediately jumped. It wasn't fear. It was an excitement he'd always felt when anticipating seeing Mia. But this time felt different. It was tempered by a nagging doubt about pulling off the con. She had known him better than anyone. He hoped the years apart had ground those memories down to nothing and with it, her ability to see right through him.

Moving up the leaf-covered aggregate-concrete walk, past the trimmed evergreen shrubs and the trees still holding on to their reddish-purple fall leaves, the noise of the city gave way to the sound of rushing water. Four stone columns spouted a thick stream of water that danced down the terraced fountain at the center of the small park. When Ike reached the circled walkway around the water feature, he spotted Mia sitting on one of the stone benches on the opposite side. A satchel sat beside her. Ike knew it might hold the answers he'd been seeking all along about his parents' deaths. Over the sound of the cascading water, he could hear his pounding heart. As hard as he tried, he couldn't stop the smile from forming on his face. As he got closer, she looked up. Despite the concern on her face, she still looked radiant, her red lips parted and her dark eyes narrowed on his.

"Still all clear," Amelia said.

Ike walked up, then sat next to her, placing the duffel on the bench between them. He leaned forward, grabbed the concrete edge of the bench with both hands, looked straight ahead at the fountain and battled the memories of the past.

"How are you doing?" she asked.

"I've been better," Ike said, still staring at the fountain.

"I know what you mean."

Ike couldn't resist any longer and turned to face her. She, too, stared ahead at the fountain. But there was something different. He could sense it. She lacked her usual glow and seemed weighed down by something. While their time together years ago was relatively short, their connection had been deeper than anything he'd felt with anyone else, before or after. Knowing what he had to do, sadness began to seep into his heart. He missed her already.

"Is that it?" she asked, looking down at the duffel.

Ike coldly buried his guilt. "It's in there. It's a teleprinter output from the bottom of the ocean."

"Anything else?"

"No. That's it."

Mia seemed surprised at first, but then looked at the duffel, gently pulled it to her, and settled back on the bench, apparently trusting him. Pulling her satchel closer, she fixed her gaze back on the fountain. It was done, but Ike hid his anguish with a smile.

"Your guys will back off now?" he said, forcing his best poker face.

"I'll pull the surveillance." She reached over and covered Ike's hand that was still gripping the edge of the concrete bench. "But be careful, Ike.

These people mean business. I'm not sure that you giving me this will shut them down."

"What about the information on my mother?"

She placed the satchel on her lap.

Ike noticed her lower lip trembling. "What is it, Mia? What aren't you telling me?"

Her gaze left the fountain and focused on their hands. "Ike, do you think we could try again after all this is over?" She raised her head and her eyes locked on his.

He hadn't even thought about that option. She probably wouldn't either when she discovered what he'd just done. But for now, his body suddenly felt light, as if free from gravity. The thought of a new relationship with the woman he was sure he could love freed him on so many levels. He hadn't considered that this case was fleeting, and that a fresh start waited on the other side.

He lifted her hand from the bench and held it in both of his. "I'd like that," he said, holding her hand and kissing it. "I'd like that very much."

Mia squeezed his hand. But Ike still sensed something holding her back. He heard a crackle in his earpiece.

"Sniper! Sniper! Get down, Ike!" Amelia yelled in his earpiece. Ike shoved Mia away, and the bench between them shattered.

"Sniper, Mia!" he yelled.

Mia grabbed the duffel and the satchel and dove for the cover of the fountain.

Ike pulled out his Glock and lunged forward too, seeking the cover of the tall stone columns. He hadn't heard the rifle fire. The sniper had a suppressor. He'd have to rely on Amelia.

"You got him, Amelia?"

Ike ducked when another shot hit one of the columns, spraying water and rock on both of them.

Mia, with shock on her face, said, "Who are you talking to?"

"Is this one of your guys?" Ike asked.

"No!"

"Are you sure?" Ike could see the doubt weigh down Mia's face.

"Ike. I have him on the second building down Sixth on the right, northeast corner." Amelia said.

Ike peeked around the columns and spotted a figure targeting them on the corner of the roof.

"Got him. I can't hit him from here."

"Ike. Who is that?" Mia asked again.

He pointed to the sky. "Amelia."

Two more shots hit two columns on Ike's side.

"I'll get him," Amelia said.

Ike peered around the fountain and saw the drone dive toward the shooter like an angry wasp.

Ike scrambled next to Mia. "She's got him occupied." He nodded toward the closest building to their right. "Let's get to that building."

Mia pulled out her phone. "I'm calling this in. You'd better get going. We'll take care of him."

"You don't have backup here?"

"No. I was doing this on my own."

Ike's body locked up for a second.

"Don't ask," she said as she turned and headed toward the building, leaving Ike behind.

Ike knew he had to go. Getting tied up in this mess wouldn't be good. He scrambled in the opposite direction, using the building across the street as cover and dodging traffic as he bolted across Grant Street. Once across, he stopped and looked back at Mia, who was hugging the building across the street, eyeing the rooftop, and talking into her phone. He was sure it was the last time he'd ever see her this way.

CHAPTER 51

IKE RENDEZVOUSED WITH Amelia outside the parking garage on Fifth Avenue. After checking the three lower floors for any sign of trouble, they climbed the stairs to the fourth floor, got into the Shelby, and headed out of the city. Ike was haunted by one question: Who was the sniper targeting? At that distance from an elevated position, the killer had a clear line of sight yet the first shot hit the small space between them. Not a likely outcome for even an average marksman. Like a bad dream, Mia's pensive demeanor and begging eyes cycled through his mind again and again, fueling a growing frustration. The reason behind those cues eluded Ike for now, but there was indeed something she was hiding.

When they cleared the Liberty Tunnels, Ike's ire burned away the adrenalin from the attack. He gripped the wheel tighter and tighter until his white knuckles ached. While his ploy bought them the time they needed, he'd been screwed out of the information on his mother, either by Mia or the sniper, and he didn't know why. During their entire encounter, she'd looked as if she'd swallowed all the troubles in the world and had refused to let them out. Years ago, Ike had learned to read her emotions, even though just like him, she kept them deep inside herself. Back then, her eyes usually gave her away. Today, her eyes had said *help me*. Ike was sure his read wasn't mistaken, but it was the reason behind her helpless silence that haunted him.

Amelia sat next to Ike, swapping out the battery pack in the drone and checking it for damage.

"Thanks for saving us back there," he said.

"You're welcome. That sniper is toast. They had the building surrounded even before I cleared the area."

"You're pretty good with that thing."

"I've had lots of practice. Although I had never given any target a haircut like that one," she said, sending Ike a sly grin. She finished with the drone and placed it in the back seat. She turned back and stared straight ahead. "It was weird, though. The sniper had longer hair. Could have been a man or a woman."

"A woman?" Ike hadn't considered that possibility.

Amelia shrugged. She turned and studied Ike. "You don't look happy. Did you do what you needed to with the FBI?"

"I think so." Ike decided to stay quiet about his mother's information for now. "We bought ourselves at least a day or so."

"Good. Glad I could be of help. You have an idea about who that shooter was working for?"

"I was just thinking about that. It's whoever is behind this mess."

She meticulously recounted what she saw from the drone for the balance of the short drive. Ike imagined it was muscle memory from the thousands of debriefings she'd given during her time piloting the Predator then the Reaper. Their discussion didn't solve the mystery of who the sniper could be, but they were on the same page. Break the code and get the answers.

The pre-lunch hour traffic was light, and they made it to the Falzone hangar in less than thirty minutes. Frank and Dominic were waiting inside, and they boarded the Citation X together. In minutes they were on their way to Kiawah. Frank and Dominic took the two seats facing each other farthest aft, and immediately after takeoff, they pulled out the table and continued their work. Ike and Amelia faced each other in opposing seats in the front of the cabin.

Amelia was gazing out the window, her face slack, and her eyes focused on some faraway place, not of this earth or time. Ike knew the look. It had been his twenty-three years ago. Amelia had lost the two people closest to her. Her father was an ass who never gave her the time of day. And her alcoholic mother had summoned her to receive a message that, according to her, was life-changing. Ike could sense her suffering behind her proud veneer, a silent burden buried inside. He didn't know Amelia well. But he knew one thing they had in common: the pain and suffering of not knowing why the most special people in their lives had been taken from them. That shared humanity had driven him to take action in the face of her suffering in the first place. And those actions had brought them to this point. He looked back at Frank furiously scribbling with his pencil. They'd have their answer soon. Then the gauntlet of truth would be laid before them, and they'd have to sacrifice something to follow it to the end. It always worked that way.

Amelia caught Ike staring at her. "Can I ask you something personal?"

Normally, that question rallied Ike's defenses. But Amelia deserved more than that. "Sure," he said, bracing himself for her question.

"What's it like—not ever knowing?"

"Not knowing what?" He knew what she was asking; he was just buying time to think of an answer.

"Your parents were killed twenty-three years ago, and they *still* don't know who did it and why. What's that been like?"

Ike looked toward Frank and Dominic. "That's not going to happen here."

"Maybe. Maybe not. So, what's it like?"

"It's like feeling different from every human being on the face of the earth. It's never really being comfortable, settled. It's like being a ship at sea with no port in sight, never belonging anywhere. It's like being angry and guilty and ashamed and determined all at the same time."

"I can relate to that," Amelia said.

"How so?"

"Most of my life, I've never fit in. Even in my own family. The only time I felt like I did fit in was when I was with my older sister and a little bit while I was in the Air Force. My father had been on me to change ever since I can remember, telling me I wasn't measuring up to his standards.

We've never really connected. It's like he doesn't give a shit. My mother can connect with me, but only when she doesn't drink. As a young kid, I used to think if I could just be good enough, she'd stop. That didn't work. But that feeling of not being enough never went away. Then my sister left to pursue her career and died three years ago. But Aunt Bessie and Uncle Billy were always there for me. They got me. They didn't judge me, and they always encouraged me to follow my own path. Now they are both gone." Amelia looked back out the window at the passing clouds. "Taken because of one call I made. What if I never find out who did it and why?"

"We'll find out."

"How do you deal with it?"

Ike didn't have to think about that one. "I deal with it by doing this, giving closure to others. It keeps me going. If not for me, then for them—for you."

"That makes sense, now." Amelia's grin returned as if she was about to tell a joke. "You know when I first met you, I thought you were just a washed-up jock trying to prove something."

"That's harsh," Ike said, holding back his smile. "What about now?"

"Now I think you're as tough-minded as they come. You have a unique drive to get to the truth and a willingness to sacrifice yourself so others can have that truth. You keep it one hundred no matter what it takes."

Ike swallowed hard. No one had ever said that to him before.

Amelia looked back out the window. "We call that the warrior's ethos in the Air Force, and you're one of the best damn warriors I've met."

"Thanks." Ike didn't have any more to say.

She turned to him again. "You know I couldn't sleep last night, so I watched that ESPN '30 for 30' about you. You were a warrior on that football field too. But the last half of that special broke my heart. You could have been the best there ever was, at least had a shot at it."

"Football player," Ike said, locking his eyes on her.

"What?"

"I could have been the best quarterback. Instead, I chose to be the best brother I could be." Saying the words for the first time publicly took his breath away.

He saw Amelia's eyes glaze with tears. The corners of her mouth turned up a little and quivered, and she gently nodded and looked back out the window.

After a few minutes of silence, Ike refocused, got up, and headed back to check in with Frank and Dominic.

"How's it going?" Ike said.

Frank looked up. Ike could see the rows of characters on the paper. All were crossed out except the last one. It was composed of three words in German.

"I'm close. Very close." He picked up the tablet and pointed to the last line. "The last words before Hitler's signature say *destroy all records.*"

"That's what the U-boat commander was doing. Looks like the Germans tossed it overboard then headed closer to shore," Ike said.

"Probably back into the shipping lanes. That's where they hunted," Frank said. He put the tablet back down on the table and started working. "I'm working on the wheel pattern. I'll have the settings soon. Then it's just a matter of Dominic inputting the information into his simulator. He's already loaded the raw coded message."

"That's great. Thanks, guys." Ike returned to his seat to let them work. The Airshow digital map display mounted on the bulkhead showed they'd land in twenty-eight minutes.

"How are they doing?" Amelia asked.

"Almost there. Probably another two hours at the most."

"I can't wait," she said with a touch of sarcasm.

"What do you think your mother has to say?" Ike said, hoping to get some insight he could use to prepare for the next steps.

"It's not good. I know Mom well. When she uses that tone, she's got bad news."

"Bad for who?"

"Sounds like for me."

"What could that be?"

She thought for a few seconds, then said, "It could be something we already know. But she said I was in danger, and the people after me were dangerous. Maybe she knows who they are."

"I think we may know that in a few hours, no matter what," Ike said.

"The thing that bothers me is that she asked us to wait. To not do anything with what we had."

"Maybe it's something that involves your family and whoever is behind this."

Amelia's eyes widened. "You think someone who knows us is behind this?"

"Then her warning would make sense."

"It would." She shook her head. "But I hate waiting to hear bad news."

"One thing I've learned is that you never know when a moment in time will change your life forever. It happens to all of us in one way or another. What you do after that, is the secret to life."

CHAPTER 52

AFTER LANDING AT the Charleston Executive Airport, Amelia exited the plane carrying her road box that contained her drone. The warm humid air put her skin into an immediate sweat. It was still hurricane season, and the water that surrounded South Carolina's Lowcountry was still boiling at over eighty degrees. She slipped on her aviators to deal with the bright sunshine piercing her eyes and followed Ike to the black Suburban he'd arranged to take them to Kiawah fifteen miles away. He had her refuse her mother's invitation for McCallum and his men to come pick them up. Neither she nor Ike trusted him.

Half an hour later, they arrived at the rental cottage Shannon had arranged through one of Falzone's subsidiaries in a fictitious name. While it was beachfront, the Cape Cod–style cottage sat behind the large dunes that protected the island. Its cedar-shingled exterior had weathered, giving the faded brown shingles a bleached gray patina, showing their age like an old man. The structures were elevated by thick piers, raising the first floor by one story. Ike pulled into the parking space beneath the cottage, and they all headed up the stairs.

Once inside, Frank and Dominic immediately set up around the rickety kitchen table. Without a word, they began to work. Amelia set down the road box in the living room. For a moment, she admired the view of the beach just beyond the seagrass-covered dune.

"Okay," Ike said as he walked up to her. "Show me how it works."

Amelia opened the box, removed the blue controller, and proceeded to show him how to pilot the drone using the live video feed, how to lock it into position to hover over a target, and how to scan an area using the high-definition camera. Together, they took the drone out on the deck, then Ike launched it.

"I'll take the boardwalk over the dunes and start down the beach," she said, putting the coms earpiece in her ear and handing a headset to Ike. "Let me know if there is any threat. It's late October and the beach should be relatively empty. It will take me about twenty minutes to get to my parents'. When I get close, expect to see McCallum's men."

"Copy that," Ike said. "If there's trouble, I'll get to you."

"Okay. This won't take long." She looked inside through the sliding glass doors. "I want to be here when they break it."

"You'd better get going. They're working fast." Ike stepped closer and put his hand on her shoulder. This time she didn't flinch. Instead, she felt his strength. "Good luck. I hope the news isn't too upsetting. Just remember, we'll work through whatever it is. Let me know what you find out as soon as you can. And keep your head on a swivel."

"Thanks, Ike. See you when I get back."

Amelia left the cottage and climbed the stairs of the boardwalk, stopping at the top. The sun was warm, and the ocean breeze cut the humidity down to a tolerable level. Inland, not more than a few miles away, a line of white clouds blossomed higher in the brilliant blue skies, converting the offshore breeze and warm landmass into thunderheads. Amelia walked down the steps and onto the beach, choosing a position halfway between the dunes and the surf. The beach was wide and stretched eastward until it curled out to sea, at least eight miles away. A few couples strolled along the ocean. Some holding hands, others cooling their feet as they sloshed in the shallow surf. A squadron of two dozen pelicans soared in formation just above the dunes. They reminded her of her time at one of the forward bases in Afghanistan. The butterflies stirred in her stomach, just as they did back then. She noticed the scent of the salty sea breeze and felt the intense afternoon sun broiling her skin. The rhythmic sound of the breakers was broken by the occasional screech of a seagull battling a fellow seabird in the surf for their next meal.

She looked up and saw her drone, floating in the sky above her.

"You're clear," Ike said through her earpiece.

She kept a visual perimeter about the length of a football field in front of her and thirty yards on either side. If someone entered that box, she adjusted her path forward until she verified they weren't a threat. Each time, Ike had identified them as friendly. She worked hard to not daydream about the meeting with her mother. Being present now would keep her alive.

In what seemed like minutes, she'd passed the second-to-last boardwalk before her parents' house.

"Here they come," Ike said in her ear. "Looks like four of them. One may be McCallum. Heads up and good luck."

She saw the four men, three dressed in their signature black polos, move single file over the dunes on the boardwalk next to the house, then fan out on the beach. They faced her and started closing on her position. She consciously kept her pace, her heart rate rising with each step. She reached behind her and checked the Beretta holstered on her waistband. In less than a minute they were face to face, McCallum standing in the middle of the formation. She stopped and he stared at her in silence. His typical intimidation.

"I'm here to see my mother," she said with her shoulders back and chin up.

"That you are," McCallum said with his stone face and black eyes focused on her. "We have to search you."

Two of the men stepped up to her.

"Keep your hands off me." Amelia slowly reached behind her. The two men drew their handguns.

"Easy," Ike said in her ear.

She glanced up and could barely see the drone above her. She slowly brought the Beretta around, grabbing the barrel with the other hand and presented it to one of the goons.

"Turn around," McCallum said.

She slowly did a three-hundred-and-sixty-degree turn. There was no need to pat her down, dressed as she was in a tight black t-shirt and skintight black stretch jeans. As McCallum's eyes moved over her, she felt like she needed a shower.

"Follow me," McCallum said as he headed back to the house.

Amelia counted at least ten men outside the house, roaming with the coms on. While they were each armed with a pistol on their belt, she knew their AR-15s, hidden to keep the neighbors calm, weren't far away. As they entered the house from the back deck, the three men peeled off to join their comrades outside. Amelia felt the chill of the air conditioning. It was colder than usual, and a shameful dread rose inside her knowing her mother always turned it down when she was drinking. She followed McCallum down the long hallway. When they passed the family portrait, she had to stop. She looked at the lonely expression on her face. That said it all. She admired Harper's beaming smile and whispered, "I miss you, Sis."

McCallum impatiently waited until she caught up, and they entered the living room. Her father was waiting. With his arms crossed, chin up, and condescending look pointed directly at her, she knew what was going on.

"I'm here to see Mom," she said flatly.

"I want to talk to you first."

"I don't think so. I think I'd rather talk to her first."

"I don't think you do. She's having one of her episodes."

She bristled at the word. *Episodes.* That's what he called it when her mom's drinking got out of control. He always had. The first time she noticed it she was five years old. Never an explanation. Never any comforting words for his young daughter. They never spoke about her drinking. It seemed to happen when her mother was in emotional pain. After Harper's death, it lasted for a year. Amelia wasn't sure it was alcoholism because it ebbed and flowed like the Lowcountry tides that cleansed the coastline of debris and flushed the marshes of their waste. They'd never had a professional evaluation because it was one of the best-kept worst secrets in her family. They never spoke of it, with each other or anyone on the outside. Her father insisted on that.

"She's bad. I think she's starting to hallucinate. I don't know what she's going to tell you, but take it with a grain of salt."

"I think I'm old enough to make that decision myself. Where is she?" Amelia started to walk toward the stairs. McCallum blocked her path at the base of the staircase.

"Get out of my way!"

McCallum wagged his head and crossed his arms.

She called out, "Mom. Mommm!"

Then she heard it. It sounded like a wounded animal. The cries were loud, oscillating in intensity as if battling terrible surges of pain.

"I'm clumimg, Melia." It sounded like she had a mouthful of marbles. The words were slurred, barely discernible, and were squeezed out instead of spoken. The clinking of ice cubes against a glass was like an arrow through her heart. She was five years old again. Her mother, dressed in a light-gray nightgown hanging from her bony body, staggered to the top of the stairs.

"Get her before she kills herself," her dad said, disgust and contempt dripping from his words.

McCallum shook his head, rushed up the stairs, grabbed her under one shoulder, and guided her down. With a highball glass half full of bourbon sloshing in one hand, her feet haphazardly hit each step like a marionette's. All the time, her wild red eyes were locked on Amelia.

When she took the last step and made it to the floor, she ripped herself from McCallum's grip and nearly fell. She wavered, then gripped the end of the banister, steadied herself as best she could, and took a long drink. She swallowed and dropped her head, then looked up at Amelia.

"Amelia," she said sadly. "Oh, Amelia." She started to cry again. Her mother reached out to her. "I have something to tell you."

Amelia looked at the woman standing before her and barely recognized her. Her mother could be the most articulate, together woman on the planet, sober. But this wasn't that woman.

"I'm here, Mom," Amelia said. She tried to keep the tears in her eyes, but she felt them roll down her cheeks.

Her mother stumbled backward, sticking her drink straight out in front of her, saving it, then catching herself as she plopped down on the first step hard. Her head bobbled as she tried to focus on her father. "Leave!" She roared in a deep growling voice.

"Please go, Dad," Amelia said.

Her father eyed her mother in disgust, huffed, then walked out of the foyer. McCallum followed. Amelia took a seat next to her mother on the stairs. Her mother took another long drink and leaned into her, steadying herself. Amelia put her arm around her. Her mother dropped her head onto Amelia's shoulder.

She began mumbling Amelia's name. Each time her voice got slower, weaker, and more unintelligible. Amelia reached across her and gently slipped the glass from her hand, setting it on the step. Her mother stopped mumbling, and Amelia felt her mother's full weight against her. She was breathing heavily, eyes closed and mouth open. There wouldn't be a conversation for a few hours.

Her father came back into the foyer, a condescending smile on his face. Amelia wanted to slap it off.

"I told you," he said, scolding her.

McCallum stepped around him and headed for Amelia.

"Take her upstairs," her father said.

McCallum reached down to pick up Tess.

"Keep your hands off my mother." Amelia swatted his hands away.

McCallum's dark eyes flashed and his nostrils flared. He balled his fists.

"I'll take her up," she said.

Amelia stood and scooped up her mother. She was shocked by how light she was. She'd lost more weight. As Amelia walked up the stairs and headed to her mother's bedroom, she wondered what message her mother had for her. It clearly was a painful one. Painful for her mother and probably for her. After laying her mother in bed and covering her up, she stared down at her and wiped the tears from her own eyes.

"I'll be back, Mom."

She made her way downstairs. Her father said he wanted to talk again but she ignored him and headed outside to the beach. McCallum tailed her and was joined by the three goons again. She got her Beretta from one of them as they headed down the boardwalk. Once on the beach, she turned and surprised McCallum by walking up to him, her face inches from his.

"Don't follow me. You *or* your goons. If you do, I promise,"—she pointed to the sky— "you'll never see it coming, and you know I'm very capable of that."

While McCallum looked up at the drone hovering over his head, Amelia headed down the beach, hoping there was better news at the cottage.

CHAPTER 53

KARA WATCHED THE news report from CNN on the muted TV mounted on the wall in her office. A terrible panic began to rise from her gut. She hadn't received any details yet, but the headline said that a sniper had fired on an FBI agent and her confidential informant in Pittsburgh. She flipped through the news channels. It was carried on every network as breaking news. She suddenly felt as if she was living a recurring nightmare she'd been having. In it, she was scaling a rock face, maybe Yosemite. She suspected it might represent her climb to the precipice of politics. But in the nightmare, she lost her grip, suddenly free-falling and clawing wildly for a handhold. She'd never reached the bottom in her dream, but something said she might hit it tonight.

Knight, who never rushed anything, came rushing in, glanced at the TV, and closed the door.

"That wasn't us," he huffed out in a whisper, catching his breath.

"They were firing on our agent? The one you said you had in your pocket?"

"Yes. We still have her compromised, and she recovered a World War II teleprinter tape from Garcia and Rossi. Now what the hell is going on?"

"Did you decode the message?"

"No. Not yet. We can't go through the normal channels, so we'll have to use outside resources to break it."

"Are you crazy? Don't do that!"

"What aren't you telling me?"

Kara knew she didn't have a choice. She needed to tell Knight only part of the story. The whole story would give him, and anyone else that acquired it, too much blackmail leverage.

"That's a message from a German U-boat. It was sunk under orders from the OSS in order to destroy that message. Apparently, the commander of the boat had decided to dispose of it himself in much deeper water before we could kill the messenger."

Knight's astonishment was obvious as his mouth hung wide open. "That was almost eighty years ago. What the hell does it say?"

"I don't know." Kara thought that was a good lie. She'd told herself she was a patriot protecting her country. "But we have to get that teleprinter tape here now."

"Okay. My contacts can have it here in two hours."

"Do it. And not a word to anyone. Got it?"

"Got it." He pointed to the TV. "I'm worried about this even more now."

"I am too. Who was the shooter?"

Knight shook his head. "We have no idea. Neither do any of the agencies. Either someone is off book or there's another actor after the same thing we are. Either way, someone knows what we're doing. Based on what you just told me, that's a shit show."

Kara agreed with Knight's assessment. She knew what she had to do, but when that thought hit her, a sadness began to crush her. It had only been a contingency, one she'd never thought she have to use.

"Where are Garcia and Rossi?"

"We lost them, and the FBI agent had to pull surveillance to get the tape."

She thought for a minute. "If you were to guess, where do you think she'd go?"

Knight watched the TV screen. "I'd leave Pittsburgh for sure." He shook his head back and forth. "I'd probably go home. Benton has security there. Kiawah."

"Okay. Get that tape here and quietly get me on our NetJet to Kiawah."

Knight walked out the door then stopped, holding on to the doorknob. "Open or closed?"

"Open."

Kara took a moment to calm herself and focus. She headed to the Oval Office, taking in everything, knowing this could all be gone if she didn't implement her contingency plan. It had risks, too, but it was their only chance to survive this crisis.

She passed his personal secretary seated just outside the Oval Office. "Is he alone?"

Mrs. Stevenson nodded. Kara kept her brisk pace and went inside. Her brother was seated but reading his iPhone.

"We need to talk."

He looked up and laid his phone on his desk. "You sound worried?"

She stopped in front of his desk. "I am. We have a problem. A big one."

Her brother's jowls tightened and face reddened as his eyes narrowed on her, and he hit the desk with his fist. "What the hell did you do?"

She ignored her brother's trademark bluster. He could bully others, but not her. "I'm saving your ass, Mr. President."

He leaned back, apparently realizing who he was talking to. "Go on."

"Amelia Garcia has become a problem."

His face turned crimson again, but he didn't speak. Kara thought she detected a slight frown. The same one she'd seen on his face as a child when he'd done something wrong.

"What aren't you telling me?" she said.

"Nothing. Go on."

"She has uncovered something," she said. "Something I was warned about decades ago. It's no longer in her possession, but she's still a threat."

"I knew it. We should take her out!"

Kara winced. "You need to stay above all this. We've talked about that before. You must maintain a position of plausible deniability. In all this. Especially this. This is the greatest threat that can be used against us."

Her brother's eyebrows rose and he leaned back, apparently realizing what her words really meant.

"Is it that bad?"

"Yes." For the first time in her political career, Kara felt the ground liquefy under her feet. She couldn't believe what she was about to say. It was the only thing that could save them and the country.

"I have an emergency plan—a contingency, and I have to execute it."

Now her brother's eyes widened further, concern wrinkled his forehead, and he sagged deep into his chair. "I've faced worse. Got the media by their short hairs."

"It could end it all for us."

"In the reelection campaign?"

"All of it."

Her brother scanned the Oval Office, then slowly shook his head.

Kara waited until he stopped and returned his attention to her. "You know I've always done what's best for us."

"Of course."

"And what you and I are doing to save this country and make it great again is our patriotic duty. It has to continue."

The president leaned forward. "I can't lose. I couldn't live with that. I can manage an impeachment to a point, but if the Senate were to vote me out …" He stopped and fell back into the chair again. "I don't know. That just can't happen."

As the words formed in her mind, a sadness stuck in her throat. "I agree. Thomas, I have to do something to save us that you may not understand. I can't tell you what that is. I have to protect you. I'm sorry. But you can be assured, I'll take care of it all. It's risky but there's no other choice. I may be able to do it without anyone knowing, but there's a chance it may come to light."

Her brother started to speak but she cut him off. "You have to sever all ties to this thing. Don't ask anything else. I love you, brother."

"I love you too."

She turned and walked out of the office.

CHAPTER 54

STANDING ON THE deck of the beachfront cottage, Ike watched Amelia walk down the sand. Her shoulders sagged, and she gazed out to sea as if what she'd needed had just sailed over the horizon. It was obvious her mother hadn't delivered.

The cool ocean breeze had gained speed, turning cooler as it fed the approaching storms behind him. The smell of rain filled the air. The sky was dark, and the rumbling thunder made Amelia pick up her pace. Ike suspected that Amelia suffered under the weight of her unmet expectations. Something out of her control blocked her from getting the information she needed from her mother that she could act on and get closure. Based on his experience with a long list of clients, no one was immune to that pain and suffering. He saw his younger self in her, and as she made her way up the boardwalk over the dunes, they locked eyes. In that moment he knew he needed to help her transform that frustration into focused anger that would spur her to take action in the face of seemingly insurmountable challenges. Something he knew how to do very well.

Ike headed inside. Frank was feverishly writing on his tablet, while Dominic leaned against the chairback, eyes closed, head tilted back toward the ceiling. Ike met Amelia after she closed the door. They quietly walked into the kitchen.

"Not good?" Ike asked.

Amelia looked down and shook her head. "She was drunk. Really drunk. She blacked out, and I had to put her to bed. I can't believe that's my mother."

Ike reached up and squeezed her arm. "I'm sorry. That sucks. I know you were looking forward to hearing what she had to say."

Amelia looked crushed; her eyes glazed with tears. Ike imagined it was both the fact that her mother was drunk and the disappointment of not getting the urgent message her mother had for her.

"I need a few more hours. She'll be better by then."

"I'm not sure we have that. You saw what happened in Pittsburgh."

Amelia wiped her eyes and raised her voice. "We can't do anything before I talk to her."

"We could be dead by then. Time is something we don't have. I'm sorry."

Amelia pulled her shoulders back and put her hands on her hips. "You don't get to—"

"Got it!" Frank yelled from the dining room table.

Ike and Amelia both turned to see what was going on.

Frank held up a sheet of paper with a few numbers on it. "The wheel settings."

Ike headed over to the table. Amelia followed.

Dominic rubbed his eyes and pulled his laptop in front of him. After a few keystrokes, he said, "I'm ready."

Frank read the settings and Dominic adjusted each of the twelve wheels shown on the virtual Lorenz machine with a series of clicks.

When he was done, he looked up at Ike. "Here we go." He hit enter.

Frank got up and came around behind Dominic where Ike and Amelia stood. Nobody moved, eyes locked on the screen. The virtual machine whirred and clicked as it decoded the message. Ike felt Amelia grab his forearm, squeezing it hard.

The output flashed onto the screen. Ike let out a huge sigh when he realized the message was in German.

Frank inched forward and squinted, reading the screen. "Oh my God." He turned pale and reached for the back of a chair to steady himself.

"What is it, Frank? What's it say?"

"Hang on," Dominic said. With a few mouse clicks, he copied the message and pasted it into an online translator. Ike's body shivered when the words appeared in English. He couldn't believe his eyes.

April 13, 1945

The infant is to be delivered on April 21, 1945 at 35.374, -71.495 at 11 p.m. Acceptance will be consent to end my reign. The US will agree to raise him as a citizen and destroy all records.

Adolf Hitler Fuhrer

"Does that mean what I think it means?" Ike asked.

Frank nodded. "Hitler cut a deal with Truman. He traded an infant for his suicide."

"There's only one reason he'd do that," Ike said, not believing what he was about to say. "It was his kid."

Frank's face lit up. "Lebensborn."

"What's that?" Ike asked.

"It roughly translates to 'Wellspring of Life.' It was a eugenics project started by the Nazis to propagate the master race. They 'recruited'"—Frank made air quotes—"pregnant unmarried Aryan women after the Nazis ordered all SS officers to create as many babies as they could, inside or outside marriage. The women needed to pass a racial purity test to show their Germanic/Nordic heritage. Blue or green eyes and blonde hair were preferred. They also kidnapped at least two hundred and fifty thousand children all over Europe that met those criteria, stripping them from their mothers, and put them into Lebensborn to eventually place them in Aryan homes in Germany. The women were kept in about two dozen Lebensborn homes around Europe during pregnancy and delivery, but their babies were torn from them by the SS and put in more Aryan homes in Germany. Babies that were slow in their development, had special needs, or didn't meet the strict racial values were executed."

"That's disgusting. Those poor women and children. How come I never heard about that?" Amelia asked.

"When you exterminate more than six million innocent people, it dominates the list of war crimes. Believe me, when we entered those concentration camps, we couldn't believe the cruelty and horror. It dominated everything," Frank said. "But the real kicker was that the judges for the Nuremberg trials had reached an incredible decision that Lebensborn was just a welfare organization."

Ike didn't want to believe what he'd just heard. He imagined hundreds of thousands of kidnapped children and the terror they must have experienced. Unwed mothers, graded like cattle, placed in homes until their babies were born, then having them ripped from their arms by the SS. His heart suddenly felt like lead, and the horror of the war crime he'd never heard of sucked him down like quicksand.

"What happened to all those children and their mothers after the war?" Ike asked.

"Many of the mothers were labeled as Nazi whores, and the Lebensborn children were ostracized when they were returned to their native countries. Even in postwar Germany, they were ostracized. Just before the end of the war, the Nazis had destroyed the confidential records that were kept at the homes. The babies' new documents were forged. The Lebensborn children all were forced to face their past cloaked in silence and shame. Some never found their real parents, and some who did, didn't find out until the 2000s."

Ike was crushed when he thought about the shame forced upon all those innocent children.

"Guess who ran the program?" Frank said.

"Who?" Ike answered. Already wanting to rip their head off.

"Heinrich Himmler. Hitler's right-hand man. As a rule, none of the fathers' names were recorded. So it's not much of a stretch to think that Hitler secretly participated and produced a child to propagate his master race."

"Holy shit," Amelia said.

Ike noticed Amelia was looking at the screen and furiously typing something into her burner. "What is it?"

She looked at Ike, her eyes wide with surprise, her jaw locked in determination. She held up the smartphone. "Those coordinates are just north of Avon, North Carolina, on the Outer Banks."

Ike looked at Frank, then Dominic, then finally at Amelia. The facts fell into place in Ike's mind like tumblers in a cracked safe. He smiled. "We've got them, now."

They all appeared confused.

"Amelia. You said you took a picture of the box on the seafloor?"

"Yes."

"That probably shows time, date, and location. Correct?"

"It does," she said.

"We have the box and still have the tape, therefore we have chain of custody, so to speak."

"That's good," Frank said. "But were still missing the who."

"Let's think about that," Ike said pacing around the room. "We know their age."

"Yeah. Born in forty-four or forty-five. That puts them in their late seventies," Frank said.

Ike patted his chin with his index finger. "And most likely, they're in DC."

"I can go with that," Frank said.

"That narrows it down to a third of the Senate, half the administration, and probably two dozen or more in the House," Dominic said with a hint of sarcasm.

Ike stopped and stared out over the dunes at the churning ocean. "But who would have the most to lose?"

"The Senators, the cabinet members," Amelia said, then paused just as Ike turned to face them.

"Or the president," Ike said. "And who has the power to mount such an attack on us and drive this cover-up?"

"You think it's him?" Frank asked.

"I think we should start there."

"We're going to need a hell of a lot more proof to accuse the President of the United States of being the son of the most despicable man in the history of our planet," Frank said. "He controls the narrative in the media right now. We'll be dismissed as political stooges unless we have irrefutable proof."

"So how do we do that? If all the records were either destroyed or forged?" Dominic added.

The group silently chewed on that question for a few moments. Then Frank said, "Someone had to raise him."

"Right," Ike said. "The president's mother. She'd certainly know. She's still alive?"

Ike saw a light go on in Amelia's mind.

Her jaw jutted out and her nostrils flared. She took in each of them, one at a time, with her dead-eyed stare. "She is. I know her. And I know where she is."

CHAPTER 55

IKE DROVE ALONG Flyway Drive and leaned forward as he battled to see through the molten sheets of rain overwhelming the wipers. Rumbling thunder drowned out their rhythmic thumping. Heading toward the entrance to the beachfront mansion, he gave them less than twenty percent chance of getting what they needed. He couldn't imagine *his* mother ever turning on him, let alone the mother of the President of the United States doing it on the record. But it was the only shot they had. After giving Ike turn-by-turn directions, Amelia fell silent in the passenger's seat. In the rearview mirror, Ike saw Frank, his head resting on the seatback with his eyes closed. He didn't know how much more of this Frank could take. One thing was certain: this visit would be a trip wire. If the president was the son of Adolf Hitler, alarms would sound in the White House and all hell would descend on them. When they exposed the truth, they'd throw the entire country into violent turmoil. Whether or not they got what they needed from his mother, they'd have to move fast.

Their plan was simple but risky. Amelia would get them inside, and Frank's age and demeanor would provide a generational bridge to the older woman. His knowledge of events at the end of World War II would ensure they asked the right questions.

"You sure you can get us inside?" Ike asked.

"I'm sure," Amelia said. "My father set her up down here when the president left the governor's mansion in Texas for the White House. The island was secure, on the east coast, and with the Secret Service detail, he assured the president that his mother would be safe. That was two years ago. Since then, my mother and I have gone over regularly to visit her and check on her care. She and I hit it off. We have a connection, and Secret Service knows me. With Frank posing as her old friend and you his protégé and former sports figure, they'll let us right in."

"That is," Frank said, "as long as the president and the Secret Service aren't on to us."

A chill skittered up Ike's spine. Frank was right. If they were on to them, this would be the end of the road. But after weighing that risk, Ike was encouraged by the fact that there had been no mention of them anywhere on social media, the president's primary first-strike weapon. He shoved the concern aside. "We're good. And at one hundred and one years old, it's no big deal if she doesn't remember you."

"She still rocking along, though. She can still get around and only uses one of those wheeled walkers with a handbrake every now and then. And despite a few little memory problems, she's still very lucid," Amelia added, squinting to see through the windshield. She pointed ahead. "It's the next drive on the right."

Ike turned past the two palm trees guarding the entrance and headed down the smooth pebble-stone driveway. It wound through the lush, manicured grounds filled with palmettos, pines, and elegant live oaks draped with Spanish moss. They crossed over a lagoon on a weathered gray wooden bridge. Through the rain, Ike saw a large alligator, his prehistoric head and dark lifeless eyes lurking barely above the waterline. A shingled guard shack came into view ahead on the right. The gate's arm blocked the road.

"Just pull up," Amelia said, sitting up and placing her finger on the window control.

As Ike pulled up, a man stepped from the shack in a rain slicker and umbrella and put his palm in the air. Amelia rolled down the window and waved him to her side. A second agent stepped out and eyed Ike.

"Miss Garcia. We weren't expecting you."

"I know, Agent Keller. I was worried about the storm and ran into one of Isabella's old friends in town and decided to drop in and check on her."

His stern face softened. "I'm so sorry about your aunt and uncle. You and your family must be devastated."

"We are. Thank you."

His concerned look hardened again, and the agent leaned in and studied Frank. Then he shifted his focus to Ike. "I know you."

Ike smiled and gave a little wave and nod to the young agent.

Keller remained serious. "Are you Ike Rossi?" Ike wasn't sure why the agent recognized him. Without signaling the alert sparking inside him, he readied to shove the SUV into reverse.

"That '30 for 30' on ESPN was a hit job," Keller said. "I have a little sister too. I would have done the same thing."

Ike blew out the adrenalin rush and shook his head. "I appreciate that, Agent Keller. It was nothing special. I always said others would do the same thing in my shoes."

"You're damn right," the agent said as a grin spread across his face. "But I still would have loved to have seen you in the NFL."

"I hear you."

"Can I still get your license, please?"

"Sure." Ike handed it to the agent.

The agent looked back at Frank. "And who are you, sir?"

"Franklin McNally." He handed a driver's license to the agent who examined it. "I know Isabella from the old days in Texas. Ike and I are down from Pittsburgh helping Amelia deal with her family tragedy. When she said Isabella was here, I had to try to see her."

"Thank you, sir," Agent Keller said. He took the licenses and met the other agent at the shack. The second agent took the licenses from Keller and went inside.

"Do we need to be worried?" Frank asked.

"Yes. But not about that, I hope." Ike said, looking at the young agent still standing outside staring at them. "I'm sure it's just a background check. I just hope it's not a call to the president."

"No. You're right. I've seen them do this to any of the new medical providers we bring in," Amelia said in a reassuring tone.

Despite her assurances, Ike moved his right hand to the shifter. All three were silent as they monitored the gatehouse for the agent's return. The only sound was the slapping of the windshield wipers against the base of the windshield. After a couple of minutes that passed like hours, Ike saw the other agent trot out of the shack and hand the IDs to Agent Keller. Carrying the licenses in one hand and holding an umbrella over his head in the other, Agent Keller went to Ike's window. Ike rolled it down.

The young agent handed Ike the licenses. "You're good to go, Mr. Rossi." He bent down and looked at Amelia. "Nice to see you again, Miss Garcia. Give your mother my best. Park in the usual spot and leave your keys."

"Thanks, Agent Keller. Have a good evening," Amelia said. Ike closed the window and drove ahead to the house. The beachfront mansion was three stories high with thick white columns, white trim, and light-gray shingle siding. A brick stairway led to the thick mahogany door on the covered front porch that stretched along the front of the house. The carriage lights on either side of the door glowed yellow in the storm-darkened twilight.

Amelia pointed to a single parking space just off the circle driveway in front of the house and next to the three-car garage. As Ike pulled in, he noticed a large platform in front of them whose color matched the house.

"What's this?" he asked, pointing ahead.

"A generator. It can power the whole house."

"Impressive," Frank said from the back.

"Wait till you see the rest of the house."

The rain looked like it wouldn't let up anytime soon, and Ike knew they had little time left. He grabbed the door handle, stopped, and looked back over his shoulder. "You lead the way, Amelia. When we find the president's mother, chat her up, then introduce us. We'll have Frank make the ask, just like we'd planned."

Ike thought the plan was solid based on the limited information they had available. Dominic had pulled up Isabella Reed's biography at the cottage. Isabella was an impressive woman. The daughter of a US senator from Connecticut, she was one of the few women to earn a Yale law degree before World War II. With her bachelor's degree in political science and political connections through her father, she went to work for the State Department. After the war, she and her husband, who'd she met at the State Department, left government service and moved to West Texas. With money she inherited from her father, she and her husband invested in real estate, including buying ranch land south of Midland. That ranch covered a small portion of one of the most prolific oil-producing areas in the Permian Basin.

As their fortune grew, they moved to Dallas, where they continued to work in commercial real estate. But in the oil crash in the 1980s, they got caught overextended and lost most of that fortune. They were able to keep their ranch and a home in Highland Park but were forced to sell everything else to stay afloat. All along, she was a proud Republican donor and active in supporting veterans, especially those from World War II.

They had two children. Thomas, the current president, was the oldest, born, they claimed, just after the move to Midland. His sister, Kara, was born eight years later in Dallas. Both grew up in Texas high society and followed in their mother's footsteps with undergraduate degrees in political science and law degrees from the University of Texas.

Isabella's husband died following the oil crash, and the tough-minded, well-respected widow kept what was left of the family's business running while guiding her son through the political landscape of Texas. With the backing of the wealthiest families in the state, led by Benton Garcia, her son had landed in the White House two years ago.

Ike agreed with Frank and Amelia that the best way to approach Isabella was to appeal to her staunchly conservative values and her great respect for World War II veterans. Frank was well qualified to make that pitch.

Ike jumped out of the car and waited for Frank to gingerly extract himself from the back seat. Amelia joined them on the other side of Frank. Despite the soaking cool rain, they walked at Frank's pace until they reached the brick stairway. Frank looked up and stopped.

"You good, Frank?" Ike asked, as he wiped the rain from his face.
"Let's go."

Together they climbed the thirteen stairs and reached the shelter of
the front porch. Ike wiped his face, squeegeed his hair with his hands, and
shook the water from them. Amelia did the same, then rang the doorbell.

Ike heard the footsteps, then the mahogany door opened. A young
woman in neatly pressed slacks and a blouse appeared. "Amelia. I didn't
know you were coming, or I would have made tea."

"That's okay, Nancy. I wanted to check in with Isabella and see if she
wanted to see an old friend. This is Frank and Ike."

"Nice to meet you both." She firmly shook Ike's hand, then
Frank's. "Please come in." She held open the door and directed them
inside. "Isabella is out on the screened porch watching the storm."
She closed the door and walked past the grand piano in the foyer. The
dark Brazilian cherry floors glowed against the beach-blue walls that
were trimmed by thick, brilliant-white, handcrafted millwork. Light
upholstered furniture in blue-and-white pastels was neatly positioned
in the living room, and they passed through the dining room with an
entire wall of beautiful walnut cabinetry framing two wine refrigerators
and a collection of fine dinnerware and delicate ceramic art. They
reached a pair of open double doors that led out to the screen porch.
Ike heard the waves crashing onto the shore and saw the flashes of
lightning dancing behind the clouds that were drifting out to sea. The
ocean breeze cooled the porch, and the soft LED lights gave the wicker
furniture a warm glow.

Isabella was sitting alone in a chair, rocking gently with a blanket on
her lap, and staring out to sea.

"Isabella," Nancy said, "Amelia is here to see you and she bought
some friends."

The woman swiveled in her chair. She wore a matching sweatsuit, and
her white hair was short and combed over her ears. While she appeared to
be old, she didn't look like she was over one hundred. Ike assumed that
was partly due to her still lean figure. Just like Frank, her eyes glowed with
the intensity of a much younger person. Before Amelia could get to her,

Isabella's mouth dropped open and shock filled her eyes. She froze for a moment in her chair, clearly stunned. She was staring at Frank.

Ike turned and looked at Frank. He had the same expression on his face. He tried to speak but couldn't. Then, he finally choked out his words.

"Claire?" he asked.

Isabella's mouth softened and stretched into a gentle smile. Then, in a weak, creaky vibrato, characteristic of a voice that had lasted a century, she said, "I can't believe it's you, Frank."

CHAPTER 56

IKE WATCHED THE tsunami of emotions surging across Frank's face. It was as if he were witnessing the climactic scene in a 1950s boy-finally-gets-the-girl movie live on the set. As Frank stared at Isabella, shock, joy, and a deep emotional tie to the woman all seemed to emanate from his cascading expressions. She looked equally struck, her eyes locked on his, as they participated in some kind of telepathy meant only for lost loves or estranged family members suddenly reunited. Ike looked across the room at Amelia, who turned away from Isabella and gave Ike a wide-eyed shrug. Ike reminded himself they were here for a purpose and time was not a luxury they could burn on an old reunion. The Secret Service could barge into the room at any moment because of one routine call from the president or his sister.

"Amelia, can you make introductions?"

"Sure. I—I guess."

"You don't need to introduce Frank," Isabella said without looking away from him.

Amelia seemed confused for a second, then caught herself and pointed at Ike. "Okay. Isabella, this is Ike Rossi."

"Ma'am. Nice to meet you. May I ask how you and Frank know each other?"

"You're Isabella now?" Frank said, finally finding his voice.

She kept her smile. "Yes. I had to change my name when we came back to the States after the war. For security reasons."

"What happened to Noah?"

"We married when we got back home," her mouth drooped, and sadness entered her eyes. "But he died after the oil crash in the eighties. I've been on my own ever since."

"I'm sorry," Amelia said, "but how do you know each other?"

Frank gazed at Isabella, raising his eyebrows. "Is it okay?"

"It's been long enough. I think we're good."

"Claire, uh, or Isabella, was with the OSS during the war. She and her partner helped run a safe house just outside of Geneva that provided assistance and safe haven to the French Resistance and gathered intelligence. We met when I was wounded. I made it to the safe house, and Isabella helped me get back on my feet."

"That's right. What Frank didn't tell you is that he and a few other members of the OSS secretly parachuted into occupied France to help some trapped resistance fighters. He saved quite a few of them from the Nazis. Got them safely out of France to us. He got wounded in the process. Once he got to us, Frank was a crucial part of the team that gathered intelligence and intercepted and deciphered Nazi messages that led to the war's end," Isabella said. Then to Frank, she said, "Where have you been?"

"After we shipped out, I went home to Bloomfield to get married, then moved to Virginia. My wife and I had a son, and I was working for what's now the NSA. Later, when my son died, I moved back to Bloomfield, taught high school, and helped our friends in Washington on the side."

Ike was enthralled with their connection. Still, he didn't think it would make what they were about to ask of Isabella any easier.

"Well, Frank, it is great to see you're still here," Isabella said.

"You too, Isabella."

She turned to Amelia. "Now sweetheart, why are you all here?"

Amelia's shoulders sagged. "My aunt and uncle were killed this past weekend. Murdered."

"My goodness. Here on the island?"

"Yes, ma'am. Anyway, we need your help to find out who's behind it."

Isabella leaned back in the chair and rocked while she eyed Amelia, then Ike, then Frank. "That's why you're here?" she asked Frank.

"Yes. Unfortunately, the evidence has brought us to your doorstep."

"You know I work for my uncle,"—Amelia hesitated and took a deep breath—"and I operate remotely operated vehicles on the sea floor. Last week I recovered something off the East Coast."

At that moment, Ike saw Isabella's jaw go slack, and the corners of her mouth turned down again. Worry wracked her wrinkled face. "What's the matter?" Ike asked.

Isabella shook her head. "Go on."

"It was a sealed box with German markings on it. I called my uncle about it and that got him and my aunt killed."

Isabella looked as if she was going to faint.

"Can I get you some water, ma'am?" Ike asked.

She bowed her head, looking at the floor, and held her palm up. "No. No thank you."

"Clair—Isabella," Frank said. She looked up at him. "It contained an encrypted message from a Lorenz machine. I deciphered it. It points to an infant delivered to the US in return for Hitler's death. We think it's his child."

Isabella closed her eyes. Ike could see she knew what was coming. The pain had already arrived. Ike knew the next words would end her life as she knew it. After one hundred and one years on this earth, her last days would be spent alone. From their basements, behind their keyboards and cellphones, and in their newsrooms, the haters would come out and excoriate her. What was left of her family and her legacy would be destroyed. But there was no way around it.

Ike choked on the words. "We think the infant was your son."

She looked up and opened her eyes. Tears ran down her wrinkled cheeks, filling the crevasses that marked her years. She swiveled her chair and gazed out to sea. The rumble of distant thunder echoed over the sound of breaking waves. It was as if the ocean was drawing her back in time. She started rocking again, her back to the group.

"I knew this day might come. But I thought I'd made it. The secret would die with me. And even though my children have been a disappointment to me, I still love them. They seem to have forgotten the things I've stood for all these years. Peace, freedom, justice, and liberty for all. I saw so many die for it. To save the American way of life."

She kept looking out to sea. "There were five messages sent by Hitler. All said the same thing. As Frank knows, you had to do that in those days because some of the messengers would be killed or captured. In this case, it was U-boats. I was told that all of them had been destroyed. Five U-boats all at the bottom of the sea. The OSS had assured me. Only Noah and I, my OSS contact, and someone in DC knew what that message said. We picked him up on April twenty-first, 1945, just before midnight north of Avon, North Carolina, and went straight to Midland, Texas. We raised him as our own. And it worked."

She stopped rocking, pulled a Kleenex from her sleeve, and wiped her eyes. She turned and faced them. "He doesn't know."

"The president?"

"Yes."

"Then who's doing this?"

"Kara. His sister. She knows." Isabella shook her head. "I told her years ago. After I'd gotten sick. I wasn't sure I'd beat the cancer diagnosis. I didn't want him to go into politics for obvious reasons, but he did anyway. And she helped him. I had to tell her. She's just protecting her brother." She began to cry again. "Is there any way we can forget this?"

Amelia stepped closer to her. "No. She killed my aunt and uncle. She killed the deputy attorney general in the Department of Justice. If you really believe in peace, freedom, justice, and liberty, we have to expose them. They need to pay for what she's done."

"Isabella," Ike said. "It's the only way to end the killing and do the right thing. I think you know that."

She shook her head. "Kara's been the biggest disappointment—and she's all mine." Taking a moment, she eyed Frank and smiled. He smiled back. Then she looked at Ike. "Tell me what you need."

"We'll need a recorded statement from you, and when the authorities come to ask, we need you to tell them what you just told us."

Isabella swiveled back to the ocean and stared. The rain had stopped but the sea was still churning. It was close to sunset, and a red glow haunted the beach. Ike knew that Isabella wouldn't be the only one to make a life-changing sacrifice to set things right and, as Isabella put it, return to the American way by providing peace, freedom, justice and, liberty for all and maybe closure for Amelia. The cost they'd all pay would be high. The president and his supporters would see to that. But standing with Amelia, Frank, and even Isabella, he knew he was with people who'd done that before.

Isabella stopped rocking. "I'll do what you want," she said. "I need some time alone now."

As they went outside and headed to the car, Ike said, "Let's get this out now. We can get it to the paper, newsrooms, and get it up on social media. We need to get the evidence in the hands of the right people. Fast."

Amelia grabbed Ike's arm and turned him around. "Not yet. I need to talk to my mother. Then we can nail the bastards."

CHAPTER 57

AFTER GIVING KNIGHT an impatient glare, Kara leaned across the console of the black Navigator and checked the speedometer. This was taking too long. The call from Secret Service had come in when they'd landed at Charleston Executive Airport thirty minutes ago. Amelia Garcia, Ike Rossi, and some old man named Frank McNally had just paid her mother a visit. If they'd gotten what they came for, she had very little time before she lost everything she'd worked so hard to get: the money, the power, and maybe even her own shot at the presidency.

"Can't you drive any faster?"

Knight shook his head. "We can't without drawing the attention of the county sheriff deputies, and we're keeping this trip off the books."

The thought of being slowed by the threat of some county deputy pulling them over almost made her puke. Rules, when it involved her or the president, meant nothing. Maybe for the common people, but not for them. They were running the damn country—saving it from itself. She'd been on this very road with the president's motorcade doing seventy. But she quickly realized Knight was right. They'd used part of their NetJets allocation from the family office to make this unofficial trip and hide it from the public. An encounter, even if no ticket was given, would greatly increase the risk of being caught. She leaned back in the seat and focused on what she might say to her mother.

Fifteen minutes later they were on Kiawah and past the second security gate. In no time, Knight pulled the black Navigator up to the gate of her mother's house. Agent Keller waved and lifted the gate, and they pulled up to the house.

"You keep them busy. I'll only be a few minutes. Just tell them I was in the area and decided to stop by to check on her. Then do what we planned."

"Will do." Knight got out of the car.

Kara stepped out, walked up the front stairs, and let herself in.

Nancy met her in the hallway. "Hello, Miss Williams. I didn't know you were coming."

"It's fine. I was in the area and decided to stop by and check on Mom. I understand she had some visitors?"

"Yes. You just missed them. It was Miss Garcia and two very nice men. They only visited for a few minutes. The older man knew your mother."

Alarm bells sounded in Kara's head. She'd seen the file on Frank McNally. There was nothing about any overlap with her mother. "He did?"

"What I gather is they knew each other a long time ago."

This was a problem. If her mother had a connection to Frank, it must have been during the war. Kara knew her mother had strong bonds with those she encountered back then. She thought they had all died. Any connection to that time in history was a threat. She needed to hurry.

"That's nice. Where is she?"

"Out on the screened porch. I was getting her some tea. Would you like some?"

"No thank you. But could you please get a sweater from my closet first?"

"Of course."

Nancy disappeared down the hallway headed for the stairs. Kara slipped past the double glass doors to the screened porch and hurried to the guest bath next to the media room. She opened the medicine cabinet and pulled out the small bottle with a stopper. It said *mometasone*, but it wasn't. She'd palmed several small doses of liquid morphine Nancy used to treat her mother's discomfort. It was called palliative care. Kara called it a blessing. Hiding the bottle in the palm of her hand, she went into the kitchen and found the steaming cup of tea steeping on the counter. The honey bottle was already out, so it was either already in there or would be when Nancy returned. Kara poured the contents of the medicine bottle into the hot tea. Slipping the bottle into her pocket, she headed back to the screened porch and opened the door.

When she entered the porch, her mother didn't turn to greet her. She kept watching the glow of a fading sunset against the line of thunderstorms on the horizon. She probably assumed Kara was Nancy.

"Hello, Mother," Kara said as she stepped around the sofa and faced her mother, who was rocking gently in the chair.

Isabella stopped rocking but didn't look at Kara. "You're too late."

"What do you mean?"

"You're here because they were here."

Her mother was a thorn in her side for most of her life, but she wasn't stupid. Kara's skin tingled, partly because of the cool sea air, but mostly because Isabella could still destroy everything. "What did you do?"

"What I should have done a long time ago."

"No. You didn't, Mother."

"I did. Why did you kill those people?"

Her mother's question sent a jolt through her body. This decrepit old woman had no idea what she was doing. Kara stepped to the railing, her back to Isabella, and watched the storms. "You know, sometimes people have to make sacrifices for the good of the country."

Her mother scoffed. "You don't get to make that decision for them."

"For many average people, you have to. They simply have no idea what to do—what's necessary."

"I never should have told you about your brother. I thought I was going to die, and someone needed to know the secret, just in case."

Kara remembered the day sixteen years ago. Her mother had received the results of her biopsy the day after her brother was elected governor. It was lung cancer. At eighty-five, Kara was sure her mother would die within the year. But thanks to her doctors and the treatment, here she sat.

"I'm glad you did. We never thought I'd need to know, but we were wrong."

"You and Thomas never should have gone into politics."

"You can't see what we've done—what I've done. He's the President of the United States. The country loves him."

"Keep telling yourself that. This country was built on people who gave their lives for peace, justice, freedom, and liberty for everyone. That's not what you're doing. You manufacture fear and demonize anyone that doesn't agree with you." Her mother looked up at Kara. "Whatever you're doing now, please stop. I beg you."

There it was. Once again, her mother was trying to discount her. She'd done it all her life. Kara was the reason Thomas was in the White House, not Isabella. Now, Isabella was the only one who knew the secret that could destroy Kara.

"You'll never understand, Mother."

Nancy entered with a tray holding the tea and biscotti. Nancy looked as if she didn't suspect a thing. Most likely, she'd be blamed for a medical mistake that would be swept under the rug. The small dose of regret circulating through Kara's veins subsided when she realized she was only accelerating the inevitable by a few days, maybe a couple of months, tops. With her mother off the chess board, there wouldn't be anyone who could verify the wild story the Garcia woman would tell. The president would call her a crackpot and any investigation into the issue would be called a witch hunt.

"Isabella, here's your tea," Nancy said as she placed the teak tray on the wicker table next to Isabella.

"Thank you, dear." Isabella steadied her hand and picked up the cup and saucer. She took a sip. A cold, chilling sadness returned, and a frown tried to force itself onto Kara's face, but she wouldn't let it. She needed to leave.

"Anything else?" Nancy asked.

"No thank you, dear," Isabella said.

Kara shook her head and Nancy left.

"Goodbye, Mother."

"Remember what I said, Kara. When you're in my position at the end of your life, all of this will come back to haunt you."

Kara ignored her and walked out of the room.

CHAPTER 58

STUNNED BY WHAT she'd just heard, Amelia sat in the passenger's seat as Ike drove Flyway. Her heart pounded with a deliberate and determined beat. Based on Frank's revelations and Isabella's confirmation, she now had one sole purpose for her life. A red-hot anger raged inside her and sought an avenue of escape. The clarity of her mission was stronger than for any high-value individual she'd eliminated in her time in the Air Force. She envisioned killing the president, wiping him and his sister from the face of the earth. As far as she was concerned, they were the ones who'd killed her aunt and uncle. The irrefutable facts alone would be enough to throw the son of Hitler out of the White House. But that wasn't enough for her. She found it hard to believe that the one man she'd pledged her allegiance to, by taking the Oath of Enlistment by which she'd lived her life, was the same man she most wanted to kill. She'd sacrificed everything to live up to that oath: the endless hours hunting her targets, the lonely isolation, and the killing. She'd become the warrior she wanted to be, ready to sacrifice so others could live free in the greatest country on earth. She'd shown her father the person she'd become, even though he'd never acknowledged her dedication or said that he was proud of what she'd done. But most of all, she'd proved to herself that she was a true patriot. Now, she'd throw it all away for a clean shot at her commander in chief and his conniving sister.

She bit her lower lip and turned to Ike. "We have to stop at Mom's," she said, making sure it sounded like an order and not a request.

"I'm sorry but we can't," he said, keeping his eyes on the road ahead. "The minute we left that place, Secret Service probably sent a report to the White House. They know we spoke to her, and they'll know why. We're out of time. We need to get this information out to the world. I've had Shannon prime her contacts in the media to set this up. We have to get back to Pittsburgh with the physical evidence and get it to the paper. Since they'll be watching for us at the *New York Times* and *Washington Post*, we'll give it to the *Pittsburgh Post-Gazette*. That's the only way to stop them. The only way we all live."

Amelia was feeling backed into a corner. She knew Ike was right. But that nagging feeling that her mother had something she had to hear wouldn't go away. It pushed her closer and closer to the edge of insanity. She was tired of battling with her father and trying to save her mother. The thought of facing her mother and father, maybe for the last time, became a growing weight that was slowly crushing her soul.

Amelia couldn't believe that her mother had kept something so life-changing from her. It was some sort of confession, that much she knew. Guilt and shame usually brought the bourbon to her mother's lips. But whatever this was affected them both.

"I understand," Amelia said, "but we have to go to the house. She knows something. I have a feeling about this. My sister always said that when things aren't black and white, trust your intuition. She called it emotional radar. My mother has something to tell me, and it has something to do with this. I'm sure of it."

"She's got a point," Frank said from the back seat.

Ike slowed the SUV and focused on Amelia. "Okay, Amelia. I get it. We still don't have much time."

"She'll tell me," Amelia said. She spotted their driveway approaching. "I'll make sure of that. Then we can go to Pittsburgh."

Ike turned the SUV into the driveway to her parents' house. "She has to be lucid. You know this, but she'll still be drunk."

"I know. I know. But she'll tell me." Amelia hoped she'd be lucid enough; she'd seen her go from blacked out on the sofa to a raging bull in less than an hour many times before. Her mother's message would come out; she just didn't know what she'd endure to get it. One thing for sure: she'd have to handle her father first.

Ike stopped the vehicle before they reached the wrought-iron security gate. He turned to face her. This time his eyes were soft, and he rested an elbow on the console between them, leaning closer. "Make sure you get everything you need. We can't go back. Since time is running out, believe me, you'll want to be sure you get what you need to get closure. And remember, I've got your back." Amelia sensed this was something he'd wished he'd been able to do to solve his parents' murders, but never had the chance to do. Ike looked down at her trembling hand. She tried to steady it.

"Thanks, Ike. Copy that."

Ike's words slowed the escalating loss of control she'd been feeling as they'd gotten closer to the house. The worst-case scenarios were looping through her mind. Her mother had something to do with her aunt's and uncle's deaths. Her mother had sold them out somehow. Her mother was setting some sort of trap. None of them made sense, but still, she kept thinking the worst. Her mouth was parched, and she wished she had water.

Frank leaned forward from the back seat and placed his hand on her shoulder. His eyes were tired and the lines on his face had multiplied. "Watch your heart rate. Anything over one seventy and fight or flight kicks in. That means auditory exclusion, cold hands, and shaky legs. You don't want that. You'll want to hear and remember every word. Keep your heart rate below that threshold, and you'll do fine."

Amelia guessed Frank had either been interrogated or had done interrogations during the war. He knew what he was talking about. She had the same reactions on her first mission when she'd targeted the first person she'd ever killed. With trembling hands, she'd pressed the two buttons that rifled the missile, and the flash filled the screen as it left the rail. She didn't remember hearing anything: not the missile briefing before the shot, not the JTAC saying *Time on Target, immediate!*, and not getting cleared hot before firing. She did remember switching to the daytime color camera, seeing the family members run out to pieces of the body, and realizing what she'd done.

Ike pulled forward and Amelia rolled her window down. The guard opened the gate and waved them through. He parked the SUV and eyed the steps up to the front door. Amelia got out, and Frank and Ike joined her at the base of the stairs. Amelia started to climb.

"Can you make it up?" Ike asked Frank who was standing at the bottom.

Amelia stopped and looked back at Frank.

Frank waved them on. "You two go ahead. I'll catch up."

"Bullshit," Amelia said as she came back down. She stood next to Frank and faced the stairs. "We'll go at your pace."

As they climbed, Amelia heard Frank's labored breathing. With each step, her own airway tightened. Sweat beaded on her forehead, and she wiped it away. She looked up the stairs at the door. Her father appeared in one of the sidelight windows. Her pulse skyrocketed. A familiar guilt gnawed at her resolve, as he condescendingly peered down at her, as he'd done so many times before. She knew he'd try to stop her from seeing her mother. But he had no right to do that. He'd never tried to get her mother the help she had needed. He just swept it under the rug. She told herself this wasn't home. This was the house where her mother and father lived. Her father had shunned and belittled her for the last time. She reminded herself that she *was* enough and decided to turn her guilt and shame into anger and action. Strength surged through her body and powered her legs up the last few steps. When they reached the door, she looked over at Frank and Ike.

"Are you ready for this?" she asked.

Both saw the resolve in her eyes and nodded. She opened the door, and they stepped inside.

Her father stood on the compass rose in the center of the marble foyer, arms folded, with McCallum skulking around the large staircase behind him. "What are you doing back?"

"I'm here to see Mom," Amelia said as defiantly as she could.

"Your mother is sleeping it off. She's out. Probably for the night."

"You two okay waiting here?" Amelia said to Ike and Frank.

"Sure are," Ike said firmly, eyeing McCallum.

Amelia headed for the stairs. Her father blocked her way. That set her off.

"Get out of my way!" She tried to step around him, but he slid in front of her.

"I'm not going to let you wake her up," he said.

"Don't pretend like you are protecting her." She was shouting now. "You never have. You've ignored her all along."

"You don't know what you're talking about!"

She was done playing around. "I'm going upstairs. Now, get out of the way." Amelia shoved her father aside. McCallum waited for her at the bottom of the stairs. Ignoring him, she tried to squeeze around him. He grabbed her wrist and twisted her arm behind her back. Pain shot through her shoulder and elbow. She writhed in agony and pulled to get free. Suddenly, his grip loosened. She turned in time to see Ike sweep-kick McCallum's legs from under him and pin him to the marble floor by the throat. McCallum struggled but couldn't free himself. Ike pulled McCallum's gun from his shoulder holster.

"Stay down," Ike shouted. "You touch her again, and I won't be so polite."

Ike looked up at Amelia. "You okay?"

Amelia rubbed her wrist. "I'm good."

Amelia saw Ike's attention go to the top of the stairs. She heard the heavy breathing before she saw her.

"A—Ameeelia." Her mother sounded worse than before. "Ameeelia? Are you down there?"

"Oh Christ," her father said, still standing at the center of the foyer.

Ike rose and let McCallum up. McCallum yanked his arm away from Ike and brushed himself off.

"Stay," Ike said.

Her mother made her way to the railing upstairs. Her hair was matted. Sweat soaked her face and darkened the collar of her light-gray nightgown. Her words had stolen her breath, and she struggled to get more air. Hanging on to the railing with one hand, she swung back and forth trying to find her balance. She swung one last time, then lost her grip and plopped down onto the floor. Amelia couldn't watch this. She dropped her head as a familiar sadness and debilitating shame took over. Ike and Frank were the first two outsiders ever to see her mother in this condition. She'd never told anyone about her drinking. She decided she had to stop her mother from embarrassing herself any further and started up the stairs.

Her mother raised a palm. "No!" That word was clear as a bell out of her mother's mouth. Like a gunshot, it stopped Amelia in her tracks.

Her mother's head hung down. She stared at the floor, then grabbed a baluster in front of her. She wagged her head and sobbed. "I have to tell you." Then she said it softly, "I have to tell you."

"Go back to bed," her father said, looking up at her.

Her mother took a few deep breaths, refocused her eyes on Amelia, and said, "These people will hurt you. They don't care who they hurt." She took another deep breath. "I didn't understand that thirty-four years ago." She dropped her head again and slowly shook it. "Harper was four, and I was struggling to raise her on my own."

"Bullshit," her father said, his arms folded.

Her mother pulled herself up a little closer to the baluster, raised her head, and locked her attention on her father. "It's true, you lying bastard. You know it is." She turned her attention back to Amelia and struggled to give her a drunken smile. "Your father was too busy running the company. At least, that's what I thought." Her smile disappeared, and she glowered at her father again. "Turns out, he was doing his executive assistant." Her mother started rocking and seemed to look off into some other time. "It crushed me. The man my father had chosen over my brother to run our company, the man I had chosen, betrayed me. I got mad." She searched for Amelia, locked her gaze on her, and began to cry again. "It just happened. I'm so sorry."

Her mother lost what was left of her composure and wept.

"What, Mom? What did you do?"

Her mother wiped her eyes with the back of her hand and forced herself to stop crying. "I had an affair." She widened her eyes. "It only lasted a few months." But then her eyes darkened, and she wagged her head again. "But that was long enough. I kept it from your father. He didn't deserve to know. Then you came along."

Amelia's heartbeat raced and a fissure filled with loneliness opened, devouring her self-confidence. Her body was sending her a warning. Still, she didn't understand. "What are you saying?"

Ignoring her question, her mother started rocking again. "Everything was fine until you had a blood test when you were five. We were Os, your father and I, and you were A. He knew he couldn't be your father."

Amelia found herself backing away. She ran her hand through her hair as an icy mass surrounded her heart. Something inside Amelia broke, not knowing if what had broken was bad or good. She stared at her father. "You're not my father? You're not my father and you knew it! That explains everything. That's why you treated me like shit. I wasn't enough for you."

Benton folded his arms. "I did the best I could."

That made Amelia laugh. "Yeah. Right." A strange sense of relief and contempt suddenly swept through Amelia. It all made sense now. She had always been enough. Her mother's secret was a terrible relief. And maybe, her father, whoever he was, would love her like a father should. Even at thirty-three, that meant a lot to her.

Still gripping the baluster, her mother eyed her father. It was clear that she wasn't done. "He threatened to expose me—and you," her mother said. "To my family, to our friends, to the world. He blackmailed me to vote my shares to keep him in his job or he would tell. So I buried it, and along with that secret, I buried myself. I became trapped, caged by my own indiscretions." She looked back at Amelia. "I told him I'd expose him, but he knew he'd be treated differently than you and I would—as women. Our shame is much heavier in this world."

Amelia saw her father grin. "You asshole. You favored Harper over me. I was never good enough as your daughter because I wasn't yours." She pointed upstairs. "But you're too stupid to see that you're the reason Mom has this problem. Yet you did nothing. You selfish prick." Amelia's chest inflated and she stood with her head up. She felt years of shame and anger spewing out of her. "You know what? I don't care who knows. I'm my own woman now. I'm proud of who I am and what I've done." She pointed a finger at Benton. "And I don't care what you think."

Amelia caught her breath. She looked at Ike. His eyes were wide, and he gave her a thumbs-up. Frank stood next to him, nodding his approval. For the first time in her parents' house, she felt heard and seen. It felt good, as if the weight of the world had been lifted.

She turned and looked back up the stairs at her mother, who was shaking her head again. Tears dripped from her cheeks and snot ran from her nose. There was more. Maybe it was the identity of her father. Could she meet him? What would he think about her? What would he say? Would he love her?

"Mom? Who is he? My father."

Her mother looked at McCallum then back at Amelia. "You know," she started shaking her head again. "Here's the thing. No one knows that but me. I promised I'd never tell you. But you have to know now. Your life may depend on it."

"Who is he?" Amelia said.

Her mother quivered and stopped crying. Gripping the baluster with both hands, she pulled herself up to her feet and steadied herself. She looked at Benton, shook her head, eyed McCallum, then looked at Amelia.

"Thomas Reed. The President of the United States."

CHAPTER 59

THE WORDS HAD vaporized Amelia's soul, leaving nothing alive inside her. In a searing flash, she was lightheaded and weak. Her bones seemed to liquify, and she grabbed for the newel post as she cried out and went down. Her future flashed before her with every day worse than this one. The unbearable shock left her powerless, stripped emotionally naked. She was the granddaughter of the most ruthless monster the world had ever known. Her head hung down, and she stared at the marble floor. She trembled and rocked, wanting to rip every cell in her body apart, separating herself from the biological reality she couldn't change. With no way out, she knew her life was over.

She felt a gentle hand on her back.

"Amelia," Ike whispered. "Look at me, Amelia."

Still rocking, she struggled to look up at him. Sitting on the floor with her, his eyes were kind, and she felt the warmth of his hand gently rubbing her back.

"I'm here. Frank is here. We're not going anywhere."

Amelia realized her face was wet with tears. "I'm done. My life. Everything is gone."

"I hear you. I may not know exactly what you're feeling but I know a little about devastation." Ike's eyes grew wide. "I'm here for you. It doesn't feel like it now, but you'll come back from this. What can I do?"

She kept rocking and shook her head.

"Listen to me," Ike said. "We are not our parents. We aren't destined by biology—by DNA. Who we are is determined by what we do. And you've lived a life of patriotic sacrifice for others. They can't take that away."

She saw Frank holding the gun on McCallum. He glanced at her, his penetrating blue eyes offering his support. "I'm here for you, too, Airman."

Amelia wanted to believe Ike's words but couldn't. A dense dark sadness pulled her down into a hell she never imagined. Her mother, the only real family she had, had betrayed her. She belonged to no one. She would be ostracized by the world. She'd lived her life as a patriot. Ike was right about that. But she did it with the DNA of a psychotic killer. She couldn't help but wonder if all the killing she had done to protect others had sprung from that demonic seed. She felt cold—dead inside.

"Come on," Ike stood and gently gripped her bicep and helped her to her feet. Then he wrapped his arms around her. He was strong, but gentle. Firm but soft. He held her, and she felt the dam break; she let go of trying to control what she couldn't control. She buried her face in his chest and wept. It felt good, as if poison were being drained from her body. When she was done, he leaned back, holding her by her shoulders.

Smiling now, he said, "I know you don't regret any of what you've done to help others in your life."

She thought about it. While her time in the Air Force was difficult, she wouldn't trade it for anything.

Ike apparently saw the light go on in her eyes. "Use that. Lean into that. Then lean into this with the courage you had as an RPA warrior."

She realized she'd stopped shaking. She saw her father still standing in the center of the room. She was surprised to see him with his hands in his pockets looking at the floor. Upstairs, her mother lay passed out on the floor.

Amelia had a decision to make. Try to hide or face this head on. Expose the president and his sister knowing she would expose herself to a flood of personal, and perhaps physical, attacks. McCallum or her father would see to that just to save their own asses. Either way, the truth would be out there, and she'd have to deal with the terrible label that would be given to her. Just like the other innocent victims of Lebensborn. Doing the right thing would destroy her life as she knew it. While she dabbled with the idea of hiding her secret, that cowardly thought made her too sick to seriously entertain it.

"You have no future," McCallum blurted out.

"Quiet!" Frank said, shoving the gun closer to McCallum's face.

"Your so-called father will disown you," McCallum continued. "That is unless his supporters kill you first."

Frank stepped behind him and put the gun against his skull. "Not a word more."

"He's right," Benton said, looking up. "We'll all be publicly humiliated. We'll lose our standing in the community, in the oil business, in the world. All of us. Including you, young lady." He kept his hands in his pockets. "Whatever you think you have, don't share it."

At that moment, Amelia realized Benton didn't know. He didn't know that he'd supported Hitler's son all the way to the White House. She scanned the little man that seconds ago was her father. A strange wave of empathy washed over her. She wasn't sure if she felt sorry for herself or for Benton. A little of both, perhaps. Maybe it was his choice of words or the fear hiding behind his arrogant façade.

"I'm with you, whatever you decide, but we're out of time," Ike said to Amelia. "Remember what happened at Isabella's."

Amelia knew that taking down the president and his sister would throw the country into chaos. The president would deny it, using lies and calling names. He'd fabricate a story that would prey on his supporters' fears and use them to destroy her. Nausea rose into her throat when she reminded herself that part of her biological grandfather lay hiding inside her. She was smothered by her own disgust. She couldn't cut it out or scrub it away. The evil of the Holocaust, the pain and shame of the Lebensborn children, and the brutality inflicted on so many by her grandfather hovered in her mind. A repulsive anger grew to an unbearable pressure inside her.

She stood up straight and brushed herself off. Despite the horrible heritage intimately ingrained within her, she decided taking Ike's advice was the right thing to do. The truth would always be with her. Face it now and make the president and his sister pay for what they'd done.

"Are you sure we have enough to take them down?" she said.

"I'm sure," Ike said.

"Take who down?" Benton said, panic in his voice.

"I want to do it," Amelia said. "The president will do everything he can. There will be riots in the streets. But only until the truth prevails. The VP will take over. I'll be a pariah. The battle for the soul of the country will rage, but I believe its values of justice, freedom, and liberty for all will prevail."

"You have no idea what you're doing and what you're destroying," Benton said.

Amelia walked up to Benton. "No sir. You're the one that had no idea what you were doing." She stepped within inches of his face. "You put the son of Hitler in the White House."

Benton looked like he'd been shot. He scanned the foyer, stunned. Then he locked his stare on Amelia. She knew he could see the truth in her eyes.

"Oh, God. Oh, God, no!"

A voice echoed from the hallway. "You won't be telling anyone." Michael Knight appeared from the shadows down the hallway and put a gun to Amelia's head.

CHAPTER 60

AMELIA FELT THE cold steel of the gun digging into the base of her skull. She remembered Knight from her teenage years. Each time she'd seen him, his presence had made her skin crawl like it did when she was close to a spider or a snake. Something had told her he wasn't right in the head. The steadiness of the gun against her skull said she was right. Realizing he would kill her in a matter of seconds, she was shocked that she wasn't afraid. Instead, a debilitating sadness smothered her, and her shoulders sagged as she thought about never being able to avenge her aunt's and uncle's deaths.

Ike moved toward them, but Knight jammed Amelia's head forward with his gun.

"Stop or I'll blow her head off."

Ike stopped but kept his eyes on Amelia.

"Let's see it," Knight said to Ike.

Ike hesitated, then reached behind him and pulled out his Glock, holding it between his thumb and forefinger. "Let her go. Take me instead," Ike said.

Knight just laughed. "Kick it over here. Hands behind your head."

Ike laid it on the tile, slid it with his toe, and locked his hands behind his head. The Glock stopped in front of Amelia.

"Step back," Knight ordered.

Ike took a few steps back. "Now you," Knight said, eyeing Frank.

Frank put the gun on the floor, raised his hands, and locked them behind his head.

McCallum bent down and picked it up. He shoved Frank toward Ike, moved past Benton, and stood next to Knight.

"What the hell is going on?" Benton said. "You work for me!"

"Not any longer," McCallum said, grinning.

Benton glared at Knight. "What are you doing?"

"If I were you, I'd shut up and stay out of this. You can't help your daughter now. She's gone too far."

Amelia looked at Ike. He stared back. She got the feeling he wanted her to stay quiet. Knight didn't know that she was the president's daughter. Not Benton's. She wasn't sure what he knew. But Benton didn't say a word.

Benton took another few steps closer. "You can't talk to me that way, Knight. I gave you your start."

"Apparently I can."

"Why are you doing this?"

Kara Williams stepped from the shadows down the hallway. "Because I told him to."

"Kara?" Benton said.

"Hello, Benton." She moved behind McCallum and Knight. "We'll isn't this convenient. All the traitors are here."

"No one will believe we are traitors," Frank said. His head was held high, and he stood tall despite still having his hands behind his head.

"They will when they see that you killed the president's elderly mother."

Amelia felt as if Knight had pulled the trigger. Isabella was the only corroborating witness. Williams had killed her own mother. Without her, it would be impossible to tie this all together. They'd failed. She glanced at Ike. His expression didn't change.

"Bullshit," Ike said. "She was fine when we left. Secret Service will testify to that."

"You mean the two agents you killed in cold blood?" Kara stepped around McCallum. "You see, you were all part of a conspiracy to try to take my brother down. But when our mother refused to help you, you decided to cover your tracks. Luckily, when we discovered what you'd done, we made it here and found you holding the Garcias hostage. We showed up along with the FBI and stopped you all."

"FBI?" Ike said, looking around the room.

Kara checked her watch. "Guess they're running behind."

"I won't go along with that," Benton said.

Kara's eyes flashed in anger. "You'll do whatever I say you'll do unless you want to spend the rest of your life in federal prison."

Benton looked at Amelia, then stepped back, his head down in shame.

Amelia's body trembled. Benton's spineless retreat was too much. She wanted to choke him. She didn't care about the gun to her head. "I always knew you were a coward!"

"Get her over with the others. This needs to look good," Kara said.

Knight shoved Amelia in the back of her head with his gun. "Get over there with those two."

Amelia stumbled forward then stood next to Ike. Frank, Ike, and Amelia stood shoulder to shoulder. Amelia knew this was it. She thought about Frank. He didn't deserve to die like this. She remembered Maria and knew how this would destroy her. "I'm sorry I got you both involved."

Ike grabbed her hand and squeezed it. "It's not over yet."

"It's been my honor, Airman," Frank said.

"Oh, how sweet," Kara said sarcastically. She pointed at Amelia. "Her first."

McCallum moved closer to Ike and raised his gun. "I'll take care of him."

Benton moved around McCallum and next to Knight.

"I knew you'd make the right decision," Kara said to Benton.

Knight aimed his gun at Amelia's face. A shiver traveled through her, but she refused to give these people the satisfaction of seeing her break down. She'd live what was left of her young life on her terms. If this was it, so be it.

As Knight locked his arm to fire, Benton lunged at him, wrapping his arms around Knight, and pinning the gun between them. It fired and both men froze, then Benton slid to the ground.

Propelled by her perpetual longing for a father-daughter bond, Amelia instinctively rushed to Benton, kneeling on the floor and turning him to face her. Blood bloomed on the chest of his white shirt and soaked it. His eyes were dilated, but they found Amelia. A quivering smile spread across his face as blood seeped from the corner of his mouth. He couldn't speak. He stared at her, smiling weakly. Part of her wished he wouldn't leave her now, and part wondered what had taken him so long. After all those years of knowing she wasn't his, his last act was one of a father. She wiped her eyes and smiled back. He stopped breathing and went limp in her arms. She turned back toward Ike.

"Don't move," McCallum said, still holding Ike and Frank in place with the gun.

But the front door exploded open. "Everybody freeze! FBI!" In the doorway, Mia was in a firing position with the gun pointed in Ike's direction. Knight pointed his gun down at Amelia's head, but Kara pushed it away.

"No. This is better," Kara said. "McCallum, don't kill him." Kara faced Mia. "You're a little late."

CHAPTER 61

MIA EYED IKE and Frank, then spotted Amelia on the ground with Benton. McCallum backed away, giving Mia a clear shot. Ike thought he saw a sliver of doubt in her expression or maybe just remorse over having to kill him. Either way, there was a battle going on in her mind.

"I told you to leave this alone," she said to Ike.

Ike couldn't believe she could shoot him. But the uncertainty in her eyes said otherwise. "I couldn't do that," he said.

"Agent. Take them out. They killed my mother and two Secret Service agents," Kara ordered.

Mia glanced at Kara then back at Ike. Obviously weighing her options.

"You know what will happen if you don't," Kara said.

She kept her aim squarely on Ike. "I'm sorry, Ike."

Ike knew this would be cold-blooded murder. But somehow, he believed they'd make it look as if it was justified. Still, he could see there was a part of Mia that didn't want to do it. He was shocked to think that the only woman he'd ever loved could kill him. "You don't have to do this," he said as his self-preservation ate away at his love for Mia. The longer she held her aim on Ike, the more he wanted to make a preemptive move, eliminating the threat. It was all reflexive, but his feelings for Mia paralyzed him.

"You killed the president's mother?" she asked.

It was a question to which he was sure she knew the answer. Ike decided to trust his gut and dropped his hands to his side. "We didn't do that. Think about it. Why would we do that? We have proof they are hiding the true identity of the president. Isabella is part of that fact set. We need her to pull this all together." Out of the corner of his eye, Ike could see Knight still holding the gun at his side. He wasn't targeting Amelia. Mia's stare relaxed for a second as she thought it through. When she locked her eyes on Ike again, he saw them dart toward Knight. Then she dropped her head targeting Ike through the gun sight. She closed one eye, but then winked the other. Ike recognized the signal. "No!" he yelled.

She jerked the gun, targeted McCallum, and fired. As he went down, she tried to target Knight, but she was too slow. He fired when she did. She missed, but Knight's bullet hit her in the neck just above the vest. Momentarily stunned, Mia clenched her throat with blood spurting between her fingers. Ike shook off the horror, snatched McCallum's gun from the floor, moved in front of Frank, and took aim at Knight. Putting the gun to Amelia's head again, Knight used her as a shield. Kara disappeared down the hallway.

"Don't or I'll kill her," Knight said, panic in his voice. He dragged Amelia to the open front door, then they disappeared. Ike dashed to Mia, dropping to his knees and setting the gun on the floor. A pool of blood grew quickly beneath her neck and created a bright red aura around her head. The bullet had severed her carotid. She was bleeding out. Her eyes were panicked.

"No! No!" Ike yelled. He pressed his fingers into the wound. This was the woman he loved. He knew that now. Regret put an arrow through his heart when he realized these were her last breaths in this world. "I love you, Mia."

"I love you too," she choked out. She cut her eyes to the door. Struggling to breathe, she whispered in a gurgle, "Finish what you've started." Her eyes froze on him.

"No, Mia! Stay with me!"

Her body went limp. Ike could tell whatever energy made a person alive was gone. An empty darkness devoured him, as if *his* life left his body, too. Tears blurred his vision. He caved in on himself like a collapsing black hole. In that moment, he realized he'd made a mistake a long time ago. Powerless, he looked at her limp, blood-soaked body, lifted her to his chest, and held her. Her arms dangled like a rag doll's. Like an animal he roared at the top of his lungs. "No!"

Beside him, Frank leaned in. "Go. I've got her."

Ike gently laid Mia on the cold floor and closed her eyelids. Then, a fuse lit inside him. Anger spun up like a tornado and took over every part of his body. He remembered what she'd just said. *Finish what you've started.* He looked at the open door where Knight had left with Amelia. After what she'd been through, he wouldn't lose her too. She deserved a chance at rebuilding her life.

He picked up the gun and charged out the door. He spotted Knight making his way across the front lawn toward the bridge over the lagoon. Mia's car blocked the driveway. The only escape was on foot. He moved like lightning down the steps to finish what he'd started.

Knight moved slower as he dragged Amelia down the path of woodchips that cut through the palmettos and pine straw. He wasn't much bigger than she was, and she struggled against his grip, slowing him with every step, but the gun against her head forced her compliance. The pathway wound to the left then the right before terminating at the bleached gray wooden bridge that crossed the large lagoon. Ike caught up to them there. Knight stopped halfway across, holding Amelia in front of him. Standing on the end of the bridge, Ike kept his aim on Knight but didn't have a clear shot.

"Stay there," Knight said, still holding the gun to Amelia's temple.

"Shoot, Ike," Amelia yelled.

Ike took aim but didn't have a clear shot. He couldn't fire without hitting Amelia.

"It doesn't matter if you hit me," Amelia said.

"Shut up!" Knight said as he pushed her head to the side with the barrel of the gun.

"Drop it, Rossi," Knight said. "Drop it now or I kill her."

Ike heard sirens again. They were closer now. "It's over, Knight. You drop it."

"No. It's not over. You're still wanted for the killing of the president's mother."

"Don't listen to him," Amelia said.

"Drop it or I'll shoot!" Knight repeated.

An idea flashed into Ike's mind. "If I do that, I'll be in a nine-line bind." Knight knew the oilfield slang. "That's the point. I'll kill her right now!"

Ike heard the desperation in Knight's voice and knew he had no choice. He hoped Amelia correctly interpreted his message. If not, he'd be dead in the next few seconds. He gently laid the gun on the bridge in front of him. When Knight pulled the gun from Amelia's head to shoot Ike, Ike dropped his head and charged Knight in perfect tackling form. Amelia grabbed Knight's arm and slammed it against the railing. Knight fought back, saw what was coming, and got a shot off just as Ike hit him. It burned into Ike's shoulder. But Ike's momentum drove them into the railing, shattering it, and they plunged into the murky lagoon. Now underwater, Ike lost his grip on Knight, and Knight kicked him deeper, then struggled to the surface. But Ike caught Knight's foot and pulled him back under, and they both fought until they surfaced. Ike's shoulder throbbed and blood spread through the water. He took a punch from Knight, but grabbed Knight's fist and head butted him. It stunned Knight.

Amelia yelled from above, "Ike! Gator!" Gasping for air, Ike scanned the surface in front of them and saw the gator closing fast on a straight path, like a torpedo locked on its target. Knight hit Ike again and spun him toward the gator. Ike's blood filled the water. Now the gator was less than twenty feet away and closing fast. Knight swung again, but mustering what strength he had left, Ike blocked it and grabbed Knight's forearm, locking Knight's hand under his armpit. Twisting with everything he had left, he clocked Knight with his other fist, momentarily stunning him, and spun him toward the gator. Knight's eyes grew wide as he faced the gator's wide-open mouth. Ike gave him one final shove, and the gator took him under. Ike felt the gator's tail brush his legs in the water. He turned and saw Amelia along the edge under the bridge.

"Swim, Ike! There's another one!" Amelia yelled from the shoreline, pointing behind him.

Ike swam hard and made it to the shore. He looked behind him and watched the second gator turn away. Amelia ducked under his shoulder and helped him walk back onto the bridge. Exhausted, he stopped and hugged Amelia. At least one person would live to maybe love again. Over her shoulder, he looked back at the house. The paramedics stood on the front porch, empty-handed with their heads down. Amelia pulled back and looked toward the house, too.

"I'm so sorry, Ike," Amelia said.

Feeling the weight of the worst kind of sadness—that driven by regret—Ike looked back at Amelia. "I lost her a long time ago."

Amelia hugged him again, then let him go. She looked toward her parents' house. This time, she seemed sad.

Ike knew what she was thinking. "He saved your life. Just like a father should."

Amelia turned back to Ike. "I know." She leaned her head into his chest. Ike wrapped his arm around her.

Two men approached the other side of the bridge. At first, they were only dark silhouettes. Then Ike recognized Agent Sherman. The second man was Black, lean, dressed in a tweed sports coat. Both had their guns drawn as they approached.

Sherman recognized Ike and dropped his gun to his side. As he got close, he apparently recognized the expression on Ike's face. Sherman looked as if he'd been shot himself. "I told her to wait for us. Where is she?"

Ike shook his head slowly. "In the house. She's gone."

Sherman holstered his gun and looked over the side of the bridge. "Knight?"

Ike nodded. "What about Williams?"

Sherman flicked his head in the other man's direction. "I think Detective Wilson's men have her."

Wilson holstered his gun. "Got her trying to run away down the beach. At seventy-two, it wasn't much of a chase."

Amelia looked at Detective Wilson.

"Are you all right?" he asked.

"I am," she said, lying to him for the second time.

"Next time, just tell me the truth," Wilson said.

Amelia, still soaking wet, gave him a self-deprecating huff.

Ike realized it was over. He pulled out his phone, still soaking wet, opened the email app, and pulled up the draft of the message addressed to all the media outlets. In addition to the detailed explanation of the evidence they'd gathered, there were half a dozen attachments including the photo Amelia took of the box on the sea floor, the translated message, the pictures of the box and its contents that Ike had taken in Pittsburgh, and an audio file. He showed the phone to Amelia.

"You ready to take them down?"

Amelia pushed her hair away from her face. She looked at the phone in Ike's hand, apparently struck by the gravity, both personally and politically, of what she was about to do. She seemed tired and maybe even defeated.

"What about Isabella? They killed her. She's the only one who can corroborate the story. We need her to make the link."

Ike took the phone and opened another app. He played a recording of their conversation at Isabella's that included her permission to record it.

Amelia's face bloomed into a smile, and she hugged Ike. He was warm and wet, but she didn't seem to care. She gave Ike a look he'd never forget. Satisfied, determined, and worried. He imagined it was the look of a warrior about to pull the trigger and a woman about to destroy her life for her country. Then she took the phone, opened the email app, and pressed send.

CHAPTER 62

Two Months Later...

AMELIA SIPPED HER glass of Cabernet Sauvignon and admired Rossi's festive holiday décor. Red and green lights ran along the outline of the thick mahogany millwork separating the walls from the ceiling. The green garland that hung from every straight edge glowed with what looked like starlight from the tiny LEDs buried within it. The stage, normally filled with an upright piano and a couple of guitars, held a massive scotch pine, decorated with silver balls, more white LED lights, and a mix of ornaments. Some were classic Rossi family heirlooms handed down for generations. Others were detailed hand-carved models of many of the icons of the Christmas season, donated by Frank.

Amelia stood next to Maria, who watched Ike and Jack laughing as they took turns sticking their tongues out while they slid the silver shuffleboard pucks through the sawdust, trying to knock the other's pucks from the table as Lauren and Jimmy clapped, cheering them on. Frank sat at the bar facing Randy, trading jokes while working their way through a plate of Christmas cookies. For the first time in her life, Amelia was enjoying Christmas. The drama of past holidays, when she'd walked on eggshells to avoid setting off her mother, was gone. She even allowed herself to drink on this special occasion without worrying about her mother's disease.

"I don't think they ever grow up," Maria said, watching Ike try to use body English to guide his puck.

Amelia looked at the grin on Ike's face. "I don't think I want them to."

Maria offered her glass for a toast. Amelia clicked it, and they took a drink.

"How's he doing?" Amelia asked, still looking at Ike.

"He's doing what he does best. Covering the pain. He's had twenty-three years of practice."

"Did you ever meet her?"

"A couple of times. Ike didn't think I knew he was dating her. I think he thought I wouldn't approve. He was trying to protect me in some weird way. But I liked her. She was like him. Full of energy. Fun. At least that was the read I had. I didn't know how much he cared for her until recently, though."

Amelia wondered what Ike thought when he watched her die. They'd never talked about it.

"How's your mom?" Maria asked.

"She's good. After the thirty-day rehab, she went back to Highland Park to meet with her extended family and the board to explain things."

"That's right. I forgot. Congratulations. Ike said you're running both Winkler Oil and Winkler ROV."

"I can't believe it," Amelia said. On her mother's recommendation, the board approved her as the CEO of Winkler Oil. Her uncle had passed control of the ROV business on to her in his will. Her cousin, who lived in California now, had fully supported that move.

"What about all that other stuff? Did it calm down yet?" Maria asked.

"A little. But I calmed down a lot. When the DNA testing was finished and proved the president was not born in this country, and he and I were descendants of Hitler, it was the worst. Haters and trolls came out from under their rocks to attack me along with a dozen media outlets. When he rallied them to go after me for exposing him, I thought it was the end. But something your brother said helped me. I *leaned* into the truth. I didn't want to hide, so I told the truth to everyone who'd listen."

Maria nodded in agreement. "I remember you on the morning talk shows. That had to be scary."

"It was. I was completely vulnerable. Emotionally raw. I put it all out there. My mom's affair. The fact that the president was the product of Lebensborn, son of Hitler and a mother taken from Norway and forced to have sex with Hitler to propagate children with good Aryan blood to expand the master race. And that I was the granddaughter of the most despicable man in history. Another Lebensborn descendant cloaked in shame."

"Well, if you want my opinion, you did a great thing. The president resigned, and I for one was happy to see him go. I can't believe he didn't know about it, though."

Amelia chuckled facetiously. "His sister never cracked. Said it was all her. That her mother and she were the only ones who knew. That's why she killed her."

"She got hers. You all nailed her for all her crimes, including the murders of your aunt and uncle." Maria took another sip of her wine.

"I used to think the president should pay for killing my aunt and uncle, but a part of me realized that maybe he didn't know, and on some level, he was once an innocent victim of the Lebensborn project." Amelia thought of her aunt and uncle. Her uncle would be proud of her, and her aunt would have been cheering her on every step of her journey over the last few months. She wished they were still alive.

Apparently reading Amelia's sadness, Maria said, "I'm sorry. I didn't mean to upset you."

"No. It's fine. I just miss them." Amelia enjoyed another gulp of the dry wine, hoping it would kill the pain. "The good news is that with my new platform, I feel like I can do a lot of good. Once I leaned in and faced the truth with as much courage as I could muster, things started to get better. Other Lebensborn descendants reached out to me. Helped me see that we were all just innocent victims of a terrible war crime. That we are not defined by our parents' heritage or DNA. We make our own lives. I feel like I know why I've been put on this earth now. To support them and people like them, and me, everywhere."

"Is that how you found out about the Norwegian woman?"

"Yes. I met a woman through a Facebook group who said that her sister had been forced to apply to Lebensborn. When she was accepted, they took her to Germany. That's where she was forced to have sex with Hitler. Ten months later, the SS took her son. That was 1945. The sister, the woman I met on Facebook, agreed to a DNA test, and the comparison with mine and with thirty-nine other Hitler descendants who were tested in 2010 confirmed her story. When the woman tried to go back to Norway in 1946, she was called a Nazi whore. She died just a few years later."

"I can't believe I didn't know that those horrible things went on during the war. I'm sorry it all happened that way."

Maria took a long pull from her glass, then seemed to hesitate, pondering whether she should say whatever was on her mind. "We're girlfriends, right?"

"The best. If it wasn't for your brother, I wouldn't be alive. And if it wasn't for your support, he might not have taken my case. But most of all, you're the only one I can talk to about all this and not feel judged."

They clicked their glasses again.

"I'm worried about you," Maria said. "About all that mess with your father. Oh, I'm sorry—I mean Benton."

Amelia had had the same concern until she put herself in her father's shoes. As her answer formed in her mind, a warmth rose through her body and a tear ran from her eye. "You were right the first time. Benton was my father. He raised me and, in the end, he protected me. In the last action of his life, he did what a father would do. And in his case, he knew I wasn't his, but he did it anyway. I wished it could have been different all those years, but I'm grateful for that last unselfish act."

A tear ran down Maria's cheek and she turned and hugged Amelia. Amelia hugged her back and didn't want to let go. This is what it felt like to belong. To fit in by being yourself.

"Merry Christmas, Amelia," Maria whispered.

"Merry Christmas, Maria."

Maria let go and gave Amelia a wide smile. "Enough of that. You look stunning. Are you going somewhere after this?"

Amelia gave Maria her best Cheshire Cat smile. "I deleted those dating apps and just relied on my heart."

Maria grinned and offered her another toast but said nothing. They continued to watch the boys play their game.

CHAPTER 63

IKE WATCHED JACK, standing next to him, as his sparkling blue eyes searched the table for the optimum path for his last shot. The smell of sawdust was comforting and reminded Ike of the many games he'd played with his father when he was about Jack's age. Unlike Ike's younger self, the twelve-year-old genius standing next to him was probably calculating the perfect angle and velocity of the silver puck in his hand, based on its mass, the friction coefficient along the sawdust-covered table, and the force he planned to apply to the game piece.

Jack broke his trance, looked over, and grinned at Ike. "Fifteen–fourteen. If I get two more points, I win!"

"That you will, but I have two pucks in the three-point zone. Miss either one and I win!" Ike said, smiling back.

Now Jack was beaming. At that moment, Ike realized he didn't have a worry in the world. This was just plain old no-money fun. He was filled with the joy of playing the game.

Jack took the shot, knocking both of Ike's pucks from the table, then the puck spun to a stop in the two-point zone. Jack jumped up and down as Aunt Lauren and Cousin Jimmy cheered from the side. He ran to them, slapping their high fives, then ran back to Ike. Ike raised his hand and Jack slapped it, hugging Ike right after.

"Great shot, Jack," Ike said as he returned Jack's hug. He looked at Jimmy. "You're up, big guy."

Jack and Jimmy ran to opposite ends of the table and began playing. Ike walked over to Lauren.

"That was fun," he said as he grabbed his Guinness off the table.

"I could tell," she said with kindness in her eyes. "It's great to see." Ike always loved her unwavering, nonjudgmental support for him and his well-being. He was happy she was here on Christmas Eve.

"You've done a great job with them both." Ike took a sip of beer as they watched the boys slide their pucks down the table.

"You've been a big part of that," Lauren said. "But I think you know it. They both adore you."

"I do. And I adore them."

"Are you doing okay these days?"

Ike took another drink. He wasn't comfortable talking about how he felt. But Lauren was a good friend with nothing but his best interests at heart. Still, talking with Lauren about the fact that he was having trouble dealing with the loss of the only woman he ever loved seemed awkward. Despite the subfreezing temperature outside, he suddenly felt warm and pulled down the zipper on his Steelers quarter-zip sweater.

"I have my good days and bad days thinking about Mia. When I think about her, the depth of my sadness seems bottomless. But then I remember the time we did have together and what she did for me, and I realize how grateful I am that she was even in my life."

Lauren paused for a moment, then said, "After losing my husband in Afghanistan, I was the same way—still am to some extent. The pain never goes away." She looked at Jack and Jimmy giggling with each other. "But life sends you moments of joy that feel much more special because of it. It'll get better. I promise."

Ike turned to her and offered her his glass. She touched it gently with the rim of her wine glass and they both drank.

"Merry Christmas, Lauren."

"Merry Christmas."

Holding their glasses aside, they hugged.

"I'll see you before you all go. I gotta make the rounds," he said.

"I'll be here," Lauren said.

Ike walked through the empty tables and joined Maria and Amelia. "Ladies."

"That looked like fun," Maria said.

"It was. You ladies look very pretty tonight. You especially, Amelia. Decide to give the basic black a break?"

"Yes, I did," Amelia said, making it obvious she was eyeing Ike's attire. "And I see you dressed up for the occasion, too. Looks like your best Steelers outfit."

Ike posed like a runway model. "Of course. In honor of the playoffs."

"I know what you'll be doing in two weeks," Amelia said to Maria.

"Hopefully all the way into February," Maria said. She offered her glass and toasted with Ike.

Maria seemed to sense the moment. "I'll let you two visit. I have to check on Randy and Frank. I don't want them to eat all my cookies," Maria said as she winked at Amelia and left.

"How are you feeling these days? You look great," Ike said to Amelia.

"I'm hanging in there. Mom's doing good and that helps. And Shannon has been showing me the ropes of leading a big organization. I think I'm starting to get the hang of it."

"That's great." Ike could see that while Amelia did look better and was much more relaxed, the pain of her losses—of her uncle and aunt and Benton—was still there. He was happy he'd helped her resolve some of the emotional trauma of those losses by uncovering the truth, but that truth had come at a great cost to her.

Amelia offered her wine glass and Ike touched it with his glass. "I was just telling Maria that I really appreciate all you've done for me," she said. "You both risked everything to find out who killed my aunt and uncle. I'll never forget that."

"It was our pleasure," Ike said. "But what we did pales in comparison to what you chose to do, no matter what the cost. Not many people would have done that." Ike took a drink. "And I know it wasn't easy watching Benton die."

A cheer went up from the shuffleboard table and Amelia and Ike watched Jimmy celebrate a rare win over Jack. Keeping her eyes on the boys, Amelia said, "I had a little trouble reconciling what he did for me at the end compared to how he treated me for most of his life. I think I've made peace with that."

"If I can offer you one observation I've made over the years, there is evil and good in all of us, but it's the little steps that take us one way or the other. I think a part of Benton felt that way all along, it was just buried under all that other stuff."

That seemed to connect with Amelia.

"I hadn't thought of it that way." Amelia faced Ike. She smiled but her lower lip quivered, her eyes silently begging for comfort. "How do you deal with your loss? I mean you lost both your parents and raised your little sister. You managed that well."

"I don't know about well. But thanks. You know, I think it was two things. The first was recognizing that the world wasn't built to serve me. I just thought it was. I had to face the pain, even welcome it as part of a greater process. The second was something my father told me. He said that if you enter the ring, expect to get punched and knocked down. He said that life is a process of dealing with pain, uncertainty, and hard work. But if you're afraid of getting knocked down and never get in the ring and just watch life from the bleachers, you'll never know the true joy of getting back up, doing your best for yourself and others, and pushing through the pain to accomplish something meaningful."

Amelia thought for a second, then said, "Hmmm. Your dad sounds like a great man."

"He was human. But I hope I don't need to tell you that you're a great woman. What you've done for your country, what you're doing now, will not easily be forgotten. I'm proud to know you."

"Thanks, Ike. Merry Christmas."

"Merry Christmas." Ike leaned in, not knowing if she'd pull away like she'd done when they first met. Instead, she wrapped her arms around him and held on. Ike could feel a couple of sobs against his shoulder. When she pulled back, he could see they were tears of joy.

"Now, you look like you're going somewhere," Ike said, making it sound like a question.

Amelia shrugged, grinned, and sipped her wine.

Ike noticed a shadow at the front door of the restaurant. A solid knock quickly followed.

Randy started for the door from behind the bar with one palm in the air. "I'll get it, boss."

Randy unlocked the door, opened it a little, and disappeared behind it for a moment. Then he came back inside, leading Agent Sherman into Rossi's. Sherman had a huge Tyvek envelope under his arm. Randy led him to Ike. Randy gently squeezed Ike's arm and leaned in, concern in his eyes, and whispered, "I got your back, boss. Here if you need me." Randy headed back behind the bar.

Sherman walked up to Ike and offered his hand. Ike shook it. "Merry Christmas, Agent Sherman." He could tell by Sherman's demeanor this wasn't a visit to wish him a happy holiday.

"Hi, Ike." He looked at Amelia. "Miss Garcia. I want to thank you both for all you've done, and unofficially, the FBI is in debt to you both. We had no idea we had a few bad apples at the top. Without you two, we never would have known how bad it really was." He looked down at the bulky light-gray envelope under his arm. He frowned, and when his eyes found Ike's, he seemed very sad. Ike braced for whatever he had to say.

"I was instructed that if anything happened to Mia to give this to you sixty days later. I was never here, and I never gave this to you. We never had this conversation. Understood?"

Ike was being pulled back into a desolate black hole at the mention of Mia's name. With a deep breath, he gathered himself, nodded, and eyed the envelope as Sherman handed it to him. It felt much heavier than it should have. The image of Mia bleeding out and drawing her last breaths barged into Ike's mind. He'd realized he had loved her from the beginning. Now he knew that only happened once in a lifetime for most people, if at all. He wondered if it could ever happen again.

Sherman leaned closer. "That sniper. He was shooting at her, not you. We've identified him as a hit man who'd done work for the Giordano family." He pointed at the envelope. "He didn't want you to have that. Be careful."

With that, Sherman turned and headed out the door.

CHAPTER 64

IKE LOOKED AROUND the room. Jack and Jimmy were still playing shuffleboard, but everyone else had their eyes on him. He studied the envelope in his hand. This was something Mia wanted him to have. He thought about his mother and how Mia may have found the answer he'd been searching for all his adult life. He wondered what Mia had wanted to give him knowing that he'd only read it after she was gone. Ike took the envelope, walked to the first booth he came to, and sat down on the deep crimson Naugahyde seat. He laid the bulging envelope in front of him. Scanning the room, he found Maria. He patted the seat next to him. If this was an answer, she deserved to see it as much as he did. She walked over to the booth, slid in next to him, and hugged his arm. "Wasted Time" by the Eagles began to play on the Sonos system and Randy pulled out his phone and turned it off. Ike looked at Maria and she nodded. He ripped the envelope open.

The envelope contained a brown accordion file folder that held a file, a three-ring binder, and a letter. The letter was addressed to Ike in Mia's handwriting. He held it for a moment and remembered her touch and the excitement he'd felt when they were given a second chance together. Now, that chance was gone. He gently set it aside. The first two pages in the file were the unredacted Confidential Informant Agreement. Ike and Maria read it together. Their mother was a confidential informant.

The controlling agent's name was Anthony Esposito. Ike remembered that name for some reason.

"Mom worked for the FBI? That can't be," Maria said, her voice high and strained.

Ike knew how she felt. His mother had been the bedrock of honesty, and she was adamant that the Mafia had given Italian Americans a bad name. Criminals were criminals. Ike and his sister had been on the receiving end of many lectures. He also couldn't see his mother risking her life, and those of her family, with such a deal. But the form didn't say what she was working on or why.

He set the form aside and began reading the typewritten notes on the next page. Each entry had a date and time. He looked at Maria and they started reading the summary together. His mother apparently worked on a murder and racketeering case against Joseph Giordano Sr., who frequented the restaurant where Ike's mother worked. The same restaurant Ike later bought and turned into Rossi's. Based on the notes, she eavesdropped on conversations while serving the family members in the old restaurant's private room. She gathered evidence of crimes, their dates, and sometimes the perpetrators. Near the end of the notes, there was a description of a conversation where Joseph Giordano Sr. authorized a hit. After that entry, a single sentence said the informant had been compromised and killed.

Maria looked at Ike wide-eyed, apparently in shock. She couldn't speak. Ike put his arm around her, and she laid her head on his shoulder. There was a small binder remaining in the larger file. Ike thought he knew what it might be.

"Can I go on?" Ike asked.

"Yes," she said, keeping her head on his shoulder.

He pulled the binder from the accordion file. It was the murder book from their parents' murder. His parents' names and the date of their murder were at the top of the cover. Maria began to cry.

Ike had seen murder books before, and skipped over the chronological record, crime scene log and report, death report, crime scene photographs, and medical examiner reports. Neither he nor Maria needed to relive that right now. He flipped to the arrest report tab first. There was nothing there. Then, he opened the suspect information section. One suspect had been identified. His name was Vincent DiOrio. Maria dug her fingers into Ike's arm, still crying. He had a long rap sheet, which was included. It was clear he worked for the Giordano family. The last line caught Ike's eye. DiOrio died three days after the murder. The man who killed his parents had died in a car accident three days later.

Ike closed the book, wrapped his arms around Maria, and kissed the top of her head. "It's all right, Sis. It's okay."

Ike knew Joseph Giordano Sr. had died a long time ago. His son was running what was left of the family. It would be pointless to go after him. Still holding Maria, he realized it was over. Maria was the most important thing in his life. Time had taken his opportunity for vengeance. Both the killer and the mob boss who put out the hit were dead. The only question left was why his mother took such a risk. It was completely out of character. The person who would know would be the handling agent. Maybe he'd try to track him down. He waited to feel the release. The thing he'd sought for all these years. It didn't come. The pain of the loss remained like a monument, looming permanently in the darkest reaches of his soul. Ike closed the murder book and Maria sat up, drying her eyes with her hands. She reached over and covered Ike's hand.

"Thank you, brother. Thanks for everything." Maria stood and pointed to the envelope on the table. "I'll let you read that." She walked to Amelia who put her arm around her and walked with her to the bar.

Ike picked up the letter. The small envelope was soft linen, Mia's personal stationery. As always, her penmanship was sweeping and beautiful. Ike opened the letter and unfolded the pages and began to read.

Dear Ike,

If you're reading this, I am sorry. I've failed. Please know that I love you and always will. I realize now that I always had. You may not understand, but I had no choice but to do what I did. A man named Michael Knight approached me and said that if I didn't cooperate, the FBI would charge my father for working with the Giordano family. His business had gotten into trouble during the pandemic, and he was forced to work for them to save it. They assured me he would have gone to prison for the remainder of his life.

I tried to get the information on your mother to you that day in Pittsburgh. But the sniper put an end to that. It's all here for you now. They can't prosecute a dead woman. I hope it gives you the peace you've sought for so long.

I'll look for you somewhere down the road. I hope it's a very long time.

Love

Mia

Ike dropped the letter. He wiped a tear rolling down his cheek. Rossi's was silent now. He looked toward the shuffleboard table and saw Jimmy and Jack standing with Lauren, staring back at him. Jack's face had turned sad. He said something to Lauren. She nodded, and Jack walked toward Ike. He stopped at the booth. Ike could see the tears in his eyes.

"You okay?" Jack asked, his eyes widening.

"Come here, Jack." Ike pointed to the seat next to him. Jack sat and Ike hugged him. Jack squeezed him hard.

"I'm okay, Jack." Ike released his hug and Jack looked at him. "You remember how you felt after the trial last year?"

Jack silently wiped his face with the back of his hand. "I cried, but I was happy that the judge said I didn't do anything wrong."

"That's how I feel," Ike said.

Happiness rocketed across Jack's face. He jumped up and ran to Lauren. "He's okay. He's okay!"

Ike had to smile. He *was* okay. He searched above the bar and found the photograph of he and his mother in the kitchen again. This time, he felt his mother's joy of being with her son. The smile on his face said he'd felt the same. For the first time, the need for revenge didn't overtake him. He knew that time had taken down her killers. She wouldn't want him to do anything else except be of service to others. He saw Jack and Amelia and knew he'd done that. Somewhere, his mother would be bragging about him.

Frank walked over to the booth with a present in his hand and sat down facing Ike. He looked at Ike. "Glad we got that cleared up."

Ike noticed the bruise on Frank's cheek. "I can't thank you enough for all you've done. I'm sorry it was so rough. You didn't deserve any of it. You've already served your country, your community, and me. You've always been my hero. And I almost got you killed."

"Bull," Frank said. "I did what I was supposed to do. If I've learned anything in all these years, it's that I shouldn't worry about dying. It's how I live each day that I'm concerned about. I'd do this all again."

"That may be so, but we never would have gotten to the bottom of this without your help."

Frank pulled out a small, wrapped gift. "I gotta get home to Bella. I celebrate every Christmas Eve with her."

"You sure you're okay alone?"

Frank gave Ike a gentle smile. "I'm never alone."

He handed the gift to Ike and his eyes went glossy. "I'm so proud of you. What you do for others is remarkable, young man. Your mom and dad are too, I'm sure. I'd like to think my own son would have turned out as well. Merry Christmas."

Frank waited for Ike to open it. When he did, it was an old hand-carved picture frame Frank had made. Ike saw the photo it contained. Frank stood next to a nine-year-old Ike on the front steps of Frank's house. Ike remembered the day Bella had taken the picture.

Frank stood, and Ike stood with him. Frank offered his hand, but Ike embraced him. "Thanks, Frank. Thanks for all of it."

"Okay. That's enough of that," Frank said, pulling back. Amelia walked up.

"You leaving?" she said to Frank.

Frank bobbed his head. "I have to go celebrate with my bride."

Amelia opened her arms and Frank gave her a long hug.

"Hey, I only got a split-second hug," Ike protested.

Frank pulled back and smiled. "You're not a beautiful young lady, either." Frank searched Amelia's eyes. "Are you going to be okay?"

"You know, the people that keep telling me I'm a traitor still get to me sometimes. Makes me wonder about everything I've done. Whether my life was a lie. But then I think about what else I would have done, and I come up with nothing."

"Make no mistake, Airman, you've lived your life as a great patriot. You've given everything for your country. Don't listen to those cowards hiding behind their keyboards."

Amelia hugged Frank again. "Thank you, Frank. For everything."

Ike noticed everyone was watching them. The others looked longingly, as if they wanted to join in. He waved them all over. "Come on over here." He opened his arms wide, and the group all piled in. They all shared a group hug, and Ike could feel the bonds between them. This was his family.

Suddenly the front door opened and freezing air blew in. A wide-shouldered man stood in the shadows outside for a few seconds. Then Danny DeSantis stepped inside. He was wearing navy slacks, a bright white dress shirt, a gray V-neck sweater that stretched across his barrel chest, and a brown tweed sports coat. He had a wrapped bottle in one hand. He bounced over to the group.

"Merry Christmas, Danny," Ike said, offering his fist. "What's up?"

Danny bumped Ike's fist and looked at the bottle in his hand. "Oh yeah," he said, raising it as an offering. "I brought this for you and Maria. Merry Christmas." Maria went to Danny, took the bottle, and kissed him on the cheek. "Don't you look handsome tonight." She smiled at Amelia as she walked past her and set the bottle on the bar.

Amelia pulled away from the group and went to Danny, who smiled, then winked at Ike. He offered Amelia his arm, and she took it as they headed for the door.

"I'll be damned," Ike said, rubbing his head.

Just as Danny opened the door, Frank said, "Airman!"

Amelia turned her head and looked at Frank. Frank snapped to attention and gave her a crisp salute, waiting for it to be returned. Amelia let go of Danny, pivoted to square with Frank, and saluted back, a tear running down her cheek. She spun and walked out the door.

THE END

ACKNOWLEDGEMENTS

AS ALWAYS, THIS book would not be possible without the help and support of my wife, CJ. Her support, understanding, and patience helped get this across the goal line. Special thanks to Steve Berry, Meg Gardiner, Robert Dugoni, Lee Child, Michael Connelly, and Joseph Finder, the ThrillerFest authors who have so generously shared their craft and advice with me. Thanks to Keri Barnum for her help and guidance and to all the people behind Mahogany Row Press. I'm grateful for Julie Miller and her wonderful editorial help. Any mistakes are of my doing not hers. Finally, special thanks to Damon at Damonza for another great cover.

If you enjoyed *The Secret That Killed You*, leaving a review will let other readers know how much you loved it. Simply scan the QR code below.

http://Amazon.com//review/create-review?&asin=B0CW1F7RH5

I'd be grateful if you helped spread the word by recommending it to your friends and family and posting on social media, too.

To learn more about new books and exclusive content, sign up for my author mailing list and receive a copy of my first novel, *The Sunset Conspiracy,* free, scan the QR Code below.

http://www.stevehadden.com
Keep reading for a riveting excerpt from
The Victim of the System...The first Ike Rossi thriller...

CHAPTER 1

JACK COLE KNEW they were coming for him next. He waited in the dense shrubs with a vengeful patience. He reminded himself he was here for a reason—one that justified the action. He fought back the dark sensation that this was wrong. *Thou shalt not kill* had been drilled into him at Saint John's. But this was the only way to end it—to be safe.

His hand shook as he gripped the heavy rifle and took aim at the front door of the mansion across the private cul-de-sac. He settled the jitter with the thought that this man had killed his dad.

He leaned back against the tree and braced for the kick. Then, through the bushes, he saw a sliver of light widen as the front door opened. He dropped his head and took aim through the scope. He'd been watching the lawyer's house for days.

The thick door swung open and his target stepped out, closing the door behind him. Jack hesitated when he came face-to-face with him through the scope. Still, he steadied the heavy rifle and squeezed the trigger.

The blast slammed his back against the thick tree. The kick felt stronger than it had when he'd fired it on his first hunting trip with his father, just two months ago. As he scrambled to regain his balance, he saw his prey— the man responsible for destroying what was left of his family—fall against the front door of the red brick home, his white shirt splattered with blood and his face paralyzed in shock. Blood smeared as the man grabbed at the door, apparently reaching for someone inside. Finally, the attorney collapsed with his contorted body wrapped around his large legal briefcase.

Jack stood and froze, shocked by the carnage he'd unleashed. When the door swung open and a panicked woman rushed out, he came to his senses.

In seconds, Jack secured and covered the rifle and began his escape. Halfway down the cul-de-sac, he was sure someone had called 911. As he calmly pulled the red wagon his father had given him on his ninth birthday, he heard the police cars responding. They raced through the expensive suburban homes toward 1119 Blackbird Court.

The two cars turned onto the cul-de-sac and slowed when the patrolmen passed a mom and her children standing in their driveway, gaping at the terrifying scene. At the deep end of the cul-de-sac, the police cars screeched to a stop. Their doors sprang open and two officers swept the area with their guns drawn. The other two rushed to the porch. The woman cradled the man's body, screaming wildly. Blood coated the porch and covered the woman's face and arms.

Jack fought the urge to run and wandered out of the cul-de-sac. Two other police cars and an ambulance raced past. Over his shoulder, he saw the paramedics rush to the porch. Then Jack turned the corner and lost sight of what he'd done—and he began to cry.

CHAPTER 2

IKE ROSSI HATED this place. Not because something had happened here. Instead, it was something that hadn't. It represented failure. A rotting failure that he placed firmly on his own shoulders. While it had been twenty-two years, the wound was as raw as it was on that dreadful day he'd tried to forget for most of his adult life. Now, after years of dead ends, he was here once again to close that wound.

He waited on the hard bench in the massive lobby of the Allegheny County Courthouse flanked by murals of Peace, Justice, and Industry. Despite their ominous presence, he ignored them. He'd never found any of those here.

As nine a.m. approached, the lobby swelled with people making their way to their destinies. Their voices and the clicks of their best shoes echoed through the massive honeycomb of thick stone archways as they wound up the network of stairs leading to the courtrooms on the floors above. Nameless faces all carried their tags: anger, sadness, fear, and arrogance. Those who were above it all, those who feared the system, and those who just saw money. While he'd always heard it was the best system on earth, he was painfully convinced that justice deserved better.

Three benches down, Ike's eyes locked on a small boy who was crying and leaning into a woman's side as she tried desperately to comfort him. When he recognized Jack Cole from the flood of news reports over the last six months, he didn't feel the prickly disdain that had roiled in his gut as he watched the initial reports on TV. At first, he'd condemned the ten-year-old boy as another killer—one who took the life of someone's parent. But as the case unfolded he'd discovered the boy had lost his father. The constant wound Ike kept hidden in his soul opened a little wider. He knew what it was like to lose a parent.

According to the reports, Jack Cole's father had committed suicide as a result of a nasty divorce from Brenda Falzone Cole, the estranged daughter of one of the richest families in the country. Jack, a genius ten-year-old, had shot and killed his mother's family law attorney—not exactly what Ike expected from a kid. When he was finally identified in video from a neighbor's security camera and questioned, he shocked investigators by admitting the act.

Claiming he didn't have a choice under Pennsylvania law, the prosecutor was trying the boy as an adult. Jack faced a murder charge. Due to his young age, both sides wanted to fast-track the trial. It was scheduled to start next Monday, just a week away.

The boy looked up and caught Ike's gaze. Despite his best efforts, Ike couldn't look away. Tears streamed down Jack's face, but at the same time, his eyes begged for help. A mix of fear and generosity accumulated deep in Ike's chest. He knew the boy sought the same help he'd sought for himself years ago, but the prospect of exhuming that pain warned him to stay away.

Still, yielding to a magnetic force that had no regard for his own protection, Ike stood, smiled, and walked to the boy, ignoring the condemning stares from the people eyeing Jack. Reaching into his jacket pocket, he pulled out a small Rubik's Cube he carried to amuse distressed kids on long flights to distant oil provinces.

He stopped in front of the pair and asked the woman, "May I?" while he showed her the toy. The dried streaks down her cheeks told him she shared the boy's pain. He recognized her from the news reports but didn't want to remind her that millions of people were now witness to her custody battle with Jack's mother's family—and the progression of her devastating pretrial defeats at the hands of the district attorney.

"Oh, that's so kind of you," she said, nodding gently.

Ike gave Jack the toy and sat beside him. Jack's smallish build and timid posture made it hard to believe he was ten—and he'd killed someone.

Jack sniffled and wiped his nose with the back of his arm.

"Here, honey," the woman said as she handed him a Kleenex. Jack wiped his nose and immediately began twisting the cube, ignoring Ike.

"I'm Lauren Bottaro," the woman said. "This is Jack. I'm his aunt."

Ike reached out. "Ike Rossi."

Her eyes flamed with familiarity. She seemed stunned. "You're Ike Rossi?"

Jack handed the cube back to Ike. "Done!"

Ike wasn't sure what startled him more, the look on Lauren's face or the fact that Jack had solved the cube in less than a minute. "That's great, Jack." Ike offered Jack a high-five, but Jack awkwardly hesitated. Finally, he slapped it and Ike returned the toy. The tears were gone, replaced by a proud smile. Ike looked back at Lauren, who'd apparently caught herself staring at him.

She seemed to regain some composure, and a serious expression swept across her face.

"Mr. Rossi, can I ask what you do, now?"

Ike hesitated, hearing more than just that question in her voice.

He looked up and saw Mac Machowski, grinning.

"I'll tell you what he does."

Ike could have kissed Mac for the timely rescue.

Mac counted on his thick gnarled fingers. "He fixes things that can't be fixed. He keeps fat cats from getting kidnapped—or killed if they do—and he's the best damn investigator I've ever seen."

Ike noticed Jack had stopped playing with the Rubik's Cube and was listening intently to Mac, along with Lauren.

Ike smiled. "Mac, I'd like you to meet Lauren and Jack."

Mac tipped the bill of his Pirates cap to Lauren. "Ma'am." Then, extending his meaty paw, he knelt painfully and came face-to-face with Jack. "Nice to meet you, young man."

Jack nervously looked away but reached for Mac's hand and shook it.

"Jack. What do you say?" Lauren said.

Jack faced Mac. "Nice to meet you, sir."

Mac's joints creaked as he reached to the floor and pushed himself up. "You ready there, partner?" he said to Ike. "We gotta catch him before he leaves the courthouse at nine."

As Ike stood, Lauren rose with him. "So you're a detective?"

Ike threw a nod toward Mac. "He is—a retired homicide detective. I'm a private security and investigative services consultant in the oil and gas business."

Lauren tipped her head back, as if enlightened. "That makes sense now."

"What makes sense?" Ike said.

"I saw your name written on my brother's day planner."

The claim jolted Ike. "My name?"

Lauren nodded again. "Did you speak to him?"

"No, I've never talked to your brother." Ike was sure investigators would have checked the planner, but he'd never been questioned.

Jack reached up and tugged on Ike's forearm. "Can you help me?"

Those eyes were begging again.

Lauren gently pulled Jack's hand from Ike's arm. "I'm sorry," she said. "He's been through a lot."

Jack kept his eyes, now wet again, locked on Ike. "My dad wouldn't do that to me. He wouldn't kill himself."

Ike was frozen by Jack's stare. It was as innocent as any ten-year-old's. A primal desire to protect Jack stirred in Ike's heart. He didn't want to believe the kid—but he did.

Lauren hugged Jack. "It's okay, honey." She looked back at Ike and Mac. "We have no right to ask you th—"

A thick, towering woman with dark brown hair and a stone-cold stare wedged into the space between Mac and Lauren. She studied Mac, then Ike. "What's going on here, Lauren?"

Ike immediately recognized her from the news reports. Jenna Price represented Jack. For the last two months she'd been billed as a hopeless underdog, and the string of losses so far—other than prevailing at the bail hearing—supported that label. A basketball player-turned-lawyer, she was battling a DA who so far showed little mercy. She worked with her father in their tiny firm, and every talking head said she didn't stand a chance.

Lauren said, "Jenna, this is Ike Rossi and Mac ... I'm sorry?"

"Machowski," Mac said as he shook Jenna's hand.

Jenna gripped Ike's hand and held it as she spoke. "My dad said you were the greatest quarterback ever to come out of western Pennsylvania."

Ike always had one answer to that comment to quell any further discussion of his accolades. "That was a long time ago."

"What are you doing now?" she asked.

Jack leaned around Lauren and nearly shouted, "He's a detective. He can help us!"

Lauren hugged him tight again. "Shhh."

"A detective?" Jenna said.

"A private security and investigative services consultant."

Jenna nodded and held her gaze but said nothing.

"We gotta go now," Mac said, looking at his watch.

Ike stepped back from Jenna. "Stay strong, Counselor." He nodded to Lauren. "Ms. Bottaro." Then Ike offered a handshake to Jack.

Jack sheepishly held out the Rubik's Cube for Ike. Immediately, Ike felt Jack's awkwardness.

"You keep that, Jack." Ike raised his hand for another high-five. Jack took the cue this time and slapped it. "Ladies," he said, turning with Mac and walking down the hall.

As they reached the stairs at the end of the corridor, Ike glanced over his shoulder. He could see Jack edging around the two women to keep his eyes on Ike, with the Rubik's Cube clutched in his hand. Ike turned back to the stairs.

"You okay?" Mac said. Ike nodded and started up the stairs to meet a man he despised. A man who might finally deliver the key to *his* parents' murder.

If you enjoyed the excerpt, you can buy your copy of
The Victim of the System here:
https://www.amazon.com/dp/B07BMHTMK3

ABOUT THE AUTHOR

STEVE HADDEN is the author of *The Sunset Conspiracy, Genetic Imperfections, The Swimming Monkeys Trilogy, The Victim of the System, The Dark Side of Angels* and *The Secret That Killed You.* Steve believes powerful thrillers lie at the intersection of intriguing stories and intelligent characters in search of dramatic revelations with global human impact. Visit his website at http:// www.stevehadden.com

Made in the USA
Columbia, SC
29 September 2024

43269022R00198